PRAISE FOR DENISE HILDRETH'S NOVELS

Savannah by the Sea is the winner of the Bronze Award from *Fore*[illegible]

"*Savannah by the Sea* is a skillfully crafted story that will have you laughing till you cry . . . I guarantee that you won't be able to put it down. For those who have not had the delightful opportunity to read either of the first two books about Hildreth's heroine, that doesn't need to keep you from reading this book. The characters and their stories are fully developed in each book. However, if you have some spending money left in your vacation fund, I highly recommend you buy the first two books, *Savannah from Savannah* and *Savannah Comes Undone*."

—Paula K. Parker, www.lifeway.com

"Denise Hildreth is one of my favorite writers. She writes with more Southern wit and comedy than should be legal. I can't read her books on a plane for fear of drawing too much attention to myself. Between the lines, Denise's stories speak life, they remind me that loss happens for a reason, and that laughter is good for the soul because it breeds hope."

—Charles Martin, author of *When Crickets Cry*

"You'll savor Denise Hildreth's Southern voice and humor. Savannah is a strong-willed and funny character."

—Michael Morris, author of *Slow Way Home*

"Savannah is both charming and shrewd, and the boisterous cast of Southern characters with whom she must contend is in rare and authentic form."

—Beth Webb Hart, author of *Grace at Low Tide*,
referring to *Savannah by the Sea*

"Denise Hildreth has quickly become one of my favorite authors. I love her amazing wit, her comedic timing, her style . . . she's got the whole package."

—Rene Gutteridge, author of *My Life as a Doormat*

"Denise Hildreth really captures the vulnerability of every young woman as she is faced with making her own mark in life. As a reader, you become so involved with *Savannah from Savannah* that you want to absorb every morsel."

—Lynnette Cole, Miss USA 2000

"I thought I'd skim this book to offer first-time author Denise Hildreth some constructive criticism. Only I discovered she's such an engaging writer of real life vignettes and relationships that I read it cover to cover. While being entertained as Savannah discovers her beliefs, values, and passions, the reader will be looking into their own 'mirror of truth.' Denise, like Savannah, has great promise."

—Naomi Judd regarding *Savannah from Savannah*

"Hildreth has approached a topic containing as much controversy as you'll find today with grace and wit. A reminder that at the heart of any issue is the heart itself."

—Michael Reagan, author *Twice Adopted*
regarding *Savannah Comes Undone*

SAVANNAH

BY THE SEA

OTHER BOOKS BY DENISE HILDRETH

Savannah from Savannah
Savannah Comes Undone

For more information about Denise,
visit: www.denisehildreth.com

SAVANNAH
BY THE SEA

DENISE HILDRETH

THOMAS NELSON
Since 1798

NASHVILLE DALLAS MEXICO CITY RIO DE JANEIRO BEIJING

This book is dedicated to my two precious parents, who have—in forty-two years of marriage—been such wonderful examples of how both to love and to forgive.

Published in Nashville, Tennessee, by Thomas Nelson. Thomas Nelson is a trademark of Thomas Nelson, Inc.

Thomas Nelson, Inc., titles may be purchased in bulk for educational, business, fund-raising, or sales promotional use. For information, please e-mail SpecialMarkets@ThomasNelson.com.

Library of Congress Cataloging-in-Publication Data

Hildreth, Denise, 1969–
Savannah by the sea / Denise Hildreth.
p. cm.
ISBN 10: 1-59554-160-8 (sc)
ISBN 13: 978-1-59554-160-4 (sc)
1. Savannah (Ga.)—Fiction. I. Title.
PS3608.I424S277 2006
813'.6—dc22

2006003502

Printed in the United States of America
07 08 09 10 RRD 8 7 6 5 4

CHAPTER ONE

The racket coming from behind the black painted wooden doors declared mayhem had stopped by. But me and mayhem had become friends years ago. Why not? I had two options: become permanently addicted to a drug of choice, or just open the door for mayhem when he arrived and pat him on the back as he left. I chose the latter. Well, okay. The former and the latter. Why make choices? While mayhem was around, I'd sit on the front steps, drink a Coca-Cola, and hope he didn't hang around too long. And truth be told, mayhem always provided me with a great story by the time he left. The only unfortunate part was, my mother usually found a way to insert me inside his story.

I opened the large door and peered inside cautiously. "What's that yapping?"

Dad was standing by the wrought-iron console, laying down his morning paper. "It's your mother's new friend," Dad informed me while Duke, our golden retriever, sat whimpering at his feet.

My eyes narrowed in on the recently purchased creature as it rounded the corner of the foyer at full throttle and came to a halt on the Persian rug, way too close to my feet. It looked like a white rat but barked up at me like a Rottweiler seeking lunch. "How in the world did you let that happen?"

Dad talked as he headed to the kitchen. We all followed. "You moved out. She moved in. Plus, your mother's a grown woman, and this is her house as well as mine. I wasn't going to tell her she couldn't have a dog."

"That's not a dog, that's a . . . a . . . a . . ." I lifted my heels so it couldn't take a bite out of my ankle. Duke barked his own thoughts. "Yeah, like Duke said, that's a"—I cocked my head—"well, it looks more like a disheveled bag of packing peanuts." I hopped on top of a stool.

The white ball of fur looked up at me, a pristine pink ribbon holding back its scraggly puppy bangs. Its toenails matched the color of its ribbon. If I hadn't known better, I would have sworn Amber Topaz Childers, the recent first runner-up (again) to Miss Georgia United States of America, had just been reincarnated as a Maltese dog. Duke leaned against me while the little white mongrel yapped at me like a broken car alarm.

I plugged my ears. "How long will she do that?" I hollered.

"Until Duke helps her realize he's the alpha male." Dad eyed him curiously. "At the rate he's going, it could take a while."

I laid my hand atop Duke's sinfully beautiful honey-blond mane. "Buck up!"

He hacked in my direction.

"Ooh, hairball."

The hacking noise, however, stopped the little white yapper. Her head cocked.

"*Hack*!" Duke offered again in her direction with a slight glint in his eye.

Her tail tucked between her legs, and she started backing into the foyer.

Duke let one paw extend beyond the others in her direction. "*Hack*!"

"Did you know he's a genius?" I offered my father.

He raised his eyebrow with the upturn of his lips. "I knew he'd realize his power eventually. So, sure you don't want to come with us?"

The heels clicking on the foyer hall reinforced my original decision. "Jake!" my mother hollered.

"I'm certain," I said

Mother rounded the corner in full vacation regalia, her linen dress flowing behind her as her hand patted down her pearls. "What's my boo-boo-baby-sweetie-pea-pickin' little pooh bear up to?"

"Mother, please, I'm way too old to be talked to in—"

"Savannah darling, I didn't hear you come in," she said through muffled tones with her lips pressed against the top knot of her latest acquisition.

"I'm not surprised." I could see only the right eye of the yapper peeking from behind Mother's red lipstick.

"Are you sure you can't make the trip with us?" Mother asked, echoing Dad's question regarding our yearly vacation to Seaside, Florida.

I stood and pushed the stool back under the black soapstone countertop. "I know it's hard to believe that I have a real job, but I do. I can't just take a week off from the paper."

"You've been there for ten months, Savannah," Mother said, as if the time frame of my job was somehow lost on me.

"I know, but I don't get vacation time until I've been there a year. Plus, this is a really busy season for me."

"Those two articles a week are killing you, aren't they?" Dad said with a chuckle.

"Those *two* articles a week take time and energy to produce. And I take great pride in what I do, so with my work ethic, it is very important that I make sure my commitment to my employer and to my craft is unquestionably clear."

They both cocked their heads at me.

You would have thought I was speaking Greek. "What?"

"Well, that's okay. Amber's going with us anyway," Mother said nonchalantly. "She can take your bedroom."

Duke and I looked at them simultaneously. "Amber's what?"

Mother turned to pull down her picnic basket from the top shelf of her pantry. "Didn't I tell you?"

"I think you forgot that little detail."

"Well, it's no big deal. Your father and I just thought it would be good for her. Eating at Criolla's." The woman was vicious. She knew that was my favorite restaurant. The lump crab meat over saffron rice in the flaky phyllo shell, drowned in butter.

"You might want to . . ." Dad wiped his lip to insinuate the need to wipe my own.

"We'll take her to the beach and let her enjoy your father's wonderful grilled specialties and my phenomenal chicken salad." She was a sadist. "Amber's just had such a rough time, you know, with her loss and all . . ." You'd have thought Amber's grandmother had just been laid to rest.

"It was a pageant."

Mother's eyes darted in my direction. "It was a dream."

I looked at Dad for sanity. "You agreed to this?"

He walked over and patted me on the hand. "We'll miss you. We'll really miss you." He turned to leave the kitchen.

"Well, you know, there is this story that the paper really needs to address. I've been pondering it for . . . well . . . a while now." Two minutes *was* a while longer than one. "With all the hurricanes last year, it might be . . . no, in fact I think it really *is* vital to hear some of the stories of revitalization and restoration on the Gulf."

Dad stopped and turned around. "We're going to the panhandle. They came through okay."

"But, they were . . . well . . . they were close, yeah, really close, to all of the devastation. The psychological effects alone are just unfathomable. And I think we've neglected their story. In fact, we don't need to neglect it a day longer. I slapped the counter for effect. I'm letting Mr. Hicks know today that we have wasted entirely too much time neglecting these people and their trauma. I'll be back in thirty minutes. Let me grab my stuff, stop and see Mr. Hicks, and I'll be ready to head out with you."

Mother and her new canine friend glanced at my father, then back to me. "Are you sure, darling? It's very sudden." I ignored the glint in her eye.

"Of course. It's essential. Give me just a few minutes."

I headed through the garage with Dad. "My, my, my, how quickly a *while* can alter a morning."

"This city would want to know," I said, continuing my gait toward my car.

"I have no doubt." He chuckled. "I have no doubt."

The vibration startled me. I reached over to grab my bouncing cell phone, which I had left on the seat of Old Betsy.

It was Thomas.

"Where are you ?" I asked. "Our parents are leaving in about an hour. I thought you and your new *friend* were going with them."

"Are you alone?"

"Incessantly."

"Can they hear you?"

"Dad, no. Mother, I've never completely ruled out telepathy. But I am in my car, almost two blocks away, so I'd say your chances are good."

"I'm not leaving today."

"What?! Mother will freak!"

"Me and Mary Francis broke up." I could hear him pacing. A pitiful habit he had learned from me. Thankfully that was the worst one.

"Mother will freak again! She thinks that girl is the cream of the College of Charleston. She hated Charleston until Mary Francis. She has your children named."

"Yeah, well, so did Mary Francis, and we've dated all of three months. But she's not coming."

I jerked Old Betsy to dodge a tourist. However, with that attire, a quick jaunt to the ER might have resulted in something more fashionable. "So, you're like broken up, broken up?"

"Like, there's a box in front of my door with all of our pictures cut in half. She sent me my half."

That made me laugh. "I guess she thought she looked too good just to give all the pictures to you."

"Well, she is a fine specimen of a woman."

I could see his face. "Don't succumb. She was crazy."

He was faltering. "She was beautiful."

"Your son was going to be named Jethro Seville."

"You think that's bad, you ought to have heard what she was going to name our daughter."

"You know you will have to tell Mother."

He adamantly protested. "No way. Not until our vacation is over. I'm not ruining a perfectly good vacation because Mother has no self-control."

I glanced up at my rearview mirror. "You can't lie about it."

"I don't have to lie, I just don't have to reveal everything I know."

"You'll regret it. It never works. You should know from me."

"You're just not good at it."

"Oh my word!" I yelled into the phone.

"You don't have to take it so personal."

"I'm not talking to you. Amber just passed me in her little Mercedes doing close to 45 around the square. Ooh, here comes the cops. Sick 'em, tiger!"

"You're pitiful."

I hollered again. "You have got to be kidding me!"

"Well, you are pitiful."

"Not you! I'm getting pulled over! Can you believe this?" I slowed up so I could get close to the curb and out of the sight of the entire Lafayette Square.

"You better get out of this one, Vanni. Dad will not pay your ticket."

"I don't need money from my father, thank you very much." I looked out of my side mirror and saw Sergeant Millings get out of his patrol car. He hiked his pants up, obviously failing to realize that they already exceeded the floodwater stage.

Thomas continued, "Well, you still owe Paige two hundred dollars, so you won't get it from her anyway."

"How do you know . . . oh, never mind. I've got to go. And I will not, and I do mean *will not*, tell Mother why you are not coming today. Do I make myself clear?"

"Hello . . . hello . . . I can't . . . you're breaking up . . ." The line went dead.

"Chicken!" I hollered into the phone before tossing it back into the seat.

"Well, well, well . . . who do we have here?" Sergeant Millings asked in his annoying way, flicking what looked to be a three-day-old toothpick through his teeth as he came in line with my open window.

"I do believe you have the wrong car." I pointed in the direction of the blue blur. "That is the young woman you should be tormenting."

"You think so, Miss Phillips? Well, you'll be lucky to know I clocked you at twenty-two in a twenty."

"Well, let's just change my name to Lucky!"

"Okay, Lucky! If you'll give me your license and registration, please."

"Sergeant Millings, you have got to be kidding me! You are going to give me a ticket for doing—"

"License and registration, Miss Phillips." He sucked air through his teeth. They should have used *him* in the *Dukes of Hazzard* movie. It would have gotten better ratings, I'm certain.

"Would you like blood with that? I'm sure I could draw some for you." Especially had the steering wheel been my arms, because my nails were now embedded in it.

"Don't be smart. Now, hand them over, missy."

"It's Lucky, remember!" I said, wanting to toss them across the street.

He took the paperwork from my hand, and the sun bounced off of a gold wedding band. In all these years I had never met Mrs. Sergeant Millings. Poor woman had probably taken to hiding. If she was smart, she had hidden from him as well. Amazing to me how a man like that can find love while I'm relegated to the companionship of crazy people.

"Well, Miss Phillips." His voice called my mind back from its thoughts of vehicular homicide. "Here you go. You can send your check by mail, or you can see me in court."

"Are you serious?" I jerked the ticket from his hand. My eyes got to what mattered most. "A hundred and fifteen dollars? For two miles over the speed limit?"

"No, forty dollars for two miles over the speed limit, and seventy-five dollars for verbally assaulting a police officer."

"You are being absurd!" I could cover my rent and have just enough money left over for food. This would sure put a dent in that achievement.

He flapped his little black notebook in my face. "I have more tickets."

"Well, do tell me, Sergeant Millings, what orifice would you like to pull this money out of? Huh? Because I've already exhausted all resources of my behind!" With that, I tossed the ticket in the passenger's seat and rolled up my window. Old Betsy gave him a sputter of her thoughts as well as the black smoke choked him.

A week away just might be exactly what I needed. Granted, I was going with a crazed mongrel and a morbidly depressed beauty-queen reject, but it was Seaside. What could happen in Seaside?

CHAPTER TWO

When I arrived at the paper, it seemed just as busy as a weekday. Of course, Saturday and Sunday still required a paper. But the staff was predominantly different. My small cubby-hole that rested at the back of the first floor had slowly come to feel like home. I had brought in some of my favorite books, placed pictures of my friends around the Styrofoamish walls, and even hung up a beautiful oil painting created by my best friend, Paige, who owns her own art studio in the back of her parents' antique store. Door or no door, this had become my world.

I jogged up the three flights of stairs to Mr. Hicks's office. He was always here.

His booming voice responded to my knock. "Come in."

I breathed deeply before opening it, hoping the *opportunity* I had rehearsed between my tirades of financial ruin would prove convincing. "Hey, Mr. Hicks. How are you on this beautiful morning?"

He sat his coffee cup down rather firmly on his lacquered desk and picked up a handful of peanut M&Ms from the candy jar on his desk. Rumor had it he refilled the jar twice a day.

"Savannah Phillips, what are you doing in here on a Saturday? I thought you did nothing but read books on the weekend."

The man knew me better than I thought. "Well, I've really been laboring over a deeply rooted concern. I feel that our paper has been insensitive and abandoned a truly humanitarian voice regarding the desperate plight of the hurricane victims along the panhandle."

His brow furrowed. His candy crunched. "What do you want?" he asked through peanuts and chocolate.

I leaned over his desk so he could see my sincerity. "I feel I need to go."

"Go where? The panhandle?"

I leaned in farther. He retreated. "They've been through so much."

"Most of the hurricanes hit the Gulf."

"And yet the psychological trauma spared no one. The packing up, the unpacking up, the one-minute-it's-coming, the next-minute-it's-retreating chaos. The hurricane season always looming on the horizon . . ." I moved my head in circles for effect.

"A story, huh?" He folded his arms across his expansive chest.

"A *real* human-interest story."

"On the panhandle?"

"It will only take a week."

"A week!" he yelled, his chair squeaking as it projected him forward. It was a good thing he'd swallowed already, or he might have choked. I backed my own self up. "You think you're going to go away for a week to some beach and call it work?"

"What would you like me to call it?"

"Call it for what it is, Savannah, vacation."

"Humph. I don't get vacation for two more months. This is not a vacation, I assure you." If I told him Amber was coming, he would agree. "This is a lesson in living. A lesson for our city, which has been spared much trauma from the perils of the sea."

"You should have been an actress." He was softening. "A week, huh?"

I looked into his blue eyes, largely hidden by his gray bushy eyebrows. "For a real story."

"It better be Pulitzer worthy."

I tried to hide the fear. "Lilly Pulitzer?"

"You know what I mean." He ushered me out. When he closed the door behind me, I was certain I heard him chuckle.

I gathered my pink *Arrevidderci* OPI fingernail polish from the top drawer of my particleboard desk. And a few other things I might need while I was gone. Like my ability to pull a story out of my—

"I'll only be gone a week," I heard Joshua's voice call out.

I tried to listen without revealing myself from behind the Styrofoam wall that separated us.

"Stay away from the girls," an unknown voice called out.

Joshua laughed as he approached his workspace opposite mine. "Yeah, yeah, I'll try."

I slid farther along my wall, trying to scrunch toward the corner out of his line of sight. I didn't have it in me today. A woman could only do so much.

"Yeah, yeah, I'll try," I mouthed to the dust particles flying in front of my face.

I heard papers shuffle and drawers open and close in Joshua's cubicle. In a few minutes, his flip-flops stopped at what seemed to be my entrance. Had his curls turned the corner and his black eyes scanned the four-foot cell, he would have caught me like a rat in a trap.

Finally Curly Locks flip-flopped away.

I exhaled.

He had tormented me since my arrival. And his torment became incessant the moment my old boyfriend made his way down the aisle without me.

Grant Lewis married almost nine months ago. I didn't go to the wedding. No need: Vicky gave me a play-by-play. Not that I had asked. I spent the next month sulking, and Joshua spent the next nine months assuring me I was not destined to become a sequestered old maid.

I crawled from my hole and peeked around the corner. He was gone, to set his sights on other maidens, I hoped. I scanned his small cubicle and noticed the book lying at the corner of his desk. I didn't even know he liked to read. Truth be told, I didn't know much about him at all. Except that his dark chin-length curls were always in his dark eyes, his skin was always perfectly olive and perfectly flawless, his favorite pair of flip-flops were the brown leather ones with brown stitching, his favorite drink was Dr Pepper, his favorite sandwich was a ham, cheddar, and tomato on wheat (which he brought in with him almost every day), and his favorite color was blue. I mean, why would I notice that he read? Not much of anything he did mattered to me. I spun his chair around and looked forward to a week away. Just another week of not noticing anything that had to do with Joshua North.

Katherine's Corner Bookstore wasn't far from the newspaper office. And I was officially in desperate need of new fiction. As I stepped out of the car, I heard my name called. Well, my name to Savannah's Honorable Judge Hoddicks.

"Betty!" the white-haired, distinguished man called from the other end of the sidewalk. He had called me Betty since I was thirteen, when I petitioned him to change my name. He got nowhere with my mother, so I changed hers to Vicky for a while. His beautiful wife, June, was on his arm. "How's that brother of yours and his lady friend?" he called.

June nudged him.

At a certain age, a wife's nudge is nothing more than wasted elbow effort. Judge Hoddicks was just that age. "Oh, well, can't say I've seen either one of them lately." And that was the truest gospel there was.

Thomas worked with Judge Hoddicks every summer. They had a mutual respect. "Won't you see them on your vacation?"

If I didn't know the man was my father's closest friend, I would have blabbered Thomas's news across the square. "Well, all the details haven't been worked out yet."

"Well, tell him I want to hear all about her when he heads back this summer."

"Will do." Oh, everybody will hear all about it. Of that I was certain.

Katherine was ringing up a local socialite with some book on flower arranging. Paula Deen, Savannah's resident celebrity, had a new cookbook out; it was on the edge of the counter. It was a cookbook with her friends, Mother being one of them. There are even pictures of some of her friends on the cover. Unfortunately Vicky was at the edge. Got clipped by a hair. A couple actually. A couple of her brown hairs that you can actually see on the edge of the cover. That had Mother's goat for a week; then she found out Paula was starring in a movie. Well, that had Mother going out to get head shots, and me retrieving antacids. The world couldn't handle Vicky on the screen. I even called Miss Paula myself and asked her to avoid all conversations of agents, acting, and the union. She promised she would. That bought us a week.

Katherine's face lit up when she saw me. She had the same effect on me. She was just the kind of lady that you simply enjoyed being in the room with. Natural, graceful, real. No mayhem on her doorstep.

She tucked her salt-and-pepper bobbed hair behind her ear and walked my way. "Savannah Phillips, what are you up to on this fine day?"

"About to leave on vaca—I mean, on research, for a story, as a matter of fact."

"Oh, now you're traveling for stories?" She laughed.

"You've got to go where the story is."

Her red painted lips turned upward. "I completely understand. But vacation sounds a lot more fun."

"Well, Mother has a new pet and another *vibrant* traveling companion, so a vacation it certainly will not be."

"I'm not sure I even want to know," she said, replacing the old *Southern Living* with the new.

"Trust me. You don't. So, I need some reading material."

"You've already finished those two books you picked up last week?"

"It was two weeks ago, actually. And yes, I have. And I want fiction. No self-help. No autobiographies. Just plain other people's issues. Worlds that aren't my own. And I've never read this," I said, picking up Tolstoy's *Anna Karenina.* The weight of it caused my arm to sag.

Katherine's dark brown eyes registered their shock. "You've never read this?"

"No. Not even when Oprah made it mandatory. I was into something else and just haven't ever picked it up."

She took the book from my hand. "Well, my dear friend, since you've never read *Anna Karenina,* this one is on me." Her dainty hand placed it on the counter.

"Katherine, I—"

"Now, hush! You buy enough, but classics are a must. So you must."

So I did. I had planned on buying a couple books, but this one held enough verbiage to prevent me from spending insufferable travel time with my mother and her mongrels—I mean *mongrel*—either coming or going. But come to think of it, I didn't need to travel this insanity completely alone. I mean, books are good and all. But companionship was better.

"I need you, now!"

"Where have I heard that before?" Paige retorted.

"Pack your bags for the beach, and get here in nine minutes. Eight minutes if you argue."

"I can't leave the studio for a week, Savannah. My mother would have a conniption."

"Tell her you're with my mother, and she'll end up wanting to come herself."

"She's out of town."

"Good, because the car's going to be crowded anyway, and plus she won't even know that you're gone."

"Why?"

"Why what?"

"Don't play dumb. Why will the car be crowded?"

"I can't tell you or you won't come," I said.

"*Don't* tell me and I won't come," she said.

"You won't like it. It's downright disabling."

"Amber's going on your vacation."

"How—"

"It was either that or your mother has gotten a dog."

"Ooh, now, that would be horrible," I said.

"I can't endure a week with her," Paige confirmed.

"It's Seaside."

"Ooh, I love that place," she cooed.

"And you can reschedule that meeting with the J. Proctor Gallery that you missed last year," I coaxed.

"You're brazen."

"Come on. Pretty please! Everything is better in pairs. Please! I'm begging you. I am on my knees in the middle of the street, begging you to come with me." I dropped to my knees. "I cannot endure such torment alone. Amber is teetering on the brink of a collapse. I'll need therapy when I get home. And I can't afford it! You of all people know this!" Thomas was right, I did still owe her two hundred dollars.

"I'll be there in a minute. I'm caught up here. Just let me lock up and pack a few of my paintings."

Now we're talking. "Okay, but you've wasted five minutes, so get a move on."

"Well, shut up so I can pack."

I hung up. Life was always more tolerable when the ratio of sanity to insanity was at least even. Three against two. It wasn't pretty, but it could be worse. Of course Paige had no idea "pink toenails" was coming too.

I noticed a new ding in my car door. That ding magnet I bought off the TV infomercial hadn't done anything yet except destroyed the muscle in my right shoulder by trying to actually suck the dings out of my car. The dings had remained; the muscle had taken six weeks to recover.

I sat down softly. Old Betsy groaned. I groaned.

I shifted the pillow on the driver's seat. I purchased this new pillow because the seat had caved in a little more and I needed extra cushion.

I say it's the heat. I say that hoping when winter arrives, the springs will constrict and raise me up a hair. But I'm not looking for too many miracles. After almost seven years of being driven hard by me (after two years by someone else), the budget is going to have to find a car payment in it eventually. But me and Old Betsy have memories. Our parting would be traumatic.

This old girl knows the streets of Savannah like she knows the guts of her transmission. She knows my favorite places to eat and hide and eat again. She could make a direct path to The Lady & Sons and then to the Gryphon Tea Room for dessert without having to be steered. She has carried me to school, to home, to Grant, to my world. And I'm not ready to let her go. Who cares if the knob to the gear shift comes off in my hands twice a week. There's duct tape for those things. And there's love for the rest. Hers for mine and mine for hers, and we'll worry about the rest as it comes.

I pulled her into her new home: the carport behind Dad's coffee shop. She was happy. I was happy. A Coke for me would make both of us even happier.

CHAPTER THREE

"Don't come in here today if you ain't going to work, girl," Richard said. His black hand scooped coffee grounds into a filter.

"You throwing a party while the owner's away?" I laughed at the right arm of my father's coffee shop, Jake's. Richard had been here fourteen of his sixty-six years.

His scooping was rather determined. "I don't know how I'm going to make it with those two old birds for a week without your father."

As if on cue, Louise came through the swinging door, hollering, "I heard that, Richard!"

"I hope you did. You've been going on out there all morning."

"Yakety-yak!" She scurried through the kitchen like a Swiffer on speed.

I poured me a BIG Coke. "Can we order bigger cups?"

She and Richard jerked their heads around at me in unison.

I took a step back. "Maybe we'll check into that on another day." I peeked my head through the door and saw the clamor.

Mervine, Louise's twin of seventy-five years, was pouring coffee as fast as her wrists could tilt.

"Savannah Phillips?"

I looked up and felt the Coke burn its way up through my nostrils. It was her. The woman I had successfully avoided for nine months, ten days, and—I caught a glance at my watch—sixteen hours. "Yes?"

"Elizabeth Lewis," she said, extending her hand. My ignorant look worked. "Grant Lewis's wife."

The dagger went in deep. What was left to destroy? My mother had a dog. Amber was encroaching on my vacation. Now this.

The bling-bling from her left hand caused me to stumble backward. The swinging door hit me in the hiney. I could see Mervine watching me. I cast her a glance. She gave a knowing smile of pity. She didn't talk anyway, so who did that surprise?

"Oh, Elizabeth, yes. I've heard so much about you. What a pleasure to meet you." I scanned her together ensemble, with its complementary toned handbag and shoes to match and wondered why I didn't think Saturday required organized apparel. The blue running pants that stopped above my ankles and white T-shirt didn't say, "Ooh, America's Next Top Model has just arrived on the premises." And the New Balance tennis shoes that I had just purchased were still shining like a beacon on a stormy night.

"Oh, and I've heard so much about you. Grant has told me ever since we got married"—dagger is now being turned —"that I had to meet you. And I love your articles. They just touch my heart every time. Especially the story about the elderly lady named Joy, who lost her memory and was wandering the streets of Savannah. Oh, girl, I cried for a week."

Well, Grant couldn't be a complete waste. He *had* loved me for years. "You liked that, huh?"

"Oh, yes, it just felt like she was part of my family." Her red, curly hair lay perfectly on her shoulders.

I ran my fingers through my ponytail, and they got caught in a tangle about midway through. I jerked a little too hard and about lost my balance.

She grabbed my elbow. "You okay?"

I recomposed myself quickly. Mervine snickered. I gave her another glance. A little more assertive this time. "Yes, I'm fine, thank you."

"Well, I know you're busy. Must be headed out to run, it looks like."

She would never know I had already run and showered for the day.

"Tell your dad the coffee is perfect as usual. And maybe we can get together sometime. Maybe do a double date," she said with a wink. A genuine wink.

I winked back. Not so genuine. "We'll see what we can do." I'd die a thousand deaths. She walked out.

Louise poked me as she passed. "She really is a nice girl, Savannah."

"Yakety-yak."

Richard popped my arm as he followed her. "Don't you be disrespectful to your elders, young lady."

I stared at them all in disbelief. Mayhem obviously was no respecter of doorsteps.

I hate the taste of coffee. Go figure. Fortunately for me, however, I love the smell. Because the smell is continually seeping through the floor of my home. I considered this as I climbed the back stairs to my apartment to grab some clothes. I walked into my freshly painted, Indian Ivory striped, tone-on-tone bedroom and clicked the answering machine on my bedside table. "Darling, bring that pretty new outfit I got you. It will look great when we go to Criolla's."

I opened my closet and stared at the blue and white sailor

pantsuit Mother had purchased for me. Not nautical. Sailor. Hat and all. I walked to the answering machine and hit *erase*.

"Savannah, it better be a story that knocks my socks off, or you'll be paying *me* for this week," Mr. Hicks announced on the machine.

I pulled out my rolling bag and laid it on the bed. I crammed all the comforts of life inside: T-shirts, jeans, flip-flops, a few sundresses, and last year's bathing suit. SPF 15, so I could get the perfect tan without the complete look of leather, because all work and no tan make for a, well, perfectly wasted week at the beach.

The beep indicated another message. "Whatever you do, don't tell Mom and Dad about Mary Francis. I'll deal with it when I get there. Just tell them I'll see them later."

"I will not do your dirty work!" I screamed to the next beep.

"SAVAAAAANNAH," the voice wailed. It could only be Miss Amber Two-Time-First-Runner-Up-to-Miss-Georgia-United-States-of-America Topaz. It had happened two weeks ago. She lost for the umpteenth time, and this one had plumb near sent her over the edge. I had pledged to be her friend. She had taken me up on it. "I'm so glad you're going with us." Word travels fast. "I JUST NEEEEEED TOOO BEE HELLLLD!!!"

I studied my suitcase, about to return it to the closet. "I'll put her in the front seat."

I turned off all the lights, checked the air, cut off the stove. It was so nice to have something that was mine. All mine. I turned back to survey everything once more as I left. The light struck the crystals of the crystal chandelier that hung over the breakfast table. Okay, so maybe it wasn't completely mine. Well, maybe "most" of it was mine.

The chandelier, however, was delivered with a note that read, "anonymous contributor to future happiness." This for a girl who doesn't even have a dining room. I have an eat-in kitchen. Mother came over, oh so pleasantly surprised, right after its arrival. She informed me every woman needs a crystal chandelier. I reminded her of my budget, my very tight budget, in hopes that would remove her need to actually hang it. It didn't. So, I gave in. Probably the first time in my life. But I gave her that one. Had I known she would tell most of the city, I would have fought harder. And when I find something I actually like to replace it with, I'll put it in storage and save it for a charity auction.

I closed the door with a sigh. A rather loud sigh.

I heard her before I saw her. That was enough. The reigning Miss Savannah United States of America and now never-to-be Miss Georgia United States of America was sitting on the steps in our garage, crying as my dad loaded the car. Amber Childers Topaz, speed demon, had made a beeline for my house. The little white ratty mongrel, encased in a hot pink vest, came running out the door, fangs bared, headed in my direction.

"GET!" I hollered. "Or I will squash you like a bug!" That did it. She retreated to Amber's feet and started trembling.

"Oh, Savannah!" Amber said, barreling toward me as the rat had done only moments before.

She wrapped me in long, expansive arms that were attached to her six-foot frame and rested her head on the top of my own—not hard considering she's six inches taller than I am. Our bodies shook in unison as she heaved.

Dad looked up from the Louis Vuitton luggage he was putting into the back of his brand spankin' used Lexus LX470 and chuckled. Dad never bought new cars. Vicky never bought anything someone else's behind had sat in.

I patted her back and pried her hands from around my shoulders. "Oh, Amber, it's okay. Just go inside and relax until we leave."

She pulled herself back. "It's just sooooooo hard."

I nodded my assurance. "Go rest. It's best."

"I will. I've close to extinguished myself."

Dad eyed me.

I shook my head.

She walked dejectedly back into the house. The rat had her nose attached to Amber's leg the entire journey.

"She meant *exhausted*," I explained. "You get used to it. Which piece is hers?" I asked, eyeing the luggage.

"The pink one."

I grabbed it. "Let's make it stay."

Mother heard me as she rounded the rear of the car in two-and-a-half-inch sling-back pumps, just how every woman should travel . . . in a car . . . for six hours. She carried a cooler. "She is going, Savannah, and you'll be nice. The poor child's been through hell since she lost the Miss Georgia United States of America Pageant."

"Excuse me, did you just say hell?"

"Savannah! Don't you make it sound like I was cussing! I was just trying to reference the depth of her despair." Mother placed the large cooler in the back of the car.

"Mother, we're talking *beauty pageant*." I spoke slowly, trying to make it clear the child hadn't just amputated a limb or something.

"Savannah, you will never understand." She turned on her heels, rather gracefully, I might add. But she's had centuries of practice. "And she is coming," she added in a yelled whisper over her shoulder. Then she called out to the tragic figure inside the house, "Don't you worry, precious girl. Miss Victoria will make this the best week of your life. We'll go to the spa, paint pottery, go shop . . ." The words faded as they drifted back inside. However, Amber's moans continued to waft through the garage. The little white ball of fur encased in hot pink came back to the door and yapped at me for good measure before following Vicky.

"Yap, yap, yourself." I hollered with a stomp of my foot. She tucked her tail between her legs and beat it.

"Savannah, quit." Dad nudged me playfully. "You'll scar her."

"*Me* scar *her*? You're about to travel with two women—no, make that three women, if you include the little white varmint, who seriously could be the poster children for 'This is drugs, this is your brain on—'"

"Cut it out." He gave me a raised eyebrow.

I returned the gesture. "Seriously, you'll need a vacation from your vacation with all of this estrogen."

"Maybe you can help Amber get through this difficult time. After all, you did offer your friendship, remember?" He closed the trunk.

"Me?" I pointed to myself. "Do you have any idea what I have already helped this girl through in the weeks since she lost? The dinners, the movies, the emptied tissue boxes? Lord have mercy, man, the *sleepovers*."

"Careful."

"Well, I haven't forgotten. And all I can say is, if you are resolute on this point, then I'm resolute that Paige is going with us."

"We don't have room, Savannah. Thomas is going to have to share the backseat with Duke as it is." He walked around the side of the car and checked the straps on the rooftop luggage container.

"Well, rumor has it Thomas is delayed."

He eyed me.

"And another rumor has it that I have already asked Paige, and she said yes."

"Well, I guess I should be grateful I have Duke along for the ride." He gave the luggage strap one more tug. "And we'll deal with the Thomas rumor later."

The amazing thing about Jake Phillips: he always found time for later.

CHAPTER FOUR

Does Pink Toes have a name?" I asked my father as he filled the cooler with Cokes from the refrigerator in the garage. I was avoiding the house at all costs. Not having to see my mother or Amber offered a little hope that maybe this nightmare that was supposed to be a vacation would all go away.

"She does. Magnolia." He smiled.

"Well, why did I ask?" I really should have known. *Magnolia* was what Mother had wanted to name Duke. It was in fact one of the reasons she despised Duke and he despised her. Her animosity: he wasn't her Magnolia. His animosity: she had wanted to name him after a tree. Granted, the dog liked to pee on trees and flowers, but he didn't want to be named after one. A dog had his pride. They hadn't cared for each other since. She hid his treats; he ate her shoes. It was an equal trade. But his life had now successfully been destroyed. At least at home. I doubt Pink Toes would make it to Jake's Coffee Shop for daily siestas.

"I think I'll call her Maggy," I said as a declaration.

"If you dare." Vicky hated anything ending in *y*. That's why I wanted to change my name to Betty. Why I still called her Vicky in my head. And why her friends Cindy, Lucy, and Chloe have been renamed Cynthia, Lucinda, and Chloina. The woman doesn't care that Chloina isn't a name. Nor is she apparently cognizant of the fact that Chloe doesn't end in a *y*. But if Chloe doesn't mind, who am I to protest.

"Oh, I dare."

Dad disappeared into the house to round up Mother and Amber. Paige rounded the corner of the garage about the same time Maggy came running out of the house, barking as if she had no idea one swat would fly her into next week.

My friend halted in her tracks at the edge of the house, suitcase in one hand, art portfolio in the other. She set the suitcase down. "Savannah, you better tell me that dog doesn't belong to your mama."

"Okay. That dog doesn't belong to my mama. Now, let's put your little bag here in the trunk." I tried to lift her two-ton bag from the concrete into the back of the SUV.

"Oh no you don't!" She jerked her luggage from my hand. "You are not going to corner me in a car with all of this"—her jutting neck indicated the surrounding chaos—"and then sit me in a house with it for a week."

I grabbed both of her shoulders and made her look into my eyes. Her messy, short, bleached-blonde tresses were in exceptional disarray today. But I stared into her blue eyes. "You can do this," I assured her. "We can do this," I assured myself. "We are competent, able women."

She met my gaze. "You are certifiable."

"I just need to go."

"Why? Why do you need to go? You could have a week's vacation from all of this if you stayed here. Why in the world would you want to follow the havoc?"

"Because . . . well, there's a story. A necessary story that I need to tell. And the only way it will be told is . . . well . . . is if I tell it."

"And you couldn't just make a phone call, take an interview, write your little story, and prevent this madness?"

"Please, no more questions. My little mind is full of riddles. And it can't take all this riddling. Please, you have to do this with me. We'll get there and leave these people to their own devices. We'll lie on the beach far away from them. We'll eat at different restaurants. We'll sleep outside in a pup tent if necessary."

"That will not be necessary."

"Good!" I sighed in relief. "But I would have done it for you. Plus, the tans that await us will be spectacular."

"You will owe me for the rest of your life."

I removed her luggage from her death grip. "I probably already do."

"Oh, you do." She glared. "You do."

"Okay. Let's get a move on," Dad declared as he returned. He opened up the back and let Duke in where he had created enough room for Duke's expansive pillow. Mother came out of the house with one arm wrapped around the sniffling Amber, and the other arm carrying a pink-pillowed basket with Pink Toes resting inside. Few ever returned from the place where we were about to travel. One could only hope the spiral downward would offer directions back up.

Like all things Amber, even her getting "settled" into the backseat was a performance. Paige and I, not being the sharpest knives in the drawer, just stood and watched as Amber "settled" herself into the middle. Had we been a tad more astute, we would have pushed her long-legged behind over to the door.

She placed her purse between her legs. Set her makeup bag on top of that, and then nestled a box of tissues in her lap. She put her seat belt on, attentive to its potentially crushing effects on her seersucker sundress. One leg stretched itself onto my side, the other reached over to Paige, and then Amber reached into her rather colorful Louis Vuitton bag, which probably cost as much as a month of my rent, and pulled out some rather sizable white-framed sunglasses. "They'll cover the puffiness," she informed the two lamentable gawkers witnessing her invading their space. Truth be told, the child looked like an albino fly. Further truth be told, I might just pawn her bag to pay next month's rent and the speeding ticket that should have been hers.

Paige only entered because I shoved her.

"*Grrr*," Maggy offered.

"Grrr," Paige retorted.

Maggy returned to hiding. This was going to be fun.

I squeezed in beside the retail store, and Duke sat in the back, none too happy either. He leaned his head over my right shoulder mighty close to Amber's rather large white hoop earrings and about ripped her ear open with his nose when it got caught in the center of the ring. That caused a brief interruption, but with Duke's nose set free, Amber's earrings placed inside next month's rent, and Paige's huffing slowed to a heavy sigh, we finally made it out of the garage. Nothing transpired as planned. Had it, we would have all started looking up for Jesus' return!

As we pulled onto Oglethorpe, I felt the familiar tug of my city. The tug that reminded me I really never liked leaving this place, even if it was only for a week of vaca—research. Odd for a woman who had been gone six years and only returned ten months ago. But even through those years of college and graduate school there was always an aching for home. My home. The city that mocked me as its "Savannah from Savannah," an identity forced upon me by years of Victoria-induced introductions.

I, however, finally accepted it, realized only one man would ever call me Betty, and now ended each of my columns declaring my own self "Savannah from Savannah" to the very readers who taunted me. The hope was that the self-assertion would end all ridicule. It wasn't completely successful. Today, I simply disregarded the pockets of resistance. Well, most of the time.

But Savannah the city had come to define me. It had allowed me a place to fail miserably and yet survive. Few places allow such grace. And even though I had let go of my one-time goal of literary acclaim, I settled into a nice rhythm of literary life, examining the essence of our humanness and telling its story through the eyes of a less-than-perfect journeyman. The city had welcomed me. Begrudgingly but eventually. I had accepted it. Begrudgingly but eventually as well.

The foghorn of Amber's nose blared beside me.

Let's hope my return would be better than the departure.

CHAPTER FIVE

Seaside had been the official Phillips-family vacation site since I can remember. I know people say that a lot, but it really is true. My parents started vacationing in Seaside in 1982 when I was only two and Thomas just a thought. In all honesty, Thomas might have been created at Seaside. Ooh, now, that's a thought a child shouldn't have to have.

Seaside provided Dad the ability to get away from Atlanta's craziness and get to the ocean. That longing for the water is one reason he finally decided to hang his hat in Savannah, but when you see his face in Seaside, you have to wonder if maybe this isn't the place he would rather have retired.

The small community of Seaside was only four years old at the time of our first visit, an ocean community that was the dream of Robert and Daryl Davis. A place of honest-to-goodness community living, of brick streets and neighbors who stop and chat when they see you sitting on the front porch. A place where the pace doesn't lose you; you lose the pace. Actually, it was eighty acres of land that Robert's grandfather purchased in 1946 for a hundred dollars an acre. He had a dream of building an employee summer camp called Dreamland Heights. And though he never saw his dream come to pass, many a passer through has enjoyed or created a few dreams of their own in the place now called Seaside.

Another reason I'm sure we continue to drive south for our vacation instead of travel to far-off, exotic places, is because Vicky refuses to fly anymore. And after her last trip (which entailed an overdose of Xanax and some shameless pictures Thomas and I took of her), she prefers vacation sites that can be reached by car. However, Dad still forces her on a plane once a year for his annual fall vacation.

We also go to Seaside due in large part to the fact that we can rent homes with full kitchens there. Not that Vicky gets to cook, though. No. Vicky is only allowed to cook breakfast on vacation and a few beach-going offerings. Seaside week is Jake's domain. He is the grilling king, and this is his week to shine. Plus, his are about the only offerings she will actually eat without inspection. She doesn't do this often. The woman has culinary phobia. If it's not hers, it might not be from scratch. And if it's not from scratch, well, the Lord will have to raise the South again. So, Seaside offers nice, fully furnished homes with clean linens (she still brings her own) and functioning kitchens and outdoor grills.

On the nights Dad doesn't feel like cooking, we go out to eat. With or without her. So she's learned that if she wants to eat with him, she'll have to make some concessions. Just like at home, she's found some restaurants that meet her standards. Criolla's does because it's been featured on the Food Network. It's my favorite. The Fish out of Water restaurant at the new Water Colors resort next to Seaside won her approval because its shrimp and grits are, frankly, better than her own. Even she has trouble hiding the sheer pleasure on her face.

The masterpiece lay open on my lap. *"Happy families are all alike; every unhappy family is unhappy in its own way."*

"You know, I was thinking." Amber crashed into my reading mode, returning me to the reality of an endless car ride with my legs up under my chin.

Did Tolstoy know us?

"What were you thinking about, sweetheart?" Mother responded.

"I was thinking . . ." She began to sniffle. Paige reached her arm around the back of Amber's neck and attacked my shoulder with a death grip. "I was thinking that there are no people I would rather be with in the world than you, my new family . . . during this, this, this SEASON OF DEATH!"

I grimaced. Paige bristled. Duke poked his head over Amber's shoulder and sniffed her hair and cocked his head. Mother reached back and patted her knee. And Pink Toes dared to peek her head out of her basket.

Duke saw her. "*Grrr.*"

Paige growled too.

Pink Toes got the message and returned to hiding. The only thing visible from the top of the basket was a sprig of white hair sticking out from her pink bow. Duke put a paw on the back of the seat as if he was going to come over. I informed him there wasn't room for his hairy behind. He conceded and returned to his pillow with a thump and a sigh. He and Paige were more alike than I had realized.

"I know this is a hard time for you," Paige said. "So we don't want you to have to talk about it. You just sit here and rest."

"Actually, I'd love to tell—"

"Yes, you rest." I patted her bare shoulder. "We'll even make sure you have plenty of space when we get to Seaside. I'm sure this is really close quarters for you during such a difficult season of your life."

"Why don't we sing a happy song?" Mother offered.

"Why don't we strangle ourselves?" I offered. Quietly.

"Savannah." Dad shot me a glance through the rearview mirror. Obviously not quiet enough.

I stared back. "I said, why don't we sing something from the Bangles?"

"Oh, Savannah, quit being a smart aleck. Singing will do us good. Amber needs to be cheered up. Don't you think so, darling?" she asked my father.

He looked back at me with that face. I gave him one of my own. "I think that would be a great idea." He smiled.

That was all it took. On came the CD player and out came Harry Connick Jr. leading a chorus of some more woeful singers in "You're Never Fully Dressed without a Smile." From *Annie.* That tone-deaf creature in the front holding a frightened little white rat started singing to the top of her lungs, making it unclear why she had turned on the CD at all. A CD I had thoroughly enjoyed until that moment. Because from then on I would never be able to hear it without having a petit mal seizure.

In a few minutes, the blubbering one beside me was doing her best to sing along. I had heard her sing once before. The event caused me to propel my forehead into my steering wheel. It hurt. Twofold. Today was no different. I was hurting in duplicate again. Then the rat starting howling, and I was hurting in triplicate. Then I saw Paige's head start to bob to the music. And before I knew it, I had lost her too.

By the time they were through, even Dad was humming along. It was all just plain wrong. Duke had buried his head in his pillow and wrapped his paws over his ears. I retrieved my ear plugs, but they offered little buffering. I even attempted to climb in the back with Duke just to create some distance, but he was still holding a grudge. At their climax, I popped four Advil and hoped they were "fast acting." Of course "time release" would be okay as well, because I was certain I would need relief all along the way. After all, we hadn't been on the road for more than thirty minutes.

By the time they were finished, I was humming, "Why Me, Lord?" They didn't care. Why would they? They were all fully dressed with a smile.

"Oh, that was fun!" Paige laughed.

I leaned my head around the Amazon beside me to catch a glimpse of the woman who had officially migrated to loolooville. "Fun, huh?" I replied.

"Savannah, you're just wound too tight."

Amber said, "You know, that's it! I've wondered all along what exactly was Savannah's problem." Now my life had officially fallen into a chasm, never to be retrieved. I was being analyzed by a kook. "Savannah, you are just too uptight. You need to relax, be young, be foolish"—she started singing again—"but be happy."

I wasn't smiling. The rest of the car joined in, officially sinking us to the depths of a karaoke bar. I leaned my head back on the headrest and closed my eyes. Paige was right. The real vacation would have been back in Savannah, far, far away from this car of nuts. This wasn't going to be a vacation after all. This was going to be my own *Survivor.* To be honest, all bets were on the rest of them. After less than an hour, I didn't even have the energy to open my eyes.

"Ahhhhh! Watch it!" Mother screamed.

I opened my eyes just in time to see her slam on her imaginary brakes. Which really didn't faze me all that much, because we had already endured the "Jake, you're going to be listening to that semi's stereo if you get any closer."

We had endured the clutching of the chest.

We had endured the endless gasps.

After all, the woman lived in the land of "all objects are closer than they appear."

How Dad had survived the last twenty-five years of her riding in the passenger seat of his car was beyond me. I stopped allowing her to ride with me years ago, after she screamed so loud that I ran smack-dab into a city square and came to rest with my bumper attached to a statue of General Oglethorpe, all because she was certain I was about to hit a trolley car that was a good football field away. The accident made the front cover of the *Chronicle*. She was seen smiling in the picture. The photo caught me eye to eye with General Oglethorpe's family jewels, separated only by the cracked windshield.

"Victoria, I'll make this clear once," Dad declared. Now, Jake wasn't one to make many declarations. But when he did, you could pretty much bet your mother's weekly appointments at *Day Spa of Deliverance* that he was going to follow through on whatever it was he was declaring. "I will not ride the next six hours with you gasping and grabbing and telling me how to drive."

"You about hit that car."

He remained calm. "I wasn't anywhere near that car."

"You were riding his bumper."

"How can you ride a bumper that is too far away to even see?" He had a point there. I couldn't even read the bumper sticker.

"How do you not get in wrecks without me in the car?"

"Just lucky, I guess."

That makes two of us "lucky" people today.

"Well, you better be careful. You've got precious cargo in this car."

"Precious cargo that will enjoy your driving abilities if you scare me again."

"Jake, be nice."

I was certain that was nice.

I wondered if that would settle it. It might have if they were driving from Savannah to Tybee Island, but if that man really thought that woman was capable of not gasping the rest of this trip, then maybe he wasn't as bright as I had thought for the last twenty-four years.

"Happy families are all alike: every unhappy family is unhappy in its own way." I began again.

"I've got to go tinkle." Amber interrupted again.

I knew what made *us* unhappy in our own way.

"What?" Paige asked. "We haven't even been in the car for an hour."

"I know. But I've got a tiny bladder." To me, that seemed impossible for a woman the size of a camel.

"We need to stop anyway." Mother's bladder was just as tiny. "Magnolia's bladder is very tiny right now, too." Oh, new rule: Magnolia will be blamed for Mother's needs. "The little thing will probably need to make quite a few stops along the way."

Dad pulled off at the nearest rest stop. He didn't mind. He was never in a hurry. He spent his life just enjoying living. He didn't mind stopping. He didn't mind driving. Being told how to drive maybe, but not the actual driving itself. He didn't mind walking Duke. He didn't mind Duke taking thirty minutes to take a dump. Jake was just the kind of man who had no agenda other than enjoying the moment. Plus, he knew Duke always loved the opportunity to sniff around a rest area.

We got out of the car. Paige first. Amber rushed around her and daintily trotted to the restroom. Mother followed immediately. Paige's face was contorted to a slight grimace as I rounded the front of the car.

"You're never fully dressed without a smile, remember?" I said in my best singsong voice. "And from the looks of that expression, you're about half-naked right now, sister."

She didn't care. She lost sight of me as soon as the good-looking fella drove up in the Audi convertible. He headed to the restroom. All of a sudden she had to "tinkle" too.

CHAPTER SIX

"You afraid he might fall in love with that little thing?" I asked Dad as he walked Duke through the dogs' section of the rest area.

Mother had returned and was walking in front of us, holding a hot pink, rhinestone-studded dog leash that connected to a hot pink rhinestone-studded choker. The little thing was dragging Mother through the area where Mother had to dodge wads with her two-hundred-dollar heels.

"That dog better not touch my pookie." Mother directed this remark at Duke while trying desperately to get back to the sidewalk.

Duke came over to little Maggy and sniffed her, and the poor thing jumped about ten feet in the air.

"Shoo!" Mother hollered.

Duke got bored with them both and came to sit between me and Dad. Dad reached down and rubbed his head. Duke leaned into his hand with mutual affection. "I don't think you'll have to worry about Duke messing with Magnolia. I think she's a little overprocessed for him."

You think?" I asked, offering Duke a rub of my own. My cell phone rang, interrupting Duke's moment in the spotlight.

"Hello . . . hello." Silence on the other end. I looked at the dead receiver. "Disconnected," it announced. "My stars, I have disconnected more people than I actually talk to."

"When did you get that new phone?" Dad asked.

"A couple weeks ago. But I can't figure out how to work it. I get my e-mail on here too. At least that's what the guy at the store told me."

"Why would anyone want to get e-mail on their phone?" The man had no agenda but coffee and conversation.

I stared at my phone. I would have responded, except I wasn't exactly sure at that moment why I did want to get my e-mail on my cell phone. "It sounded good to me when the guy told me what it could do."

It rang again.

"Hello," I said, pressing the *talk* button gingerly.

"What are you doing?" my friend Claire asked. I laughed into the phone and excused myself from present company. Claire and I caught up for a few minutes while the world of "rest area" whirled in the background.

The odd pair of Amber and Paige exited the restroom together. The gentleman Paige had followed drove off minutes ago. But it seemed she had forgotten him.

Amber climbed back into her seat, and we all took our places.

"I think I left the door unlocked," Paige said to the air.

"What?"

"I think I left the door to the gallery unlocked."

"Well, call Bill next door and have him go check it."

"He and his wife went with Mom and Dad."

"Well, call Jeff on the other side."

She grabbed her phone. "Yeah, he can do it for me."

Duke wasn't interested in Paige's issues. He lifted his head up over the seat as soon as the car backed out of the parking place. He began to make a low growling sound in the depths of his throat.

Pink Toes inched lower into her picnic basket, desiring not to be lunch.

"Calm down, boy. She's not taking your place," I assured him. "No one is taking anyone's place." Maybe I was trying to convince myself.

The whole thing, however, seemed to be just a little more than he could bear this time. I mean, as soon as we got back on the interstate, Duke lost it. Before anyone could stop him, that seventy-five pound animal leaped over my seat, ran his right paw through Amber's hair, got his left paw hooked in the handle of her handbag, slapped the phone from Paige's hand, and let absolutely none of that stop him. He jumped up onto the armrest between Dad and Mother and hopped into Dad's lap with his tail wagging like a fly swatter in Vicky's face. If Magnolia could be a lapdog, so could he.

Vicky screamed. Dad tried to stay on the road. And we missed careening into a road-construction barrel by inches. Dad pushed on him to get back, but no one in the backseat wanted him returning the way he had come. Poor Amber was back to crying, and Magnolia was whimpering like a whipped puppy, and Vicky was spitting and sputtering, all while trying to extract red dog hairs from her red lipstick.

Dad pulled the car over and returned Duke to his pillow with a pat of the head and a whisper in the ear. Who knew what those two talked about. But Duke wasn't easily deterred. He returned to his growling over Amber's shoulder. She whimpered and moved closer to Paige. Paige groaned and tried to smooth Amber's disheveled hair. Amber reached into her purse to grab some Advil and a bottled water.

Paige snatched the bottled water with one hand while dialing Jeff with the other. "You just had to go pee."

"But I need some Advil."

Paige wasn't budging. "Take them dry."

"Paige!" I momentarily felt bad for the soul next to me.

Paige didn't care. "This has already been an eternal trip, and I'm not stopping every thirty minutes for sister here to take a potty break."

"I just need a sip."

Paige hesitated but finally laid the phone down, opened the bottle, and handed it to her. "One sip."

Amber complied more out of fear and exhaustion than anything else. She took the cap from Paige's hands. "Oh no, you don't. Give it back."

Amber didn't want to, but she did. And from then on Paige was the regulator of all Amber's liquid consumption.

Jeff wasn't home. Gone for three weeks, his voice mail declared. Paige took of swig of the water herself, her expression making it clear she wished it had been stronger.

"There it is, ladies. Lunch," Dad pronounced.

Every head looked up.

Except mine. There was no need. I had seen my father's on-the-road restaurant of choice many times.

"What is this?" Amber asked.

"What is this? This is Southern feastings at their finest," my father informed, turning the car off with a smile.

Thomas and I had been tortured for years. Thomas and I hated country ham and breakfast for lunch. Dad loved both. Cracker Barrel had both. So Cracker Barrel it was. Only the country store saved us. Knowing we would leave with access to a sugar coma inside our individual brown goody bags, we entered each Cracker Barrel experience without the weeping and gnashing of teeth.

I saw the wooden rocking chairs on the front porch swaying away. Every grandmother passing through was encased in her sweater of the season. Why elderly people feel the need to wear seasonal attire is beyond me. I mean when the Christmas sweaters come out in Savannah, I prostrate myself and thank the good Lord Christmas only comes once a year. But when women actually pull out Halloween sweaters, it's certain they have unresolved, deeply rooted issues.

At least spring sweaters offer a variety of colors and vegetables. Truth be told, it's one of those ideas I wish I would have thought of myself: grow you a garden, wrap you some gifts, carve you some pumpkins and hot glue those puppies on some knitted cotton sweaters, and by George, I'd have me a collection called "Seasons by Savannah." But no, as with most lucrative ideas, I'm usually left somewhere in the land of "if only I had thought of that."

"Victoria, what are you doing?" Dad asked, eyeing the pink basket that she was trying to take into the restaurant.

"Well, I hope you don't think I'm leaving her in that car with Duke. We'll come out, and her tail will be hanging out of his mouth."

Dad reached for the basket. He was met with resistance. "You can't take her in there, honey. She'll be fine. Won't she, Duke?"

I could have sworn Duke grinned.

"If he harms one hair of her fur, Jake Phillips, he'll be shipped to an island for castrated retrievers."

Dad winced. Why is it men always wince when someone talks about castration or vasectomies, or when they watch an episode of *Funniest Home Videos* and those skateboarding idiots make contact with railings? But they do. Dad took Maggy from her anyway.

"I'll put up the netting to keep Duke in the back."

I laughed.

"Why is she laughing?" Mother asked my father.

He turned and raised his eyebrow at me. "Because she thought of something funny. Isn't that right, Savannah?"

"That is absolutely true." The truth that Duke chewing right through that netting wouldn't take more than ten minutes caused me to downright laugh hysterically.

We walked inside. I looked back, wondering if the car would even survive what was capable of transpiring inside it while we dined on biscuits and gravy. Oh well. We'd know soon enough.

My cell phone rang three times over lunch. Just to let me know I had e-mails.

"I will throw that in the trash," my mother offered. Loudly.

Dad concurred, "Savannah, really. We want this to be a peaceful vacation."

I eyed them both, wondering why nothing had been said to Paige about her ringing cell phone.

The focus was eventually removed from me, because right in the middle of Uncle Hershel's breakfast and Amber's egg-yolk omelet, the request for which caused the waiter's eyebrows to rise, my mother's scream came loud and furious. "He's got my baby in his mouth!"

That Pink Toes had become her baby in no less than a week was proof of Mother's ability to bond easily. It had taken me years to break free of a little of that Super Glue bonding, but I was glad to realize in that moment that she had shifted her attentions to another subject.

Vicky took off out of that Cracker Barrel quicker than Paige could inhale her last bite of hash-brown casserole. Amber screamed and followed. Dad paid the bill. I refused to leave without grabbing a pecan log, and Paige stuffed the rest of her biscuits in her purse. By the time we got to the car, Duke was licking Magnolia's head with a rather sinister expression. I didn't think he had murder in him, but one had to wonder. Vicky might just have saved her little munchkin. Or even sicker still, Duke might have fallen in love with a Lilliputian.

Nah.

CHAPTER SEVEN

"Happy families are all alike; every unhappy family *is unhappy in its own way."*

The hacking sound came from the front seat.

"What in the world is that sound?" Amber asked me.

I slammed my book shut. "I have no idea." Then I saw it. The little white fluff of fur was leaning over the edge of her basket in the first throes of heaving. I knew what this was. Duke had done it a thousand times. Usually after a gorging of beans and weenies. Whatever just went down was about to come back up.

So maybe we had more than one way to be unhappy.

"Jake!" Mother screamed. "Stop the car! Stop the car! Magnolia's about to be—"

There wasn't enough time for her to even finish her sentence. Miss Magnolia got sicker than a dog. And the evidence was cascading down on Vicky's lovely "car riding" outfit.

Dad swerved to the side of the road. "Ooh Lord, have mercy. That stinks."

No sooner had he got the car pulled over than Mother was opening the door, making some pretty good gagging sounds herself.

All while holding the little basket containing the sick puppy out the door.

The smell was so putrid the three of us in the backseat decided getting out into fresh air might not be such a bad idea. Amazing that something so small could produce something so lethal.

"Paige, take her," Mother said, trying to hand the basket to Paige. Paige reluctantly obliged because of her respect for her elders, all while holding her nose.

"Savannah, I've got some wet wipes in my makeup bag in the back."

I walked around to the back of the car, and Duke came billowing out, sucking half of the air from the atmosphere. The poor thing must have been holding his breath ever since we got out of the car.

"Now you know how we feel," I whispered to him as he fell over in the grass, playing dead. "You should have gotten rid of her while you had the chance."

As Dad was helping to clean up Mother, we heard the gagging sound again. "Oh no, you don't, Pink Toes," Paige said, setting the basket on the ground.

"Savannah, get Magnolia out of the basket and hold her while she throws up," Mother hollered.

"Do what?"

"You heard me."

Maggy gagged again. I gagged in response.

"For Pete's sake, Savannah, help her!"

"We aren't talking *dying roadside victim* here. We are talking *carsick rodent.* Potent rodent at that," I added, trying to hold my breath. I was certain the thing could take care of herself, but I gingerly picked her up by her heaving sides and held her over the grass. I turned my head away from the horrors of the odors. No good. I was downwind. And every aroma Pink Toes offered to the environment, the environment offered back to me.

After it finished its regurgitating, the thing went to shaking and quaking.

"Come here, my little sweetie pie," Mother said after Dad had done all he could. "Let Mommy wipe your little mouthy-wouffy." She cooed and gagged at the same time while wiping the rat's mouth off with a wet wipe as if it were a toddler.

"It's all my FAAUUULT!" The wail came loud and shrill.

Paige and I jerked to the heap of seersucker and honey-brown hair on the side of the road.

Paige nudged me. "If we had a video camera, we'd have just won a hundred thousand dollars."

Mother waddled toward Amber with Maggy and her basket hooked over one arm.

"I'm BAAAD luck! I mean, look at us. We're sitting by the side of the road. Your precious little princess can't keep her lunch down."

How she saw precious and princess in that was beyond me.

"And your outfit is ruined. And here I am, a beauty queen, sitting by the side of the ROOOAAAD!"

Paige and I leaned against the car. Had they offered a million-dollar prize, we would have taken that home too.

Mother set Maggy down gingerly and pulled out another baby wipe. She lifted Amber's chin. Paige and I had to turn away. Even beauty queens could not cry pretty!

"Sweet baby girl. You don't worry about Miss Victoria's dress. We will go shopping and buy us both new dresses. We are going to pamper ourselves all week long, because this is all about making you feel better and taking your mind off your heartache."

"Think we could get in on the clothes buying?" Paige whispered.

"Humph. We don't need them or their money. We are going to take care of ourselves. Because we are grown women with real jobs and *real* lives."

"We're on vacation with your parents."

"*You're* on vacation with my parents. I'm researching a story."

"Okay, Sherlock. Tell yourself what you will, but sister ain't here for no story. Sister's here because she's getting replaced by a dog and a beauty queen."

"You are ridiculous."

"You are—"

Fortunately Dad interrupted her and rounded all of us back to the interior. Maggy got a case of the shakes that would have made a salsa dancer look docile.

Amber pulled a bottle from her purse and sprayed the air in front of her nose.

"What did you just spray?" I asked the companion sitting next to me.

"It's Vera Wang." Amber smiled.

"Great! Now we get to enjoy the rest of the trip soaking up the aroma of flowers and puke." I couldn't have described this vacation better myself.

"Watch out for that buzzard!" Mother screamed as the little black crow flew from the side of the road. And as a man true to his word, she left Jake Phillips no option.

Right there in the middle of I-10, he pulled the car over, placed it in park, opened the door, and got out. He walked around to Mother's side of the car and opened the door for her. "Your turn."

She laughed that surely-you-jest kind of half laugh and said, "Jake, don't be silly. Get back in the car."

"No, Victoria. I told you that if you screamed again, I was going to let you drive. You screamed. You drive."

"Jake, I'm not driving." Her face flushed with momentary embarrassment, a rather odd occasion. I studied it carefully. "Now, get back over there." She reached for the door. He didn't budge.

Amber began wringing the handles of her Louis Vuitton. Paige, Duke, and I were enjoying the episode. I wouldn't have minded some popcorn.

"Victoria, I said you are driving. Now, either get out and walk around, or climb over."

He removed the quivering basket from her hand. At least the man was kind enough to hold her rancid dog. I thought the trade showcased humanity in its finest form.

She looked at him incredulously. He stared at her, expressionless. In a few moments she flipped the skirt of her dress around, slid her heels out of the car, and stood at the car door as he climbed into her seat. Her eyes narrowed as she glared at him one more time, waiting to make sure he wasn't going to bust out in hysterics. He simply closed the door. She came around to the driver's side and climbed in. And proceeded to take her time hooking her seat belt, finding a station on the radio, and trying to convince each one of us this was all her idea. Had we not just witnessed the fiasco, we might have actually bought the act. At least we were able to enjoy the whole scenario.

Off we went. Jake leaning back in his seat, determined not to arrive at his vacation stressed. Duke growling ceaselessly, not even attempting to hide his sense of betrayal, ready to pounce on the puking princess on his master's lap. Mother tried to maintain her composure. The woman would need a good three days before she unwound from this event. She'd have plenty of company. The only person who wouldn't need therapy would be the man who was holding a doggy basket on his lap. He was already sleeping.

The sniffles started again. "It's been such a trying time in my life."

"And trying times need to be dealt with in much more pleasant circumstances than these," Paige interjected as she rolled down the window. "Here. I bet you could use some fresh air." She grabbed Amber's head and directed it toward the window.

"Ever gotten a spanking in the car?" I called out, searching for a new topic.

Amber jerked her head inside and tried to reconstruct her hair and wipe her nose at the same time. "Oh no. My parents didn't believe in spanking." Who did that surprise? The woman was named Amber Topaz. How could you spank that?

"Mine either," Paige offered. I didn't believe her for a second. "They gave me whuppin's." Now, that was more like it.

Dad woke up unannounced and entered the conversation uninvited. "Savannah Phillips, neither you nor Thomas got nearly the spankings you should have gotten." He chuckled.

Amber gasped. "Miss Victoria, you believe in corporal punishment?"

Mother still wasn't in the greatest moods for talking, so she simply said, "Uh-huh."

I couldn't let her get away with that.

"Uh-huh? She doesn't just believe in corporal punishment, Amber. She believes spanking should be administered with a fly-swatter." Amber's face contorted in horror. "And she spanks with one swat per syllable. 'You-will-li-sten-to-me-when-I-talk-to-you,'" I mimicked in my best Vicky, all while swatting the air with my hand.

Paige interjected, "And heaven help those whose mothers are so deeply Southern that words that should be one syllable turn into two. 'You-a-re-go-ing-to-re-gret-th-is . . .' Those beatings just go on forever." That one even made Mother laugh. But she refused to take her eyes off of the road.

"The worst is when we were on road trips like this, and Dad would be driving, and Thomas and I would get into it, and he would try to reach behind his seat to get us. We'd get as close to the car doors as we could to try to get out of the line of fire."

Dad laughed. "So I'd just stop the car and take you beside the road and give you a whipping."

"I just can't imagine any parents whipping their children," Amber said.

I pointed to the front seat. "Well, now you don't have to

imagine it. You have two actual participants sitting right in front of you."

Something forced Amber to look out the window. Mother had finally gotten off of the interstate and pulled up to a traffic light. "Ooh, Miss Victoria, you just technically ran that red light."

"No, I didn't. The light's still red, and I'm sitting here perfectly stopped."

"Well, actually, if your front wheels have crossed the large white lines at the end of this lane, then technically you have run a red light. You could get a ticket for that."

Paige looked up from her phone, which she was studying as if it would tell her who else to call about her unlocked door. "How do you know that?"

"Oh, I spent eight hours taking a defensive driving class."

Paige gloated, batting her short eyelashes. "What? The beauty queen couldn't get out of a ticket?"

"Actually, the 'beauty queen's'"—Amber batted back in mock appreciation—"platform at the Miss United States of America pageant was the benefits of defensive driving training in an era of reckless and self-centered vehicle operatives." Then that bottom lip began to quiver. "So, not only did I not win, but I spent"—and there she went, wailing the rest of her sentence—"eight hours with a bunch of HOOODLUUUMMS!"

"Hey, don't be so quick to judge," I said. "I took that course, and I'm not a hoodlum."

Dad turned to look at me and raised his right eyebrow. Paige wrapped her arm around Amber, doing her best to offer comfort. "It's okay. Look at all you've learned."

Amber brought her wails down to managed heaves. "Ooh, Miss Victoria, when you make a turn, you need to stay in the inside lane." She dabbed her eyes with tissue. Paige and I really could learn a lot from her. "Unless there are two turning lanes, then you stay in the lane you are in."

I noticed that little muscle in Mother's jaw begin to pulse. And all would have been fine had Mother not gotten into the turning lane to go to Wal-Mart a tad too soon for Miss Defensive Driver of America.

"Uh, Miss Victoria, not to, uh, be a nuisance or anything, but you really aren't supposed to get into this lane until you're at your turning destination. Turning lanes aren't for our driving pleasure; they're for turning."

Mother made a turn of her own. She turned to look at Amber, who sat wide-eyed and amazingly unmascara-clotted. Fortunately for Amber was that the woman wasn't armed with a fly-swatter. "Amber, if you mention my driving one more time, *you* can drive the rest of the way."

"Ooh. Trouble in paradise," I mouthed to Paige, who had peered behind Amber's shoulders.

With that, Miss Victoria squealed into a parking place, got out, and headed into Wal-Mart all by herself. Dad remained seated, smiling with extreme satisfaction.

Amber looked at the three remaining humans in the car, whose eyes were locked on her. Her lip began to quiver one more time.

"Ah! No, you don't, missy," Paige said, grabbing her arm. "Get out of the car, and we'll go buy you some ice cream. I'll even let you get a bottled water." And with that Paige and Amber followed Miss Victoria into the land of every need supplied.

CHAPTER EIGHT

"You really thought this would be a good idea?" I asked the man in the front seat, holding the quaking mutt.

He leaned his head back. "It became rather peaceful after I made your mother drive."

"Until our personal driver's handbook decided to entertain."

"I found it rather informative."

"You gloated."

"I deserved to. After twenty-five years of that woman trying to tell me how to drive, I found those five minutes rather enjoyable."

"How does she think you get anywhere without her?"

"I have no idea."

"You would think she would have eventually quit commenting."

"You'd think."

"Ever wanted to slap her?" I knew that would make him turn around.

"No, just you," he said with a wink.

I slapped him on his shoulder. That caused the pink-bowed princess to start a low moaning sound. Duke looked over my shoulder and growled at her. She whimpered. "That dog is pitiful."

Dad rubbed the top of her head, and she pushed it into his hands. "She's a sweet little thing. She just doesn't like road trips."

That officially made two of us.

Vicky never ventured into Wal-Mart except for our annual trip to Seaside. She's a Target kind of girl. I had come to discover, however, that the store was by far one of the greatest inventions of a generation. It had been my best friend since my college years. It had all the necessities of life: food, makeup, suntan lotion, CDs, and books. And it was always the first pit stop right after we turned off Interstate 10 to Highway 331. We'd backtrack north for a mile and hit the Super Wal-Mart before trekking the last thirty miles to Seaside.

"Has mother spent the night in a Target lately?" I asked Dad with a snicker.

He laughed that knowing laugh. "No. I think the last venture about did her in for sleepovers in lonely, dark places." He referred to the time Mother found out a new Sunbeam iron was about to hit the shelves. She watched the advertisements for a week.

"Did she ever actually get the iron?"

"She thinks irons are cursed."

"So is that why all of our clothes go to the dry cleaners?" I was finally figuring it all out.

"That's why your underwear has been starched all these years, baby girl."

This iron Mother wanted was "magical" for its time. It turned itself off, had a retractable cord, and came with purple or blue accents. Your choice. She wanted to be the first in line, as if the entire female population of Savannah was going to be spread out across Target's entrance in sleeping bags for an appliance and thus confirm they really were destined for a destitute life of housekeeping. Every other woman in Savannah was biting at the bit for such a declaration.

And Vicky agreed. So one night she hid in the store until it closed.

"Did you ever tell her that Don knew he locked her inside that evening?"

He laughed again. "No. He said she had pestered him all week about what day the iron was *actually* coming. So when he saw her Via Spigas sticking out from the zippered front of the tent in the camping section, he thought he'd let her enjoy her evening."

"He better be glad they don't sell guns at Target, because the way that Big Bird blow-up doll scared her, she might have shot holes in that place from kingdom come." I was getting downright slaphappy.

Dad was laughing so hard Pinky got to bouncing on his lap.

"*Hack*!" came the sound.

I laughed harder. "Be careful, or she is going to hurl all over you." I tried to breathe. "Did she ever say what made her actually spray the pepper spray in her own face?" That one got me tickled again.

Dad was holding the basket up in front of him so he could laugh without shaking Pink Toes to death. Duke was eyeing us both.

"She said that she could have sworn that that Big Bird was Big Foot, and when she went to spray him, the bottle was turned backward."

"What did the paramedics say?"

"Nice aim!" he blurted right in the little rat's face. He finally had to set her in the driver's seat so he could let loose. Poor man probably hadn't laughed this much since that night.

"Ooh . . . that is funny. Did they ever repair all the damage she did to the bicycle aisle?"

"No. She helped repair it, remember? I made her go to work there every day for the next two weeks when she got off at the chamber." He wiped his eyes, referring to her position as head of the Savannah Chamber of Commerce.

"Yeah, you went with her, you pitiful old man."

"Ooh . . ." He tried to catch his breath. "She had suffered enough."

We both sighed heavily while the tension in our stomachs began to loosen. We stared back at the doors to Wal-Mart, knowing perfectly well what was transpiring inside.

Wal-Mart on Seaside trips was where Victoria Phillips stocked up on all essentials, to be cooked under her supervision. Her shopping cart would consist of all things fresh. Fresh meats, fresh fruits, fresh vegetables, and fresh bread. She would bake a ham and a turkey and make us sandwich meat so we could have sandwiches at the beach.

We longed for Lunchables, but the woman wouldn't let people she loved eat pepperoni thinly sliced and packaged in plastic. She would graciously buy me an abundant supply of canned Cokes and a bag of ice. Because if I couldn't have McDonald's Coke from the fountain, then canned Cokes were as close to it as you could get. Unless you were fortunate enough to find the glass bottles.

Now that Paige was with us, there would be a substantial amount of Diet Cokes and Doritos, and with Amber coming on the trip, there was no telling. The child had eaten her weight in sweets since she had come in first runner-up. A couple evenings ago she spent the night with me, and the woman finished off two pints of Purity O'Charley's Caramel Pie ice cream without offering me so much as a spoon. I was pretty certain substantial amounts of sugars would be in her purchase.

Jake wouldn't require anything specific. Just enough meat to cook out. All he truly *required* were early morning walks with Duke down to Modica's Market to get a paper and to share a cup of coffee with Mr. Modica before anyone else arose. He and Duke would take the scenic route home and greet the other people they had become friends with through the years. Then he would sit on the front porch and rock in the rocking chair with his best friend beside him and Vicky (okay, maybe she is his best friend).

In any case, he would read his paper and drink his coffee. Mother would fix him a substantial breakfast, and they would eat outside together and laugh and talk. And you would see them fall in love all over again.

And some evenings Dad would slip me a twenty and ask me and whoever had traveled along to go entertain ourselves for a while so they could be alone. I would have to control my own gag reflex and would refuse to look at either of them for a full twenty-four hours. The mere thought of my father and mother being intimate was just too much. You know it has to happen—you just don't want to think about it. But something about them getting away from all the craziness of home allowed them to concentrate on each other a little differently. And even though it was disgusting and not a visual a child would want to dwell on, it was charming and provided a sense of safety. So there Dad sat, across from me, not needing to go into Wal-Mart for anything, because Victoria provided everything he needed. Happily, I might add.

Dad and I enjoyed our hour in the car together. It would have been perfect had Duke not attempted, no fewer than ten times, to take out the canine in the front seat.

The three women returned with enough groceries to feed a family of ten for no less than a month. Amber had been privileged to partake of liquid. Paige had a Diet Coke herself. And Mother had a smile. She had just spent money, hadn't she? And in what should have been no more than a six-hour trip, we entered Seaside, Florida, in a mere nine, each of us holding three Wal-Mart shopping bags on our lap. The Beverly Hillbillies had officially arrived.

I rolled down my window and smelled paradise.

My cell phone snapped me out of it.

"You think Sylvia Lancaster is home?" Paige asked from the other side of the car. "Maybe she could go check the door."

I reached behind Amber and slapped Paige on the back of the head. "It's fine. Your door is locked. You're on vacation. And no one is going to run away with your paintings. Now look out the window and enjoy the view."

"A little pent up?" Amber asked.

"It's called anal retentive," Paige said.

"If I hear those phones again, I will throw them out the window." So Mother's offer still stood.

A cell phone immediately started chirping. Both Paige and I swallowed hard as we looked down to check our caller IDs. It wasn't us. The chirping continued. Dad turned his head in the direction of Mother's rather large and obscenely expensive handbag.

"I think it's for you," I said with a huff toward the big brown eyes that had turned around to stare at me. Then I turned to give Duke a brief glance. He gave me a nod and turned his gaze back out the window. At least one of us cared to look at the world we were entering.

I turned my attention back to the highway. There was something almost magical about turning on Highway 30-A off of County Road 283 that takes you into the quaint recesses of Seaside. It hits you as soon as you pass Criolla's that life has just changed. Maybe it's the bike path that parallels the street, or the coastal dunelands that sneak up on you and offer a peaceful preview of the ocean that awaits. Whatever it is, when you hit the white sand dunes just across the first small bridge, a smile creeps across your face. And when the first tin roof comes into view, well, every part of your body just melts into the leather that surrounds you. You roll down your window so you can smell the salt. And when you do, your entire being enters vacation mode, and every being in the car, human and animal alike, exhales.

Today was especially beautiful. Because those tin roofs, picket fences, front porches, and towers perched atop many homes that overlooked the ocean meant liberation from this bench seat. We had officially started our working vacation. And everyone knew it. Seaside had grown immensely since we started this journey over twenty years ago. When we first started coming, there was nothing on 283. But now the colored shops of Grayton line the highway. And on 30-A, Grayton Market has taken over the corner, hiding Pandora's restaurant.

But the most noticeable difference is how the entrance to Seaside has changed. Used to be you were welcomed by the Seaside sign and the yellow home on the left with the peach and seafoam-green trim. It was the first house you would see before you took a step back in time. But that all changed in February 2002, when Water Colors was created, a seaside resort that made luxury retreats available to working families. But Water Colors arrived with condominiums as well as a beachfront hotel, and a few more fabulous restaurant selections to add to 30-A. It brought quaint little shops and a market of its own. And in spite of the excitement of the development's arrival, the certain familiarity about Seaside remains, making it feel almost like home.

And then we saw it, the small, rust-colored, stained wooden sign with white letters spelling out *Seaside*. The three little red and white umbrellas let you know what life here is all about: sun, sand, and sleep. Amazing what one little sign and the beginning of white picket fences can do for a weary soul.

The large beachfront homes that line the street are each named. And each plaque bearing their names makes a clear declaration of what that home represents to the family that owns it. Names like *Four the Girls, Same Time Next Year,* and *Julie Got Her Way.* But the names change through the years as the owners change. And though Seaside boasts many more actual year-round residents these days, most homes are rented out to pilgrims like us for the majority of the year.

We drove right through the heart of Seaside, the spring sun reflecting brilliantly off the tin roofs, a standard in Seaside and the perfect complement to a rainy evening.

Amber crawled over me and planted her perfectly reconstructed nose against the car window. "Ooh, what's that?"

I spat her hair out of my mouth.

"That's Central Square." Dad began his commentary of the town he loved. "That's the heart of Seaside. It's actually modeled after places like Charleston and Savannah. Or like Italian piazzas. It was built as a gathering place to offer all of the people around here the opportunity to get to know each other."

"Kind of like shopping," Amber said.

"Amen, sister," Mother offered.

"And food, because that brings people together too," he continued.

"Preach it, brother!" Paige shouted from the backseat.

Amber pointed. "What's that grassy area there?"

I tried to catch a glimpse of it with my left eye. That was the only thing that wasn't obstructed by her rather looming mass.

Dad's tour continued. "That grassy hill there in the middle of all the stores is the amphitheater. It's also called the Town Center, and it's the only actual grass you'll find around here. All the front yards are filled with native plants. But this is where they'll show movies, or the rep theater that started a few years back will perform a play. And people just head out there with their lawn chairs or blankets and wine or coffee . . ."

"Or Coke," I offered.

"Or Coke. And enjoy the production of the evening."

"Like a drive-in without the cars," Paige interjected, still examining her phone. Paige was an old pro at Dad's tour too. She had come with me almost all of the thirteen years since we had become joined at the hip.

The amphitheater lay nestled inside the curvature of the heart of Seaside. It was the place where all the action happened. A semicircle of shops and eateries, it had matured beautifully through the years.

The small silver camper *Frost Bites,* which offered frozen

delights, sat on the edge of the amphitheater. A delight for hot beachgoers. And then we passed the small post office that sat on the edge of the road in front of the amphitheater.

"See that little post office?" Dad pointed, causing Maggy to duck. Poor thing would need years of therapy just to recover from this car ride. "Mr. Davis, who designed Seaside, actually designed this post office himself. If my memory serves me correctly, this is actually one of the most photographed post offices in the nation."

"So you can send postcards and torture those you love with where you are and they aren't," I retorted.

Paige closed her phone and looked out the window. "I always hated postcards. Who wants to be reminded of all the fabulous places someone else is? What do they think you're going to do? Hang them on your refrigerator or something?"

Amber turned and looked at her.

"You have postcards all over your refrigerator, don't you?" Paige asked the long-tressed species hanging over me like a baboon on a summer day.

"You'll never know," Amber offered through pursed lips. She turned her head back to the Town Center.

"For a long while, all that was there was Modica's Market and Dreamland Heights," I said, pushing her back over to her seat while I finished off the tour. "They filmed *The Truman Show* here, you know."

Her eyes grew wide. This was a woman who dreamed of being famous. Or infamous. I'm not sure it would matter. "That movie with Jim Carrey?"

"Yeah, that's the one. And when they started the production, they built quite a few of these buildings. Like the one that we just passed with the spa and the pottery place."

I made a mental note to visit the spa. Why not? I was already worn-out.

"Are there a lot of famous people that come here?"

"You see a few every now and then," I responded.

"I saw Susan Lucci once," Mother mused. "She looked much *older* than she does on television." I was certain that made Mother feel better.

"Most are just your everyday people, Amber," Dad said, rubbing Maggy's head while he surveyed the landscape. "A lot of people save up all year to have a vacation here that their family can enjoy. You do have some who have a lot of money, and these are their summer homes. A few have made this their permanent residence. Then there are others like us who come once a year, every year. You get to know people that way, which is nice. But for the most part it's just a place where people come to get away from life and its pace."

"It looks expensive." This from a woman who had clothes from the most expensive boutiques in Georgia.

"It's not cheap. But few vacations are."

I brought us back to the tour at hand. "And those buildings back there with the bookstore and the other little shops were all built for the movie set as well."

Her bleary, aquamarine, contact-colored eyes lit up as this world of brick streets, bicycles, and bathing suits began to engulf her. Odd for people who live so close to the beach to get excited about coming to one? Yes. But going to the one nearby just feels like a Saturday. Coming here, to this haven in the middle of the Florida panhandle, feels like, well, dare one say, paradise.

"I think she's going to be sick again," Dad said, holding up the heaving pink-gingham picnic basket.

Well, as close to paradise as we'd ever see this side of glory.

CHAPTER NINE

I can share a room with Savannah!" Amber declared as our luggage hit the bottom of the steps.

"No, we want you to really be able to relax, after all you've been through." Paige placed her arm around her. I love Paige. "You deserve your own space for the week."

Amber rested her head on Paige's shoulder, a rather contortionist type of move considering their height difference. "Thank you, Paige. That is so sweet of you."

One of the beauties of Seaside is that you can come for years and never have to stay in the same house. So each year we would pick one with enough bedrooms for us and usually some friends and make it home for a week. Mother preferred to stay in Savannah Sands, and not because it was on the ocean. If that wasn't available, she'd take any house big enough on Savannah Street. Such things need no explaining. That is, until the String of Pearls was built on Seaside Avenue. Then Vicky found her resting place.

String of Pearls was Mother's favorite. Truth be told, it was my favorite too. Vicky loved it because it was painted cream. Her favorite color. Not that I think cream is a color. I loved it because of the

French doors stained a rich pecan that lined the front of the house on both floors. And because of the magnolia tree in the front yard, which reminded me of home. Everything about it was clean and pristine, just the way I desired my life, yet a far cry from how it actually existed. So, at least for a week, I could pretend my life was as perfectly aligned as the eight Adirondack chairs in a row on the front porch.

In no less than ten minutes, Paige and I were settled in and unpacked. We peeked into Amber's room, and she was unpacking a wardrobe that made grown women lust. Two that I knew of specifically.

"Where did you get this?" I asked, running my hands across a soft polished-cotton sundress. "It's beautiful."

"I got it at Saks. It was for . . . my . . . my . . ."—the tears and wails started coming before she could finish—"queen's breakfast at the pageant."

Paige snatched the dress from her hand and hung it in the closet for her, and then wrapped her arm around her shoulder. "Come on, Miss Amber, me and Savannah are going to take you to get a bathing suit. That will make all of us feel better."

"But I already have a . . . "

"Oh, don't argue," Paige said, bringing her toward the door. "You need a bathing suit with no memories attached to it."

"You think?"

"We're certain," I assured her.

Amber's eyes held sincere appreciation as she batted away the tears. "I probably need to get a complete new wardrobe to get rid of all my memories."

"Ooh, that many, huh?" Paige glanced back at me as we descended the stairs.

I offered her a shrug.

"Worse. I even have memories of other people's wardrobes."

Paige and I looked at each other but didn't even bother. "We have no idea when we'll return," Paige hollered out to my mother and dad. "Absolutely no idea," she whispered to herself.

"We have dinner reservations at seven," Dad informed.

"Well, then we'll be back by six forty-five," Paige shouted as we exited the building.

PER-SPI-CAS-ITY Market caught Amber's eye first. It was the first outdoor market to open in Seaside in the summer of 1981. Originally it was called the Seaside Saturday Market and housed a few tables shielded from the intense southern sun by canvas awnings. But with the brutality of summer's humidity, it changed into the Seaside Saturday Sunset Scene.

Eventually, though, in 1983, architect Deborah Berke arrived and designed multiple stalls that looked like tin-roofed beachfront cottages. And it is there that now a woman can find any item necessary to enjoy a week at the beach. Each clothing cottage offers linen dresses, hats, belts, straw bags, and flip-flops. It is a woman's paradise.

"Maybe I should just go total bohemian," Amber said as she stopped to fondle a pair of woven flip-flops.

"Too drastic a change." I plopped down on the blue and white cushion that sat atop the white wooden bench. "You just need to loosen up a little. I mean, your face is pretty enough without makeup. Ever thought about wearing a little less?"

Her perfectly manicured hand reached up to touch her face. "You think I could get away with it?"

"Absolutely. And then if you would just loosen your hair up a bit. I mean, I think your hair looks great just straight and shiny."

"Straight and shiny?" I didn't miss the sarcasm in Paige's voice.

"Well, it does." I glared. "Just natural."

Amber's hands ran across a long, layered cotton skirt.

"Ever owned a pair of jeans?" I asked.

"No," Amber responded flatly.

Paige's face contorted. "You have never owned a pair of jeans? How old are you?"

"You shouldn't ask a woman her age," Amber said shaking her head as her hand moved up to the army green tank that rested on top of the skirt. "And no, like I said, I've never owned a pair of jeans. I did have a lovely linen ensemble once that had the *look* of denim, but that's as close as I've ever been."

I eyed her long legs. "Amber, your legs were made for jeans. You are a jeans dream."

She looked down at her lean legs sticking out from beneath her sundress. "Really? So why would you want to cover them?"

"Don't think of it as covering them," I informed her. "It's more like accentuating them."

"Swimsuits first, then jeans," Paige said, taking the flip-flops out of her hand and directing us toward Fabs. "You will be a new creature by nightfall."

Fabs has some of the most beautiful swimsuits I've ever seen. There would be no new one for me this year, however. I usually bought one every year just because I wore it so often it fell apart that fast. But this year my budget had no room for extras. Mother would buy me one if I asked. After all, she would be in here by tomorrow morning getting herself a new one as well. But I had decided I wouldn't ask this year. A free vacation was enough. I would enjoy that. Plus, the thought of parading my Coke-loving thighs in front of Amber's perfectly proportioned body didn't excite me much anyway.

My point was proven when she exited the curtain, poured into a fabulous taupe number. She looked as good as *Entertainment Tonight*'s host and former beauty queen herself, Nancy O'Dell. The small spaghetti straps and slightly squared neck complimented her shoulders and bosom to perfection. But the small matching belt that sat at the top of her hips with the tortoise buckle just made me want to scream, "I hate you!"

"Ahh!" Paige screamed as she exited her dressing room and

caught sight of Amber. Once she saw herself, the scream turned into a moan.

"Whose pitiful idea was this?" she asked the mirror. It mocked her. "I drink Diet Cokes, for goodness' sake. Where did this come from?" She jiggled the barely visible little piece of skin hanging over the top of her bikini bottom. She had obviously forgotten the Doritos. Her hands moved on down to her hips. I almost thought I saw a tear in her eye.

"You look wonderful, Paige," Amber offered.

Amber, however, looked almost inhumanly flawless. Her legs went up to there. Her breasts were the perfect size for her body. Her skin was the perfect tone for her bathing suit, and neither her hands nor feet were disproportionate to her frame.

"This is a sad comparison," Paige stated as they stood side by side, Amber's six-foot frame towering over Paige's five foot five.

"Just look at it like this, Paige," I tried to encourage. "If you had a slightly greater area of distribution, you would look just like her."

She turned and glared at me, and then headed to the one-pieces with skirts. "These hips should not be forced on anyone's eyes."

"You need a bathing suit like this," Amber said, reaching up into a mass of two-pieces and pulling out a red halter-style top with bikini bottoms that had a short red and white stripe sheer skirt. "The top will lift you up and give you wonderful support. And the bottom is cut high enough to make your legs look leaner. Yet the sheerness of the skirt hides that slight . . . well, that slight . . . extra."

"How do you know this?" Paige asked, yet to be comforted.

"I know bathing suits, Paige. I've competed in them for more than half my life." Neither one of us could argue with that. So we didn't. And when Paige made her second entrance, she looked fabulous. We both stared at Paige's reflection in the mirror.

"That is unbelievable," I said, walking up behind her to get a better view myself.

"It wasn't that bad before," Paige responded.

"Well, it didn't look like *that*, I assure you."

Amber laughed.

"You are really good at this," Paige told her.

My word. If I'd had the money, I would have let that girl turn me into a calendar model. I sure hoped I didn't look like Paige's first attempt once I donned last year's suit. But I was certain these two would inform me tomorrow. Paige grabbed a matching pair of flip-flops. Amber purchased that divine suit she had had on, with a beautiful pink-and-taupe floral wrap, and I decided I just might have to come down with the flu tomorrow. Then my muumuu wouldn't be any big head turner.

We walked to dinner. Me, Dad, and Paige in flip-flops. Victoria and Victoria Jr., in three-inch heels. Victoria's were Stuart Weitzman pumps, and Junior donned Stuart Weitzman wedges. But the girl was wearing jeans and had let us straighten her hair and do her makeup. Vicky had eyed her curiously when Amber descended the stairs. Paige and I almost regretted talking her into them at *Venus*, a women's clothing store on the square. When we looked down at our own stubby legs in our own jeans, we realized we should have left the woman in sundresses. And when she slung that beautiful mane of hair, we were regretting that too. But for the first time in our almost fifteen hours together, Amber was smiling. So we would endure the double takes she would get for an evening with no tears. It would be our sacrifice for the cause of peace. World peace, that is.

CHAPTER TEN

"Watch out!" Paige hollered. Four adolescent boys who had lived all fourteen of their years befriending ding-dongs about careened into us on a bicycle built for six small people—or four of them.

They laughed.

So did I.

Joshua would enjoy this place, I thought to myself. My workplace compatriot rode his bicycle everywhere. I didn't know why. I just knew it gave him some of the most beautiful-looking calves I'd ever laid eyes on.

Paige nudged me. "What land did you just travel to?"

"*Amityville Horror*."

"Ooh, thinking about a guy, huh?"

"Let's change the subject."

"Okay, let's talk about how stupid we were to put that creature up there in a pair of jeans."

"Let's change the subject again."

"Okay, let's talk about how lame we are to still be taking vacations with our parents. I mean, how old are we?"

"It's free."

"Okay, let's talk about how brilliant we are the older we get."

I turned to her and smiled. "Yes, I like that subject."

In Seaside you've not much need for a car, unless you're going to go shopping or to the movies in Destin, or plan to eat at a restaurant outside of Seaside (thus the reason for bicycles built for small football teams). And if you're perfectly content with the restaurants within walking distance, you wouldn't even have to pick your keys up off of the counter for the duration. Tonight, we would eat at the Water Colors Fish out of Water restaurant, which was so close that driving wasn't a necessity at all.

We rounded the sidewalk that led the way to the hotel restaurant. Although Water Colors didn't have the maturity of Seaside, it had done an excellent job in maintaining the integrity of the area. The pale yellow beachfront hotel gave way to the welcoming building that housed the reservations desk. The lime-green, full-length door shutters that flanked all the windows were subdued by the ivy that grew up the walls. The restaurant was just beyond the lobby. Its plain wooden doors with pewter handles were no reflection of the bold statement of style and color that awaited inside.

The bright mosaic fish that greets you on the first level is as tall as your mama. Well, mine anyway. And the kaleidoscope of color emblazoned upon it hints at what awaits the eyes upstairs. The restaurant is on the second floor, offering a fabulous view of the white dunes and the ocean. Near the hostess station, two hanging porch swings face each other, so the nuisance of waiting on a table can be overlooked with a front-porch experience. A fabulous idea, I might add.

The walk to our table led us through the bar. Most restaurants are that way around here, making it clear everyone likes a little vino on vacation. Or that on vacation all clocks are on after-five time. And that's when the explosion of color hits you, from the bar stools with their multicolored seats to the iron railing that looks like dancing seaweed topped with crystal balls in primary colors.

The hostess led us past the terra-cotta walls, past the grills with the expansive copper hoods, straight to a table that overlooked the water. I pulled out my chair and noticed that the lime green on the cushion matched the shutters outside. Mother gazed up lustfully at the hand-painted light fixtures.

Yeah, don't let that lady fool you. She has a lust demon or two she needs to get rid of.

The hand-painted shades in their subtle Tiffany-blue tones have fishes painted on them in the same terra-cotta tones of the walls. And as the scene laid itself out, I realized the writer in me rarely missed the details of life. Whether in a restaurant, on a face, or the mere nuisances that surround.

Vicky sat across from me and almost melted into the sunset that backlit her hair color.

Good for the sunset.

Not so good for Vicky.

"These men haven't taken their eyes off of Amber since we walked through the door," Paige whispered in my ear. Her breath moved my dainty silver earring. "It's as if they are celebrating her."

"Vicky ain't doing too bad herself," I noticed. "And I do believe that woman just ogled my father!"

She sighed heavily. "I guess we'll just pull up the rear."

"I hope these jeans have magic powers, if that's what we're supposed to do!"

She snickered.

Paige and I pulled our chairs up to the curved booth that faced us. "Scoot over, honey," Dad said, pushing Mother around the booth. They had shared the same side of the booth since I can remember, regardless of whether anyone was sitting opposite them. So weird, wasting a perfectly good booth like that.

We watched the rest unfold. He opened the menu; she peered inside. He placed her order and his. And the evening was spent with them eating off of each other's plates.

I scooted the stone-gray placemat with the fish design closer to me. I didn't want to be the one who ended up with remnants of dinner attached to my blouse. I had chosen a sheer cream crepe top with dainty capped sleeves and a cream tank underneath. White enough to announce whether I had had the filet mignon or the beef short ribs.

But no matter how appealing everything on the menu looked, I would have the same thing I had every time we ate here: the low-country shrimp and scallops, minus the scallops, with creamy grits and asparagus.

When dinner arrived, I placed the first bite of grits in my mouth. "Hallelujah!" I shouted a little louder than I had intended.

Paige snorted.

Mother glared.

"I can't help it. These are the best things I've ever put in my mouth."

"Ever?" The queen of culinary inquired.

I could not lie. "Next to your fried chicken, yes. Ever."

I laid another bite on my tongue and rolled them around, searching for a remnant of grain. None could be found. By the time the chef had cooked those grits in chicken stock, heavy cream, and enough butter to make Paula Deen look stingy, they tasted more like mashed potatoes.

Slurp! Paige licked the first of her short-rib beef bones, her lips smacking rather loudly. Vicky eyed her. Paige picked up another and ran her tongue across it.

In the time we cleaned our plates, I do believe three verses of "How Big Is God?" could have been sung.

Vicky never commented. There was no "This is absolutely wonderful." No "Someone go see if that man in the kitchen is married, 'cause Savannah needs a good man." Nothing. She doesn't compliment many chefs. Well, she does compliment Miss Paula. But that's because the two women are so close they go to the spray-on tan booths together and stand there buck naked! If someone knew me that well, I'd compliment her biscuits too!

Mother caught Amber's bloodshot eyes. "You know what you need, darling? You need a good man."

"I have one," she stated matter-of-factly as she flaked the crust from her bread.

Mother sighed. "Darling, Joshua North is not necessarily the man for you."

I looked up, trying to disguise my shock that Mother knew how crazy Amber was over Joshua. Of course, she pretty much knew this girl's underwear size. Why wouldn't she know she was crazy about Joshua? Amber's lip began to quiver.

"But if Joshua is what you want, then we'll just hope that happens for you. Then maybe we can help Savannah find a man. Ooh, Savannah, what about that cute little blond over there?" Paige and I turned slowly.

I gasped. "What? The forty-year-old?"

"He's not forty."

"He is if he's a day."

"Well, you need someone mature," Mother said. "Like I got with your father."

"Victoria, you make it sound like I need to purchase my own defibrillator."

"They say every home should have one," Amber said.

"I'll keep that in mind," Dad assured her.

I felt my butt vibrate. I twitched, realizing it was my phone. A few glances stole my way. I looked down, knowing I couldn't answer it. I had been told it would end up in the ocean if I didn't cut the ringer off, so answering it at the table wasn't necessarily a good idea. I tried to be discreet and took a peek. It was Thomas. I sent him to oblivion. I refused to be his alibi. I refused to be his anything. He would tell the whole truth and nothing but the truth, and he would tell it himself. And I wasn't going to listen to him go on about me keeping his secret.

I twitched again. He had just left a message.

"Victoria . . . Jake, so good to see you both," Dennis Starling said as he exited the kitchen of the restaurant he managed. "How are things in Savannah?"

"Oh, Dennis darling, they have been wonderful. Never a dull moment." This from the woman who controlled all moments.

"Dennis, great to see you," Dad said, standing and gently folding his napkin by his plate to greet the familiar friend. "Dinner was amazing, as always."

"We're so glad you joined us. I'll have some dessert sent out to you, on the house." Amber's eyes lit up and it faintly seemed as if she licked her lips.

"Dennis, we don't expect dessert." Dad returned to his seat.

Paige coughed loudly. She prevented me from having to kick him.

"I know you don't expect it, that's why I enjoy doing it. Victoria," he said, turning his gaze to my mother, "word has it your good friend the president might be coming through this way in the next couple weeks."

Mothers eyes lit up like a lighthouse calling in the entire Coast Guard. Sad, first of all, that people who only saw my mother once a year actually knew her and, second, knew that she was insanely infatuated with the president of the United States. This woman would never be selected to guard the briefcase that carries the codes for our national security.

"Oh, he is, is he? When? Do you have any idea when?" She practically bounced.

"Not sure. They talked about the Secret Service coming through sometime the end of the week or first of the next."

"Oh, he's got one Secret Service agent, George, that I just fell in love with when we went to the state dinner a couple months ago." Her dainty wrist flopped around.

Dennis rested his hand on the table. "You went to a state dinner?"

Paige moaned. She knew she wouldn't see dessert now for another thirty minutes.

"Oh, I love this story," Amber mused in a bemoaning sort of way as her fork tickled her salad leaves.

I do believe not a day has gone by since we went to the White House that Mother hasn't brought it up. You would have thought her own self-penned write-up in the newspaper would have gotten it out of her system. And if not that, then the special she did on the public access network, where she showed her pictures of the event and a video clip that she had gotten from C-Span, all while wearing the same evening gown that she had dined in. But amazingly enough, none of these outlets emptied her of her excitement. So we were forced to listen to the account often.

"How did you get that invitation?" Dennis asked.

"Well, I was part of a left-wing conspiracy."

"Mother, that is ludicrous." I took over for the sake of truth in reporting. "Mother was making a statement in front of our courthouse. The president was headed around the square in his motorcade, and his driver had a heart attack behind the wheel, which caused him to careen into Mother, which prompted an invitation to the White House."

"Breathe, child, breathe," Paige said.

"Like I was saying, Dennis," Mother said, staring at me, "a left-wing conspiracy to take me out failed, allowing the president to meet me and Jake and wonder why we had never made it to a state dinner before."

Dad took a drink of his sweet tea and leaned back into the deep lime-green cushion.

"It was for the prime minister of Saudi Arabia," Mother continued.

"He's one of those men who wear dresses," Amber clarified.

"But you must tell him how you prepared for months before the actual event," I coaxed.

Now Paige was kicking me. Obviously, backtracking increased the distance between here and dessert.

"Don't be catty, Savannah."

"Mother bought a flag, hung it beside the door, and piped 'The Star Spangled Banner' through our outdoor stereo system for the rest of the day. Until Dad came home." I gave him a wink.

"The neighbors didn't care for the entertainment," Dad offered.

Dennis smiled knowingly.

"Well, Savannah and Thomas both went with us. Savannah would have dressed more appropriately had she worn the first dress I bought for her."

I couldn't believe her. "That dress had more crinoline than a tulle factory."

"I saw that dress, Savannah," Amber said, raising her glass of lemon water. "I thought it was lovely."

"I don't think Dennis cares about all of this, ladies," Dad interjected.

Paige reached across the table and patted his hand.

"You're such a wise man, Mr. Phillips. So very wise."

"I wore a Carolina Herrera." Mother eyed me again. "What? You were in a buying mood. I've always wanted one of her dresses."

"The first lady looked beautiful too, I must say," Mother stated begrudgingly. "But that Bushie—Mr. President. He was simply dashing. He looked at us and said, 'Mrs. Phillips, what a pleasure to have you here at the White House this evening.'"

I could see Dad holding his breath. About the same way he did that night.

She tilted her head as if a spirit of meekness came over her in waves. "I told him. 'Oh, Bu—I mean, Mr. President. it is my pleasure to share this evening with you as well.'"

"Then he said"—she covered her mouth to stifle a giggle—"'Hope you haven't found yourself under any concrete lately.' And then he gave that chuckle. I said, 'No, not lately.'" That was when Dad pulled her onward down the line.

I tried to help the story go a little faster. "They made us sit at separate tables. That was the biggest mistake the White House staff made during this event. Had they known Mother often needs restraining, they would have sat a personal agent at her right hand. But no. They sat us at different tables. So all we could do was watch."

"This must have been how you met George?" Dennis inquired.

"Oh, no. She met George about the time she said good-bye to her table companion—"

"Sean Connery!" Mother said.

"—and made her way to the podium."

My butt vibrated again. I about tipped my chair over. When Dad quit staring at me, I looked down. It was a text message. "Shut up," it read. Paige. I didn't even look at her.

"You did not!" Dennis laughed in disbelief.

Mother looked at him as if it was strange he would find this hard to believe. "Well, I had something to say." And say it she did. Every eye in the White House dining room stared at her as the beauty bedazzled in her diamond-and-sapphire necklace and matching sapphire-blue *peau de soie* silk evening gown made her way to the podium.

Fortunately for me, I had never pointed out to my table guests, Senator Bill Frist and Senator Kay Bailey Hutchison, that my mother and father were just across the way.

"Actually, President Bush had just risen to say good night to the guests and invite us to the ballroom for an hour of dancing. And as he was thanking the people for coming, Mother got up and raised her hand slightly and made her way to the head table," I said.

"He nodded at me," she insisted. "He wanted me to come up there and address the people."

"Oh, so that's why the Secret Service came from all directions to pounce on you, along with Dad, I might add." Then I turned back to Dennis. "The president stayed them, but Mother kept striding right up to the microphone. Talking all the way."

Dennis was trying to stifle his mere pleasure at the story. Paige had taken to pounding her fist against her forehead. And Amber was delightfully quiet for a few moments. She had teared up at the talk of ball gowns but quickly regained her composure. "So what did you say when you got to the microphone?"

"I just said, 'Uh, Mr. President, there's just one little thing I need to say before we leave this evening.'"

"So you were standing right there by the side of the commander in chief of the free world?"

"Fortunately for her, she was still free herself," I commented. "Because, by the looks of the Secret Service, they'd have her chained up before the last dance." Dad gave me a look followed by a smile that he covered with his hand.

"I said"—Mother acted as if she was ignoring me—"'Excuse me, ladies and gentlemen.'"

She tapped the microphone at that point. As luck would have it, it worked.

"That was when Bush—I mean, Mr. President leaned over me and said, 'This is Victoria Phillips from Savannah, Georgia. I invited her here along with her husband, Jake, and their two children.'" At that time I hid behind my napkin. Thomas was so excited to be sitting by Dennis Hastert that he hadn't even noticed Penelope Cruz sitting across the table. So, trust me, Mother's actions were totally lost on him. "Then he turned back to me and said, 'Mrs. Phillips, did you have something to say?'"

"I said, 'Uh, yes, Mr. President . . . I just wanted to thank you for having us, and thank your beautiful wife.' And, oh my goodness, about that time I noticed the vice president and said, 'Hello, Mr. Vice President. You look sparkling in a tux.'"

Nothing else on him was sparkling at that moment, I assure you.

"Then I said, 'I just need to tell these people here tonight that while we're here celebrating the Saudi Prime Minister'—and I gave him a nod—"'you need to get a grip on those gas prices.' I said, 'I mean, my stars, sir, you've got enough oil to saturate an ocean, and I've got people in my city who can't hardly afford a tank of gas.'"

Well, poor Dennis laughed out loud.

"'But this isn't about you right now,' I said." I could tell he was grateful. Increasingly irate, but grateful. 'But I just need all of you fine Washington people to know that this man is one of America's finest.' And I just rested my hand on the president's shoulder. And then I told them that when his motorcade ran over me, he sat with me and talked with me and made sure I was okay. And he even made sure it wasn't a left-wing conspiracy . . . which I'm still not totally convinced of."

"You did not say that!" Dennis said.

I responded, "You bet your sweet bottom she did!"

"Wait, I'm not finished. Then I told them how he took the time to care about me, though I'm not a corporation. Not an organized group. Just me. A woman fighting for justice in an increasingly unjust world." She pounded her fist on the table. "'So, in case you've forgotten because of the state of politics in Washington,' I said to them, 'I just wanted you to know that my family and I are here tonight, not because we bought our way here or schmoozed our way here, or even because we deserve to be here at all.'"

When she said that in the White House, I did believe my mother had crossed into the land of humility. I actually peered over my napkin just to check.

"I told them, 'In a world where leaders focus on polls, he

focused on me. Granted, I wasn't easy to miss, encased in rubble, but we've got a leader who cares about us as individuals. And I just needed the room to know that tonight, Mr. President, before I went home. Thank you for this wonderful evening. A superb meal. And exquisite company. And even though Sean Connery is a handsome man'—then I nodded to my table companion and he nodded back—'you are the reason why all of us are here.'

"That's when I saw Helen Thomas sitting in the back, and I let her know that if she got snippy again, I was going to ask that our president here move her to the back of the press briefing room." Mother had found great satisfaction in that moment. I, however, had lowered myself even farther under the fine damask tablecloth.

"Then I just gave him back his microphone, and that was when George came and accompanied me for the rest of the evening. The president thought it would be nice if I had a personal escort."

He and the rest of the room.

"Oh, and did I mention the president and I shared a dance, and Jake here got to cut a rug with Laura?"

"My word, Victoria Phillips, you never cease to amaze me," Dennis said, wiping his eyes.

"Want to check on that dessert?" Paige finally voiced after enduring all she could.

"I think you deserve it," he said with a wink.

Amber eyed Mother from across the table. "That was a lovely story, Miss Victoria. You left out the part though about—"

Paige raised her knife. "I think we've heard enough stories for one evening." Dad took the knife from her hands and laid it by his own plate.

But we still let her be served first when dessert arrived. And Amber didn't waste time scarfing down hers either.

"What about Dennis?" Mother looked at me, eyebrows raised.

"Mother, seriously. My love life is not so deficient that it needs you to increase its activity."

Paige mumbled through her chocolate torte. "No, your love life is so deficient you need to borrow your dad's defibrillator."

On the way home, the conversation turned toward the two who had remained at home. Maggy had been left in her kennel. Mother felt that would keep Duke happy and Maggy safe. Not that he would eat her. No, he'd just terrorize her. Come to think of it, he was probably sitting at the door of her kennel right now, terrorizing the tar out of that little thing just by licking his lips.

When we got home, we discovered he hadn't terrorized her at all. Why should he? He had found a large bag of peanut M&Ms in Paige's room and dined like a king. The chocolate hadn't killed him. But the poor thing was going to have a rough night of it, if the moans that he was offering up were any indication. Maggy was sleeping as pretty as a picture. Morning could possibly reveal the little "princess" had fed them to him herself. That dog could be wooed with anything edible. If she was smart, she might have just gained the upper hand.

CHAPTER ELEVEN

Some things don't vacation. For me, tilling time is one of them. Tilling time is my everyday-for-ten-years habit. It is my time. My time to reflect, request, and listen. I've never been much good at the listening part. But with the changes in the course of my life over the last year, in which I've had to face the inevitability of actually growing up, listening has become a new priority. I had brought a special CD for the week, one I had been saving for a while. No words, just music. With the continual influx of words in my environment every day, I wanted tilling to be a time where none were needed. So me and the instrumental sounds of Jim Brickman headed out to till.

"Up already?" I asked Mother and Dad as they sat on the front porch, drinking coffee and reading the paper Dad had already fetched.

"It's eight, Savannah." A declaration in and of itself. Of course, this was coming from a mother who didn't know what a day without makeup was.

"Obviously Duke needs a little more exercise," I said, noticing the frighteningly human animal sitting at the top of the stairs with his leash at his feet. I spoke to him. "Obviously the rumbling and tumbling of last night haven't done you completely in." I attached his leash. "We'll see you two later."

And with that we entered the world of our familiar routine, because even now, since my move, Duke often spends the night so we can till together. I think Dad lets him stay because it makes him think I'm safer.

Plenty of other morning joggers were partaking of the same. They came in every shape, size, color, and age. The morning sunshine was no respecter of persons. Nor, unfortunately, was it a respecter of attire. Because some people were prime candidates for the "don't" section in the back of any fashion magazine.

"I spy with my little eye something coming up the street jiggly and encased in Lycra. That could be Exhibit Number One."

Duke agreed and gave them a bark as they passed.

Fortunately, the sun had the ability to spotlight those in black pretty favorably regardless of fashion deficits. You just had to hope that you could reach the end of the workout before the perils of the heat reached you first. Because when heat hit black Lycra, it didn't matter what the sun made you look like, you just were what you were. And more of it. Unfortunately, I hadn't gotten up early enough for that. So I donned cotton. And only moments after the sun settled against my face, the April humidity slapped me upside the head.

Few things in life are as majestic as the ocean. The mere sight of it reveals to me something greater than myself. It has the same effect on me as the live oaks draped in moss that consume Forsythe Park. They let me know that only something superior could create such stately offerings. It was the perfect environment in which to communicate with greatness. So I did. Duke and I ran along the quiet sands, the music played in my ears, and the familiar majesty of my Creator whispered to my soul. It truly was a perfect morning.

I jogged closer to the water, because the compact sand made the running easier. Duke kept in perfect stride, and thirty minutes passed before either of us realized it. We both finally collapsed in the sand near a staircase leading up to one of the pavilions. I do believe we both were wearing smiles. I looked out into the vastness of the water and was overcome by the way the sun reflected off of its surface. The glare refused your gaze for any length of time.

"Ready to head back, boy?" I rubbed the top of his head. "I've got to get to work on my research." He knew exactly what I meant, and he made it clear what he really wanted to do. "I can't, boy. Dad will make me bathe you, and I don't feel like that this morning."

He pleaded anyway.

"Okay. Why ruin a perfectly good morning?"

With that, I released the dog from his prison and *finally* let him enjoy *his* vacation. Within seconds he was running rapidly through the waves. I pulled out from my pocket the new ball Dad had bought for him before we came. It floats. A new one is required for each vacation, because the previous one inevitably ends up on the ocean floor. For the next thirty minutes, I wore us both out. We were headed back toward the stairs when I heard that familiar name.

"Joshua, hey, wait a minute."

I turned to see who shared the name of my newspaper coworker. And all I saw were some dark curls on a perfectly fit, sculpted body wearing swimming trunks and walking away from me.

"There's no way," I said to Duke, who had turned to look himself. A bouncy blonde was skipping her way toward him and grabbed him in a bear hug. When they turned to the side, I could tell perfectly it was Joshua. My Joshua. I mean, my working colleague right here, standing on my beach, with his arms encased in some rather sassy little blonde number. "Oh my stars! It is him.

What in the world is Joshua North doing in Seaside?" Duke let out a dog moan.

"Wonder who *she* is?" He cocked his head in his own wonder. "Maybe it's his sister." I assured Duke and myself. "Of course, I don't even know if he has a sister." Then she reached up and touched the side of his face in an intimate sort of way and kissed him. Duke looked up at me, making it clear that was in no way, shape, or form the kiss of a sister. "I agree. That ain't his sister." I pulled Duke behind the stairs, where we could peer through the slats and somewhat conceal ourselves.

"You think this is spying?" I asked. Duke didn't care; he watched them through one of the slats below mine. If he didn't think so, why should I? "It can't be spying. They're in the middle of the beach. A public beach." So we continued watching.

Joshua wrapped his arm around her waist, and she wrapped hers around his. As they continued to walk up the beach in the opposite direction, she laid her head on his strong, beautifully defined arm, and he kissed the top of her head. Neither of us took our eyes off them until we couldn't see them anymore. As I led Duke up the stairs, he let out another soft moan. I tried to conceal my own. After what felt like an eternity I pulled myself together and yanked Duke's leash. "You're right, my friend, Amber will never be able to handle this one on top of everything else she's been through. So we'll keep it our little secret." And we walked back in the direction of the house. We walked like ninety-year-olds with osteoporosis. But we walked all the same.

"Here, let me help you with that." I offered to the black-haired gentleman who was in a battle with his three bags of groceries and the white picket gate that led to his cottage. The gate was winning.

"Thank you. I appreciate it," he responded with a nod of the head and a soft Spanish accent.

"Have anymore you need me to grab?"

"No, this is it."

"Thank you for helping him." The voice came from the far side of the porch. I looked over to see a stunning woman sitting back down in a rocker on the porch. Her exotic features and beautiful accent matched that of her husband. She laid the latest novel in the Sue Grafton series on her lap. "What's your friend's name?" she asked through her warm pink lips.

"This here is Duke," I said, walking up the steps. "Duke, can you say hello?" He walked over to the lady and placed his paw on the top of her book.

It startled her at first but caused her to laugh. "Well, aren't you a charming gentleman, Sir Duke."

"Don't let him fool you. He's not all high society. He's been known to crash many a party in his time."

She rubbed the top of his head. "Everybody deserves to crash a good party or two. I'm Lucy." She extended her hand.

I reached mine out to take her own. "Nice to meet you, I'm Savannah, Savannah Phillips. Lucy, is that a family name?"

She laughed. "Actually it's Lucia. The closest my mother could get to Lucy, a character from *The Lion, the Witch, and the Wardrobe*, one of her favorite books. Lucy was the youngest of four, and so was I. Eventually everyone called me Lucy."

"Lucia was my name in Spanish class. There wasn't any way to translate Savannah," I said, explaining before she asked. "I had requested Savananiña, but that didn't fly."

"I can see why not."

"Your mother must have introduced you to her love for books, huh?" I pointed to the one lying across her lap.

"Yeah, she loved to read to me at night. Eventually, I was the one asking her instead of her asking me. And it's become one of my favorite things." The gentleman returned with his arms free of their burden. "This is one of my other favorite things too," she said with an illuminating smile. He bent down and kissed her softly on the lips.

"Manuel, meet Savannah. Savannah, this is the love of my life and my husband too. Can you imagine both of that in the same person?" We all laughed. Manuel's eyes danced like a schoolboy's. His goods looks reminded me of a slightly older Antonio Banderas.

"You're welcome to stay for breakfast," she offered. "Manuel's great at eggs and toast. Plus, our kids don't get here for a couple more days, and we're missing them already. It'd be nice to have someone their age around."

"There's no way you two could have kids my age."

"I love her, Manuel," Lucy said, looking up at her husband. She rubbed her face. "Olive skin has removed the need for sun and its aging device."

"Lucky you," I said, staring at my challenged golden arm. "Lucky" seemed to be the state of affairs these days.

"Actually, we have twins, a boy and a girl, who are twenty-four, and our baby, who is twenty. They're coming up on Tuesday. We haven't seen them much since we left New Orleans. So, until then, you have a standing invite to breakfast."

"Did you say New Orleans?"

"Yes, our home was destroyed in Katrina. We have some precious friends who have let us live here for . . . well, nothing compared to what we should be spending. We are still trying to work everything out with our home and our land. It's been a tremendously long and difficult process." Her black eyes grew distant for a moment.

Her voice was rich and exotic. Soft and enchanting. And I'd found my story. I rested against the porch railing. "I can't imagine what you've gone through."

"We couldn't have imagined it either," Manuel said, running his hands through his thick black hair.

"I'd be interested to hear about all of it sometime, if you have a few moments."

Lucy's eyes brightened. "Over breakfast would be perfect."

"Sounds wonderfully tempting this morning, but my friend

here can eat the kindest person out of house and home," I said as Duke and I headed back toward the unyielding white picket gate. "It was a pleasure to meet you both."

Manuel threw his hand up in a wave. "Thanks again for your help, Savannah. We'll see you around, I'm sure."

"I'm certain," I said. As I turned back to close the fence, I looked at this couple one more time. Manuel had leaned down over Lucy, and his face had concealed hers. After three kids, you'd think they'd tire of each other. Obviously they hadn't. I tucked the visual away. Maybe I'd ask her secret about keeping her man happy while I got my story. On the other hand, what use did I have for such secrets anyway?

All parties had moved to the back porch for breakfast when Duke and I arrived home. Miss Maggy was lounging on a furry pink pillow at Mother's feet when I saw them through the screen door from the kitchen. Duke growled when he saw her, and she did the unhappy dance until Mother picked her up and placed her on her lap. Maybe she wasn't so vicious after all. More food than five mouths could possibly eat still rested on the table, even though all plates were licked clean. I, for some reason, had no appetite at all.

"Nice walk?" Mother asked when she heard Duke.

"Yes, ma'am," I mumbled as I stayed inside to avoid conversation. I grabbed a Coke.

Paige came through the screen door and walked into the kitchen. "I'm going to take a shower and get ready for church."

I grabbed her and pulled her into the hallway. Her eyes widened. "What? What happened? You look like you've seen a dead person."

"I saw Joshua!"

"Close enough."

"Stop it, Paige. I saw Joshua on the beach with a girl who was all but licking his face. And he had his arms all wrapped around her. It was disgusting and simply reprehensible."

"Disgusting, yes. Reprehensible, how?"

"Paige . . . it's, well . . . it's . . . My word, woman, Amber Topaz is crazy about him. She will die another wailing-induced death, which we will be forced to endure, mind you, if she finds this out, or worse, sees him with this little bouncy bleached-blonde."

"Hey, watch it." She ran her fingers through her messy bleached-blonde hair.

"You don't count."

"You're right. I'm natural."

"Give me a break."

"Give me a break," she mimicked. "But you're right. We can't tell her. I already had to spend fifteen minutes standing behind her in the mirror, assuring her that she is still beautiful and someone will want her even though seven judges didn't. I refuse to spend the rest of this trip picking up the pieces of another dead dream."

"I completely agree."

"I mean, there is no way she is going to find out on *my* vacation that Joshua North is not her entry into the realm of the Mrs. United States of America royalty. Let's keep her occupied and keep our eyes out for him. Deal?"

"Deal."

She eyed me. "I'll try to make sure you don't have to see him either."

"What's that supposed to mean?"

"You know exactly what that means. But you've had enough trauma for two days, so I won't make you go there now."

I took her up on her kindness and changed the subject. "I met a Lucia today."

"There actually is one of those? I thought that name was simply for the benefit of your torture."

"Nope. And she seems pretty content with it. Changed it to Lucy but doesn't seem to bother her a bit."

"Bothered you for three years of Spanish."

"Not as bad as your name though. I think Señora Schmoltz must have hated you."

"What? You don't like Victoria? I thought it was a perfectly lovely name."

"Liar."

"We all have our crosses to bear." She put her arm around me.

I clung to my Coke. "Are you referring to the size of my behind or my thighs?"

"I'll let you know once I see. Now, go get ready for the church service."

"I look as good as Amber does."

She hugged me tighter. "Such a funny girl. Such a very funny girl." She laughed alone.

CHAPTER TWELVE

It was Sunday. It was the South. And I was Jake's child. Therefore, I went to church. Because there are some things Dad doesn't take vacations from either. In fact, Dad is pretty much the most consistent individual I know. He doesn't see vacations as much more than a change of scenery and the removal of a work schedule. But he still gets up at the same time. Still walks one companion and endures the other. Still reads his paper over breakfast. And still requires church attendance on Sunday.

The Seaside Interfaith Chapel was always a part of the Seaside vision but wasn't realized until 2001. Before the chapel was built, Dad used to deliver a message to us in the living room of our rental. Now, Dad's not bad at that, but even so, we were glad to move to the actual pews of the picturesque wooden-plank church that stands across from the Forest Street Park.

What is it about people who go on vacation and still go to church? Maybe it's a Southern thing. Or maybe it's the fear that hellfire and brimstone might seek you out on Monday if you sleep in on Sunday. Maybe it's the family bonds that vacations seem to nurture. The relaxed atmosphere, the feeling of gratitude that needs a place to express itself. Or maybe it's the soul's innate need for communion with each other and with their Creator. Whatever it is, by nine forty-five, the sanctuary of Seaside Interfaith Chapel is pretty much full, and a few young men in their button-down shirts and khakis, carrying their Bibles, are still making their way up the brick streets.

"Does she know she's on vacation?" Paige whispered in my ear as my mother descended the stairs like royalty.

"I would say, she's rather understated."

She scoffed. "In comparison to what?"

"To that." Amber descended the staircase in rather regal attire herself. And a hat slightly larger than my mother's.

They walked out the front door in front of us. Paige and I followed like Cinderellas in pre-prince fashion with sort-of-pressed skirts and complementary dressy T-shirts. The two beauties in front of us clip-clopped all the way to the church. Paige and I flip-flopped behind. It *was* vacation.

"Oh my Lord, have mercy—"

Paige cut me off. "Honey, we're almost to the church, and you can praise Jesus all you want to there."

"No, I just had a horrible thought."

"Worse than the thought of the two of us continually entering places after the two of them?"

"Yes. What if Joshua is in there?"

Her eyebrows perked up. "Ooh, yes, that could be worse."

"How is that worse?" Now I wanted to know.

"Well, he'll be catching a glimpse of us after them."

"They look that good, huh?"

"They always look that good."

"Why don't we dress up more?" I said, stopping Paige in the middle of the street.

She looked at me, and we both got our own selves tickled.

We let the two beauties enter first. We almost took seats outside in the overflow section of the grassy lawn, where we could listen to the message via the large speakers that flanked the doors of the church. But Dad assured us there was room enough inside.

We sat in our pews and would have used our bulletins to hide our faces in the event of a Joshua sighting. Unfortunately, someone had forgotten the bulletins at the printer. So I hid behind the two large hat heads seated next to me. If Joshua arrived, I hoped he'd never recognize the lovely attired group on pew eight.

The distinct sound of Florsheims and sandals on the dark hardwood floors caused me to look up. Two male voices, laughing as they entered, caused me to grab Paige's arm.

"They're twelve." She patted my hand. "Mere babies. No worries."

I squinted into the bright light coming through the front windows. The inside was almost as bright as the outside. I ran my hand over the back of the white painted pews.

"Looks like we dressed up after all," Paige said as the blue-jeans-and-shorts family came inside.

We watched the parade of Florsheims and slip-ons. Sundresses and sunglasses. Hats and halters. Little girls in their little white dresses, a few of whom had forgotten to change out of their polka-dotted underwear.

I saw Lucy's and Manuel's heads a couple of rows in front of us. I watched them as she nestled against him. I couldn't help but wonder what that was like. It had been so long. And even now, I couldn't remember feeling the feelings that seemed to match what I saw in this couple. Or in my parents, for that matter.

I wondered what love would look like for me. I hadn't really wondered that since Grant had walked down the aisle. But now, seeing something so real, I wondered if I had ever known real love at all.

As the song leader began to sing "No Other Name but the Name of Jesus," I felt a pinch.

"Ow!" I cried involuntarily.

The people in front and beside eyed me.

"Don't look now, but Prince Charming just entered," Paige whispered out of the side of her mouth.

"Tell me you are not lying in the very house of God."

"I may have moments of irreverence, but sister ain't stupid. No, back five rows at the other end of the pew."

"Whatever you do, do not look back."

She turned around. "Okay, I'll just use the eyes in the back of my head to give you a play-by-play."

"If he sees us, this will be horrible. So sing, woman, just sing."

The little towheaded girl in front of me with the polka-dotted panties looked over the back of her pew, inspecting my mother. Poor child probably hadn't seen so many baubles since her great-grandmother Eugenia was buried in her entire jewelry collection.

The Scripture reading that morning was from Matthew 5, where Jesus is giving his longest recorded sermon, the Sermon on the Mount. And when the sweet lady got to the part that reads, "Blessed are those who mourn," I heard a whimper come from Amber's side of the pew.

But when the Doxology was delivered, by a woman who could hold her own on any opera stage in the world, even Jake's eyes were misting. And by the time the pastor got up to deliver his sermon, every heart was ready. For a moment I forgot Joshua was there.

At the close of the service, we took communion. Before partaking, we were asked to examine our hearts for any impurity. I ran my hand across the painted arm of my pew, noticing the small chips in the paint where little fingers had probably picked at it over time. And I thought of all the things I needed forgiveness for. My quick temper with Amber. My abhorrence for Mother's new dog. My hatred for the blonde stranger on the beach. My total aggravation for Curly Locks somewhere behind me. I was still rummaging through my trash when the time came to eat the bread.

After the benediction, I could have kissed Bill the usher when he stopped at our pew to greet my parents. He looks amazingly like Walter Cronkite, and if he'd interviewed them for an hour, I wouldn't have given a hoot.

"He's gone." Paige informed. "You can breathe now."

I exhaled. Loudly.

"We had over eight hundred Easter Sunday in the pouring rain," Bill told Dad as they walked slowly to the door.

"That's amazing. A long way from the thirty-five you started with," Dad said.

"Sure is, Jake. A long way. Want to come with us to Bud and Alley's for lunch?" My mouth salivated at the thought of the fabulous restaurant once touted by *Vogue* magazine as "favorite new restaurant in the world."

"Appreciate the offer. But I'm gonna take these girls to the beach for the afternoon."

Bill gave us a smile. "Well, enjoy yourself. Hope to see you again soon."

Lucy and Manuel were at the back of the chapel as we prepared to exit.

"Good morning, Savannah." Lucy's ebony eyes caught my smile.

"Good morning, beautiful lady. Come meet my family."

I introduced the Phillipses and our vagabonds. Lucy and Manuel were as welcoming as few people I'd met. Her arm was hooked gently through his, and every time he spoke, she watched him in unashamed admiration and affection.

As we headed out the door, Mother stated her evaluation. "She's beautiful. Penelope Cruz exotic. You know, kind of like I'm Lauren Hutton exotic."

"Oh! I see that, Mrs. Phillips," Amber gushed. "I can really see that!"

Blind and delusional, I returned for my Bible, which I had left on the pew. As I stepped back into the aisle, I heard a sound coming from the altar. I saw no one but did notice the stucco-and-seashell cross on the altar table that sat directly in line with the front door. It made me think of the crosses I had had to bear throughout these last few months. My mother, returning home, the loss of a dream, the loss of the love of my life. Then I thought of the faces, bright with smiles, with peace, with contentment, that had come and gone through this same front door this morning. I found it hard to believe that anyone would need a cross or the walls of a sanctuary on vacation. But just in case, I guess it was a good idea it was all here. Just in case.

CHAPTER THIRTEEN

Does pain have a painometer?" I asked Duke as we sat on the front porch, watching Vicky exit for her beach excursion.

Her presence reminded me why we never go to the beach with her in Savannah. The beach and Vicky are work, not a vacation. She came armed with large hat, large cooler, large sunglasses, large beach bag, and high heels. She really could have starred on a soap opera. It wouldn't have been a stretch. Just the perfect opportunity to get paid for living this way. Surely that would have made more sense than living this way for virtually no reason at all. And come to think of it, it wasn't Lauren Hutton she looked like at all, but Susan Lucci. Maybe that's why Mother resented her so.

"Let me take that, baby," Dad said, removing the cooler from her arm and using his other hand to hold her free one. Her red and black floral sarong was wrapped around her strapless red bathing suit. The expensive one that had been in the window of Fabs just yesterday. I knew she would get there. The skirt swayed with her prissy walk. Amber followed closely behind, as if she had just gotten released from the "Victoria's School of Beach Going." And poor Paige. She had wanted to branch out. The swimsuit shopping trip with Amber had set her mind on a dangerous course of action. She exited the house in her new suit and cover-up and heels. Yes, sister said *heels*.

I gasped. That caused her to fall. That caused me to laugh. That caused her to get mad. And before we left, she had thrown Amber's borrowed shoes into the foyer and put on her flip-flops.

"We can't be everything," I said.

"But look at them." She pointed to my mother and Amber as they pranced along. "How do they walk like that?"

I patted her arm. "They came out of the womb wearing them. But we didn't. So we have to do it *gradually*. You can't go from these"—I pointed to my beach-going flip-flops—"to those." I pointed to Amber's three-inch heels. "But do you really want to walk like that anyway?"

Paige eyed the two of them curiously. "You mean exactly like that? Hips swaying, wrists dangling, hats flopping?"

"Yes, like that."

"Can't say that I do."

"Well, thank the Lord and call off the cavalry. Sister thought you had crossed into the land of the certifiable. Now, get a hold of yourself and stay out of Amber's room if you don't have any more willpower than that."

"But it's hard. She puts stuff on and it looks so good and you just want to be able to look half as good as she does."

"But we're not her."

"What, Amazons?"

"Right."

"Right. We're not leggy or lean."

"No, we're squatty and stout."

"Speak for yourself."

"You know what I mean, Paige. So you need to start smaller and work your way up if necessary. Start with a wedge. You can balance yourself better. Trust me, I've learned that the hard way. Then work up to a smaller heel. But no matter how we start, we really do need to lie up the beach from the two of them."

"I agree. We don't need to be too close for comparison. But we need something to eat first. Want an ice cream?"

"It's only ten thirty, and you just ate a huge breakfast."

"But my hips are hungry!"

"Well fiddle-dee-dee. Then by all means, let's eat ice cream."

Heavenly Shortcakes and Ice Cream wasn't open at ten thirty in the morning. Apparently only Paige felt ice cream fit into the breakfast category. "It is dairy," she told me. But we were forced to make our way onto the beach.

"Yoo-hoo! Girls! Over here."

So much for lying upstream. Dad had already situated himself in a nice lounge chair and propped the latest John Grisham novel across his chest. Come to think of it, Dad and John favor each other quite a bit. Dad has acquired a few more gray hairs, but it really was quite uncanny. And I had never even thought about it until that moment.

Mother was doing battle with her umbrella. Wasn't quite sure why she needed it. Sister's hat could protect a small settlement. Amber had chosen the chair beside Mother and reserved two more next to them for Paige and myself. We would have chosen the two by Dad, but *People* and *Us Weekly* protected our places.

Paige laid her new wrap delicately at the foot of her chair, and I tried to ease out of my lime-green skirt, which matched my white two-piece with the small green leaves and pink flowers. The suit had been hanging in the window last year and caught my eye immediately. It fit perfectly, and I had worn it ever since. Good thing I loved it. Money (or lack thereof) would make it mine for another year.

Paige and I plopped onto our loungers. I adjusted my straps to avoid tan lines. Every summer required the perfect tan. And the perfect tan required the perfect lotion and no strap marks. But the commotion next to us caused us to turn our attention to our beach buddies.

First, Mother and Amber tugged on their loungers until they landed predominantly beneath the umbrella, as if any sun could actually muscle its way under their hats. As if that wasn't enough protection, they slathered their bodies with SPF 80. Amber's came in an orange tube. Mother pulled out a brown Tropicana bottle that looked very similar to my suntan oil. They both slathered themselves like chickens getting ready for the frying pan.

"May as well get comfortable," I told Paige. "Watching this could take up most of our morning." So we turned over, and Paige laid her head on her arms, but I placed my arms to the side to make sure everything got equal exposure, and then we continued to enjoy the show. The panhandle's hurricane season was about to start off with a bang. Two perfect storms had just landed at once on the beaches of Seaside.

Then the two sorted their magazines and laid them neatly across the bottom of their loungers. They each retrieved a bottled water and finally, after they had straightened their towels twice, laid their bodies to rest. And in no less than ten minutes, each of them was fast asleep: Victoria sputtering, Amber downright sawing logs. And both of the bottom of their legs gradually taking on more and more sun as it shifted in the heavens. By now, even the sun seemed to move slower. I think they wore it out too.

"Ooh, champ should cover his bum," Paige said, causing me to set Tolstoy aside on page one line one, again.

I noticed the dark, leathery-looking thirty-something walking up the beach in a thong. The oil slathered across his body made every defined muscle scream out.

Paige let her eyes rest on the top of her magazine. "Well, champ's got a nice bum at least."

"You make it sound like you've seen worse."

"Don't you remember that vacation I took with my parents to Europe? We went to the beach that turned out to be nudist? Honey, I saw things on that trip that shouldn't have been allowed to see the sun!"

Dad laughed from behind his book. "Girls, you are pathetic."

"Just don't even think about it," I warned him.

"What? You don't want to see your daddy's pretty legs?" He yanked his shorts up to midthigh.

"Stop it! That's a visual a child should never have to endure."

Our banter woke the sleeping beauties. "Oh Lord, have mercy," Mother said as she caught sight of the two cheeks sauntering up the beach.

"That behind could win a beauty pageant," Amber observed.

Paige and I looked at her, puzzled. Well, I guess she would know.

"Savannah wore a thong once."

"Paige!" I said, slapping her.

"Well, you did." She rubbed her arm.

"I know you did not, Savannah Phillips," Mother called.

"So pitiful she put it on sideways. Didn't even notice till it got wedged in the middle of the church service."

"That is what thongs do!" I said, slapping her again. "And you have just been completely barred from all of the remaining embarrassing moments of my life."

Amber found herself amused. "How do you put a thong on sideways?"

"If it can be done, sister here can do it."

I picked my book back up to ignore them all. Until I caught a glimpse of a man with blond spiky hair and the petite brunette alongside him. "Oh my word, that looks like that singer. You know, the one I like, Jonathan Pierce."

Paige looked up. "No way. That's not him."

"It is. I really think it is. That must be his wife?"

Paige crinkled her eyes against the sun. "If it is, she's a midget."

"You shouldn't say that," Amber scolded. "She's petite. And he is fine." She slid her Jackie O sunglasses down to the top of her nose.

"I know. I was hoping he wasn't married. But he is. I heard she's a fiction writer."

Amber looked closer herself. "What kind of fiction does she write?"

I squinted for a better look. "I hear they're books about crazy people from the South."

Paige threw the towel over her head. Her voice was muffled through the cotton. "Well, don't let her see us. She'd have enough stories to tell for years."

"I heard she writes about her husband's music in her books."

Paige let the towel fall beneath one eye. "That is shameless cross-marketing."

"I think it's charming." Amber's face contorted into a rather odd smile.

They drifted up the beach, and our line of sight was overtaken by an eighteen-year-old with a perfectly taut teenage body in her little itsy-bitsy, army-green bikini.

"Those were the days, weren't they, sister?" Paige looked at the young girl with woeful countenance.

"Yes, they were, my friend. Yes, they were."

"Girls, you are sad creatures," Mother said.

Paige uncovered the other eye. "I bet her boobs are fake."

"Paige! That's horrible." I turned to look for myself.

"No. They're not fake," Amber said.

Paige turned her eyes toward her. "And how, pray tell, would you know?"

Amber rolled her eyes. "Paige Long, I have seen enough fake boobs in my life to know when they are and when they aren't. Fake boobs sit high, like little balls in the top of your chest. Do you see hers? No ball. No sitty-uppy. Therefore, no fake boobies."

Had cameras been watching us, they would have caught four I-spiers flanking one fake boob expert turn their heads in unison like a bunch of Charlie McCarthy dolls. Well, if her assessment was correct, those were the real thing.

We watched the woman continue her stroll up the beach, and her departure caused Paige and me to examine Amber's boobies.

"They're mine, girls, all mine," she said with extreme satisfaction as she took a bite from a Snickers bar.

We leaned to look over her in the direction of my mother.

"Don't you dare even ask me such a question. That is totally inappropriate," she retorted.

"All real," Dad said with a shameful grin. "All real."

"Jake!" Mother said, slapping him with a totally enjoyable smile.

"Sick!" Paige and I blurted in tandem.

Amber crinkled her nose. "Oh, Mr. Phillips, that's just not right. I'm certain that is not right."

Paige and I looked down to examine our own. "Where'd they go?" I asked. "Ooh, there they are." That caused every one of us to laugh hysterically. I even think Jake had to wipe his eyes.

Paige couldn't let it go. She had one final assessment of our situation. "Yep, no ball. No sitty-uppy. Perfectly real. Too bad for us."

"Look on the bright side, ladies," Dad said. "You could look like that." He nodded his head to the man walking down the beach with man boobs.

For the first time in twenty-four hours, all women were speechless.

CHAPTER FOURTEEN

"Happy families are all alike; every unhappy family *is unhappy in its own way.*"

"Ahh! Get off of me!" Mother screamed.

"What is it now?" I asked, peeking over Paige's red top, which offered little obstruction.

"It's those love bugs. Those nasty little horny creatures."

"Mother," I said in mock shock. "You shouldn't use such words."

"Well, they are. Have you ever seen anything so disgusting? That they're bugs is bad enough, but to be attached by the tail is just . . . well, it's just"—she shivered, very closely resembling her new pet—"it's simply sordid."

She sounded like she was writing a tawdry romance novel. Wish I could read the novel I brought.

"We studied them in my biology class once," Amber said.

For some reason that didn't surprise me.

"In fact, their whole way of reproducing is rather interesting."

"I'm certain we're not interested," Mother advised.

Paige leaned over in Amber's direction. "No, we're interested."

"Well, let's just say there is a lot of rivalry between males, and the women die quickly after they lay their eggs."

"Well, that's the most wonderful and depressing thing I've ever heard," Paige said, rolling onto her back. "You finally have men fighting over you; then they get what they want and kill you in the process."

"I told you that you didn't want to know."

For the first time, Paige might have actually agreed with my mother.

Mother had packed a masterpiece in that cooler. That was why Dad was so willing to carry it for her. Homemade chicken salad. And a perfectly complementary bean, onion, and tomato salad in a balsamic vinaigrette. And crunchy garlic melba toast bites to eat with it.

"No Doritos?" Paige asked.

Mother looked at her and smiled. Then she dipped into that magic bag of hers and pulled out a grab-size bag of Doritos.

"I love you."

"I know you do."

The cabana boy in red trunks and wavy sun-streaked blond hair distracted all of the females' attention. Paige stuffed her Doritos bag up under her chair while he settled the bill for the chairs and umbrellas with my father.

"Hey," I whispered, poking her. She wouldn't turn back toward me. "Hey." She still couldn't exit her trance. "Hey!" This time all heads turned toward me. Even Mr. Cabana Boy's. I smiled, trying to assure them I still had one leg outside of Kookooville. All heads turned back to their business, and this time I pinched Paige's arm.

She turned to me in disgust. "Wipe your mouth," I said in my newfound whisper. "You've got nacho cheese dust all over it."

She wiped in panic mode without turning back to the visitor. Then she looked up at me for my inspection and approval.

"Say thank you."

"Thank you," she mouthed, and with that she stood up to flaunt her confidence in her "Body by Amber." Paige's little red and white striped skirt followed Cabana Boy back to his cabana, and they disappeared in a sea of red.

The Gulf Coast hasn't been called the Redneck Riviera for nothing. In fact, the actual definition of *redneck* descended the stairs from the East Ruskin Beach Pavilion about the time Paige made her exit. It was the bleached-blonde hair that vied for the color of mustard, French's to be exact, with the year-old perm that stuck out from underneath the hot pink cowboy hat that gave her away. I could see the matching fingernail polish on her two-inch nails as they tugged at the front of her hat. But it was the black-and-white zebra-striped bikini with hot pink straps that wrapped the garland on the tree. How she managed to slather herself in oil without clawing her skin was indeed a feat.

I was ready to swim. However, the gnawing fear that I would drown if I didn't wait thirty minutes after eating had remained with me these twenty-four years. As hard as I tried, I couldn't break the phobia that I would walk into the water and the load in my stomach would somehow drag me to the deepest floor of the ocean. So I decided to take a trip to the bathroom. That would occupy some time. No one wanted to join me, since everyone else had gone at different intervals throughout the morning. Amber Topaz and Mother multiple times.

I noticed a familiar face walking into the surf store. "Adam!" He turned toward me, and his eyes rewarded me with immediate recognition.

"Savannah. When did your family get here?" He walked over and gave me a hug.

"We just got in yesterday. How are you?"

"Doing pretty good," he said, fiddling with the buckle of his belt awkwardly.

"Well, I thought I might see you and Kate this morning. So how is she? Where is she? And the boys? How are they?"

He raked his hands through his short brown hair. "Well, a lot happens in a year, Savannah."

I read between the lines. I had met Adam and Kate ten years ago. I was fourteen, and they were twenty-four-year-old newlyweds whose wedding gift from their parents was a home in Seaside. They took to me and I took to them. And each year we would catch up on the year before. And each year brought news of no children . . . until fertility treatments after seven years of marriage resulted in gorgeous twin boys. And Kate and Adam, as if they weren't already a perfect family, multiplied their perfection with twins. "Yeah? What's going on, Adam?"

"Well, it's too much to tell standing out here. But Kate's at the house, so I'm sure she can fill you in, and I know that she would love to see you. I'm grabbing a few things for the boys before I go over and get them. She'll be alone this evening, and I'm sure she would love the company."

"Why is she alone?" I prodded.

"Savannah, really, it's all for the best."

"If you're trying to tell me that you two aren't living together, then I don't know how that is for the best of anybody."

"Trust me, Savannah, it is." He fidgeted with his pocket now.

"Best for whom?"

His tone grew more frustrated. "Best for all of us." He paused to settle his temper. "Now"—he took me by the arms—"you look beautiful. And it is wonderful to see you, as always. And please, go see Kate. She'll love it." He pecked me on the cheek. "I've really got to run." And with that he slipped into the world of surfboards at Roxy. I stared at the door, feeling as if part of the earth's spinning had just slowed down. Surely this all had a perfectly logical explanation that could be remedied. I just needed to find the logic.

Lucy and Manuel were sitting at a small table outside Roly-Poly's when I exited the bathroom. It looked like my story would be pretty easy to get after all. She had donned a hat befitting my beach partners. Vicky would love her all the more. "Good morning again, you two."

"Well, hello again yourself, Miss Savannah," Lucy said, setting her fresh-squeezed lemonade to rest on the table. Manuel just smiled and pointed to his full mouth. "Want some?" She lifted her chicken-caesar wrap.

"No. Just ate, actually. A few of us are about to go swimming. Maybe we could talk about New Orleans some. Would you like to join us?"

"No, not today," Lucy offered. "Today I am taking my Manuel shopping."

"Ooh, Manuel's lucky day." I eyed him with a wink.

"Oh, yes. Lucky man am I."

The sight of Joshua and some guys coming out of one of the shops past Manuel's head caught my attention.

"What's wrong?" Lucy asked. She looked up to see the group exiting the store. "You know them?"

I sat down quickly in their extra chair and rested my elbow on the table, using my hand to shield my face. "I know the one in the white shorts. Please tell me when they've gone."

"Okay . . . wait . . . one more minute, they're looking in a window . . . Now they're talking . . . Now they're laughing . . . Okay, they're moving . . . they're moving . . ."

"Lucy." Manuel laughed. "You're crazy."

"Okay . . . one more second, they're about to round the corner. Whew." She let out a sigh. "All safe."

"You're sure?"

"Totally."

I looked up at the two of them smiling at me. "I'm an idiot."

Lucy reached over and patted my hand. "No, it's precious. So, how long have you loved the man in the white shorts?"

I looked up to make sure the guys were out of view and responded without thinking. I laughed. "Me? Love Joshua? Oh no, I don't love Joshua. He's just a guy who works with me. Who torments me. Who drives me crazy. I mean, my stars, he was just kissing some girl yesterday . . . no, I don't love him . . . can't even stand him most—"

Lucy wiped her face calmly. "Savannah, you talk a lot."

"I know. I babble."

"But you do love him. It's all over your face."

"No. It could be a bout of indigestion from Victoria's chicken salad I had for lunch, but trust me, love for Joshua North it is not."

"Call it what you will. But don't you agree, Manuel?"

He looked at me sympathetically. "Yep, my new friend. I do believe you're hopelessly in love."

"You two are so silly." I laughed. They really were cute and crazy little things. "I *couldn't* love him. I'm absolutely certain there is no way I could love Joshua North."

"Love will do things for you and to you that nothing else will," Lucy said, eyeing Manuel.

Manuel responded, "Yes, it will. Thankfully."

I stood up. I needed to go. I really did. These were sweet people, but the heat had no doubt triggered early onset dementia. "Well, I'm so sorry to interrupt your lunch."

"No bother whatsoever. I'm glad we could be your lookouts."

"Oh, thanks for that. I'm really sorry."

Manuel looked up. "You're no bother, Savannah. You helped me. We helped you. Enjoy your day."

I tucked the chair back under their table and walked away. The loathsome love bugs alighted on my shirt. I flicked them off. "Get a room!"

CHAPTER FIFTEEN

Luck seemed to be stalking me like a cat stalks a rat. I do hope I didn't just refer to myself as a rat. I heard the laughter of boys before I slammed into their bodies. That was one of the consequences of looking down instead of up. A big one caught me and apologized quickly. I looked up to see his blue eyes catch my own. "I'm sorry, Miss. We weren't paying any attention."

One of the guys with him turned around, and we saw each other simultaneously. "Savannah!" Joshua announced. "What in the world are you doing here?"

"No way," the green-eyed smasher responded. "You two know each other?"

"Yeah, yeah . . ." Joshua hesitated, obviously still stunned at seeing me. "Savannah and I work together at the *Chronicle*." He just looked at me and smiled as if he forgot his friends were around.

I looked down and spotted some sand on my flip-flop and tried to wipe it off with the toe of my other shoe. "Well, Savannah . . ." Mr. Blue eyes said, wrapping his arm around me, "tell us all you know about Mr. North."

I laughed.

Joshua pulled his arm off me. "Leave her alone, Mark." Mark released me and stood back to be introduced. "Okay, Savannah. This is Mark Greene, this is Brady Fletcher, this is Hank Davis, and this"—he flung his arm toward the even taller guy at the end of the line—"is Johnny Deal." Johnny smiled from ear to ear. "These, Savannah, are my best friends in the whole world."

"A pleasure to meet you, gentlemen." I offered a smile in return as I retrieved my hand from the last handshake.

"So, Miss Savannah," Johnny said, fitting me nicely underneath his arm, "can Joshua really write? I mean, we just can't imagine it."

I turned to look back at Joshua. Torture would be sweeter. "He's actually a very fine writer."

"A *fine* writer, huh?" Johnny chided. "Imagine that, fellas, our Joshua, a *fine* writer."

Joshua's face flushed. I'd never seen him do that before. Few things ever embarrassed this man. Amazing what friends could do to a person. "Okay, fellas, that's enough. Go to your little surf shop, and I'll meet you on the beach in a few minutes."

Johnny smiled again. "I do believe we have just been given the brush-off, gentlemen."

"I believe you would be exactly right," Mark said. "Savannah, a pleasure to meet you. Please do not wreak havoc on our dear friend here. We know women have a way of doing that to him."

Yes, we certainly did do that, didn't we? "Then I'll be ever so gentle," I assured them.

They turned to leave, only after Johnny had kissed my hand and declared the entire "run-in" to have been a pleasure.

That left Joshua and me to stare uncomfortably at each other. After all, the last time I had seen him, he was playing tongue aerobics with a woman who, "sitty-uppy" or not, was unequivocally a bleached blonde. "Charming," I finally offered to break the silence.

"What are you doing here?" he asked, still finding it hard to believe we had accidentally ended up at the same place.

"Working. And you?" I couldn't wait to hear this.

"For a wedding, actually. This is the first time my friends and I have seen each other in a couple years."

"Friends, huh?"

He frowned. "Yeah, friends."

I looked into his dark eyes. It was clear he wanted to talk, but I didn't have it in me to be gracious. I didn't want to know the life story of his *friends.* "Well, I really need to get going." I turned to head in the direction of big hats and beach fodder. How exciting.

He grabbed my arm. "Why are you in such a hurry? Where are you headed, anyway?"

"My parents and Paige and . . . uh, your friend Amber are all waiting for me on the beach." I turned my attention to the empty wine cartons outside the back door of Bud & Alley's kitchen.

"Ooh, Amber's here." He rubbed his curly black head.

"Yes, Amber's here. So, if you don't want to run into her, you might better avoid me."

"Well, you could come hang out with us for a while. You would love it." His dark eyes started to dance. They did that whenever he had come up with a new idea or some witty comment. "The guys would love it. And we have some other friends there who would love to meet you as well."

I raised my right eyebrow. I couldn't help it. The man was either deficient or unbelievable. Who could be certain? "No, thank you. I've met enough of your friends."

He frowned again. "That's really rude. My friends were nothing but kind to you, Savannah. You know, you really can be a royal little twit."

My mouth dropped open. How could this man be so self-righteous? I wasn't the one who was kissing all over some other man one morning and then inviting Joshua to come meet my friends as if he were today's prize. I paused before I spoke. Two intertwined teenagers passed by oblivious to our presence. "I beg your pardon?"

"You heard me. So maybe my friends don't drive Saabs or live in mansions, but they're some of the nicest, most enjoyable people you would ever meet. You know, maybe I was wrong about you. Maybe there really isn't anything in you but pettiness." And with that he turned to leave.

"How dare you say all of those things and walk away," I said, flopping over to him. I noticed a few people staring. I had no idea why drama always seemed to find me in public places. I grabbed his arm and pulled him out of the center of the public area to a covered walkway that connected the two Seaside shopping areas. "This has nothing to do with the quality of your friends, but everything to do with your . . . your little rendezvous this morning."

He really did look at me then as if I were from Kookooville. "My what?"

"Oh, please. Don't act like you don't know what I'm talking about. I saw you today swapping spit with some little blonde on the beach. And now you want to prance me over to your friends like I'm today's lucky number. Well, I'm through being lucky!" He stared at me. "Well, anyway, I don't think so, mister. I have a little more pride in myself then that." I straightened my wrap just to make sure he got the picture.

He smirked at me. I hated when he smirked at me. "So you saw me this morning, huh?"

"Yes, I *saw* you this morning," I said, whispering as a man in some scary-looking attempt at shorts passed us talking on his cell phone.

"You were spying on me?"

I turned my gaze back to Joshua. "What?" I huffed. "No, I was not spying on you. I was walking on a *public* beach, watching you make a *public* spectacle of yourself."

"You saw me kiss another girl?"

"Are we playing *Jeopardy*? You know exactly what I saw."

"You are so . . . so . . ." He shook his head and laughed irritatingly. "Absolutely . . . beautiful."

"So what? Did you hear what I just said?!"

"Yes, I heard you. And I realize it bugged you. It bugged you bad." He stepped closer to me.

"You need to back up, mister."

He inched closer again. "What you saw was a simple hello kiss between two college buddies who haven't seen each other in two years."

"I saw more than college buddies. That was . . . well . . . it was downright inappropriate." I held my hand out against his firm, T-shirt-clad, expansive chest. A rather nice chest, actually.

"Inappropriate? It was a peck."

"Not from my standpoint."

"Your standpoint lacks perspective. Your standpoint saw what you wanted to see, not what actually happened. It was a simple kiss. But, yes, you're right."

I had forgotten why I should be right. "About what?"

"About us being more than friends. At one time we were more than college buddies. In fact, Celeste and I were a couple."

"Celeste? What a name for a beach swinger."

"Savannah. Just stop it. She is a wonderful girl who I dated for a year and a half actually. Until we broke up and she fell in love with my best friend and roommate, Mark. And now they're one week shy of getting married. And that's why we're all here. For the wedding. *Her* wedding. A wedding she just got in town for yesterday. This morning was the first time we had seen each other in two years."

"Married, huh?" I scoffed as the kitchen of Bud and Alley's penetrated the breezeway with their aromas and sounds.

"Yeah, married." He moved my hand out of his way. "So things aren't what they had seemed, now, are they?" He moved in a little closer.

I backed up, feeling the stucco wall come into contact with my bare back. The shade from the trellis overhead and the building across the breezeway removed the sun from my face. "I guess not," I said, refusing to remove my eyes from his. He looked at me in a different way. Deeply. Confusingly. Scaringly. I know it's not a word, but it fits here. And I knew what he was going to do. He had toyed with me before, but he wasn't toying with me this time. "I guess I should—"

He put his finger over my lips. "You should say nothing. You talk way too much as it is."

"You think?" And with those words the softest lips this side of creation touched mine in a way they had never been touched before. True, Grant had kissed them on multiple occasions. But they had never been kissed like this before. Passionate, yet gentle. Strong, yet tender. Territorial yet perfectly free. And I kissed his back. It was the only polite thing to do.

He leaned back, and I rested my head against the wall. I couldn't open my eyes. I was officially paralyzed. "Savannah?"

I still didn't open them. "Huh?"

He laughed. "You okay?"

"Uh-huh."

He laughed again. "Are you sure?"

"Uh-huh."

"You can talk now."

"Uh-huh."

"Oh, excuse us." I heard Manuel's voice and opened my eyes. Hoot-owl style.

I laughed awkwardly. Okay, pathetically. "Um, oh, hi. Uh . . . how are you . . . um, um . . ."

Lucy giggled. "Hi," she said, extending her hand to Joshua. "I'm Lucy, and this is my husband, Manuel."

"Oh, yes, yes, that's right, Lucy and Manuel, and this is . . . um, this is . . . um . . ."

"Joshua North. And it's a pleasure to meet you." He extended his hand as well.

"Well, we'll let you two get back to your, um . . . discussion," Manuel said politely.

"Yes . . . our discussion. We were discussing how hot it is . . ." I said, fanning myself rapidly. That was stupid. Because they left giggling.

"Okay. Look," he said, turning my head north. "See that house over there? The one on the beach?"

"What? Proteus?"

"That's where we're staying. Mark's parents rented it for the week for us guys. Everyone will be there tonight for a cookout at seven, and I would love for you to come." He spoke the last line slowly to make sure I understood.

"Oh, I don't know." I ran my hands through my hair hastily. "I've got a really busy schedule. I'm here to work, and I can't really be fooling around . . . I mean, I can't be slacking off."

"You can't work all the time." He smiled and leaned over to kiss me once more. I leaned my head hard against the stucco. This one was slightly more awkward.

"This took too long, Savannah."

I didn't speak. Imagine that.

"Tonight," he said, turning in the direction his friends had gone.

"Don't wait by the door."

He smiled anyway. And I watched his curls disappear. I leaned back against the wall to catch my breath. A soft gray cat came and rubbed against my leg. I looked down in time to meet her eyes. She made it clear she had observed the entire episode.

The love bugs flittered and attached to the pink bow on my bathing-suit top. I scooped them up and sent them back to flight. "You cute little things, you!"

CHAPTER SIXTEEN

Savannah, baby, what's wrong with you?" Mother asked as she looked up from her *Southern Living*. The woman couldn't get away from her roots. Either of them, the Southern kind or the ones on her head. Truth be told, her roots could be the real reason she was wearing a hat. Since she had gone back to her "natural" dark brown, she was having a little trouble—dare I say it—hiding the gray.

"Nothing's wrong. Why in the world would you think something's wrong? My stars, can't a girl go to the ladies' room? I can't swim for thirty minutes, so I wasted them before I went in the—"

Paige got up to rescue me. "Ooh, Savannah, let's get in the water. I'm simply sweltering."

Her use of the phrase "simply sweltering" was an obvious clue she was trying to save me from myself.

"Let's go."

"There's something seriously wrong with that child," my mother said to the snoring princess on one side of her and the bespectacled bookworm on the other. I looked back to see Dad lower his glasses and raise his right eyebrow at me. I turned away immediately. That man could hone in on things quicker than Paige could hone in on the smell of nacho cheese.

We waded through the water, speaking from the sides of our mouths, trying not to talk above a whisper. Waves were incapable of completely concealing sheer exhilaration. I shifted my straps to make sure I didn't get marks.

"What gives?"

"What are you talking about?"

"You leave to pee and you come back humming 'The Way He Makes Me Feel' from *Yentl.* And we are probably the only two people in the world who think *Yentl* was Barbra Streisand's best piece of work."

"It's my favorite movie," I said, splashing water across my chest. "What are you doing spying on me anyway?"

"I don't have to spy on you, Savannah. I can read you like a book."

I laughed. "Oh, well, that's not saying much. This from a girl who hasn't read a book since junior high."

"Maybe so, but you've tortured me with every song on that sound track since *junior high*, missy, and you've never hummed that song. Plus, your lovely MAC lip gloss in the shade of Entice is now efficiently smudged all around your mouth. And unless you've spent the last thirty minutes licking your lips free of your mama's chicken salad, I'd say sister's been swapping spit with someone. And since you are so obsessed with *where* Joshua North is at any given moment, I would say that you just laid one on him. How is that for how well I know you?"

My jaw came unhinged. I started to scream at her knowledge. But a wave nearly swept us back to shore, and we both came up sputtering. I didn't answer until we safely made our way through two more onslaughts and were able to ride the perfect little swells that come before the waves.

"Just so you'll know you don't know everything, *he* kissed *me.*"

"Oh, excuse me." She laid her hand mockingly across her chest. "I knew it!" she screamed loud enough for them to hear in Tampa. Vicky's head perked behind her magazine, and Dad smiled a sly little smile.

"Shut up, you crazy woman! Do you want Victoria Phillips to know that I just kissed the man who referred to her as 'Vicky' in the first article he wrote for the paper? She has disdained him ever since. And do you want Amber to know that her only remaining hope for the throne has been dashed by the friend who just stole Mr. Husband United States of America?"

"What about the woman you saw him kissing just this morning? It was his sister, wasn't it? It's always their sister. When they write stuff like this in novels. They always make it the sister."

"An old girlfriend."

"Ooh. Don't you wish this had been a novel?"

"An old girlfriend who's marrying one of his best friends this weekend."

"So it wasn't as elaborate a kiss as you remember, huh?"

"It looked like it. It looked like two people intensely in love. Enraptured with each other's presence. As if they were the only two who existed this side of creation."

"Okay, enough drama."

"Okay, you want the truth. I felt like I was going to puke."

"Thank you."

"It was perfect," I said, shifting my straps again to avoid prolonged exposure in one place.

"Puking?"

"No, loo-loo, the kiss. Focus. It was soft and yet strong."

Paige's eyes glazed over. "All that?"

"All that."

"Not like Grant?"

I thought of that for a moment. I had fought so hard to keep Grant. Even gave it one last-lamentable-ditch effort. But I failed. And even though Joshua had known all along that I was only after Grant so I wouldn't lose him to someone else, I wouldn't admit the truth to myself. "No, not like Grant. Grant's kisses were always kind of mushy and pure. This held things in it I've never felt before."

"Yeah, right."

"No, really! I felt things I've never felt before . . . Well, I take that back. I'm not sure what I felt. It was just weird."

She wrapped her arm around my shoulder while we bobbed like two bobble heads in the surf. "I know."

"You know it was weird?"

"No, I know *you're* weird." She nodded toward the beauties on the beach. "Can you disguise your glee for the rest of the afternoon?"

"There is no *glee* to disguise."

"Well, you better do better than you did a few minutes ago."

I furrowed my brow. "How's that?"

"Perfectly, Savannah."

I punched her. She punched back. Then the wave punched us both right upside the head.

The water pounded me in the face as I hummed. I loved the feeling of a shower after swimming in the ocean. The cleansing of the water as the salt runs down from the top of your head to your feet. And the way you can feel the sand fall away from your hair and slide between your fingers is purifying.

Afterward, I looked in the mirror to gauge if I had any strap marks. All seemed okay, so I exited my bathroom wrapped in a towel and a smile.

Thomas was waiting outside the bedroom when I came out.

"Ahh!" I screamed.

My brother screamed back.

I slapped him on the arm. "Why are you screaming? You are the one standing outside my door."

"Because your scream scared me. Why are you humming anyway?"

"I was not humming. And when did you get here?"

"Whatever." He plopped down on the bed. "So, you didn't say anything, did you?"

"I told them absolutely nothing. It's not my story to tell." I eyed him meaningfully and returned to the bathroom to put on my robe and makeup. "But it is yours. And you need to tell them. The truth too. Not just little tidbits to keep them off of your back."

"I just need a week to rest. I'll tell them when we get back home and I can get back to school."

"You're a chicken."

"But I'm a cute chicken." He smirked. He was right about that.

"Well, cute or not, there is nothing cute about lying, Thomas, and you know that. So you need to decide when you're going to tell Mother and Dad what's going on. I think tonight would be the perfect opportunity. It will just be you and Vicky and Dad."

"Where are you and Paige going?"

"I don't know." I hesitated. "We're just going to grab a bite to eat and relax some."

"No! Head up! Up! Up! Up!" I heard Mother's voice from down the hall.

"Who is she talking to?" Thomas asked.

Maggy barked.

"Her latest protégé."

"What happened to Amber?"

"She's already got the 'head up' part!"

He laughed. "Well, anyway. We're not telling Mom and Dad our little secret tonight," he said as he gave me a peck on the cheek.

"Hey, Thomas." Paige entered as he departed.

"Hey, Paige. Want to come catch a movie with me tonight?"

Paige eyed me. I eyed her harder. "I told you Paige was going to hang out with me tonight," I said.

"I'd love to, Thomas. Besides, Savannah has been invited out for the evening, and I think she needs to go."

"What is this?" Thomas walked back in the room. "Savannah has a date?"

"Savannah has no such thing," I said. "You know, you were right. You two need to go to a movie together. Have a wonderful time. But you do know you'll have to take Amber."

Their heads jerked in tandem. I mocked them. "We have to do what?" Only Thomas's mouth moved. Paige's was still agape.

I closed it for her. "Yes. Encouraging her was going to be mine and Paige's responsibility tonight, but since you and Paige are so bent on me going out while you two catch a movie, then you will have to take Amber."

Paige ran to the window, jerked it open, and hoisted her leg through. "What are you doing?" I screamed.

"Killing myself. There are deaths far worse, I assure you."

Thomas couldn't help but laugh from his comfortable position against the door. I grabbed Paige's arm and pulled her back inside. "Better yet," she said, "how about I throw you out? Then no one will ever know you told us to take her."

I jerked my arm free. "She's not that bad."

"Your mother would much rather have her company," Paige said.

Thomas agreed. "And she would much rather have Mother's, I'm sure. Plus, I'm not sitting around here for a whole four-course dinner to be interrogated about where Mary Francis is. It would be brutal and so nonproductive."

"Either you will take her, or I will tell everyone that your upcoming nuptials are off." I dared him to make me prove it.

"I was never getting married."

"Tell that to your mother."

"You're evil."

"You're eviler. Now, get." I pushed them both out the door and closed it in front of them.

I swung the door open after the knock. "What?!"

Amber peeked her head in.

"Oh, sorry, Amber."

"Are you having dinner with us tonight?"

I tried to keep my eyes from bugging out. "You got a lot of sun," I said. "How'd you get all of that with the hat and the umbrella and the sunscreen?"

"I soak it up like a sponge. Got this on my trips to the bathroom, I guess." She looked down to inspect her beautifully elegant arms herself.

"Well, ten trips to tinkle in an afternoon will do that to you." Paige came back in and plopped on the bed.

Amber walked over to my closet. "So what are you girls doing?"

"Oh . . . nothing really." I gave Paige that look. "Just inspecting what I brought." It was a struggle to sound nonchalant.

She pulled out a light-green silk sleeveless blouse with cream lace trim on the top. "Ooh, this is pretty,"

"That is nice. He'd love that—" Paige clapped her hand over her mouth.

"Who's he?" Amber asked.

I glared at Paige. She was about to die a thousand deaths, and as far as I was concerned, I'd be privileged to administer each one. She would wish she had jumped.

I tried to group my thoughts. "Just a friend I saw who's here for the week."

"Savannah has a boyfriend?" Amber chided.

"Well, no, not exactly. Just a friend who, well, who asked me to come by this evening. But I'm not planning to go. I'm planning to sit right here and read my book." I said, plopping down on my bed and opening Tolstoy to page 1.

She completely ignored me. "Well, in that case, we need to pick out something fabulous for Miss Savannah." She scanned through my clothes quickly. Then she said, "Okay, that's nice.

Now let's go check out my closet." She walked out of the room. I crawled over to Paige's bed and slapped her.

"I didn't mean to! It slipped." She rubbed her arm.

We headed to Amber's closet, and all three of us stood staring inside. Everything in it was fabulous. "Ooh, this would be great, she said, pulling out a beautiful chocolate silk sleeveless dress. Your mother bought that for me a couple weeks ago. She handed it to me and I held it against myself. It dragged the floor. It was beautiful. A beautiful gift from *my* mother. "Oh, so maybe we need to just look at top options." That Amber was a quick study.

For the next thirty minutes, Amber laid every top she had brought across her bed. The last piece she pulled out was a beautiful taupe linen strapless number trimmed with pale pink tulle and a matching rose. It was beautiful and would have been a perfect complement to my Stuart Weitzman wedges and a pair of jeans.

"That's gorgeous," I responded.

She held it in her outstretched arm. "Then tonight it is yours."

"Amber, I can't take—"

"Savannah. You are like a sister to me. If this man is worthy of you, I'd be honored if you wore my top tonight."

I felt like dirt. Worse. Dirt below the dirt. Even worse. The minuscule pieces of muck that make up dirt. "Thank you. I really appreciate it. But I won't be needing it. I really have all intentions of staying home."

"I'm sure you do." Amber winked. Paige and I walked out the door. Paige had restrained herself from saying a word for the last thirty minutes. At least God wasn't *completely* out of miracles. "Oh, what's his name?" Amber asked, causing us both to stop dead in the doorway. I couldn't move. Paige moaned. Well, I could face it head-on or spend the rest of my life hiding behind shrubbery.

I turned to stare at this kind woman. "His name is . . . it's . . . actually, let's just keep this all a surprise. I'll introduce him to you at some point. It's just way too premature. He's just a friend. It really isn't anything more than that."

"Ooh, honey shoo . . . shoo . . . go make yourself beautiful for your man."

I stood there wearing, I'm sure, an expression of utter confusion. "Would you mind us not telling my mother about this right now?"

She used her perfectly manicured nail to zip her lips and lock them shut. Then she muffled something like "mum's the word" through her tightly pressed lips.

Paige took advantage of the moment. "Well, I guess you would much rather stay here than go with me and Thomas to a movie, wouldn't you? I mean, knowing how you love to be with Miss Victoria and all."

Apparently Amber wasn't aware that her mouth really wasn't zippered shut, because she continued to mumble without opening her lips.

"I knew you wouldn't." Paige patted her arm even though Amber's head was shaking up and down yes as hard as it could.

I smiled at her. "You can talk, sweetie."

"I'd love to—"

Paige went to interrupt.

I didn't let her. "What, baby? You can say it."

"I'd love to go, Paige. I haven't been to a movie in weeks. Could we go see that romantic comedy with Tom Hanks and Jennifer Aniston? I hear it is such a tearjerker. It might give me some pointers on how to win Joshua's heart . . . you know, completely." She batted her four-inch eyelashes, and we could feel the breeze across the room.

"Oh, I'm sorry, honey, we're going to see *Die Hard, Part Sixteen*. I knew you'd hate it. Maybe later in the week we'll take you to see that."

Amber's eyes began to squint. They narrowed in on us in a strange way like something out of *Poltergeist*. "Ooh, I love Bruce

Willis. And I love how he shoots them and strangles them." She played it out in front of us like Jackie Chan. We backed up toward the door. "And then, he—"

"Alrighty then. Be back in a few." And Paige jerked me back into our bedroom.

"I am going to hell," I announced.

"Yes, you are. For what you just did to me, I'm sure there is a special area of torture reserved for wicked people like you."

She was unbelievable. "I mean for the lie *you* made me tell."

"Me? I didn't make you lie. Anyway, you didn't lie."

"I didn't expound."

"It's not the right time. There will be a right time, and this isn't it. Now, get dressed and leave before I kill you myself." She kissed me on the cheek. "And have an absolutely wonderful time."

"I really have no intentions of—"

"I'll expect to hear every detail."

"If you utter a word, I'll—"

She duplicated Amber's recent lip-locking mime and then slammed the door in my face. She slammed it with the utmost respect, I'm certain.

Dad was stretched out on the back porch in an Adirondack chair, veritably floating in the aroma of steaks being grilled on the patio below. This chair had been a constant in Seaside gardens, patios, and porches for years and years. Thomas Lee designed the very first chair in 1903. He needed some comfy lawn furniture for his summer home in upstate New York. He shared the idea with a friend. The friend patented it and made a fortune. But that was in no way any relation to what I was doing to Amber. I think.

"Good book, huh?"

Dad lowered his reading glasses and looked up at me from his reclining position. "Very."

"Where's Mom?"

"Where do you think?"

"In the bathroom."

"Yes, in the bathroom."

"What's she doing? Primping?"

"Actually, no. She's soaking in a bath, because she's got highly sunburned legs from the calves down."

"Sounds attractive."

"Let's just say it cut her wardrobe options in half."

"A perfect excuse for a new one."

"My thoughts exactly."

I sat down and tucked my robe up under me. I eyed him head-on. "So I guess you're all staying around here tonight, huh?"

"Smells that way." He sniffed the delightful aroma.

"You saw Thomas?"

"Yeah, he's avoiding us though. I have a feeling it has something to do with Mary Francis."

This man was amazing. "I think I might go walk around for a little while. Enjoy the evening. Maybe stop and see if Lucy and Manuel are out. I really need to talk to them and start my story. I've got to get something in by Tuesday."

"Don't you want a steak first?" He opened his book back up.

"Nah. Too many Cokes." I patted my stomach.

He laid his book across his chest and slowly removed his glasses, folding them neatly and placing them on top of his book. This man knew how to torture a soul. "Have a wonderful time."

"I will." I gave a quick peck and tried to scurry out.

"Oh, Savannah. Did you know Joshua North was in town?"

I felt my saliva dry up immediately. I tried to be nonchalant as I turned around slowly. Wish that defibrillator was hanging around nearby. "Um, I . . . How did you know that?"

"I ran into him this morning when I went to get my paper. We chatted over a cup of coffee."

"Oh, well, isn't that interesting. Small world, huh?"

"Yeah, I guess it is." A smile slowly crept across his face. "So you *didn't* know he was here?"

"Actually, I saw him this afternoon. But I haven't given it much thought since. Well, I'll see you later this evening."

I stared at the top of his head. He even resembled John Grisham from the back. Let's hope the man didn't feel the need to take up investigative law. At least not tonight.

The taupe linen top leered at me from my bed as I entered my room. Amber must have brought it in for me. I turned to my closet and pulled out a black lace top with small capped sleeves, a ribboned waistband, and small pearl buttons. I pulled out my jeans and a pair of black wedges that laced up my calves and studied myself in the mirror. I put on some makeup and pale pink lip gloss. Once I dried my hair, I let it lay neatly across my shoulders. I could hear voices on the back porch and knew that they would never hear me leave. As I went to close the door, I looked back at Amber's beautiful top lying across the bed. It was such a kind gesture. But just in case I did see Joshua, I didn't want Amber thinking I had worn her own clothes to see "her" man. I picked it up and walked it back into her room and stowed it safely inside her closet. I only hoped I could be as gentle with her heart.

CHAPTER SEVENTEEN

The gray-headed gentleman slapped his partner's bum. I hoped it was his wife's. Then he pulled her to him and planted a juicy one on her orange lipstick. Maybe it was the saltiness in the air or the sound of my humming—who could be certain?—but romance had broken loose over this haven in the South.

The stickiness of the air brushed against my face as I passed the couple, now both wearing orange lipstick and huge smiles, and continued my walk through the perfect evening that had settled in.

Wonder if I had looked equally happy this afternoon?

This afternoon. This afternoon had changed everything. I think.

I glanced at the bricks that were intricately laid in the street and laughed at how unintricately my own life had laid itself out. Less than a year ago I was about to enter the literary world by becoming an author. It never happened. I unwittingly threw that chance away because I thought my mother had rigged my success. Come to find out that was actually one thing she hadn't felt the need to control. I found out a little too late.

So I returned to Savannah, a place I never thought I'd end up, and found out my man had ended up with a long, gangly looking redhead named Eliza, or Elizabeth, or something that starts with an *E*. I began writing for the newspaper. Took over the human-interest column of my deceased mentor, whom I never actually met in person. My first few offerings left me flat on my face. But over the past ten months, I've gained some footing and my sense of voice. Don't always know when to keep that voice quiet, but I'm slowly learning when it matters.

Thrown into the middle of this entire whirlwind was getting my own apartment and meeting this man I had come face-to-face with this afternoon.

On our first encounter, he had almost run me over with his bicycle. I do believe I noticed almost every detail about him that day. The curly dark hair. The penetrating black irises. The perfectly white smile. The immersing grin. And those beautiful legs and tightly honed arms. And with each encounter, my heart had fallen for him harder and harder. And with each smile, and each word and each brush of the arm, he had driven me sufficiently insane.

When he finally confronted me about six months ago, declaring that my attempts to regain Grant's love had absolutely nothing to do with love at all and everything to do with not wanting to lose, I knew then that he thought he knew a little too much about me.

"Manuel, I would say Miss Savannah looks beautiful this evening, wouldn't you?"

I looked up at the two sitting on their porch, playing a game of cards. Their smiles washed over me. I returned them. "Beautiful? You think?" I asked, opening their gate.

Manuel laid his card down. "I'd say extraordinary."

"Well," I said, placing my hand daintily across my chest, "I do believe you just made me blush."

"The tall stranger?" Lucy asked.

I walked to the top of the stairs and pulled a chair out from their small table. "The tall stranger?"

"Well, surely that's where you're headed looking like that?"

"Actually, I was coming to see you."

Lucy turned to look at Manuel, then back at me. "Coming to see us, huh?"

"Yes, I . . . well . . . I told my boss I would write my next human-interest story while I was here. I thought maybe your story would be very interesting to the readers. Would you be willing to share it with me? I don't have anywhere else to go." Well, not in a hurry anyway.

They laughed. I wasn't sure why, but they laughed. "Well, we'd love to," Lucy said, "but we're about to go out and eat." I noticed a perplexed look cross Manuel's face as he eyed Lucy.

"Oh . . . yes . . . We were actually finishing up this hand before heading to dinner. I guess you'll have to get with us tomorrow." His expressive Hispanic tone rose.

I watched them for a moment, feeling as if I had intruded. Lucy sensed my feelings and turned back to me. "I hope you can find *something* to do with your evening."

"Yeah, sure . . . I've got this book I've been trying to start since I got here. So tomorrow, then, 8:00 a.m. Would that be okay? After I run?"

"Tomorrow," Lucy said with a wink.

The construction team from the new home being built on the oceanfront property was putting their coolers away in the back of their truck. I could eye Joshua's house and see the lights over the roof of their cab.

I gave them a nod as I passed. The tool belt on one of them triggered a brief memory of my last encounter with construction workers. Actually, it was Mother's encounter. Vicky had issues with construction workers. Well, no. Vicky had issues with everyone on some level, but recently had a rough time with a few construction workers.

Our neighbors were doing some remodeling. They claimed Mother's extensive gardens had devalued their property. Well, honestly the gardens had. They made the distinction obvious. Vicky's garden: pretty. Their garden: not so pretty. So they were putting on the dog. They were planting gardens that overlooked our gardens and redoing features on their house that honestly didn't need redoing for ten more years.

Their construction team worked hard. And that meant they came in early and worked late. Now, Mother is always in her office by nine, but she doesn't get up at the crack of dawn. But these construction workers would show up around five every morning. They'd nail. They'd saw. They'd talk. Loud. Anyone familiar with downtown Savannah knows that talking at your neighbors can be heard, well, by your neighbors.

So sister Vicky, who is head of the Savannah Historical Preservation Society, knows two things. And what she doesn't, she'll make up. Convincingly I might add. She knows that work isn't to start before seven on weekdays and before eight on weekends. So she called her good friend Cynthia, who is Hispanic, and asked her how to say, "No working until seven," followed up by, "No working until eight."

Had Cynthia known how those poor workers would be abused by Mother's incoherent Spanish, she never would have told her a thing. But every morning they'd come early, ready to earn an honest day's wage, and Vicky would pop her head out of the front door, often with silken eye mask still propped atop her forehead, and start hollering "*no hombres comiencen hasta las ocho de la mañana*." Those poor men were afraid to work before *eight thirty* after she got through with them.

But the new team that showed up one day to reshingle didn't know Vicky's rule. And that day, in exasperation, she hollered, "*Hombres castrados a las ocho de la mañana.*" Those men screamed at each other and took off like streaks straight up Oglethorpe. I'm not sure they quit running until they reached Atlanta. Come to find out she was telling them, "All males will be castrated by eight." The Johnsons couldn't get workers after that. They tried two states in all directions, but everyone had heard about the lady with the machete. And few ever wondered who had mutilated Mother's little "fountain boy" that resided in her garden.

The workers eyed me curiously as I passed laughing, laughing at the memory and that my mother could intrude on my evening even when she was nowhere around.

The pleasant moment faded the second my feet touched the welcome mat of Proteus.

How in the world had I gotten here?

Fortunately, Joshua's friend Johnny saw me. He was approaching the house with arms loaded with Modica's Market bags. I opened the door for him. The beautiful beachfront home was quiet inside.

"They're all out back. Let me put this stuff up, and I'll walk out there with you," he said, setting the bags down on the counter.

"What you got in there?"

"The fixin's. That's what we call 'em 'round here. The pickle, the tomato, the onion . . . but don't touch that if you're going to get you some sugar tonight."

"Excuse me?" I raised my eyebrow.

"Girl, it is what it is. We knew something was up with Joshua, but he wouldn't tell anybody. So, now we know. Savannah, and I'm not talking the city is what's up with our boy. So, like I said. Stay away from the onions."

He was not going to be stopped.

He grinned like a Cheshire cat. "And every good cookout needs chips. So I've got any variety these hounds could want." With that he folded up his brown-paper shopping bags and laid them on the counter. "Now, let's go meet everybody." He put his arm around me. "You're nervous. I can feel it."

"You can?" I asked, trying to make my feet walk toward the screen door.

"I can feel anything. And right now I feel a Southern girl about to darn near jump out of her skin. They're just people, Savannah. Good people. You'll love them." He reached his other hand out to open the back door that led to the patio. "Now, go sic 'em, lady," he said, prodding me into the realm of strangers, gas grills, and the eyes of a strangely familiar man standing across the back porch, holding a Dr Pepper.

CHAPTER EIGHTEEN

Barbra's voice really needed to get out of my head.

"Savannah, I presume," came the voice of a stranger with an outstretched hand. "I'm Luke Greene, Mark's father. It's a pleasure to have you here."

"It's a pleasure to be here. How do you know my name?" I asked with a slight laugh as I leaned down to shake his hand. He returned it to the arm of his wheelchair. I tried not to stare.

"Joshua's been talking about you all day. I do believe you have stolen his heart." I looked for the door. The stately gentleman twisted the small lever at the front of the arm, and the motion of the wheelchair caused my head to turn as he twirled himself around. Joshua was positioned right in front of him. He acknowledged me alone.

"You look beautiful," he said, walking around Mr. Greene. He wrapped his arm around me and moved to kiss me on the head. I retreated instinctively. My stars, the man was trying to kiss me in front of strangers. He grinned and never missed a beat.

"Savannah, please make yourself at home," Mr. Greene said.

His interruption caused me to blush, embarrassed that I had so easily forgotten his presence.

A beautiful lady in her early fifties with frosted blonde highlights and piercing blue eyes came around to Mr. Greene and placed her hand comfortably on his shoulder. "You must be Savannah."

"Yes, baby, that's her."

"And you're as lovely as Joshua told us. Welcome," she said, extending her other hand. "Please, get something to drink. Dinner will be ready shortly."

"Thank you."

Mrs. Greene shooed Joshua off. "Now, go introduce her to the others, Joshua."

"It sounds like I've been introduced already," I whispered, trying to hide my agitation. "I guess you were pretty certain I would be here."

"I was absolutely certain." He tugged me to the other side of the porch. I immediately caught sight of the blonde head that had kissed him this morning. I looked down at my top to make sure all of my buttons were fastened. Not sure why. Just felt a little undone. A rather common occurrence.

No unbuttoned buttons. No price tags. (I'd done that before too.) No, all perfect. Well, almost perfect. See, this woman was supposed to be dog ugly. And not only was she not ugly, but she was surrounded by three other stunning women, another beautiful blonde, a breathtaking African-American, and a beauty-queen-material Asian. The latter two had lustworthy black locks. But since the Ten Commandments had arrived and then departed from our fair city, I had really tried to work on the coveting aspect of my character.

"Savannah, this is Heather, Deneen, Linda, and Celeste. Ladies, this is my . . ." And there came the deciding moment. I held my breath. I had no idea what was about to come out of this man's mouth. Shoot, I had no idea what had come out of his mouth all day long. Instead, he said, "This is the lady I've been telling you about." Well, that answered a thousand questions. "Savannah Phillips."

They all "ahhed."

"Savannah, these are some of my closest friends."

Each girl leaned over to hug me. And I had officially entered Joshua's world. Dinner. Laughter. Stories of college adventures. Some tame. Others needing taming. Most of those were Johnny's stories. Dessert. More stories. More laughter. And then slowly the group began to dissipate.

The guys had taken to a postdinner game of volleyball. I watched perched atop a blanket.

"Can I share your blanket?" Heather asked.

"I'd love that," I said, scooting over and moving the shoes I'd slipped off out of the way.

She smoothed the crease beneath her. "I haven't seen Joshua North this happy since I've known him."

"I find that incredibly hard to believe. The man of a thousand women."

Her dark eyes reflected the soft red hues of the sunset. "Don't let his looks fool you. Joshua was never a player. No. Joshua has always been more serious. Settled, Mark would call him. Only dated Celeste steadily. Never anyone else seriously. Come to think of it, I'm not sure he ever really dated anyone else, period."

Now, there was a curious fact. I returned my attention to Joshua, who was high-fiving Johnny over some extraordinary feat of testosterone. Plus, women were watching. He caught my eye and winked as he brushed the sand from his impeccable calves.

"You're a perfect fit," she assured me.

"Why would you say that?" I asked, looking down at my bare feet covered in sand.

"I can just tell. It works by the heart, Savannah. The best thing you can do is not overanalyze it. I did that for years."

"You did?"

"Yeah. You see that guy over there?" She pointed to Brady.

"Who, Brady?"

"Yeah. He loved me for years. But he's white. I'm black. And black and white in the South mean one thing—well, I'm not sure what, but it certainly isn't marriage. Plus, neither of our families appreciated us going outside of *their* definitions of love."

I looked up at her, able to see she still carried a deep fondness for the blond-headed man across the fire. "What did you do?"

"I married him anyway."

"Oh my stars! What did your families say?" I knew perfectly well what Victoria Phillips would have said, had I brought home Gregory, my wonderful black legal advisor and friend from Jackson, Mississippi.

"Well, they didn't sing a chorus of 'Ebony and Ivory.'" We both laughed. "Actually, they had a plethora of colorful commentary. Then my family met him and his family met me, and neither could deny the love that we had for each other. So they don't anymore, and we're about to celebrate our second wedding anniversary. And another addition in, oh, about six months." She patted her hardly distinguishable pooch.

"That's wonderful," I said, touching her knee.

She put her hand on my shoulder, revealing a simple platinum eternity diamond wedding band. "Wonderful and sometimes painful. We've heard every horrible thing you can imagine from the mall to the church. We get stares and remarks behind our backs, or loud enough for us to hear. But we have the things that matter. We have common morals and a common faith. And there are many 'matching' couples, as I like to call them, who never even bother to see if they share those two most important traits. Yet *we're* the odd ones. Oh well, we deal with it."

"How have you been able to handle all of that?"

"Oh, did I forget to mention we have an undeniable attraction?" she said with a glint in her eye.

I smiled. "I can see that."

"Okay, just checking. Honestly, as long as the core of who you both are is the same, I've learned you can't overthink love, Savannah. You'll find enough obstacles along the way. Enjoy the good parts. Know bad ones will appear. And just determine that you'll go through them together. Mr. and Mrs. Greene are perfect examples of that."

"Do you mind telling me what happened?"

"A car accident. Mark's senior year in high school. Mr. Greene had been an alcoholic for years. One night he was driving drunk, and a tree stopped him before he even laid a foot on his brakes. The trauma left him paralyzed from the waist down."

"Oh, how awful."

"Yeah, it was a painful story."

"How did Mrs. Green make it through all of that?"

"There aren't many like her. But she recognized immediately how this shook up Mr. Greene. And he never touched alcohol again. She said if it took this to give her the best years of her life with her husband, then she would spend the rest of her life enjoying their time together. Mark will tell you the same thing. He and his dad have actually had a real relationship since the accident. It changed Mr. Greene forever."

"I'm not sure whether to be horrified or amazed."

"I think you can be both. We were. Real amazement can come out of horrific moments."

"How true."

"Yes, it is, my new friend. You never know where love will go." She stood up and brushed the remnants of sand off of her shorts.

"Do you think Mrs. Greene has any regrets?"

"If she ever did, I would say she doesn't anymore."

I held the silence, taking in the story.

"We'll see you soon," she said.

"I'll look forward to it."

"You'll be sick of us, I assure you." She smiled. "Come on,

Daddy," she said to the vibrant fella who had just flown face first in the sand.

He popped his head up. "Who you callin' Daddy?"

"You, lucky man." And with that he brushed himself off and they walked arm in arm up to the house. Chocolate and vanilla. In the direction of Mrs. Greene, who was sitting on Mr. Greene's lap, watching.

The water felt cool. Not tepid. Not freezing. Just cool. I walked with my shoes in my right hand and let the water wash over my feet with each passing wave. For a long time we didn't say anything. We just walked.

"They liked you." His strong yet gentle voice pierced even the sound of the crashing wave.

"I liked them too. The jury's out on you, though. You obviously led everyone to believe I would be there. I didn't even know I would be there, until, well, until I got there."

"I had no doubt you'd be there, even if you had a thousand."

"You're incorrigible."

"Ooh, big word for a human-interest writer." He nudged me.

I nudged back. Harder. Ran him right into the incoming wave. We both laughed. "I did like you with them, though."

"What do you mean?" His long legs slowed to allow mine to keep up.

"Different people have a way of bringing out different things in us. Paige brings out my wild side. Mother brings out my maniacal tendencies. Dad brings out my thoughtful side. And each of your friends brought out something different and beautiful in you."

"Like what?"

"Like your laugh. Your confidence, yet a shyness. Your gentleness and your smile. They complement you."

"You noticed all that?"

"I'm not as self-absorbed as you think I am."

"What do I bring out in you?"

I had to pause for that one. There were so many things he had brought out in me. "Rage. A tightness in my chest." I turned his direction. His head was down and his feet brushed the sand. A loose curl hung in his face, but I could see the outlines of his smile. I felt his hand slip into mine. The warmth of it removed the chill from my own. "And a thousand questions with no answers."

He stopped in the sand and turned to look at me. "What questions do you have, Miss Phillips, that I need to answer?"

I looked into those eyes that looked into mine far deeper than I had ever allowed anyone to see. I felt remotely exposed. I shrugged. "Oh, the simple things. You know, who are you? Where do you come from? What makes you crazy?"

"Joshua North," he stated matter-of-factly as he stepped in closer. "Jacksonville, Florida." And then his right hand moved gently around my waist. "Savannah Phillips." He moved his other hand, which still held my own, around the other side of my waist. And with that declaration, the same lips that had taken me to new places this afternoon took me somewhere else beyond our recent travels. If I didn't know better myself, I would declare sister saw those stars she had been declaring she owned for years!

He leaned back and looked at me. I asked, "Did you just say I drive you crazy?"

"Yep. You've been doing that since the day I met you."

"Drive you crazy how?" I raised my right eyebrow.

"In every imaginable way." He kissed me again. I returned it with everything a kiss could hold. I couldn't help myself. The man was downright fine. "My, my . . . how long has it been since you've been kissed?" I could feel my face flush immediately. "No, no," he said, lifting my chin. "It's wonderful. Everything about you is wonderful." He held me tighter.

"It's been a long time." I felt as vulnerable as one could.

"Well, I'm glad you saved them for me and didn't give any more to that Grant fella," he whispered in my ear.

"You're about to ruin a perfectly good evening."

He pulled our hands from behind my waist and led me up the stairwell to the East Ruskin Street beach pavilion. "Then let's head back to the place with food so I can shut my mouth."

We walked toward the pavilion with its extensive latticework, which is found throughout Seaside.

"So what got Joshua North from Jacksonville, Florida, to Savannah, Georgia?" I asked as we climbed the endless set of stairs.

"A job. A man will go anywhere for a job."

"The one you have now?"

"Yeah. I applied right out of college. I knew to become a writer for a larger paper, I would have to start with a smaller one."

"Do you have aspirations for the *New York Times* or the *Washington Post* or something?"

"Did."

"Did?"

"Yeah. I wanted to be an investigative journalist. But then I came to Savannah and grew fond of the pace. The city. The girl."

"So you determined you were fond of me and just decided to stay? I find that one hard to believe."

"Actually, the day you walked into that office, I was headed to turn in my resignation."

"Nuh-uh!"

"Uh-huh!" he mimicked. "I was tired of covering the shenanigans of your mother and Amber. I wanted something more. And then something more walked in wearing those gray slacks and that pink sweater . . ."

"There is no way you remember what I was wearing."

". . . accompanied by those gray slip-on shoes with matching Kate Spade satchel. And when I saw you, I remembered that I had almost run over you . . ."

"Almost?"

"Okay, slapped you flat on your back that morning in front of your house, when you were about to take Duke for a walk. And the same feeling came over me again."

"What feeling?"

"That goose bump feeling," he said, shaking.

"I did not give Joshua North goose bumps," I said, laughing.

"You did. And then when I saw you in the office that day, I knew."

"Knew what?"

"That I wouldn't leave that paper until I knew that I had done everything in my power to make you love me."

I stared at him there. "You say that so easily."

"What? Love?"

"Yeah. We don't even know each other. I don't even know your mother's name, so how can I love you?"

"Her name is Vivian."

"Vivian?"

"Yes, mighty close to Victoria, isn't it?"

"Worlds apart, I'm certain. For your sake, worlds apart."

CHAPTER NINETEEN

So when do you get to meet the family?" Johnny asked as he poured another Dr Pepper. I believe it was his fifth.

"I'm not sure she can handle the family," Joshua said, pushing his empty plate out from in front of him.

"I told you. If I can handle mine, I can handle yours."

Johnny sat his cup down deliberately. "You mean she doesn't know anything about your family?"

"I know his mother's name is Vivian."

"Okay, and do you know his father?"

Joshua tilted his head to the side and shot me a look. Not a look of fear or of discomfort. Just a look. A look that seemed to let me know I'd find it all out eventually. Why not tonight? Johnny was perfectly content to oblige.

"His mother is quiet," Johnny started.

"Uh-huh. And his father?" I asked.

"Well, his dad is . . . can I just be honest, Josh?" He turned and looked at his friend.

Joshua nodded.

"Well, his dad is a rather, shall we say—"

"Be gentle," Joshua said.

"Well, he had trouble being faithful."

I tried to hide my expression. It didn't work.

"Joshua, I'm sorry."

"Nothing to be sorry about," Joshua said tipping up his own Dr Pepper. "My life is what it is."

"But his mother is great," said Celeste, who was still sitting at the end of the table. "A little wounded but a sweet lady."

"She never outgrew being the victim," Joshua added. "She's not strong like your mother. She would take him back tomorrow and let him cheat on her for the rest of her life." I heard a hint of the remaining frustration.

"I wouldn't say my mother is strong. Stubborn maybe. Strong, well, that's my dad's department."

"Well, my father married affair number umpteenth. She's my age, dumb as a rock, and living off the money of her last husband. Just the kind of woman your mother would love."

"She'd have my grandmother flopping in her grave."

"Your mother's mother?"

"Yeah, she was my mother to the millionth degree. All the grace and class and all the drama and, well, drama. Where are your parents now?"

"Well, my dad is living somewhere in Las Vegas. He sends a birthday card to me, and to both my sisters on my baby sister's birthday. That way it only costs one stamp instead of three. He calls sometime around Christmas if he remembers. But he never remembers."

"Well, it doesn't matter, Josh. You and your sisters came out wonderfully," Johnny reassured him.

"You have sisters?"

"I have two. Hannah, who is three years younger than me. She just graduated college and moved back to Florida to work in my mother's jewelry store, which is a wonderful influence for my mother. My baby sister, Lauren, is still at the University of Florida and just turned nineteen. I love that girl," he said, appreciating anyone who appreciated his Gators. "She talks like a lawn mower, but she's always making sure everyone's okay."

I turned my body toward his and took in his face for a moment. There was a tiny scar underneath his left eye. I placed my finger on it and traced it delicately. "And where did this come from?"

"I gave that to him," Johnny said. "It was a brutal fight over a woman named Savannah." He grinned from ear to ear.

Joshua laughed, and the small scar curved upward toward his ebony eye. "It came from a ruthless linebacker who hated me for four years of high-school football. That came on year number four. He wanted to leave me with a little something."

"Coach Robbins and his wife really are what saved Joshua and his sisters," Celeste added.

"Is that your football coach?"

"Yeah. My dad showed up my first day of practice my freshman year to let me know he was leaving. 'For good,' he said. He had left 'for good' about ten other times. But coach overheard our conversation, invited me to his house for dinner, and pretty much kept me around ever since. He coached every game I was in and came to every one I played in college. His wife became like a second mother to my sisters and has tried to encourage my mother endlessly through the years. And they both still call every Sunday afternoon to make sure I'm in church and not out drinking or smoking."

"That's amazing that you would have someone like that in your life who wasn't your actual parent."

"His example really was what caused me to realize I wanted more for my life too."

"In what way?"

"In every way. In my thoughts. In my lifestyle. In my passions. In my determination. And I wouldn't trade the things that I've learned through the hard roads, because every road has led me right here." He raised his eyes to meet my own.

Johnny made gagging noises. "Okay, gush, gush. You just need to introduce her to the family and get on with it."

"I was planning to do that at our wedding." The words flew out of his mouth like second nature.

The Coke I had just swallowed lodged itself in the far recesses of my brain and set my eyes on fire. Wedding? Was he crazy? Right here in front of his friends?

"I will be the best man," Johnny announced.

Celeste caught the look in my eye. "Johnny, hush."

"What?" Johnny stood up and yelled, "We're having a wedding, everybody!"

I wondered how I could pull my blouse up over my head to cover my face without exposing myself any further. I reached for Joshua's hand. I squeezed it. Hard. "Could you excuse us just one moment?" I tugged him back in the direction of the beach.

"What? You don't want to marry me?" he said as I dragged him behind me down the stairs.

"First, you tell all of them I'm going to be there tonight without me even knowing. And I let you get by with that. But now you go and plant a seed in their head that we're getting married, and I've only even kissed you once."

"Twice."

"Oh, whatever! This is insane! You just make me crazy! You've always got to one-up me. Show me you're the man! Well, I'm not a prize. I'm a person. And I just think you're way too presumptuous for your own good. So I'll leave you now to undo all that just got"—I flailed my arms in a vain attempt to undo—"done up there."

"Why can't you see what everyone else can see?"

"What? I see two strangers. Okay, two work associates. I'll even give you that much. But love? How in the world could you love someone you don't even know?"

"The same way you love me."

I know my mouth flew open on that one. "Love you? Love

is special, Joshua. I don't throw those words around. If I ever tell you I love you, it will be real. Right."

"What I'm saying to you is real." He stepped in close to try and calm me down. "This is completely real to me. I don't throw these words around. I've only told one girl in my life I loved her, and I did."

"Who? Celeste?" I tried to hide my disgust.

"Yes, and you shouldn't say her name that way."

"This is just too fast. Too much, too soon."

He pulled me closer. "And one day you can tell me the same. But not until you're completely ready. Besides, I already know." He winked one set of his extravagantly, disgustingly long eyelashes.

I sighed heavily, removed myself from his arms, and turned to walk up the beach to another pavilion and home.

"I'll see you tomorrow, then," he said with that lilt in his voice.

I turned and glared. All I could see were the whites of his teeth. His irritatingly perfect teeth.

"Potty, precious. Go potty. Come on, now, go potty," Mother cooed at the white ball of fur dangling from her hot pink leash, sniffing every shrub in the front yard. Mother was outside in her high-heeled bedroom shoes and Christian Dior pale pink nightgown and matching robe. She held a bottle of baby powder in her free hand.

How did I deserve such a perfect evening? Lucky, I guess.

"Now, come on, Magnolia! It is time to go potty."

"Do you think you can get her to potty on command?"

"Ooh! Savannah Phillips! You about made me go potty! Don't ever sneak up on me like that again. What in the world are you doing out so late? Where have you been?"

With that the little thing squatted and saved the day. "Ooh, look, Mother. There she goes."

Mother flipped around just in time to catch sight of Maggy going potty. Mother started jumping up and down, clapping her hands like a child. Maggy got so excited over the fact that Mother was so excited that she came running and ran smack-dab into a tree. Thing let out a yelp, and Mother went over to attend to her boo-boo.

"There, there, precious. Let's get you powdered now and off to bed."

All of which allowed me to crawl into bed safely, where I longed to get at least to page 2 on my book. Give my mind an escape from the events of the day. Unfortunately, lying by my pillow was a note in pink stationery embossed with the words *Miss Savannah United States of America*. The handwritten lines on the inside read, "I hope your evening was perfect. You deserve it so much. Thank you for sharing your vacation with me. Love, Amber." I slammed my head into the pillow. My head was still there come morning.

CHAPTER TWENTY

The smell of baby powder had infiltrated his world of sweat and drool. So Duke was even more eager than usual for our tilling time this morning. The ocean offered us both what we needed. Me an opportunity to dissect my thoughts. He an opportunity to dissect the crab that he had conquered after I pulled it from his ear. His pent-up rage was released on the crustacean. I pitied the helpless hermit, but the poor dog had suffered undue trauma, and even the best of us could break under such burden.

When I grew tired of watching Duke paw at his new conquest, I stared into the ocean. The heat of the sun had already permeated my clothes and my body, but the breeze off the water felt as if the world was offering me its finest gift. Tilling time had been loaded with questions. Questions of love and its fear. Questions of unsteady hearts and undue pain. And heaven had whispered a message of stillness. A stillness to allow love to prove itself, and an assurance that I didn't have to figure out life before life actually revealed itself. So there I sat. Still.

Duke eventually looked up from his conquest and turned in the direction of the staircase that led back to the street. I turned as well and saw Amber Topaz, not sauntering, but more like lumbering down the lumber. Duke whined and ran toward me.

"Maggy not the only one who has you troubled, huh, boy?" I patted his head and attached his leash to his soft, brown leather collar. A Jake purchase.

The cries of the plodding princess were a familiar tune. Duke and I made our way to her and awaited her arrival at the bottom step. The queen looked haggard. It was my hope that she hadn't asked the mirror today who was the fairest of them all. It might have offered her few condolences. But the white shorts that she had on revealed the prettiest legs this side of . . . well, this side of the stairwell. Her white small-heeled sandals and white cotton sweater had her looking like a beach bum's dream.

"Have you seen the paper?" she asked as she made her way to the bottom step.

"No, I haven't had a chance to look at it this morning."

"Well, don't bother." She started blubbering and marching toward the water. "Because on the front cover of the 'Life and Living' section is the reigning Miss Georgia United States of America and Miss Florida United State's picture, declaring them joint spokeswomen for . . . for . . . for TAN PERFECT! I WEAR TAN PERFECT!" she screamed to the heavens. I almost feared she would keep walking straight through the ocean until she reached China (okay, Mexico, but China sounds much better). Of course, she'd come to a watery grave before she received another stamp on her passport.

I ran after her, stopping her just before she reached the packed sand, where the shadow of the last wave still remained. "What in the world are you going to do? Drown yourself?"

She looked back at me incredulously. "You've got to be kidding me. I have far too much life to live to kill myself. I was just going to . . . going to . . . GOING TO SWIM TO THE DEEP END OF THE OCEAN!" She started wailing again. Maybe the woman really did read.

"Amber, get ahold of yourself." I turned her face to me. Actually, she looked right over my head, but I cocked her face toward me, so she could at least see my eyes. "There is nothing in life worth taking yours. Especially not Tan Perfect. My stars, woman, have you smelled that stuff?"

She looked at me as if she did not understand the question.

"Well, I have." But I refused to elaborate on my own run-in with the tanning lotion, an episode in which I believed the house was on fire. "The stuff smells like smoke! It's not even worth shedding a tear over."

"Savannah, this is *my* dream. Do you understand that? Do you have any idea how hard I worked and deprived myself of fun and french fries and watched the news until I could have taken Dan Jennings' place myself?"

"I think it's Dan Rather, but that doesn't matter right now. Plus, he's retired and replaced now anyway."

"Oh, who cares? Dan Rather. Dan Plather. Ugh!" she screamed into the wild blue yonder. "I'm so sick of all of this. I'm sick of being second. I'm sick of being an intruder on other people's vacations. I'm sick of being alone." And with that she plopped herself into the sand, covered her face, and wept like a baby.

I hovered over her there as she sat in the sand. I didn't rush the moment. Stillness, remember? Plus, it was so rare that I actually had the ability to hover over her at all. "You are not alone," I finally said, kneeling down and wrapping my arms around her. "You have not been alone for a long time. Certainly not since you met my mother. She's been crazy about you since the first day she met you."

"But she's the only one. My mother only likes me as long as I wear a tiara, and I wouldn't know what my dad looked like if he came to the door selling the Ginko Knife."

Those words exposed her soul. A soul whose existence I had never even acknowledged. I felt a huge force lodge itself in my throat. "But look what you have now. A woman who thinks you're great no matter whether you're Miss Turnip Green or just Amber Topaz. A man in my father, who would be anything you needed him to be, and then there's me and Paige who lo . . . lo . . ."—I tried one more time—"who love being your friends."

She looked up at me with a face that had no mascara streaks whatsoever. She really had amazing gifts. But her face was so lifeless and sad. It broke my heart right there at the edge of the ocean, even though her desperation did revolve around a tiara. But as Vicky had taught me months ago and continued to remind me, a dream is a dream, no matter how it presents itself.

"It's okay, sweet girl. You will never be alone again." And there on the beach, I held Amber Topaz Childers in my arms. I could only smile politely at those who passed with their wide-eyed stares and strange glances. Duke wouldn't even act like he knew us. He had extended his leash as far away from us as he could. That was how he caught the eye of the new arrival.

"Hey, Duke, what are you—"

I turned as soon as I heard Joshua's voice. Amber looked up from her embedded position in my shoulder. And faster than a moth can turn into a butterfly, that sister had arisen from her grave of grief transformed. Those eyes scanned Joshua North more thoroughly than an X-ray machine at the airport scans my flip-flops.

"Well, Joshua North!" she exclaimed, bounding in his direction. I caught his eye from behind her and shook my head violently, making it clear she had no idea of our previous evening, or afternoon, or past nine months of, well, of absolutely nothing. "What in the world are you doing here in Seaside?" She ran her fingers through her hair and wiped the sand off her beautiful behind.

"Oh, I'm just here with some friends."

"Savannah, can you believe Joshua is here?" She turned to me with eyes so wide I could have driven a truck into them. I'd have liked to throw myself under the wheels. "It's fate," she mouthed for my eyes only. "Well, Joshua . . ." She turned back to him and put her arm through his. "I believe it was meant to be that you and I are here at the same time. You have got to come spend the afternoon with us. We're going to lay out here by the ocean and have a wonderful afternoon. Don't you think that's a brilliant idea, Savannah?" She turned back in my direction and stretched her face out in a rather awkward contortion.

"Well, I think we need to make sure Joshua doesn't have other plans."

He looked at me with his own large eyes. "Actually, Amber, I appreciate the offer, but I have some friends here, and we have some things to do to prepare for my best friend's wedding on Saturday. So we've got a really busy week. But maybe we'll run into each other again."

"Well, you won't be able to avoid me all week, Joshua," she said, running her fingers up and down his T-shirt like she was doing hand motions to "The Itsy-Bitsy Spider." I determined then and there that she was either schizophrenic or I was. I was beginning to place votes on the latter. "Because I do believe this is preemptive of something very special." And with that she ran her long hand across my man's strong and deeply tanned forearm and sauntered back up the stairs. I know I did not just call him *my man*. Then she turned around and gave me a wink, and we heard a screech of sheer joy as her clamoring heels reached the top of the stairs. My, how the weight of the world could evaporate so quickly. No, not evaporate, just relocate. Right to my shoulders.

"What did she mean by *preemptive*?"

"She actually meant *predictive*."

"Well, thank the Lord. I thought she had a plan of attack or something."

"Well, maybe you heard her right the first time. Anyway, you get used to it. Thank you for not saying anything." I tried to relax every muscle that had called itself to attention in my body.

"Well, she can plan her plots, but the only one I'm spending time with this week is you. So you'll join me for lunch?" He wrapped his arms around me. "Eew, you smell like fish."

I pulled away and glanced up just to make sure she hadn't returned with her preemptive assault. "I've been running and sweating."

"Well, fortunately for you, I love fish." He wrapped his arms around me again. "So, lunch?"

"I'll have to play it by ear. I'm just not sure it's a good idea."

"What do you mean *by ear*? By what you hear everyone else is doing in your house?"

"By what I determine I want to do." I placed my hand on my hip. I felt like I was two, so I casually dropped it back to my side.

"You will have to tell them all eventually, Savannah." He ran his hands through his curls.

"You know, there are a lot of things I will have to do eventually. I will have to go to the gynecologist this year eventually too, but who wants to rush such things? Plus, do you remember that to tell anyone about you would result in a face-to-face encounter with my mother?"

His eyes didn't hesitate. "It may take years. It may even take five grandchildren." I officially gasped. "But I will win her over one day. Even if I don't, I'll still be completely in love with you."

"Excuse me, did you just say grandchildren?"

"What? You only want one baby?"

"Is this *The Truman Show*?" I scanned the beach for cameras. "This is a joke, right? Get the girl for the vacation. Go back home, tell all your friends. Say things that are completely insane while you're here, but play it up so big, there's no way she'd think you weren't telling the truth."

"You watch too much television."

"Well, if you're serious, I'm even more certain that you are the most pompous, self-appointed Don Juan of the panhandle, and I'm not sure that is anything I want to be a part of."

His right hand reached for me, and the flicker in his eye let me know what he was going to do. "No, you don't, mister. I am not a . . . a . . . a . . . kissing machine! Put your compliment in, get your kiss out! No, you are just going to have to take a holiday from such pleasures!"

He kissed me on the cheek. "I'd love to see you for lunch. We'll be surfing this morning. I'll keep my eyes out for you."

"Ha! I've got an appointment with my mother and Amber."

"Well, they're welcome to come too."

"Well, they're welcome to come too," I mimicked.

He gave Duke a rub on the head. "Take care of my girl, boy." Duke pawed Joshua's leg. "Yes, you can come too." Duke settled completely down. The dog knew exactly what Joshua was saying. Well, that and a lucky sand dollar wouldn't get him anything out of my kissing machine! My word, I had just officially called myself a kissing machine. I wouldn't be avoiding him for his arrogant ways today. No, I'd be avoiding him for my ridiculous attempt at a metaphor.

CHAPTER TWENTY-ONE

I knocked on the white-framed glass door attached to the pink cottage off of Rosewalk. A diaper-clad toddler passed in front of the door, trying desperately to balance himself and waddle across the four-inch planked heart-of-pine floor. Kate's blond hair swung in her face as she scooped him up and planted kisses along his chubby, creased neck and headed to the door. Her eyes reflected recognition, but her face registered worn out.

"Savannah Phillips. I didn't even realize it was that time of year. Come in, come in."

I motioned to my companion. "We'll wait out here."

"Let me put this rascal in his playroom, and we can sit and talk for a minute." She scurried away without time for me to respond.

I scanned the front porch and the familiar rockers where Kate and I had spent many an evening talking about life. She had always been so wise and kind. We would stay up late and play cards and drink Coke, and Adam would ask about Grant if Grant wasn't with me. And yet now something was missing here today. Some element of life. I wasn't sure how the absence of one person could make it so different, but even the pink on the wood siding seemed as if it were a different color.

Kate returned, pulling her loose strands of sun-kissed hair back into her ponytail holder. "Here, I brought you both some water," she said, handing me a bottle and setting a Tupperware bowlful down for Duke.

We both thanked her.

"My mom's in the kitchen, cleaning up from breakfast, so she'll keep her eyes on the boys," she said, throwing her body down into a white rocking chair and sighing heavily. "Sit, Savannah. Sit."

I sat down, and Duke made music in his water bowl. "I can't believe how they've grown."

"I know. It's amazing. It's like you see their legs extend before your eyes. And they're into everything." She laid her head back.

"You look exhausted."

She lifted her head slowly and laughed. "I feel worse than I look."

"I saw Adam." There was no need to skirt the issue.

She turned her head toward me. "When?"

"Yesterday."

"So what did he say?"

"Enough for me to know that you two aren't together." I rocked gently.

She turned her head back to the center of her rocker and stared across the street.

"Do you want to tell me what happened? You don't have to, but if you want to, you can."

She shrugged. "I'm not even sure what happened. One late evening became two late evenings. Then two late evenings became weekend business trips. Then weekend business trips grew to a final showdown where he simply stated he didn't love me anymore. Granted, the babies took up a lot of my time, but we had waited so long. He had eight years of my undivided attention.

And now that he wasn't the center of my universe anymore, I guess he found someone who would allow him to be the center of hers."

I looked over at her weak blue eyes. "Do you think there is someone else?"

"Think?" she said, whipping her head around. "I'm certain. That's why he's gone. I can do this without him. My mother did it without my father, and we can do it without him."

"Kate, I don't know what to say. Honestly, I don't know what to say." I'm certain there were people who would have loved to witness that statement. "How are the boys?"

"They're too young to really understand." Then her eyes ignited with rage. She was always so soft-spoken and loving. But what was coming back at me was a hostility I'd never encountered from her. "I think they need a man of honor and integrity and all those things Adam isn't. I mean, he even came around a month ago apologizing and crying and acting like all of that would get him back into my house, into my bed, into the lives of my boys. But it will never happen. He's lucky he gets to see them at all. And when I'm done with him in court, I'm going to do my best to make sure he doesn't get to see them ever again." She turned her head back toward the gravel pathway.

I was glad. He didn't deserve to see them. "You deserve better than that anyway."

"Yeah! I agree. He is completely delusional. I'm taking everything. And when this is over, he'll wish he had never given me his name."

I looked down at Duke and back at Kate's hardened face. I reached over and touched her arm to try to offer some tenderness. "I'm really sorry, Kate."

She kept staring at the gravel path.

"Thanks for the water."

"You're welcome. It was good to see you, Savannah. Come back by when you get a chance."

I would come back. And Lord help Adam the next time I laid eyes on him. I would say he didn't want to talk this afternoon, that little lyin', cheatin', two-timin' . . . I sang that song as I walked away until the thoughts of my article interrupted my solo.

The truth was, Kate was in her present state because Adam wasn't truthful. The epiphany hit me as I swatted at the bee that had charged me from the honeysuckle I just passed. Thomas was going to be in a pickle for the same reason: he didn't know how to be truthful. Truth be told . . . Oh, that was funny. But honestly, truth be told, the problem with so much is our lack of truth.

That's what people need to hear, I decided. They need to hear about where people are, what people are really going through. And this is it. Real life. Real pain. Real betrayal. They need to know what lies produce. What with all the muck and mire in the world, someone needs to help liberate it from such, well, muck and mire. Plus, people are probably tired of reliving all of the horror of those hurricanes. This is better: the inability to tell the truth is at the core of most of life's issues.

And that's the gospel truth.

"That's a pitiful concept. It's overprocessed and boring. I thought you were there to come up with something that would make people cry, rip out their heart, stomp on it, and then make it all better after you were through."

I moved the phone from my ear and stared at it, wondering for a moment if Mr. Hicks was going to squeeze all two hundred and something pounds of himself through the little holes in the receiver. "Do you have an inside voice?"

"You better send me something in about hurricane victims. Call it 'Weathering a Storm.' Then maybe you'll think it has something to do with that ridiculous concept you just pitched. We've all been betrayed, Savannah. At some point you get over it. We haven't all been through Katrina."

"They both have equally devastating effects," I countered.

"But they don't both write your check."

The man was brutal. "I see your point. Any other words of wisdom you need to offer me today?" I tried to hide my sarcasm.

"Your story is due tomorrow at 2:00 p.m., that's 1:00 p.m. your time. I would strongly urge you not to be late."

The dial tone blared in my ear. And blared. And blared. And blared.

"Well, he's a man with no character." I heard Mother's voice as I made my way to the gravel walkway in front of the house. But her words caused me to retreat before I was detected.

"You shouldn't question a man's character simply because he called you Vicky by mistake in the paper." My father turned the newspaper page as he spoke.

"Amber deserves better than him," Mother said, her crispy red feet and calves resting atop an ottoman as she applied aloe to them. It was a rather pitiful picture. Her little princess sat on the ottoman at her feet.

He closed his paper and turned his attention back to her. "Victoria, it is not your business to determine what Amber deserves. What if Savannah was the one bringing him home?" My heart officially stopped beating.

She jerked her head in his direction, causing her feet to bounce on the ottoman and practically send the mongrel at her feet into the wild blue. "Jake Phillips, bite your tongue. My baby wouldn't see anything in that man. And the only reason Amber does is because she's so wounded right now she doesn't have a clear perspective on anything."

"Well, I like him." He opened his newspaper back up. "Shared quite a few cups of coffee with him over the last couple months, and he's one of the finest young men I've met in a while.

And whether Amber likes him or Savannah fell in love with him tomorrow"—those words about made me swallow my tongue, and Vicky let out a rather gruesome noise herself—"he deserves us to be nice to him."

With that she picked up her pooch and huffed into the house. Duke watched them out of the corner of his eye, then made a beeline for the ottoman and plopped himself down. I was certain he giggled.

I sat down in Mom's chair and kissed Duke on the head. "Lover's spat?"

He looked above his papers and fixed his eyes across the street. He dropped one side and picked up his coffee cup, then took a long gulp. He returned it to the table. "No, Victoria moment." That pretty much said it all. "Now, how's my girl and boy?" he asked, rubbing Duke's head.

Duke was thankful Vicky had retreated with her ball of fluff. "I guess you realize Amber saw Joshua."

"Yep."

"She thinks he is the answer to her prayers."

"I'd say by the way she came in singing 'Great Is Thy Faithfulness,' that is a pretty fair assessment."

"She'll be destroyed when she knows the truth," I said, rubbing my temples. What a long day.

He turned those beautiful green eyes on me, the eyes that could make me completely miserable or completely at home dependent upon how they peered into me. This was a mixture of both. "The truth? What exactly is the truth?" Apparently so long a day that sister had forgotten to watch her tongue.

"Well, you know . . . that he just isn't into her."

"Oh yeah, that," he said with a hint of sarcasm.

"What?"

"What?" he echoed. "Something else you need to say?"

"You know, don't you?" He always knew.

"Know what? That Joshua North is crazy about you? Pretty

much. He doesn't try to hide it." Dad grinned now. "What about you?"

I laid my head in the palm of my hands and talked to the ground. "I don't know. He's just so pushy and presumptuous." I straightened. "And so incredibly sweet and kind."

"Is that who you saw last night?" he asked, folding the edges of his newspaper.

"Yeah. It wasn't my complete intention though. But Lucy and Manuel already had dinner plans." I looked out at the street. "Amber will be destroyed if she finds out."

"She'll be far more destroyed if she finds out any other way than from you." He stood and dropped his paper into the chair. "She's a big girl, Savannah. Not as fragile as you think."

"I just stopped the woman from becoming breakfast for a shark."

He laughed. "She wouldn't have gotten her feet wet."

I recalled that she really hadn't put up much resistance when we reached the edge of the surf. "You don't think?"

"Savannah, those were a two-hundred-dollar pair of heels she was wearing. Shoes your mother just bought her."

Mother hadn't bought anything for me in a while.

"She was cleaning them with a cloth diaper when she came back. Trust me, she wouldn't have been learning Spanish by sunset, I assure you."

"Are you as confident that Mother will learn to like Joshua?"

"I'm confident that Victoria will one day like him as much as you do." He smiled. The Jake smile. The smile that had calmed a thousand fears over the past twenty-four years and found its way to the root of them once again. I heard the whisper of stillness again. My heartbeat steadied, and for a moment I was certain, no matter how it all transpired, that this force standing next to me would hold my secrets until I was brave enough to reveal them.

CHAPTER TWENTY-TWO

There was laughter and the banging of pots and pans. "Teach me the chocolate gravy," I heard Amber say.

I peeked my head into the kitchen and couldn't believe my eyes. There they were. My mother and Amber, cooking. And chocolate gravy, no less. Was nothing sacred? That was our family recipe. And no matter how much Amber thought she was a part of our family, we didn't produce six-foot women. We produced midgets.

"It's really easy," my mother said, getting the milk from the refrigerator. "I tried to teach Savannah once, but she just didn't have the patience."

Patience? I have plenty of patience. My cell phone vibrated my backside. "Hello," I whispered, irritated. It was Thomas with a proposal for a round of golf. He had no other options. "That is the most boring sport, and it goes entirely too slow."

I hung up and mumbled to the air all the ways I, Savannah Phillips, am patient.

I made my way back to the porch and its revelations. Today's revelation: vacation breeds fondness. Okay, just plain passion. The two teenagers were trying to hide behind the outdoor shower in the house across Seaside Avenue. But they weren't lost on me. I had come back outside alone, with a Coke and a smile and my book. And there they were, tiptoeing around the house in search of a secret corner, trying not to let their laughter reveal their conspiracy. They finally found a safe retreat behind the shower, but their giggles floated all the way across the street. And after what I'm certain was a rainstorm of passionate kisses, he withdrew to the sidewalk and she rested her head on the edge of the shower, plastered with the biggest smile this side of Olan Mills.

I wondered if that was how I had looked when Joshua had kissed me. And then I wondered if Grant had ever made me look that way. Maybe the day I kissed him for the first time. But there was such a familiarity between us that the kiss lacked passion, even though it held the uncertainty and innocent exploration that first kisses do. Sure, we'd shared moments of passion, mostly when we would see each other again after long absences, but never what I felt yesterday: worlds spinning, heart pounding, upper lip sweating.

I returned my attention to my companions. Two of my favorite companions. The Coke had a kick all the way down. And so I began. *"Happy families are all alike; every unhappy family is unhappy in its own way."*

"Those two at it again?" Mother asked.

Well, this was just getting better and better.

She exited the house with her pooch princess, who wore a lovely new pink leopard collar and matching bandana. Mother was as pristinely attired as well in pale pink linen, complete makeup, and heels, even though most people were still wearing pajamas and leaning back in rockers at this time of day. For most, vacation applied to morning, afternoon, and evening. For Vicky, vacation just applied to Victoria time.

I didn't even mention it. That would be asking for an explanation I didn't need. "Yeah, he just headed back up the street. You've seen them before?"

"We see them every day, don't we, Magnolia?" She cooed as she sat down next to me and spread across her lap a leopard-print blanket with Magnolia's name embroidered at the corner. Maggy jumped up and made herself comfortable.

Life wasn't right. The woman had gone to talking to dogs. If Maggy talked back, I was taking the bus home.

"We watch them laugh and giggle." She patted Maggy's front paws together, as if pat-a-cake was their morning ritual. "They sneak around that house, looking for a hiding place all the time, and then they act like they haven't seen each other for years each time he knocks on her window."

I stared back across the street, catching the eye of the young girl, who turned and ran. "I thought that's what falling in love was like."

"What? All laughter and giggles?"

"No, all aches when they're not with you and aches when you watch them go."

"Savannah Phillips . . ." She looked at me. I didn't turn her way, because I knew she thought she was reading something in me. But she would be sadly mistaken. "I know something has gotten into you. Have you met someone? Oh my word, you have!" She shifted in her chair, causing Maggy to look as if she was getting motion sickness. "I mean, yesterday you came back humming one of those Barbra Streisand tunes, which you know I abhor." She had lost all fondness for Ms. Streisand the day she sang "Evergreen" for the Clintons. Mother briefly wept over the loss of one of her favorite entertainers. But grief was soon replaced by the usual disdain for anyone who insulted her dear Bushie. Thank the Lord and celebrate the land of Dixie that Barbra wasn't at the White House dinner. Helen Thomas's rebuke would have been poppycock compared to what Mother would have rained on Ms. Streisand.

"Was that why you weren't with us at dinner last night?"

I stood up from my chair and grabbed my Coke and book. I patted the head of her little creature, who seemed about to lose her breakfast. "Mother, love hasn't visited my radar for years. But if you want to know, yes, I was with a gentleman last night. But there is absolutely no reason for you to meet him, because I'm not sure that there's much to it." And with that, I departed for more comfortable surroundings.

"We'll keep our eye on her," I heard her assure Pink Toes. "A very close eye. I actually wasn't sure if she would ever find anyone like our sweet Thomas has. My boy's found a beautiful girl, did you know that, Maggy?" Maggy responded with a hacking noise, amazingly loud for such a petite little creature. Thank the Lord above for distractions. And for Thomas. He'd taken a load off of me this time.

The love bugs landed on the front of my shirt. I swatted them. "Really, I'm not in the mood."

"Where are you headed?" I asked the rather snazzy-looking sister in the new red bikini.

Paige turned as if she were a cat caught with Tweety in its mouth. "What?"

"You heard me," I said, blocking the stairway by stretching my arms across the banisters. "I said, where are you going?"

"Savannah, really. We are at the beach. And when one is at the beach, one must lie on the beach."

"You're going to meet that little cabana boy we met yesterday, aren't you?"

A sly smile spread across her face. "Love is in the air, Savannah," she said, breathing in dramatically. She exhaled even more dramatically. "Ahh. Can't you smell it, sunshine? Of course you can smell it, can't you?" She tried to move my arm out of the way. "Now you will move, or I will reveal your secret to your mother."

I dropped my arm. "She knows my secret," I snipped.

"Ha!" she snorted. "She knows half your secret. I will give her no-holds-barred, Katy-bar-the-door, Santa-Claus-is-coming-to-town-and-all-that-stuff secret." Her nose was about to touch my own.

"You are shameless."

She gave me a peck on the cheek. "Yes, absolutely shameless. Come join me later."

"No, I'll take care of Amber for you. You were too gracious to me yesterday."

"Well, she wasn't all . . . yes, you're right! I did, didn't I? Ooh, well, have fun, because your dad went to meet Thomas at the golf course in San Destin. So it will just be the three of you today! Plus, I have an appointment at the art gallery today. Wouldn't that be wonderful? To have my work in two locations?" She laughed, skipping all the way down the stairs.

A shudder went through me at the thought that I might actually have to spend the entire day with Mother and Amber. "Just the three of us?"

I heard only sinister laughter that bobbed in through the swinging screen door as it bounced back into place.

Manuel was stretched out on a chaise that rested on the front porch. I watched as Lucy bent down to kiss him. All he did was smile.

"You two need to stop that," I said as I opened the gate.

Manuel placed his hands behind his head and returned the same smile to me. "She's a captivating woman. I can't help it."

She winked. "Savannah, how was your evening? Eventful, I hope."

I would give them nothing. "Oh, not much to tell. Just another evening trying to get a story."

They shared a look. Honestly, they were about as bad as the love bugs.

Lucy headed to the screen door. "Can I get you some breakfast? We had a big one today. Frosted Flakes and bananas."

"That would be wonderful."

"Have a seat, Savannah." Manuel motioned to the small dining table in the corner of the front porch across from his chaise. He turned on his side. "So, anymore sightings of that Joshua guy?"

"Oh, a few here, a few there."

"Don't want to talk about it?"

I eyed him with a raised eyebrow. "I'd much more enjoy talking about you."

Lucy returned with my cereal, and for the next hour they shared their story. Truth be told, I did cry some. So did they. The question was, would Mr. Hicks send me to New Orleans myself by the time this was over? I was certain he would let me know. But in the entire hour I was there, the one thing that was evident was that Lucy and Manuel would have made it through even worse than Katrina simply because they had each other. Maybe Kate and Adam needed to spend an hour with Lucy and Manuel, learn how to love without destroying each other in the process.

There we lay. The three stooges. Stooge number one was lying with her calves hidden beneath an umbrella and the rest of her body in the sun. With any luck she'd get her skin tones to match.

Stooge number two sat propped up with her binoculars, looking up and down the beach for one person and one person alone: the man solely responsible for preventing her from falling into the abyss of all loser beauty queens.

And stooge number three, trying to read a book in lieu of figuring out a way to get out of another day at the beach with stooges one and two.

Placing the straps of my bikini top underneath my arms, I began. *"Happy families are all alike; every unhappy family is unhappy in its own way."*

"Let's play the name-that-person game!" Amber said, clapping her hands together. Maybe I should have let her get at least waist deep this morning.

"The what?" I asked, trying to refrain from slamming my book shut.

"Ooh, there goes, um . . . um Jackie. Yoo-hoo, Jackie!"

I leaned forward. The girl in the pink bathing suit never turned our way.

"Well, I guess that wasn't her name. But she sure looked like a Jackie."

The child really was a rhinestone short of a complete tiara.

Mother raised her head. "So, how do you play?"

Amber laid out the rules. "You just call people by what you think their name is. Like, see that hairy man coming up the beach. What does he look like to you?"

Mother tipped her sunglasses to the bottom of her nose. "A Ted, maybe?"

I squinted.

"Let's see if it's Ted. Yoo-hoo, Ted!" Amber called out.

The man turned and looked.

Amber got giddy. "You did it, Miss Victoria, you did it! His name's Ted."

I lay down with a sigh. "His name isn't Ted, it's Big Foot. The man has as much hair on his back as he does his stomach, and you yelled at him so loud he had no choice but to look."

"Ooh, Savannah's cranky this morning," Amber said, picking up a Kit-Kat bar from the cooler.

"You try it, Savannah," Mother said.

"No."

"Come on, try it."

"Yeah, Savannah. Don't be a beach-pooper; try it."

I looked at the two of them. If I did this, I would no longer have any excuse for my stupidity. No, it would be completely my fault. I looked at a little girl in a pink polka dot bikini who was filling up her beach bucket with sand. "Angelica," I said smugly. "She looks like an Angelica."

No sooner had I said that than little polka-dot bikini's mama called, "Angelica, come get you some more sunscreen."

Mother's and Amber's mouths went agape. I raised my right eyebrow and laid my head back down. They'd never want to play with me again. And they'd never know that I had just been in the ladies' room with the mother and little girl ten minutes ago.

"Ooh, Amber. Look, sweetie, it's noon. If we want to get to the stores by two to get you a new dress, we better hurry."

"What does Amber need a new dress for?" I asked, trying to wipe away the sweat that had just slipped underneath my sunglasses and was stinging my eyes.

"Oh, well, Amber thinks Joshua might invite her to dinner this week, and I told her she just needed a new dress to make herself feel really special for the occasion." Mother wrapped her red floral wrap around her petite waist. The sun rested on her dark brown hair, which was growing out and now fell nearly to her shoulders.

"You can come with us." Amber tossed her empty wrapper into her beach bag and reached for her bathing suit wrap. She swung her long legs to the side of the chair. Her french manicured toenails underscored her perfection.

"Amber, has Joshua agreed to go to dinner with you?"

"Well, no, silly. But I could see it all in his eyes this morning. He just didn't want to seem too anxious. You know how guys are."

"And you want to buy her a new dress?" I quizzed Mother.

She shook her blanket, and the wind drove her sand right into my face. I tried to spit it out.

"Ooh, I'm sorry, darling. And yes, I want to buy Amber a new dress. She deserves a pick-me-up after all she's been through. And you are welcome to come, though I know you hate shopping." Mother laid her towel atop her matching red tote.

"I don't hate shopping," I said rather defensively.

She cast a questioning expression my way. "Oh, you don't? Well, then I must have misunderstood all of that kicking and screaming you've done for the last twenty-four years."

I turned to my side and tried to look casual while keeping a firm grip on my bathing suit straps with my armpits. "Mother, Mother, Mother . . . a woman grows into the enjoyment of those things."

"Well, that's some of the best news I've heard! Why don't you join us then?" Amber danced.

"Well, I would, but I've really got to get to work on the rest of my story."

"Savannah, come on, we'll have fun," Mother said, reaching for her own bag.

"No, please, you two go. Have some bonding time. I'm going to lie here and read. I don't get a lot of time to do that at home. Please, go enjoy yourselves."

Amber laid her wrap back down beside her. "No way. We're not leaving you here by yourself. It just wouldn't be right."

Mother didn't seem real excited about Amber's insistence.

"Honestly, go. I love to read. Alone. Please, you'll hurt my feelings more if you stay." I had never said something more truthful in my life.

"You're sure," Mother said as she finished loading up her stuff. More a statement than a question.

My cell phone rang. I could have kissed it. I looked down at the caller ID. It was Mr. Hicks. I wouldn't rush to answer it. "Absolutely. Go. Please."

"Okay, but I feel horrible about this," Amber said, wrapping her skirt around her.

It rang again. I swatted at them. "Don't. Have fun. Buy me something if that will make you feel better." I was brazen.

Mother loved that idea. "Ooh, we'll get you something great."

Amber packed up her bag. "While we're out, Miss Victoria, can I pick up a subscription?"

Mother looked at her. "You can't pick up subscriptions, Amber."

"I can't call it in to a pharmacy or something?"

"She means *prescription*," I said, rolling onto my back and settling into a peaceful position.

"Oh, sure child." Mother looked at her pitifully and patted her on the shoulder. She pulled her toward the stairs. "We'll get you your subscription." Mother looked over her shoulder and shook her head at me as if she wasn't completely certain the girl was altogether together.

"Hello?"

All I got was a dial tone. I'd have to get back to him. Right back to him.

I stared at page 1 of my book. It had been a rather interesting first page. Okay, first line. I was alone now. This was my moment. I gazed at my bathing suit wrap lying there all taunting. I *was* hungry. I could pick the book back up a little later.

Granted, for the last ten years that has been the greatest longing of my heart: time alone, a good book. But a girl did need food.

I adjusted my straps, packed up my book, and slipped on my wrap. I crammed my beach towel into my tote bag and decided I'd just take a walk. Walks on the beach were what vacation was all about anyway. But first I'd see what I could find for lunch. Plus, I needed to celebrate the fact that I'd found a story.

CHAPTER TWENTY-THREE

I hate dead people. So, I'm not altogether sure why *The Poseidon Adventure* is one of my favorite movies, seeing as how so many people die in it, even Shelley Winters, but there it is. So it had never made any sense to me why someone would name a house by a boat that sank and killed people, until the day I realized that what I thought was the Poseidon was in fact the Proteus. I was glad I never mentioned that story to anyone.

Not far away, bikes rested against the stairs that led to the beach. I knew that was the direction that I should head, even though I had come up other stairs just a few moments ago in search of food. As I came to the Tupelo Beach Pavilion in one of the oldest sections of Seaside, I gazed down at the white sands of the Gulf Coast. Heads bobbed in the water, and I could hear the sound of their laughter. I watched quietly. They would go through waves and come up shaking their heads. An odd thing boys do. They would wipe the saltwater from their mouths and noses and then do it all over again. As I was about to head their way, I stopped to watch as Mr. North rose up out of the water.

"Oh my stars, I do believe I might need to cover my eyes."

The man coming up out of that water had a prettier chest than we'd seen in days. And his wet, black chest hair glistened beautifully in the warm sun.

It was the first time I had seen him without his shirt, and I was thankful for the chance to view without his knowledge of my scrutiny. That would have made for even a far more awkward moment than the one I was now experiencing. The man was as fine as the fizz of my Coca-Cola. That I could not deny.

I decided to descend the stairs as nonchalantly as possible. After all, this was a public beach.

Johnny gave me away. Who did that surprise. Joshua turned to see what he hadn't noticed. But the smile that swept across his face assured me he noticed now. He headed my direction, drying his curls with the edge of his towel.

"How did you get away?" he asked, wrapping his towel around the back of his neck. His swim partners raised their hands in a wave and then headed over to their beach chairs to leave us alone.

"What? I'm just out for a walk." I crossed my arms and rubbed them. A vain effort to comfort my uncomfortable self. "Everyone else had plans today. Shopping and golf, I think it was. I don't do either."

"What? You don't shop?" he asked incredulously, tugging at each end of his towel and leaning in with his shock.

"Hardly ever. Mother has left me scarred. Plus, she's more than willing to do it for me." I leaned in, making my own statement.

"Really? I can't believe I've met a woman who doesn't like to shop."

"See. You don't know everything about me." I returned my hands to the staircase rails. "But I do enjoy nice things," I said, just to make sure he knew. "But shopping with my mother for an afternoon is not my idea of vacation. So I thought I'd just go for a walk." I dropped my eyes for a moment. The first *don't* of telling a lie.

"So, since you're here, and I see you've got your suit on . . ." he said as his eyes made the observation. He didn't linger. Not like hairy Ted had on Amber anyway. He took his hand from the end of his towel and reached out for mine. "Why don't you hang out for a while and then go get some lunch with me?"

"Well, I can't stay all day. I do have work to do, you know." He led me toward two beach chairs. "That's why I'm here, in Seaside, remember?"

"Yeah. You're here to work. I remember," he said, smiling. "Got a towel?" he asked.

"Right here in my bag."

He patted one of the chairs. "Then quit thinking about work and sit down and enjoy being at the beach with me."

So I did. I wanted to adjust my straps though. I needed to adjust my straps. But I didn't want to sit in front of Joshua and start lowering bathing suit straps. It just wouldn't seem proper. So I did my best to forget about it. And for the next hour we watched Johnny get stung by a jellyfish and Mark threaten to pee on his leg, because an episode of *Survivor* showed that pee took away the sting. We encouraged Mark not to, and Mark walked Johnny to the clinic instead. Johnny screamed like a girl all the way.

We talked about life and friends and work. We shared our thoughts on our editor, Mr. Hicks, and his incessant craving for sweets, and our other thoughts on Mr. Hicks's secretary, Jessica, who adores Joshua and abhors me. And we learned even more about one another, about each other's lives and the fact that he hates butter beans and I love them. He loves macaroni and cheese out of a box, which I only get to eat when my mother's not cooking, because she won't cook anything out of a box. And I learned that his eyes light up when you mention his friends, and they get introspective and older when you mention his parents, and they get amazingly passionate when he's talking about me. And with each topic there is a different cock of the head and raising of the eyebrows. And everything about him is new yet feels old, as if I've known it all my life yet am experiencing every aspect of it for the first time.

"Interrupting something?" Paige asked. I hadn't even heard her sneak up on us.

"Not a thing," I said, patting the edge of my chair for her to sit.

"Hey, Paige. It's great to see you," Joshua said, sitting up to greet her.

I saw her eyes move down to his chest. I nonchalantly tugged at her arm. "Where is your friend?"

"Huh?" she said, not wanting to peel her eyes away.

I tugged again. "Where is your friend?" I emphasized the *your.*

"Oh, uh . . ." She finally turned her gaze back to me, offering a you're-one-lucky-woman kind of look. "Uh, he's got to work until two, and then we're going to grab some lunch together. Would ya'll want to join us? I think you'd like him," she singsonged.

"Well, I really have to go get my story ready to submit to Mr. Hicks."

"Story-shmory. You have to eat. Isn't that right, Joshua? She needs to eat."

"We'd love to join you," he said.

"You know you're craving some hot wings from Shades." She nudged me.

Few things were truer. "What time?" I asked

"Two fifteen. We'll meet you there."

"We'll look forward to it," Joshua said.

And off she went, her little red and white skirt swinging in the breeze. She turned back once and tugged on her bathing suit straps. I knew what she meant. I had successfully ruined my tan.

"Who's her friend?" Joshua asked.

"Oh, I'm not really sure. He works over there at the cabana."

He rolled over on his stomach so he could look up at me with his dark eyes. "Did she know him before you got here?"

"Know him?" I asked with a chuckle. "No, she met him yesterday."

"Yesterday?"

"Yep. Sister likes it; sister makes her move."

He rested his head on his hands. "This will be interesting."

"It always is. It always is."

Shades has the feeling of a Jimmy Buffet song. It smells of sand. You can come through the bar and grab yourself a margarita on the way to your table. The pastel colors of the benches on the front porch, which looks more like a boat dock, all resemble the shades of the Caribbean: periwinkle blue, Pepto-Bismol pink, and ocean green.

We made our way to our table across the aged wooden floors, which begged us to take our shoes off, and meandered through the artwork, some of which I was certain I could have painted myself. Joshua and I took a seat by the front window.

The view from our seats was a perfect landscape of the Town Center. We could see the little stores resembling beach shacks that sold jewelry or videos. What every couple needs. A little entertainment for her, a little entertainment for him. From here we'd be able to see our lunch companions arrive and watch the rest of the city go by until they did.

We ordered a Coke and a Dr Pepper and felt our heads bobbing to resurrected Beach Boys music even before we realized music was playing. And we found even more to talk about. And laugh about. And discover about each other. Then we saw Paige approaching. Alone. She was showered and shined and in another attempt at a heel. An apparently newly purchased wedge.

"Did you see that old red phone booth outside?" Paige asked as she sat down in the black wooden chair with its hunter green pleather cushion.

"Yeah, remind you of home?" I asked, referring to the one outside of the Sixpence Pub.

"Yeah. But just reminded. Didn't beckon."

"Where's your friend?" Joshua asked.

She laughed a nervous laugh. "Couldn't get away from work. They had someone call in sick."

"Well, this is a perfect day to be sick," Joshua offered. "Maybe we can meet him tomorrow."

"It's no big deal," she said in her way. But I knew it was always a big deal. It was one more man who couldn't keep even a small commitment. Just lunch, maybe, but that's usually where it started. Paige was a master at hiding her hurts. I was the only one she let into those places. Joshua would never know she cared. And he didn't. To the last bite of our buffalo wings, he never knew that she would struggle with the frustration of another broken date all day. Because even though she and I swore off boys years ago, I'm certain her fingers had been crossed.

CHAPTER TWENTY-FOUR

It's easy to see why you two are best friends." Joshua said as we walked along the sidewalk past the new Izod store and Modica's Market.

"She's the best friend I've ever had."

"It's easy to tell. You complement each other."

"How's that?" I noticed the tandem flopping of our flips.

"The way you hurt for her when she walked in alone. The way she tried to hide her disappointment from me." I felt my brow furrowing. "The way you tried to continually reaffirm her the entire lunch and the way she made it known, through a hundred gestures and all the words that she didn't say, that she would be okay, you didn't need to worry about her right now, but you should enjoy this week for yourself."

I came to a dead halt in front of L. Pizitz & Co. "There is no way you read all of that between us." It was more a statement of sheer amazement than an actual question.

"Every line, Savannah." He reached over to take my hand and gently raised it to his lips and kissed it softly. "Every line. And you are both very lucky to have each other. Because I don't believe

I've ever seen two women protect each other like you two did in the matter of a lunch."

"I can't believe you noticed all that."

"I notice a lot of things, Savannah."

My shock had trouble settling. "I declare you do, Mr. North. I declare you do."

My tribute to Scarlett was interrupted by my cell phone. It tumbled out as I was rummaging through my beach bag to try and find it. It crashed on the sidewalk. Joshua scooped it up.

"Hello. Savannah Phillips's phone. Yeah, uh, sure, she's here." His speech slowed as he handed me the phone. "It's a guy."

That shocked me about as much as it shocked him. Unless it was Mr. Hicks, there weren't any testosterone-bearing callers on my speed dial.

But the voice on the other end was all too familiar. "Are you with that guy? The guy that you work with that you absolutely abhor?" I could hear the "I told you so" in Gregory's voice all the way from Jackson, Mississippi.

"Don't you have a job?" I retorted.

"Don't you? What are you doing gallivanting with your boyfriend in the middle of the afternoon on a workday yourself?" I could hear his grin. And I was certain those white teeth were downright taking over his chocolate face with his great sense of satisfaction. He had seen Joshua once, when his job as law clerk for a judge in Jackson brought him to Savannah to assist with the Ten Commandments' situation. Gregory let me know in specific terms that he thought I was completely taken with Mr. North. He would make me suffer for this for years.

"I'm not *gallivanting*, for your information. I'm in Seaside, pursuing a story." I tried to smile at Joshua and whisper into the phone at the same time. "Excuse me just a moment," I said to Joshua as I stepped to the other side of the walkway.

"Pursuing a story, my eye. You are pursuing a dark, curly-headed Southern gentleman. I just hope you're being tactful."

"Did your call have a purpose?"

"Actually, it did. I was headed to Savannah with the judge and wondered if you were in town. Thought we could catch up. But consider me caught up."

"Well, have a wonderful trip, and I'm sorry I won't be there."

He chuckled. "Be there for me to gloat? Yeah, I'm sure you'll hate you missed that. Well, have a wonderful week, and I want a rundown when it's over."

"I'm sure you do."

I closed the phone and looked up at Joshua, who was sitting on a bench outside of L. Pizitz.

"Competition?" he questioned.

"Excuse me?" I asked, dropping the phone back into my bag.

"Is there something I need to know? Do I have competition I'm not aware of?" He crossed his ankles.

"Mr. North"—I chuckled like a true Southern charmer—"I am the daughter of Victoria Phillips. There will always be competition. Are you jealous?"

He stood up rather quickly. "Me? Jealous? A little competition never scared me." But the texture of his voice was strained.

"Well, I'm not sure your tone matches your words."

His arms slipped around my waist, and right in front of the store window for every accessory-buying vacationer to behold, he planted one more doozy on me. A doozy that left me a little woozy. "When he can do that to you, I'll be nervous."

And he left me there. Two old ladies about fell into the window when I turned in their direction. They both gave me big ol' winks. I winked back. After all, if competition did that to Joshua, I might make Gregory call twice a day.

From the sounds of the twin choo-choo engines on the sofa, shopping must take a lot out of a person. Mother was sacked out on one end, surrounded by, well, sacks. Amber was sacked out on the other end, surrounded by, well, more sacks. And each of their three-inch heels was resting on the coffee table.

"If you'd worn sensible shoes, you might've had a little more energy when you got home." They responded in simultaneous snores.

Paige was lying on her bed, reading a book. That behavior was the equivalent of me power-cleaning a bathroom. The woman was on the verge of cracking up. She hated to read. Reading put her to sleep, which was the goal. And to prove the scope of her sorrows, she was reading *He's Just Not That into You*. Things were worse than I thought.

I leaned against the doorframe. "Where's the perky step from this morning?"

She propped her book on her knees. "Perked."

"Did he really have to work?"

"Not until the new cabana 'boy' showed up in a one-piece suit with long blonde hair. Cynthia."

"She was pretty, huh?"

"She was disgustingly perfect."

I laid myself across the bottom of her bed. "I think you're pretty perfect."

"Pretty perfectly pathetic."

"Ooh, whiney Amber has created whiney Paige." Her eyes bore into me. "That's not the way to find a man anyway."

"This coming from the woman who has liked two men in her life. Okay, Miss Dating Guide for the Twenty-first Century, how exactly should I find a man?"

"Don't be catty."

"Don't be so full of advice. You have everything you've ever wanted. And you'll get married. And you'll have babies. And I'll still be looking for a man who's simply willing to pay for dinner."

"You need to slow down this cart you're haulin' for me into the land of wedded bliss."

"Well, it's true. I can see it all over both of you."

"You're ridiculous." I didn't want to laugh. She was too pitiful for me to laugh. "Joshua thinks you're pretty great."

"He does?" She folded her book across her chest. There really wasn't any need; she was only on the copyright page.

"Yeah." I crawled into the bed next to her, wrapping my arms around her. She nestled her head against me.

"I need a man," she said.

"You need a good man. Not just any man. And don't you forget that."

"I won't. But I want him to look as totally hot as yours."

"I want him to, too, so you'll quit looking at Joshua. You were shameless at the beach."

"I couldn't help it. That was one of the most handsome chests I've ever seen."

"I cannot tell a lie. You are right. But this is about you."

"Right. Me. So, since this is about me, I need my preferred therapy of choice."

"Ice cream?"

"Yes, ma'am."

"We'll ruin our steaks."

"You can't ruin steaks."

The choo-choo trains never heard us leave.

"I did two weddings already this weekend," the apparent wedding planner stated to the three fiftyish women clad in sherbet-flavored linen outfits.

Ms. Orange replied, "How were they?"

"Pretty good."

"No problems at all?" Ms. Lime prodded.

"There would never be any problems if weddings didn't come with mothers of the brides!" he said.

Ms. Raspberry got a kick out of that, and they all parted laughing.

Paige licked her strawberry gelato. "Wonder what he'd say about *our* mothers after *our* weddings?"

I licked my chocolate ice cream on a sugar cone. "He wouldn't be able to say anything. He'd be in a padded cell, blubbering."

She laughed. We both knew it was absolutely true.

Paige loves the Artist Colony of Ruskin Place. I knew the combination of that *and* ice cream would perk up her perker. Plus, her meeting at J. Proctor Gallery was in an hour, after the gallery closed. She had brought her portfolio with her. She is certain you just never know when the opportunity will arise to promote your talents. She should be a publicist. Hmm, come to think of it, maybe she was really my mother's daughter.

Ruskin Place is a treasure trove in the heart of Seaside. Modeled after Jackson Square in New Orleans, it features quaint shops on the bottom floor of the townhouses that tower over them. Some of the townhouses actually house residents, which is evident by the landscaping. The others house people who want a different kind of Seaside experience.

The mustard-color stucco townhouse that is Lynn Field Reddoch's interior design store is first to greet visitors to Ruskin Place. The windows, framed by aged teal shutters, display the backs of the antiques. The fronts are to be enjoyed by those who actually enter. Her store sits prominently on the corner. A couple years ago she expanded to the townhouse across the walkway. Ms. Reddoch lives above her store and obviously trusts us travelers completely. Because each evening many of her antique iron chairs and chaises and mosaic-covered tables remain on the sidewalk.

"What are you ladies doing?" came Thomas's voice as he exited Quincy's, Ruskin Square's most popular arts, toys, and games shop.

We licked our ice-cream cones in unison.

"So funny."

"When did you get through golfing?" I asked, touching his red cheeks.

"About thirty minutes ago. We got in eighteen holes, and now Dad wants to head out to the beach for a while. So I came to grab a few things for later."

"What you got in the sack?" I asked.

"Party fodder." He pulled out a fork that would extend to the next table, along with two new board games of some adolescent fare.

"And you are the one dumping Mary Francis?"

"You're what?" Paige's mouth fell open.

"Savannah, I thought we had a deal."

"A deal requires both parties to receive something in return. You offered me nothing in return. Surely you were not able to keep it from Dad all day. The man is practically prophetic."

"Well, he figured it out by hole eleven." He fiddled with the strings on his bag. Tying. Retying.

"Then why would you care if I know?" Paige nudged him.

"Because you are getting chummy with Amber."

I turned and looked at her with an is-that-true kind of look.

She shrugged her shoulders, crinkled her nose, and shook her head, confirming it as a drastic overstatement.

"And if you tell her, she will tell my mother, and the rest of the week will pretty much be shot."

"So I take it you won't be at dinner?" I asked.

"Dad's grilling, I'm going. It's not nice to talk with your mouth full of food anyway. Then I'll head out and meet the fellas." Thomas hung out with the same group of guys every year. Many of them actually lived in Seaside. The boy never let moss grow on him. If he wasn't sound asleep, he was out somewhere, doing something with someone. "See you two later."

"Later."

Paige and I sneaked into Quincy's, where she pored over sketch books and oil paints, brushes, and chalks. I meandered through the stationery and notebooks. We exited two hundred dollars poorer. Well, me, only twenty. Paige called her purchase a tax deduction. I needed to find out more about those.

Then we crossed the walkway to Surfer Girl, which had relocated here a couple of years ago from the beachfront. It's welcome sign has flip-flops on it, so you can't help but go in. We left with new flip-flops as well.

Paige loves just to walk through the art district, examining the talents of others. She loves the modern and progressive style of art housed in J. Proctor's, and the vibrant Seaside-esque art found in Cara Roy's. I watched as her entire body relaxed and left behind the emotions of the afternoon. She was at home here, surrounded by people with a love for the expressions of life that she knew. Of things that she really liked. As for me, my mind kept wandering. Wandering to something I liked. Granted, I didn't know a thing about art, but I do know what I like. And I was beginning to think I liked Joshua North.

CHAPTER TWENTY-FIVE

Paige and I nestled into two of the many chairs staggered around the square at three- and four-yard increments, an artistic arrangement in and of themselves. We sipped on fountain Cokes from Café Rendezvous.

"It's like you've transported yourself from a beach resort to the streets of a small village," I said, taking a sip of my Coke and enjoying the burning sensation all the way down.

Paige set her Diet Coke down on the old tin washtub that served as a coffee table. "What do you want your wedding to be like?" she asked out of the blue.

I choked on my Coke and felt it make its way to the back side of my nostrils. "I'm sorry, I have no idea. The thought of a wedding hasn't crossed my mind in, well, never."

"Really?"

"Yes, really. And if you're referring to Joshua, we are just getting to know each other."

"Have you thought of Grant at all this week?"

I turned my gaze to the windmill spinning on the small patch of lawn in front of the nearest townhouse. "Grant's married,

Paige. I can't let my thoughts or emotions turn to him anymore. And to be honest"—I turned back to her—"there *are* things that I feel with Joshua that I never felt with Grant."

Her surprise registered. "Never?"

"Well, maybe in the beginning there were moments of excitement. But something seems different here. I can't place my finger on it, but it's different."

"They call it love."

"He *calls* it that anyway."

"You mean you haven't told him you love him?"

"You have got to be kidding."

"You have got to be kidding," she retorted. "You mean this man has confirmed his love for you, and you respond with, 'Yeah I think you're swell too'?"

"I never say *swell*."

"How do you *not* respond to 'I love you'?"

"I don't want to say it until I know for sure."

"What will make you know for sure?"

"I have no idea." I puckered my lips like Elvis.

"Why do you do that?"

"Do what?"

"That pucker thing."

"This?" I did it again.

"Yes, that."

"It helps me think."

"You're odd."

"Getting odder. But anyway, if I'm going to say 'I love you' to Joshua or Mr. Magoo—"

"You did not just say *Mr. Magoo*."

"Focus. If I say 'I love you' to anyone, it will mean I want to spend the rest of my life with that person. I'm not a spring chicken anymore."

"Well, you're not a lame duck either."

"But I want those words to mean something this time."

"They meant something last time."

"Yes, they did. But I was sixteen. Now I'm twenty-four. They'll mean a lot more now."

"You do have a point. So back to your wedding." She eyed me impishly.

"I thought you had an interview."

She looked at her watch and jumped up from her chair. All I saw was her backside and the sounds from the copper wind chimes in front of Newbill Collection by the Sea, celebrating her departure.

I waited on Paige. I should have brought my book. She came out smiling. Time would reveal what that meant.

The smell of Dad's grill accosted us while we were still blocks away. Probably because the smell of hamburgers and steaks were present every evening on the streets of Seaside. Vacation did that to people. It brought them outside and made cooking an enjoyment instead of a chore. Of course, to Vicky, cooking was a rite of passage. It was the "woman's way," she called it. I called take-out the woman's way myself. We waged war over that one. She won. She cooked a homemade chocolate cake, and I went to bed praying God would give me the "woman's way" and that I'd never let it go.

"Hey, precious darlings," Mother said, kissing us on the cheeks as if we had been gone for days. Her little white fluff was nestled in her arms.

Duke wagged his tail from his seated position by the grill. The dog wasn't going to miss the opportunity to eat beef. He was no respecter of other animals' well-being. Truth be told, if he got a real good moment alone with that other canine, she might be dessert.

"I think I'm going to invite Joshua to dinner with us tomorrow night," Amber announced over her half portion of salad.

Paige kicked me under the table. I chewed a little harder on my beef.

Thomas chimed in. "Who's Joshua?"

"A man who could possibly one day be my husband," Amber proclaimed.

Thomas's brow furrowed. Paige kicked me again and nodded her head to indicate that I better do something. Thomas eyed us both. Vicky saved me. Who would have guessed?

"Amber, I thought we talked about this. You don't invite. The man invites. You don't even know him that well. You don't need to go declaring to him that he might possibly be your future husband."

"Oh, I wouldn't do that to *him,* Miss Victoria." She nibbled her lettuce. "I'm just telling you. My new family."

Thomas's furrow ran deeper. "What have I missed in two days?"

"Bunches!" Paige exclaimed. "You missed the car trip. You missed the barfing dog. You missed the tinkling princess. You missed the educational trip to the bathing suit store. And you have apparently missed the fact that Amber is now officially a part of your family."

Thomas eyed my father.

"We told her we wanted her to feel a part of our family," Dad said.

"Feel?" Thomas questioned.

"Yes, feel," Dad said.

"And don't you think whatever man I decide to marry needs to meet all of you and get to know and love each of you exactly the way I do?" Amber said. "I mean, that way you can examine him and give me your thoughts, and then I can tell him what he will need to change in order for us to make our relationship work, and then we can talk about our future and how each of you will play such an important part. And then, Savannah"—here, her eyes began to moisten with tears, and I knew I probably wouldn't be prepared for what was coming—"I know this is strictly parenthetical . . ."

Thomas's head cocked.

I shook my head at him.

". . . but, whomever I marry, even if it should be Joshua, I'm certain he would agree that we would definitely want you to be our children's godmother."

Paige ducked just in time to miss the masticated beef that spewed out of my mouth. I snatched up my napkin and wiped my face while Mother eyed me, appalled. Dad raised his right eyebrow, and Thomas sat back in his chair and crossed his arms. "I think it's a little soon to be talking about children," I informed her.

She patted my hand as if I were a child. "Savannah, but it doesn't matter who I marry. I know there is no one I would want to be a mother to my children if anything ever happened to me and their father than you. And whatever wonderful man you marry."

"But Joshua is not really here in Seaside to see you," I said, treading carefully. "Don't you think he might be busy with his friends, I don't know, getting ready for the wedding or something?"

"Or something," Paige mumbled. I kicked her back. Hard.

"Savannah, honey. I'm not talking specifically about Joshua. But I can't deny that I have a very strong feeling that this is a destiny encounter. I just lost my greatest dream, remember." As if we could forget. "Now it's like I have a real chance of spending my life with someone whom I've been extremely fond of for a long time. And then, parenthetically of course, I could become Mrs. United States of America."

My mother was shaking her head. At least the woman knew when crazy had entered the building. Of course, she had just bought crazy a new dress for the possibility. "Amber, I want you to listen to me now." She took Amber's hand and stared into her fake aqua-ocean eyes. "You just need to let life take its course. If Joshua is the man for you, nothing will be able to keep you apart. But you don't chase boys. Boys chase you. Don't ever forget that. I still have that man over there chasing me," she said with a coy smile.

Well, if my appetite hadn't been altered enough, it totally vacated the premises at that one. Dad smiled and took a bite of his steak.

"I understand. But I really was talking in complete parenthetical."

"Hypotheticals!" I blurted. "The word is *hypothetical*!"

"That's why I don't eat beef," Amber whispered to my mother. "You're never sure when that mad cow disease is just going to go straight to the cerebral cortex."

Thomas continued to survey the meal.

"So was that a no on dinner?" Amber asked after a pause.

"How about just see if your paths cross again," Mother suggested. "And if they do, then, well, then I guess you can invite him to dinner. But only if he crosses *your* path." She waved a finger. "Not if you cross his . . . purposefully."

This coming from Miss Purposeful Path Crosser herself. She had been crossing paths on purpose for years. New neighbors who had tacky yard ornaments. New businesses that had flashy signs. New restaurants that had tacky servers. She crossed more paths than she had paths to cross. But bless the Lord and sing a chorus of "Just As I Am," sister didn't want Miss Amber crossing anyone's path. It might be downright unladylike.

Paige ran her finger across her plate to get the last bit of juice, then slurped her finger like an ice cream cone. Maybe Mother needed to take a trip down Paige's unladylike path after she finished with Amber.

CHAPTER TWENTY-SIX

"Time to go," Mother called from the bottom of the steps.

I caught a glimpse of her, all dressed in white, and almost took a moment to sing a chorus of hallelujahs. Then I realized she wasn't dead (just kidding); she was ready for our annual family picture.

"Ooh, I'm ready! I'm ready!" Amber said, skipping out of her room in a white linen dress.

I gasped. Granted, I didn't like family pictures, but it was *my* family picture. Even the little yapper was snuggled in Mother's arms, donned in a white polo dress for dogs. We would never return from such depths.

"Savannah, hurry up!" Mother shouted.

"I forgot. You'll have to give me a minute." I stared at Paige lying across her bed, rubbing the gut that had grown with the two helpings she had consumed.

"What?"

"Why aren't you getting up?"

She rubbed herself like a genie lamp. "I'm not going with ya'll to take family photos."

"Come on," I whined. "I don't want to go by myself."

"You're a big girl. Spread your wings."

"They're broken."

"They've never developed."

"Okay, that'll work. They've never developed. Now will you come?" I asked, slipping on a pair of jeans and a white sweater. White was required for Mother's picture.

"No."

"You're cruel."

"Who brought who on this journey of horrors?"

The only good thing about taking a family photo on the beaches of Seaside was, first, that it always turned out beautiful. Second, I got to see Haley. Haley has lived behind her camera since I can remember. To be honest, it is as much a part of her as her auburn hair and amber eyes. And the pictures that come out of that camera are magical. Our first encounter three years ago resulted in a friendship that lives on through phone calls and e-mails.

"Savannah, my friend, it's great to see you," Haley said, her auburn hair glistening even more brightly in the setting of the sun.

"It's wonderful to see you too, sweet girl," I said, giving her a hug. I whispered in her ear, "Make this as painless as possible."

"A miracle worker I am not. But a powdered doughnut I do have." She pulled a pack from her camera bag. She always had powdered doughnuts. Paige would probably regret she didn't come.

Mother pranced around trying to find the perfect backdrop of dunes, pampas grass, and ocean. Haley had already found it for her.

Haley maneuvered us into place like an artist. She wore a prosthesis below her left knee, from a childhood accident, but it was evident that confidence had found its way in her soul. Her new husband, Tank, was largely responsible for that, I was sure. When I finally got to meet him, I would thank him.

"Ahem, excuse me. Uh . . . miss." Amber tried to get Haley's attention.

"Oh, yes."

"Um, uh, where would you like *me* to stand?"

Haley eyed my family, not sure where the new creature had come from. Amber looked so pitiful standing there by herself. Here we were, a lovely family (well, until Mother added Pink Toes), and there Amber was, thinking she was a part of it.

"Amber, why don't you come stand over here by me," I offered.

Her face lit up, and she fluttered over and spread herself out on the sand, letting the skirt of her dress lay across the white beach.

"This picture would have been much prettier if you and Thomas didn't insist on wearing jeans," Mother said through her clenched smile.

"Everybody smile," Haley said, trying to distract us from apparent conflict.

"I could have worn shorts," I offered, smiling myself.

"Savannah," Dad said.

Haley's camera clicked away.

"Great shot. Okay, now what about a mother-daughter picture."

Dad and Thomas took a moment to walk toward the beach a little. Amber and the princess in Ralph Lauren stayed put.

I could tell Haley was caught off guard. "Um, Amber, would you mind just scooting over there with the fellas for a minute?" she asked in her most professional voice.

Amber looked up at Victoria as if somehow the entire Phillips family line had been lost on Haley. I could see Mother processing. She had become a pro at that. I held my breath, realizing that she was about to actually tell Amber she couldn't be a part of this picture.

Finally, her words were released. "Amber, darling, I believe

Haley"—oh, that was good—"would like one of just Savannah and me."

Amber's aqua eyes began to glisten. Hoping for a recount. But Mother remained firm.

So there I stood. Me and my mother. I waited one more moment, for the next shoe to fall. It fell, all right. "Haley, we're ready now."

And there I stood, me, my mother, and Maggy.

"Well then," Haley responded. "All you Phillips girls should all smile and say *ruff!*"

Had it not been so pitiful, I do believe I would have laughed myself silly.

Haley snapped some more pictures and posed us for one final hurrah. Mother sat her princess down a little too close to Duke, and when Haley said, "Okay, on three, say cheese," well, Duke lifted up his leg and showered that princess with a thunderstorm.

"Duke!" Mother hollered, snatching up her whining, dripping pup.

"Duke!" Dad laughed.

"Jake Phillips, this is not funny. Your dog has defiled my baby." She stomped in the direction of the house. Amber flittered behind.

Thomas, Dad, and Duke laughed all the way home.

"I see little has changed," Haley said as I gave her a hug good night.

"What would we do if it did?"

"Who's going to join me this evening?" Dad asked the dinner crew regarding his evening walk. Mother was a given. Thomas declared he had walked enough today and was heading up the street to watch a movie with friends. Paige was going to stay behind at the house and do Lord knew what. Maybe pick up on her copyright page. I wanted to stay behind with Paige, but Dad really wanted me to come. Amber went because she felt so bloated from her three bites of roughage, and four powdered doughnuts.

Mother made her second exit from the house. The first time, she emerged with Maggy in a baby carrier strapped across her chest. Dad sent her back inside.

Now they were back, Mother with her little creature on a leash, and both looked miserable. I, however, might enjoy this walk a little more after all. But I had an odd feeling none of us would receive twenty dollars to get lost tonight. Especially after Mother slammed her three-inch heel on the two love bugs that alighted right below her foot.

I could smell the honeysuckle that ran along most of the white picket fences of Seaside Avenue before I even got to the sidewalk. The scent was much more subtle in the evenings than in the humid morning, more like the hint of the aroma of wine.

As we turned off of Seaside Avenue, we solicited more than a few looks as we strolled along Forest Street. Not me and Dad. No, we were normal news. Abnormal news were the two who strolled behind us in heels high enough to impale small children.

"Did you have a good day?" Dad whispered.

"Yeah, it was nice. Heard you got some interesting news from Thomas today."

"Oh yeah." He laughed. "I'm not surprised. She was a little too, well, a little too . . ."

He needed no words. I understood perfectly.

"Are we going to Criolla's tomorrow night? I've been salivating at the thought since I decided to come."

"Yeah, I think we might." He fiddled with the toothpick held between his teeth. "I had coffee with your beau this morning again."

"Who?" I sputtered.

"Who?" He chuckled. "Do you live in the land of denial?"

"No, I live in the land of the certifiable, and two of them are up our . . ."

"Don't you say it."

"I was going to say, if you would allow me to finish, kind sir, that two of them are following close behind. Plus, he's not my beau."

"Okay then. Well, your mother thought I should get to know him, since Amber is so set on the fact that he's the one for her. Now, do you see why you can't let this charade go on much longer? Someone is going to get hurt to a possibly unrecoverable degree."

"Well, let's not worry about that on our little walk here tonight." I wrapped my arm around him.

"You can't distract me. I don't distract."

"Well, let's not worry *her* little head tonight then. I'll try to tell her tomorrow."

"No try. Will."

"Okay, 'will try,' how's that?"

"You'll regret your delay."

"I regret a lot of things, Dad. But at least this one I can partially control."

"You think you're in control of this?"

"Is the pope Polish?"

"Actually no, he's not. Neither was the last one."

"Really?"

"Do you read the paper, seeing as you work at one?"

"I like the 'Life' section."

"Do you?"

"Oh yes. I love life," I said with a smile. He smiled back. He couldn't help it. He had a weakness for me.

"Ooh!" I heard Mom holler out. I looked back just in time to catch her walk begin to change. The woman had a bladder the size of a gnat. "Hey! Yoo-hoo!" Mother waved at us as if we couldn't guess what her issue was. "I've got to go to the ladies room."

Unfortunately for her, we had walked to the back of Seaside, where there was only new construction, and there was no place to go potty. Well, no place but one. A rather rough-looking Porta Potti wobbled atop a mound of gravel.

"Victoria, there are no restrooms around here but that," Dad said, pointing to our discovery.

She huffed at him. "That is not an option for a lady." This from the woman who actually had the city of Savannah build public restrooms for the parade of homes. She refused to let the women of "her" city use Porta Pottis.

Dad turned around and continued walking. "Then you'll just have to try and hold it until we can get back to the house."

We heard her heels clicking rather awkwardly behind us.

"Uh, Mr. Phillips." Amber's voice penetrated the evening. "I'm not so sure she's going to make it."

We turned and looked. Mother had intertwined her legs and was trying to walk as if she were playing a game of hopscotch for contortionists. "Victoria, if you've got to go that bad, then just hold your nose and go use that bathroom. There's no use in making yourself miserable."

Maggy's leash was extended as far as it could go, trying to pull Mother along. "I'm not going in there. It's just . . . well, it's just wrong."

"You have no other options," I observed.

Her legs scrunched tighter.

"Take her!" Mother said, extending Maggy's leash to Dad. "I cannot believe I am doing this." She reached into her purse. Yes, she takes walks with her purse and her heels and full makeup and wet wipes and an extra pair of panties in case of an accident. Don't ask. I think the picture painted here is clear enough. She had a bladder extension years ago. The only thing that got extended effectively was the invitation to find another bladder surgeon, because the one who had to endure her apparently got his fill of Victoria Phillips.

She pulled out a tissue and waddled over to the Porta Potti. As she closed the door behind her, I saw the winged beast slip in right behind her. Then I heard the locking of her door. Because for certain, one of the three of us was going to try to sneak a peek. I hoped she would think she was alone.

Not for long. Her scream was loud and shrill.

"Victoria, what is it?" Dad asked. The man should just take walks with Duke and leave the rest of us behind.

"She just realized she's not alone in there," I said, cocking my head slightly as a rather serious ruckus ensued behind those fiberglass walls.

"What's in there?" Dad began to look a little concerned.

"A wasp went in right behind her."

"A wasp?" Amber gasped.

"Why didn't you tell her?" Dad asked, tossing me Maggy's leash and walking over to open the door.

"I thought it might come out unharmed," I hollered.

He turned and gave me that eye. That don't-mess-with-my-woman eye.

"Jake! Jake! Get me out of here."

"Hold on a minute, Victoria!" he said in the flustered tone he almost never used.

"It won't open, Jake! I can't get the door to open!"

Dad desperately jiggled the handle. But it wouldn't budge. "Just calm down, Victoria! Just move the latch over."

"Ahh! Get away from me, you beast! I'll kill you and parade your squished self in front of your friends!"

"I told you the wasp has far more to worry about than Mother does!" I said, making sure he could hear me.

"Calm down, Victoria and move the latch!"

"I'm moving the latch, genius! Ahh! Get back, you little beast from the pit of hell!" The entire Porta Potti shook.

Dad wiggled the door handle while trying to hold the toilet steady. "Victoria, quit shaking the toilet, or you are going to make it fall over."

"It's trying to sting me, Jake!" The toilet rocked harder.

"It's going to sting you twice if you don't focus and move the latch!"

"I tried! It won't move! Why don't you come in here, Mr. Know-It-All, and see if you can get it to open!"

Wasn't that a novel idea.

"Ahh! Get away from my bottom!"

My family was sadder than I thought. About that time I saw a blur out of the corner of my eye. It was large and loud and jerking off its three-inch heel. "I'll save you, Miss Victoria." And with that the beauty queen slammed her shoe down on the gravel pile, the heel popped off and flew in the air, and she caught it without even looking. In ten seconds flat she had jimmied that lock, and out fell my mother. Hair quite askew. Attire quite askew. Pearls all but choking her.

"The Princess of the South has officially been dethroned," I announced.

No one appreciated the assessment but me.

"Oh, Amber! You precious angel!" Mother said, flinging her arms around Amber's neck and kissing her cheeks like a European. You are so wonderful to me! You would do anything for me! Thank you, darling, thank you."

Once Mother released Amber, Amber put her shoe back on. I'm not really sure why.

Dad made sure nothing was hurt on Mother, and I watched as the wasp flew out wiping his brow. The poor thing had probably never come so close to death.

Maggy had gone back to shaking, and Duke had lain down for a nap.

"I bet they'll have their own television show together by the time we get home," I said, obviously a little louder than intended, because Dad looked my way. I turned my head as if he had gone to hearing things.

"Miss Victoria, please don't ever scare me like that again," Amber said as she plodded home. One click. One clomp. One click. One clomp.

"Where'd you learn that heel thing anyway?" I asked.

She giggled. "Well, it's just a little trick Miss Watermelon Spitting Seed Queen taught me years ago. There was a little issue with her boyfriend and Miss Sausage Festival Queen. Let's just say Miss Watermelon's shoe wasn't the only one to meet such a fate."

One day I'd learn not to ask.

CHAPTER TWENTY-SEVEN

The sail was hardly visible from the shore. But I couldn't help being mesmerized by the solace of it rocking gently on the water. Today the ocean was like glass. A slight breeze blew from the west. Duke and I had hit tilling time hard this morning and were resting on the Odessa Street Beach Pavilion. The "stick" architecture of the pavilion provides an open feeling that allows you to feel the wind. It was my favorite of them all. I felt secure inside, yet the air is allowed to flow through. In here, I fully enjoyed the reasons why people come to such a destination at all: the sounds and the breeze. The building's design has almost a kaleidoscope effect when you look at it from a distance. Much like the feeling of my life right now. It's a bunch of enjoyable colors spinning in uncontrollable directions, even though I insisted I was in complete control.

"What do you think about love?" I asked my companion.

He raised his right eyebrow and then turned his attention back to the water.

"Ever wish you could express your love to Lucy?"

He moaned and plopped to the floor with his head on his

paws, thinking of the beautiful chocolate lab that resided in the antique store up the street from Dad's coffee shop.

"I know, old friend. Love is a crazy thing."

He rolled over so I could pet his big, old, fat beef-eating stomach.

I obliged. "I'm not sure what to do. It's all so crazy yet feels so different. And then there's Amber."

He moaned and flipped back over. I had apparently ruined the moment.

"I know, boy, but I really have to think about her. I mean, she is gaga over Joshua. I can't just break her heart. No . . . I have to be gentle. I'll just have to wait until the right time. There *will* be a right time," I declared as if trying to convince myself.

I felt a tug on Duke's leash. He was standing, trying to make his way down the stairs toward the ocean and a golden cocker spaniel. "You are shameless, Duke." I tugged back. "You really need to find yourself a committed relationship. Maybe now that Maggy has arrived—"

He turned around and glared. I swear that dog is part human.

"Come on, let's go see what merry sunshine is up to this morning." He wouldn't budge until I apologized.

I saw them before I reached them. My man and the mother of my godchildren. Did I just say *my man* again? Did I just agree to be the godmother of Amber's children? She had detained him near Modica Market. I wondered who had crossed whose path. By the look of Amber's attire, with her tube top and new jeans, which I would never forgive Paige for suggesting, I would say Amber had done the path crossing. I would never do such a thing. Dad sat at the small table in front of the market, watching the whole exchange.

When Amber cascaded away, Joshua sat down in the chair across from him. Mr. Modica came out the door and greeted the two gentlemen, then went back in to take care of a father who needed a breakfast fix for himself just to endure the two children that were tagging along.

"Looks like I'm having dinner with you this evening at Criolla's," Joshua announced to me upon my arrival. I took a seat next to him.

"You are not!"

He smirked. Dad smirked too. This was not going to be pleasant. They were both brazen. "Oh, yes, Savannah. I will be your dinner guest for the evening. Now, would you like to tell your mother and Amber after our dinner, or before?"

"I would like to—"

"I think she's hedging," Dad said.

"I would like to find me some hard liquor."

"Savannah Phillips!" Joshua rebuked. "Do you have something you need to tell me before we take our relationship any farther?"

That man had just beat my father in admonishing me. Something was terribly wrong with this picture. "I said—"

"She always does this," my father chimed in.

"I know." They both took a sip of their coffee with the same hand, mirror images of each other. For a moment I was horrified.

"I said, let's make sure Duke doesn't lick her."

Dad raised his right eyebrow. "That was one of your more pitiful attempts lately."

"She's not as quick on her feet as she used to be," Joshua informed my father.

"I think she's been distracted," my father said.

"You think?" Joshua said, giving me a wink.

"Am I here?" I offered. A rather loud offering.

"Oh what, baby girl? Are we not giving you enough attention?"

"I don't need attention."

Joshua reached over and laid his hand across my own. "I can give you all the attention you need tonight at dinner with your family."

"You *cannot* come to dinner with me and my family."

"I believe I have some say in that," Dad replied.

"It will be too ugly! The woman has declared me the godmother of your . . . your children." I waved my arms toward Joshua. Duke gagged. That was to help me realize I still held his leash in my hand.

Dad took Duke's leash. "Come here, boy." Duke was grateful and sneezed in my direction. On purpose.

"She didn't necessarily say they would be Joshua's children," Dad said.

Joshua laughed. "Wonder how I could be father and godfather at the same time?"

"Now, that just sounds gross."

Joshua looked over at my Dad. "I think she should tell them tonight."

"No, you two. I can't. Just give me one more day. Give Amber this evening and then I'll tell them. I promise. I just don't want to crush her. She'll be looking forward to this all day."

"Okay," Joshua conceded. "But I will not pretend I like her. I won't do that to her. It would just make this whole thing worse."

"You can't just hold her hand or something?"

"Savannah! Have you tipped your rocker?" Dad said. "You are acting crazy."

"Well, you would too if the girl who was one step away from becoming one with the sea was after your . . . your . . . your . . ."

"Your what, Savannah?" Joshua inquired.

"Uh, my . . . my . . . my . . ."

He and Dad leaned in with identical expressions. "Your . . . your . . . what?"

I squinted my left eye and raised my right eyebrow. "You're my . . . well, what is it? Maybe you're my boyfriend."

"Ooh, I like that." He took another sip of his coffee. "Sounded more like a question than an answer, but I'll take it. Is that okay with you, Mr. Phillips?" He looked at my father with a newfound seriousness.

Dad smiled at him, then turned to me. "Fine by me. I've just been waiting for her to admit it to herself."

I raised my eyebrow.

"Put it down, Savannah." Dad laughed.

It descended. "Oh, well, since you two are such fond friends now, why don't you just sit here and do what men do. Drink your coffee, read your paper, and all that stuff." I patted Joshua on the shoulder and headed up the street.

"You'll have to tell her eventually." Joshua's voice rang in the distance.

I had already stuck my earphones back in. But I heard him. Every word.

"Where's your friend?" Lucy asked as I walked by. She was in her usual morning position, sitting and reading.

"He abandoned me for his real master."

She chuckled. "He's a daddy's boy?"

"He goes wherever the path of least resistance leads," I said, laying my hands on the edge of her fence.

"What are you doing for lunch?"

"I have no idea. I'm still trying to figure out what's for breakfast." I offered her a knowing smile.

Her dark eyes twinkled. "What? No lunch with the curly-headed guy?"

"Well, Lucy, Lucy . . . I must say: What are you insinuating?"

She laughed. "Not a thing. Just stating what is perfectly evident."

"So you think we're having lunch together today?"

"I'm just saying if you happen to be free, Manuel and I would love for you to join us. He wants to go to the oyster bar today."

I hate oysters. "Ooh, well, I'm not quite sure what my lunch plans are, but if they do entail Mr. North, I'll be more than glad to ask him his take on oysters. However, there is the small matter of the rest of my family's agenda. I have a few houseguests who don't know about my . . . status with Mr. North."

"Is that what they call it now?"

I puckered my lips the way Paige hated. And with that I gave her a wave of my hand. "I never much liked oysters," I offered as I left.

All I heard was her laughter.

CHAPTER TWENTY-EIGHT

Okay, the red or the green?" I heard Amber ask, holding up the two tops with the tags still hanging on them. Obviously Mother felt Amber needed options. "I think the green brings out the flecks of green in my eyes, don't you?" Paige would have agreed, but no one was sure what Amber's real eye color was.

Paige came scampering to the door when she saw me pass by. "Ooh, Savannah, come in here. What do *you* think Amber should wear tonight to dinner with Joshua?"

I gave her a look. *The* look.

Amber struck a pose in my direction. "Savannah? The red or the green?"

"The red, definitely the red," I said, eyeing Paige again.

"Ladies, you just continually confuse me. Oh, well, I'll just eenie, meenie, minie, moe them."

We squinted in tandem.

"Well, ladies, Miss Victoria is taking me today to get my nails done. I would love for you to join us if you have some free time," Amber said, leaning into her closet to hang up her tops.

Paige scanned Amber's fingernails. Her perfectly manicured nails. "But your nails look fine."

"Your point?" Amber asked.

"Obviously I have no point," Paige said, shaking her head. "But I'm sorry, I can't join you today."

I stuck my chipped horrors behind my back and made a mental note to take care of those myself before this evening. "Oh, me either. I'm headed right now to write my story and turn it in. Busy, busy. But you and Mother have a wonderful time."

She offered us one last chance. "You're sure? We would have a wonderful time."

"No, we're sure. I've got to finish reading my book anyway," Paige said, turning to give me a sideways glance. I rolled my eyes.

"And I'm having lunch with Lucy and Manuel."

"Well, okay," she said picking up her multicolored Louis Vuitton, which was a perfect complement to her red tube top. "But you'll miss all the fun."

"We know." Paige assured her. "We have a way of doing that."

"Toodledoo, girls."

"Toodledoo," we offered in unison, watching her bouncy locks disappear down the stairs.

Paige threw herself down on the bed. I followed. "You stink," she said.

"It's called sweat, and that's what happens when you exercise."

"Who needs to exercise this body? Look at this stomach." She patted her pooch.

"Everything looks smaller lying down. It spreads out, genius."

"Spreads out nicely, I might add."

"So, you want to go to lunch with us?"

"No, no fifth wheel today."

"You're never a fifth wheel."

"I have officially become one." She rolled over to look at me. "Don't get too close. You really do smell like fish."

I slapped her. "You are never a fifth wheel in my life. I hope you will always know that."

"I do. But Thomas, who's still avoiding your mother at all costs, has a group of people going out on a friend's boat today. He invited me."

"Thomas? Invited you?"

"Yes. I am a rather exciting person to have around. Plus, he knows you're totally up to something. So he's looking out for me."

"He's trying to get information, isn't he?" The other reason why he was continually having her hang out with him made me too nervous to consider.

"Probably. And he is a royal pain, but he can be nice too. How are you?"

"You sure you don't want to come?" I asked, getting up and taking her hands to give her a tug. She wouldn't budge. "Serious, you need to exercise."

"I'm sure I don't want to come. And I'm even more certain I don't want to exercise. I mean, Jennifer Lopez is famous for a bum like this," she said, giving hers a firm slap. "Why ruin a good thing?"

"Of course, how silly of me."

"Yes, how silly of you."

Lucy and Manuel were already at the Hurricane Oyster Bar when we arrived. I had finished my story. Then I had happened upon Joshua. And he had happened to be available. So we happened their way. He had already been on the beach when I found him, wearing an irritating (okay, charming) look of satisfaction when he saw me.

The salty breeze that wafted up through the small Obe shopping-and-eating district made the thought of seafood all the more appropriate.

"Lucy and Manuel, I'd like you to meet Joshua North."

"A pleasure to meet you, Joshua," Manuel said, extending his hand.

Lucy looked breathtaking as usual, her deep, rich Spanish features illuminated by the sun. Her thick accent hovered over her words. "Joshua, what a wonderful treat to meet you. We've caught a few sightings of you this week."

"Oh, you have, huh?" He turned his face to me.

"Let's sit," Manuel said, motioning to the chairs.

"I love oysters," Joshua said, all but licking his lips.

"I hate oysters," I replied.

"You hate oysters? You live in Savannah, love seafood, and hate oysters," Joshua summarized.

I looked into his dark eyes and wanted to brush that loose curl off his forehead, but it felt inappropriate somehow. Too intimate. "Yes, you don't know everything about me, you know. I absolutely hate oysters. But I *love* peel-and-eat shrimp."

"Ooh, me too," Lucy offered.

For the next hour and a half we talked of our lives, Manuel's retirement from Southeastern Freight Lines, the hurricane that changed their lives, and the mother who continually changes mine. We watched their gestures and their thoughtfulness and their love. And I had to listen to the sound of oysters being sucked the entire time. Oh well, all things have their price.

We left completely full and completely satisfied.

"I'll look forward to seeing you at dinner," Joshua said as Manuel and Lucy left to stroll the beach.

"Well, I won't be hard to find. I'll be the uncomfortable one."

He leaned over and kissed me in that perfect way of his. "No, you'll be the beautiful one sitting right next to me."

"This is going to be completely disastrous. Can't you play sick or dead or something?"

"Lie?"

"Lie? I would never suggest lying," I said with my hand across my chest in shock.

"What, a half truth then? Don't you know half truth is no truth at all?"

"Oh my stars. That is exactly what my father says. You scare me."

"You scare me more. No lying. I will come to dinner. I will try to prevent your mother from hating me more. I will try to convince Amber I'm worth hating. And I'll try to convince you that you are only steps away from finally falling in love with me."

I studied him for a moment. His faint smell of cologne. His rich dark eyes. His tanned arms. For a moment I wasn't even sure what I was about to do myself. Then I reached for his hand and took it in my own, bringing it firmly to my heart. "I'm not so certain, Mr. North, that I have very far to fall."

I walked away, kicking myself for the second lame remark in a span of a couple days. He was still smiling.

CHAPTER TWENTY-NINE

Sundog Books is one of Seaside's oldest businesses. It used to be in the space now occupied by Hooch and Holly's, the stationery store, my second favorite place in Seaside. But Sundog Books is now nestled next to Shades. Its new building came when the Town Center was revamped during the filming of *The Truman Show*. When you enter, it's as if you enter another world. You won't see any of the neatly stacked shelves of Katherine's Bookstore here. Sundog's is a book lover's dream. You can tell the owner is all about books. Not magazines, not cappuccino and scones. Even the newspapers are relegated to wooden shelves outside the door. Why? Because this is a bookstore that sells books! Loads and loads of books.

The shelves are piled high with books, and then books sit on the bookshelf in front of the books. So you have to move books in order to find other books. It is absolutely captivating. And for me, at moments, a stinging reminder of what I might have achieved.

"What have you been doing since retirement?" a lady asked an elderly gentleman as he and his wife (I assumed) came through the door with her.

"He's writing a lot these days," the wife answered for him, as I've noticed wives tend to do.

"Oh, George, that's wonderful. What kind of things?"

"Oh, just short stories, mostly," he said.

The stout questioner smoothed her skirt. "Think you'll ever get anything published?"

"He could," his wife said.

"Who knows? Right now the writings are just for me. Maybe I'll let someone read them one day. But today they're just for me."

I picked up a book off the table in front of me and examined the cover—a pair of slippered feet—as their conversation slipped away. I turned the book over and studied the picture of the thirty-ish writer from Hackensack, New Jersey, who had written her story and watched it get stacked on the shelves of bookstores nationwide. The old comrade of hurt began to make its way up my throat. Even the months of fulfillment at the paper and now with Joshua couldn't completely quell the emotion that appeared every now and then over my lost dream of writing novels. It had been years in the making, from notebook pages in middle and high school to short stories in college to novels in my master's studies to the contest that I had legitimately won . . . and then lost for all the wrong reasons.

I hadn't even been able to pick up my manuscript to leaf through it since then. I just hoped for the day that it would all go away completely. The desire and the sting. And that I could just be satisfied with the place I was: the land of "almost there." I perused the shelves and left with a biography. I may not read it for a year, especially at the rate I was going with my latest novel, but I couldn't leave a bookstore without a book any more than Paige could come out of a store without something to eat.

The fragrance from the honeysuckle around the fence of Josephine's Bed & Breakfast was especially spirited today.

The afternoon humidity strengthened the aroma. And the vacated bicycles lining her walk proved I wasn't alone in enjoying their scent.

The bird that had parked his way in front of me was in no hurry to scurry.

"What did you do, fly south for vacation?"

He cocked his head, huffed, and trotted off. Maybe I had missed my calling altogether and should have become Dr. Doolittle. I laughed to myself and pulled the new book close to me. Life was bittersweet. I had let go to receive. I had let go of the dream of being a fiction writer and discovered the world of journalism. I had let go of Grant, then received Joshua. Amazing how life requires letting go to receive. But in each instance, no matter how painful, each brought me to a different place, a better place, dare I say a wonderful place. I shed tears over what I had lost, but I would always know in my knower that what I received in exchange would take me to new and better places.

"Come here, Magnolia. It's Mommy. Yoo-hoo!" I heard the sound of clicking three-inch heels on the brick street.

About that time, a white fur ball wearing a black-and-white zebra-print collar came running in my direction. I snatched her up, only to meet my mother heading down the street, "glistening."

"Lose something?" I asked, returning her prize in my uplifted right hand.

"Oh, Savannah darling. Thank you. I do declare that Duke unlocked her cage and opened the screen door himself in hopes she would end up dinner for a tomcat."

"I can't say I've seen any loose tomcats hanging around. But I do declare you're sweating," I said, mimicking her deep Southern drawl.

"Women do not *sweat*, Savannah Phillips. Women glisten."

Who knew what the difference was, but she was certain there was one. The closer we got to home, the more her little ball of fur quaked. As we opened the gate that led to the front door, I do declare I saw a glimpse of mischief in Duke's eyes.

"There's no way," I said to myself as I passed him. I turned back to look at him. He raised his right eyebrow at me. And I was sure I heard the sound of snickering. Maybe I do have a second calling, because I do believe that creature just snickered. But when I turned back around to make sure, he was scratching himself.

"Males. Nothing keeps their attention very long."

Amber's floor was littered with lingerie and belts and shirts and divorced shoes. Paige bolted out of the room with a hat hidden behind her back.

"What are you doing?" I asked as I followed her to our room.

She waved the floppy object in front of my face. "If she goes out in this, I'm ordering take-out. I mean, I know we've both been craving fresh lump crab meat"—her speech slowed and began to slur as her eyes started to roll back in her head—"drowned in butter over saffron rice." She shook herself violently as if forbidding her body to completely miss what she had been trying to say. "And I can't wait to see how this evening transpires, but that woman is insufferable. She has modeled thirty . . . count them"—she wiggled her fingers, at least the ones that weren't holding a hat—"*thirty* outfits, and nothing makes her happy. Didn't she just get a new dress for this occasion? Her perfect size-0 body is too lean, or too wide, or too this, or too that . . . *Ugh!*" she pushed the bedroom door open. "I'm not a drinker, well, not a big one anyway, but this woman . . . she might just send me right over the edge." She threw her body over the bed and tossed Amber's hat over her face.

"That's attractive," I said, opening the closet door. I stared at its contents. "I thought she was your new friend, and you enjoyed all of this."

"She's a sweet girl, but she's obsessive. I mean, that is just a trait that I can't handle. In large doses of course." She looked at me as if *I* were the obsessive-compulsive one. True, I had just been eyeing a stray hair lying on the floor of the bathroom, which would need my complete attention in about one moment. Come to think of it, our bathroom was filthy.

"Don't even think about it!" she hollered, knowing I indeed had an obsessive-compulsive disease when it came to cleaning bathrooms in moments of stress, like having dinner with your boyfriend whom your friend is completely infatuated with and your mother disdains.

"And," she continued, "if you try on anymore than one outfit, I will make you go to sleep tonight listening to . . . I don't know, maybe the sounds of Shelley Winters."

"You wouldn't," I said, still looking at the bathroom. "Anyway, she doesn't sing. Plus she's dead, and you know I don't do dead people."

"Okay, well, how about this? If you make me comment on one item of clothing in that closet, I'll sing you to sleep myself."

I turned my attention from the bathroom to the closet, forgetting that I actually had to be dressed for this dinner too. I laughed. "Would I look better in the white slacks or the black ones?"

The hat missed me by an inch. It was a big hat.

CHAPTER THIRTY

If it weren't for the sign with the exotic Caribbean face with yellow earrings, Criolla's would be easy to miss. But if you do miss it, well, slap whoever's driving, because you just missed a piece of heaven on earth. *The* piece of heaven I'd been waiting for since we got here.

Amber pushed her way past us all. She traveled past the palm trees, past the pale stucco walls, past the lamp posts lighting the walkway with teal-green shades that match the teal-green window shutters.

As she stepped through the door, she took the breath right out of the room. She did that most everywhere she went. I slinked in behind her. I did that most everywhere she went too. Joshua was waiting at the bar in the center of the restaurant. He was leaning against a table, staring at the door. And as the beautiful lady who looked more like a goddess than a human made her entrance, I watched his eyes scan her and then cross her shoulder and meet my own. And with the smile that lit up his eyes, I knew. I knew that his heart truly was for me. Every other mouth standing agape may be drooling over the vision in jeans, ones that definitely needed washing by now, but not him. Not my man. I mean, if that man could see the amazing creature in front of me and still have eyes for the midget in the black linen sundress behind her, he had something that I had never found in a man before.

Amber reached him first. Of course.

"Oh, Joshua," she said, starting to wrap her arms around his neck. He took her hands in his own, a vision of politeness, and returned them to her sides. She wasn't deterred for a moment. "I'm so glad you could come. You are just going to love my family. Family," she announced as she turned around. Paige moaned. Thomas rolled his eyes. "This is my wonderful, and extremely handsome bo—" She caught Vicky's eye. "My lovely friend Joshua."

Joshua was so gracious. He extended his hand to each member of Amber's *family* as Amber introduced him.

Mother eyed him like an inspector inspects a house for termites. He never faltered. He took her hand, held it between his own, and said so genuinely, "Mrs. Phillips, it is a pleasure to personally meet you. And I hope my mistakes of the past will not prevent you from getting to know me for my other qualities this evening."

I do believe her heart fluttered. He had her in the palm of his hand, literally. Unbelievable. Her very posture softened as Frank, the maître d', led us to the round table in the far right corner that we would occupy for the evening. Joshua stayed behind for me and whispered in my ear as he placed his hand in the small of my back, "Exhale."

I did. Loud enough for Thomas to turn around.

Joshua helped me and Amber to our seats. Thomas was ever the gentleman and sat Paige in hers while Dad did the honors for his lovely princess. "You look beautiful," Joshua mouthed as he made his way to his own seat, chosen by Amber. Next to her. Across from me.

Criolla's interior was completely Caribbean just like its cuisine. The pale peach walls were accented by deeper peach tones below the chair railing. Teal was the accent of choice in the seat cushions, the ceramic bread baskets, and the carpet.

My eyes caught a mother and daughter having dinner alone in a corner table. They conversed casually and laughed often. As I looked across the table at my own mother, who sat on the other side of Joshua, poor man, I realized I couldn't even remember the last time Mother and I had shared a meal together, alone. She looked exceptionally beautiful in her vibrant orange jacket and white tank. The color made her dark eyes even more vibrant. Looking at her there, so beautiful, smiling graciously at the man who had all but stolen my heart, I decided we would have to do that soon. Maybe even this week, while we were still on . . . vacation.

"So, Joshua, tell me exactly what your intentions are with Amber."

Or maybe we wouldn't. I kicked Dad's leg. I'm sure he would regret sitting next to me by the end of the evening. "Victoria, why don't you let us order. Give yourself a chance to get to know Joshua before you interrogate him."

"Well, I just think we need to know what he—"

"I said we will order, and then we will get to know Joshua this evening."

We all knew what he meant. Even she knew. He meant, "Sit there like a duchess and shut your yapper!" I patted his knee. It was the least I could do. The man would be bruised for weeks.

I looked at Joshua. A light band of perspiration had broken out above his lip. "Exhale," I mouthed. He did. Twice. Hard.

Drinks came and dinner was ordered. "So, Mrs. Phillips," Joshua said as he buttered a piece of bread, "it's been a pleasure getting to know your husband over these last few months. And Savannah as well." He looked at me with that Cheshire cat grin. I turned my attention to the straw in my Coke and sucked in a burning mouthful. "What with our cubicles being side by side and all. So I would love for us to get to know each other better as well." He turned his attention back to her.

Amber scooted her chair closer to Joshua. "Oh, you will have to get to know Miss Victoria. She has been so wonderful to me. Just yesterday we went shopping, and she had so much good advice, about . . . well"—Amber giggled—"about men and, well, not just men, but work and life and all kinds of things. You could learn amazing things from her." She rubbed his shoulder.

He patted her hand and placed it gently yet firmly back by her plate.

Octopus might as well be on the menu.

"Yeah, you'll love Mother," I offered. "She's charming and witty and very respectful of people's private lives." I accentuated the last part to make my point clear.

"I like to get to know people intimately," she said, eyeing me. "So tell me all about yourself, Joshua."

And until dinner arrived, he did. And with every word, and every story, and every time he made her laugh, she melted more and more. And by the time dinner arrived, I was certain Victoria thought he would be a perfect lifetime mate. For her new daughter at least.

Dinner arrived, also perfect. Never before was there a better meal, except maybe Victoria's pork-loin roast with mashed potatoes and gravy. But resting before me, in a phyllo-dough tureen, was a layer of saffron rice covered in the most delicious buttered lump crab meat you'd ever want to taste. It is sinfully delicious. Most everyone ordered the same at mine and Dad's urging. Thomas sat conspicuously quiet on his side of the table, and Paige rarely talked during meals anyway. I eyed the two of them, thinking maybe she should marry Thomas. They both loved food. But what good was food if you only ended up killing your spouse?

"So what are your thoughts on marriage and children?" I heard come from the pink glittering mouth across the table.

I felt a lump of crab lodge itself in my nasal cavity.

Joshua looked at me. I think my face had turned blue. "Are you okay, Savannah?" he asked, reaching across the table and handing me my water.

Every eye turned to me. I did the Heimlich on myself and recovered with as much grace as possible. "Fine," I managed.

Joshua turned his attention back to Amber and spoke without hesitation. Why shouldn't he? He meant every word he was about to say. "I think marriage and children and family are one of life's greatest gifts." He caught my eye. I grabbed my water and didn't stop until I had gulped to the bottom and swallowed a lemon seed.

The table's attention turned to me again. "Savannah, you're going to choke again if you don't slow down," my father said, now patting my knee.

"Sorry," I sputtered, longing for something stronger. If I didn't fear my mother building an altar there in the middle of the restaurant and anointing me with olive oil, I'd have downed a bottle of wine all by myself. It was lost on her that Catholics and Presbyterians, and who knows, maybe even Methodists, actually had *wine* for communion. She thinks Jesus turned the water into Welch's.

"You were saying?" Amber said, after turning her glare from me and reconstructing her swoon for Joshua's benefit. The woman was brazen.

"I think family is wonderful. My parents divorced when I was in high school." I saw Mother twitch. "But I had a wonderful mentor who showed me what a real family looks like. Kind of like what Thomas and Savannah have with theirs."

"And me," Amber reaffirmed.

"Yes, please don't forget Amber." Thomas finally spoke. He turned his suspicion-filled eyes to me.

What? I gestured in return. I had gone to stabbing my crab meat and simply relocating it to other areas of my plate.

What? he mimicked with a shrug.

"Ah . . . ah . . . choo!" Amber spewed daintily.

"Bless you," Joshua said.

"I've got to refill my Viagra *prescription*," she said, emphasizing *prescription* so we'd know she got it right. She wiped her nose with a tissue.

Thomas and Paige gasped simultaneously.

Mother and Dad glanced at each other.

Joshua about choked himself. "Your what?"

"She means Allegra," I assured the rather aghast party. "It's Allegra, Amber. Allegra."

"Yeah, for my allergies." As if that's what she meant all along. "So do you like sports?" Amber asked.

"All men like sports!" I snorted, rather obnoxiously, I might add. Paige kicked me. "In fact, this table would be fabulous at soccer." I rubbed my leg and glared at her.

"Yes, it would," Dad agreed.

"And prime candidates for therapy," Thomas added. "Because you are all acting very odd tonight."

"We're not acting odd." I chuckled. "Who's acting odd?" I turned to Paige. "You see anybody odd?"

"I don't see anybody odd."

Thomas sat back in his chair and decided to leave us to our odd selves. Maybe because I reminded him with my eyebrow that I knew *his* secret.

"Mother went to therapy once," I blurted before I could stop myself.

"Savannah!" Mother said, clutching her chest.

"Well, you did!"

"What I do is not for public consumption. We have newspaper people here," she whispered, as if the man next to her couldn't hear her talk to me across the table.

"Ooh, I love therapy stories," Amber said, bouncing in her seat. "I have tons. You share Miss Victoria's. I'll share mine."

Dad grabbed my knee. But this just felt right, so I continued, "She started the day she left Dad."

Mother reached across the table, trying to grab me. "Savannah, you stop right now!"

"Savannah, you're pushing it," Dad replied, trying not to get a kick out of the whole thing.

"Oh, Mother, it's really cute."

"I'm finding absolutely nothing cute about it," she said through gritted teeth.

"We'll let Joshua judge," I offered.

"And me, oh, let me. I love to judge." Amber bounced again.

Paige was doing her best to contain herself. Which was a miserly offering.

"Mother had gotten mad at Dad—"

"Jake, I swear, if you don't stop her—"

"Mother, it is not nice to swear," I scolded.

"Savannah, you need to stop. You're not going to tell your mother's business here at the dinner table." This time he meant it. He knew every deficiency in the woman next to him. But they were not going to be told by someone else. Even if he himself knew how funny they were.

"Forgive me. I will not tell how my mother left you and rolled her luggage up the street only to find no room in the motel, and how Paige's mother had to pick her up and let her spend the night at their house, all of which forced her into *one* therapy session. I promise I will not tell that story."

"Savannah." His lip was quivering.

I patted his knee. "I know, Dad. That would be tacky."

The waitress came and removed our dishes, and I watched as what I had waited days for was taken out from under me with not much more than a nibble. I glared at the woman across from me.

"Okay, now me, me!" Amber said, still bouncing in her seat. No wonder the child weighed ten pounds. She couldn't stop moving.

"The first time I went to therapy . . ." Now Mother was casting her glaring looks that meant, *Child, you don't tell the man you want to father your children about your therapy visits.* Amber never noticed a thing. "It was right after the first time I lost the Miss Georgia United States of America pageant." A collective groan went up from Paige, Thomas, and me. Joshua listened like a perfect gentleman. Mother winced. Dad ordered another dessert. And Amber talked for the next fifteen minutes about the therapist who taught her how to look into the mirror and tell herself, "Hey, you. Look at me when I'm talking to you!"

That caused the whole table to crack up. Amber really was charming in a bizarre kind of way. And she was completely enamored with Joshua, who was as polite as I've ever seen a man be.

"Please join us for our evening stroll," Amber encouraged him as he pulled her and Mother's chairs out for them.

Now it was "our" evening stroll.

"Oh no, Amber. No evening stroll this evening."

I laughed. "Yeah, after last night's stroll, I'm not sure anyone would want to—"

"Savannah!" Mother and Dad called in unison.

I lowered my voice. "We're fasting from evening strolls. It's a personal thing."

Amber picked up a toothpick as we started out the door. Mother snatched it from her hand about the time she sucked a kernel of saffron rice from her tooth. "Women don't pick their teeth in public," Mother reproved.

"But I've got rice stuck—"

"I don't care. I don't care if you got rice stuck up your—" Mother restrained herself. "Throw it away," she said quietly, trying not to force attention.

Amber chunked it in the garbage.

Joshua's bike was sitting in the parking lot. "Do you want me to ride back with you?" Amber offered.

"Oh!" He tried to hide his shock. "No. I wouldn't want you to have to do that."

"I don't mind, really," she cooed.

Thomas touched her arm and spoke up. "That's okay, I'm going to walk his bike back with him. I'd love to get to know him a little better." Amber pouted at Thomas. No love was flowing between those two.

"It was a pleasure to spend the evening with all of you," Joshua said. He shook Dad's hand and gave my mother a tender hug.

"Oh . . . well, uh-huh, it was a pleasure spending the evening with you too, Joshua," she said, trying not to let her orange-red lipstick spread from ear to ear.

"I hope all my mistakes are water under our bridge."

She smiled. "Just don't make me build any more bridges."

He laughed. "I'll do my best." He reached for Amber's hand, and she threw her arms around his neck. His responder couldn't respond quick enough to prevent that one, so he patted her back. Then he gave Paige a hug and turned to me. I reached for his hand and shook it vehemently. "Great to see you, Joshua." I reached up and slapped him on his arm like two players in a huddle.

"You too." He took my hand between his and held it softly. I tried to prevent my body from melting. And it was virtually impossible. "I'll call you soon," he mouthed.

I nodded as imperceptibly as possible.

As everyone climbed into the car, Thomas whispered in my ear. "You owe me, Vanni." I raised my right eyebrow. In my mind we were even. "You owe me big."

He knew. He always knew.

"Happy families are all alike; every unhappy family is unhappy in its own way."

"So how long?" Thomas asked as he laid himself across the foot of Paige's bed. Catching sight of her face covered in a cucumber mask about sent him toppling off the side. "My word, woman, what is that?"

She stuck out her tongue. The only colored item on her albino face. "Amber gave it to me. She said it would transform me in fifteen minutes."

"Dream—"

"Shut up!" she retorted.

He turned his attention back to me. "So, how long?"

I laid my book across my chest and cocked my head at him. "How long what?"

"How long have you been crazy about that man?"

I huffed. "You're so silly."

"I'm so owed after saving your man from having to tote Miss Attached at the Hip home on his bicycle built for one."

I grinned at him. "I really appreciate it. So now we're even. And what did he say?" I sat up in the bed and leaned in Thomas's direction.

"He said Amber looked hot!"

I threw my pillow at him. Paige kicked him with her feet, which he had planted himself on. "Ow!" He laughed. "Actually, he said that you had been crazy about him since the day you met him."

"He did not." But I knew he had.

"He did too. But he did add that he had been crazy about you since then too."

"He did?"

"Yeah, he did. Why have you been keeping this a secret?"

Paige kicked him again. "Hello. Amber was the one who invited him to dinner, in case you forgot. Not Savannah."

"She knows he's not into her."

I laughed at his naiveté. "You've got to be kidding. That woman has no idea he is not completely taken with her. She's certain he is the man of her destiny."

"So tell her the truth."

"Oh, just like that? Prance myself right in there and tell her the truth?" I leaned back against the pillow between me and my plaid-padded headboard. "This coming from a boy who's scared of his mama."

"I'm not scared of my mom. I just want to enjoy my vacation. I'll tell her I broke up with Mary Francis after vacation."

"You and Mary Francis broke up?!" The howl came from the vision in orange, who was trying to hold herself up by the door casing. She clung to her orange-clad rat with her other arm.

Thomas's face went ashen. He refused to turn around and kept his eyes on me.

"Thomas Phillips, you will come into my room and tell me and your father what in the world you are thinking. That girl is marriage material. She's smart and comes from a wonderful home, and I've already picked out your wedding china!" She forgot Maggy was in her arms as they waved up and down.

He finally turned. "Mother, it is no big deal."

"No big deal? I've made plans. Called friends!"

"We weren't even engaged!"

"That was a mistake too! I'm not sure what it is with you and Savannah that you have such trouble finding and keeping love. With what me and your father have, you'd think you'd be love magnets."

Thomas stood up and took Maggy from Mother's arms before the hairball got thrown across the room. Maggy looked incredibly appreciative. For a moment I wondered if the poor thing even liked having to dress to match her mother. "Go to your room and relax," he said, patting her shoulder. "I'll be in there in a few minutes and we can talk about everything."

"Fifteen minutes, Thomas. You have fifteen minutes." And with that she turned around and walked away. We listened to her heels as they departed, only to hear them turn around and head back in our direction. We all held our breath. She returned only to snatch Maggy from Thomas's grip. I do believe Maggy reached her paws out for Thomas to save her, but it was too late. Mother's door slammed behind them.

"Like I said, you might want to get the truth on out there, or it will blow up in your face, sunshine," he said, leaning against the door. "But I do like him."

"You do?" I smiled.

"Yeah. If you can keep him, you will have outdone yourself."

Our pillows hit him simultaneously.

CHAPTER THIRTY-ONE

I hear something," Paige said, bolting upright in the middle of the bed.

I rubbed my eyes and let out a yawn. "You're dreaming," I reassured.

The *clingity-clang* came again. This time I bolted. "Oh my stars, what was that?"

"See, I told you I heard something," she whispered, trembling beneath her N 'Sync T-shirt. She had loved them since we saw them in concert our senior year in high school. When they sang "God Must Have Spent a Little More Time on You" and Lance Bass walked right up our aisle and touched her face. Ruined her for life. "I didn't think there were mass murderers in Seaside."

"Shhh . . . what if they hear us?"

"We better go get your dad." She slithered out of the bed so she couldn't be seen through the window. The next noise caused her to stop in her tracks. "Well, if it's a mass murderer, I guess he knows you by name." She turned toward the window. I cowered close behind.

"What are you doing here?" she yellspered to the curly-headed shadow standing below our window.

"Tell Savannah to come out here." I peeked from behind her shoulder. The only thing we could see were the whites of his teeth.

"He's got it bad," Paige said over her shoulder in my ear.

"Yeah, he does," I said, running to the closet and slipping a white T-shirt on over a brassiere. Who knows why I bothered? Then I climbed into some running shorts and my Nike rift tennis shoes. A tennis shoe that is as close to flip-flops as they come. I ran into the bathroom, brushed, rinsed, and spat, and pulled my hair back in a ponytail in record time. All done with a smile.

I tried to tiptoe down the stairs so I wouldn't disturb the house. Who wanted war before the sun rose? When I reached my mass murderer, he was armed with two bicycles.

"How did you get these here?"

"I walked them over."

Paige was still leaning out the window. "Bring her back before sunup," she said with a smile. But she still didn't move. She just watched us.

"There's something I want to show you. And you can only see it this time of day." He patted the top of the seat to the extra bicycle. "Hop on."

I hadn't straddled a bike seat since middle school. I wasn't even sure if I could remember how to ride. Paige had to stifle her laughter at my first attempt, which ran me into the neighbor's fence of honeysuckle. "Ow."

Joshua rode back over to me and put his hand on the handle bar to help steady me. "Haven't done this in a while, huh?"

"A while? Yes, I believe you could say a while."

The next attempt wasn't as ugly. I didn't collide with anything, but had anyone been watching (and I knew of two young sweethearts across the street who were, because I heard them giggle too), they would have been certain a drunk was on a bicycle headed up Seaside Avenue.

"Follow me," he whispered.

And so I did. I followed him out of Seaside and to the edge

of Water Colors. When he turned up the last street at the edge of Water Colors, and then up toward a small rock path, I realized how little I really did know this guy.

"There are unsolved murders all over Savannah," I said to myself. "Maybe he is the guy. Maybe I have come to the ocean to be mutilated and sent up the river in little pieces. Why did Paige let me go?" My pedaling feet were beginning to feel like lead.

He turned back to check on me, and I was certain his smile had grown sinister. Wicked even. "Sweet Lord above, please keep me safe. You know my life has enough issues. I really don't need death on my plate this morning," I whispered.

The small rock path led us down to a dock that crossed over a pond and then out into the middle of the Western Lake. He parked his bike. I pulled up behind him and discovered that my booty had been bruised. I leaned my bike slowly up against the railing and eyed this dark stranger curiously.

"The old gray mare ain't what she used to be," I said, limping away from the dock. I was certain I'd be sitting on a doughnut pillow for weeks.

He laughed. Okay, that was a little more soothing. "You don't ever ride?"

"And that could be lost on you how?" I retorted.

"Miss Phillips needs to toughen her tushy. Come down here," he said, walking to a small ladder that led to an attached floating dock.

Maybe this was it. Maybe he was going to push me off and hold me under. Maybe he really did have a thing for Amber and needed to get rid of me and planned to do it under the cover of darkness.

"You seem a little nervous. I'm not going to kill you or anything." He chuckled.

"Ha ha." I laughed nervously. "You're so funny." I climbed down the small ladder as he stood behind me, making sure I didn't fall. He had seen me knocked off of my feet more than a couple times, so I guess he figured I might need the extra protection. We sat down on the dock, and he reached over and took my leg. I wasn't sure what he was going to do. Maybe he would just cut off my leg first. I squinted. Then I heard the sound of Velcro coming undone on my shoes. He slipped off one and laid it beside me, followed by the other. Then he turned my legs toward the water and slipped my feet gingerly into the cool liquid. "Cold?" he asked.

I cracked one eye open. No death. No knife. "Not bad," I replied.

He slipped off his flip-flops and put his feet in the water as well. His legs curved over the plank board, allowing the muscles in his stunning thighs to reveal how perfectly perfect they actually were. If he were a murderer, he would have fallen in the Ted Bundy category. Then he stared in front of him. "Right over that dune, you'll see the sky change when the sun comes up. There are few things so beautiful." He looked at me.

"Ted Bundy was a charmer," I said it before I could stop myself.

"Excuse me? Did you say Ted Bundy?"

"Ha . . . no . . . I was saying, Fred Lundy was a farmer. I'm not sure why I was even thinking about that. It just popped into my head. Ever have things just go pop, pop, pop?" I said, flitting my head about. If he didn't plan on killing me, I might just fling my own self into the water.

"You're so odd," he said, his smile never leaving his face. He turned his focus back toward the dune that concealed the shore. "I've got some things to tell you." I could see the first bit of the morning chipping away at the night.

I moved my feet back and forth through the water, forcing the lapping water to hit the edges of the dock as it rocked slowly underneath us. "What things?"

"Just a lot of things I've been thinking about. After dinner last night, I'm absolutely certain of how I feel about you." He pulled his feet out of the water and placed them back on the dock, then turned his body so he could clutch his knees up to his chest and look at me.

I kept looking at my feet. "You've been declaring how you feel for two days now. Are you saying there's more? I'm not sure I can handle many more declarations."

"I am totally in love with you, Savannah, and everything about you. I think your dad is an amazing man. He's been so kind to me. Your mother, well, I think we actually made progress last night."

"That's because she thinks you like Amber. Trust me, if she knew it was me you were after, you would have begged for an interrogation by the entire cast of *Law & Order* in lieu of Victoria Phillips."

"I don't think so. I got a sense she detected something else was going on."

"Trust me, the only thing she detected was Amber's crazy about you, and she'll learn to like you for her sake. I know this woman, Joshua. She requires strategic maneuvering."

"Well, if she never does like me, it won't change how I feel about you." There was such an assurance in his eyes. So totally calm, obliterating my own insecurities.

I pulled my feet out of the water and mimicked his position. "I'm glad you're so confident. I'm just an influx of emotion here. And I don't know what to do with all of these feelings." I felt something I couldn't name rise in my throat. He reached over and took my hands. "I mean, one day I'm grieving the loss of what I thought was the love of my life, and the next day I'm staring into the face of a man who has stirred emotions I never even knew existed in me."

"I know you loved him, but don't you see how this is different?"

"Yes. I do now. I see that I never loved him the way I should have. And that I didn't treat him the way he deserved. And that I never felt about him the way I feel about you."

"So you're saying you love me?"

"I'm saying"—I raised my right eyebrow and smiled at him—"that things are happening in me I've shut myself off to for so long, I don't know how to decipher them all."

"And I want to help you decipher them. I want to help you realize that I'm here for the long haul, but I need to know you are too. I can't play games with Amber or with your mother. And you shouldn't either. I want to tell the world. And when we get back home, I don't want to sneak around and walk on eggshells, afraid someone might see me kissing you or holding your hand. I can't throw pebbles at your window forever." He laughed.

"Those aren't bad things."

"Savannah!"

"Okay, okay, you're right. I will tell them. I completely promise. Before we leave here, Amber and my mother and Mr. Modica if you want, will all know that you and I are . . ."

"Go ahead. You know you want to say it."

"That you and I are a perfect couple." I smiled.

"They'll all know?"

"My stars, do I need to take out an ad?" As soon as I said that, I realized the real horror of all of this was that my mother probably would. If not to congratulate me, then to seek all background information on Joshua.

"Ooh, look." He pointed back to the dune. "You don't want to miss this."

And I didn't. I wished I could etch the scene into my memory. Every feeling. Every sight. As morning began to push back the lingering remnants of yesterday, I knew Joshua and I would be different after today as well. We could never go back to the way we were. We had crossed a chasm, and the bridge had collapsed. And I had no desire to build a new one.

I looked at him. He could still be Ted Bundy. But I tried to assure myself he would have acted before now. "You know," I said, looking down to inspect my wet feet, "the way you kiss me . . . it really is different than anything I've felt before. I mean, Grant never kissed me that way. And well, I've never really kissed anyone else. Do you think that's crazy?" I asked, feeling my face flush.

"No, I don't think that's crazy. I think that is rather special."

"Well, I've just always thought that was something you only share with people you really care about. And I've never really cared about anyone other than the two of you. I mean, here I am, Miss All I've Done Is Kiss! Miss Saving Myself for the Perfect Man!" I laughed nervously.

"You mean you and Grant were never intimate?" he asked.

"Of course not!" I responded rather passionately, just about scaring myself. "My mother scared me about that years ago. She said, 'Darling, boys will tell you anything to get what they want, then they'll get it and they'll leave.' I completely believed her. So, no, no, no . . . no touchy . . . no nothing."

I noticed his countenance change. Serious. His teeth bit down on the underside of his upper lip, pulling it in harelip style.

"What? You . . ."

He finally spoke, but didn't really look at me. "Celeste and I were together for quite a few years. We were really close."

"How close might that have been?" I felt my right eyebrow begin to creep up. I tried to make it come back down. It refused.

His nervous laugh frightened me. "What are you asking exactly?"

"I'm asking, *howww cloooose* were you and Celeste?"

"Are you asking if we were intimate?" He cocked his head.

"I would say that is exactly what I'm asking."

"Well, since we need to be completely honest with each other . . ." He tried to hide his growing discomfort. "I guess you do need to know that we were intimate."

My heart sank. I felt the stinging of tears creep their way to the corner of my eyes. A pressure collided with my chest with a thud. I was officially having a heart attack. Why slice and dice me when you could just give me a coronary?

"We were together for three years, Savannah." As if that were some kind of condolence. "It shouldn't completely surprise you. And it was before . . ."

"Before what?! Before you thought about it? Before me? Before all of this?" I said, flinging my arms through the air. I could feel myself overreacting, but I didn't know how to rein my emotions in.

He was perfectly calm through my tirade. "Actually I was going to say, before I made the decision that that wasn't what I wanted for my life. That I wanted to wait until *I* met the one I would spend the rest of my life with. So, since her, there has never been anyone else."

"Do you want me to lick a gold star for your achievement chart?" I stood up, which caused the dock to sway underneath me, forcing my knees to almost give way. Or maybe it was the weight of the pressure of this moment that was about to do me in.

"Don't be catty, Savannah. This is serious, and I'm trying to be as honest with you as I can," he said, rising behind me.

"I've never been with anyone, Joshua!" I screeched as the tears burned my eyes and as the lump overtook my throat. Just making it a little more clear. Volume did increase clarity, didn't it? "I've saved myself my entire life for one night, one man. Call me *crazy*!" And anyone who was watching this entire episode certainly would have. "Or call me *lucky*—that seems to be the word for the week. But I've had a vision for my life and the man who would love me, and what it would be like to never have to worry about memories or comparisons or old emotional ties." Then I paused. But it still came out. Unfortunately it always comes out. "But with you I will never know *any* of that, now, will I?"

His eyes registered immediate hurt. But I didn't care, because the tears I had been trying to conceal were running rampantly down my cheeks. And the tenor of my voice had risen about three decibels in volume and pitch. "I'm sorry, Savannah. I never dreamed . . . this is too much for you to handle right now, obviously."

"You think?" I snapped.

"Yes, I think," he said, so Joshua calm. "I think you obviously had expectations that I will never be able to fill for you. And I think you need to take some time and let all of this digest and see what you need to do with it. But you do need to know something: I've made mistakes in my life and this won't be the last one, I assure you. So, if you're looking for perfection, you won't find it here. But I've also made restitution for those mistakes. And I've dealt with them with the only One who has ultimate authority over them. And He hasn't held them over my head. I can't ask you to change your dream. I can only let you know that I've gotten the forgiveness necessary for me to move on. You'll have to decide if you can live with that." He reached out to touch me one more time. I flinched. He withdrew. And the look on his face would cause me a thousand heartbreaks. But it didn't matter. I had waited. He had caved. Good thing I found out sooner rather than later.

He climbed the stairs with a much different stature than he had come down. He walked silently to his bike and pedaled away, leaving me there on the dock, alone, in the blazing morning sun, with nothing but my *lucky* self. Had I been able to grasp the hands of Father Time, I would have wrenched them backward until they broke. But, yes, this had officially become a moment from which I could never return.

CHAPTER THIRTY-TWO

The entire city of Seaside had grown quiet. Well, to be honest, no one was even awake yet, but it was all the same to me. Death by silence. The only sound I heard was the rubber of my tires as they met the brick-laid streets. Everything looked different on the ride back to the house. My Technicolor world had been swallowed by the land of black-and-white. My life was black-and-white. This was wrong. The choice he made was wrong. And just like that he had taken with him all the color that I had finally been enjoying after such a season of shadows.

The breeze stuck the salty tears to my face. Dad and Mr. Modica were sitting at a table in front of the market, having coffee. Dad threw up a hand to wave as I pedaled through the Town Center. My arm was too heavy to lift. The only thing I could raise was my eyebrow. I saw Dad's brow furrow. When I reached the gate to the house, I leaned the bike up against the white picket fence. And as I closed it behind me, I shut out my last hopes for a *Leave It to Beaver* life. I had just arrived in reality television. And it was all too real.

"Savannah Phillips, where have you been? I know you are not just getting home." My mother's tone bounced off my numb self.

I wanted to throw myself into the shrubbery at the side of the walk.

Amber followed her out the front door.

Maybe death *would* have been sweeter than this.

"Oh my side, Savannah!" Amber's singsong voice tried to penetrate my stare. "Were you out all night with your new fella?"

Mother's hand flew up to her face. "Oh my Lord, have mercy, my daughter is a hoochie-mama. You finally meet another man, and down come all your standards!" I felt the heat in my face begin to rise.

"I was not out all night, and I am not a hoochie-mama," I said, trying to make my way down the walk.

Mother blocked the stairs. "You will tell me who you were with, young lady, and you will tell me now." I might have taken her a lot more seriously had she not been holding Maggy, who wore a silk bandana that matched the eye mask still perched atop Mother's head. Obviously she was having trouble sleeping.

"I will tell you no such thing, because you are accusing me of something I haven't done. I'm not going to lie. I was out with someone. Someone I was going to introduce you to, but there is absolutely no reason to now. So, if you'll excuse me, I'm going back to bed and may never arise."

I pushed past her.

"Ooh, I think I'm having chest pains!" I heard Mother say.

"Sit, Miss Victoria, sit. Not you, Magnolia!"

I let the door slam behind me.

"You want a Coke?" the face asked as it knelt down by the side of my bed. I had buried my face in my pillow.

I lifted my head to look up. I blew a lone hair out of my eye. "No."

"No Coke? What happened in the span of an hour that is so completely horrific?"

"I don't feel like talking." I turned my head to the other side of my pillow.

Paige would not be denied. She walked around. "You have to tell me. I'm the only one whose relationships go south in the span of less than a week. Yours last for decades."

"I've only had one," I mumbled.

"Which lasted for a decade. I rest my case."

"This one's not worth talking about. This one's over, and it never should have started. And you should be happy now, because I'll be all yours again," I said, trying to fight back the welling tide of tears.

She rubbed my head and then slapped it.

"Ow!"

"That's what you get for being so stupid. I don't want you to be alone and pathetic like me. I want us both to be happy and enraptured like you. The last thing in the world I want is both of us crying on our pillows." She sat down on the floor in front of my face. "Now you have to get a grip and tell me what is going on. It can't be so bad to justify such words."

"It is that bad." I cried. "He's a whoremonger."

She screeched with laughter. "He's a what?"

"He is, and don't laugh. He's been with that girlfriend of his. The one who is about to get married."

"Been with how? Movies, carpools, what?"

"Don't be stupid."

"He's slept with her?"

"Yes, why would I call him a whoremonger if he hadn't slept with her?"

She wiped her face. "Please try not to spit on me."

"Sorry," I blubbered.

"Sleeping with a onetime girlfriend does not a whoremonger make. At least I don't think it does. Does it?"

"It does to me. It's one too many."

"Savannah, I know you've never been with any man, but most men have been with a woman." This is how Paige comforts me.

"So, all the virgins are gone?" I wailed. "Well, we should just make T-shirts that declare it so!"

"Well, let's not get drastic. I was thinking a billboard would do." I hated her. She made me laugh when I didn't want to. "You're hurt. I understand that. You've waited a long time for some nooky."

"You did not just say nooky!"

"Well, what did you want me to say? Lovin'? Hanky-panky? Rafter raising?"

"I want you to not say anything else." I sat up and pulled the pillow that I had soaked to my chest.

"I know you've saved yourself. And that is your greatest treasure to give to the man you love. But had it never occurred to you that you might meet and fall in love with a man who had already been with someone else?"

"No." That was completely honest.

"Oh, my sweet sister Savannah," she said, rising to sit on the bed and rub my head.

I raised my hand in defense. "Do not hit me again."

"I'm not going to hit you, crazy." She kissed the top of my head, which had nestled itself under her arm. "He's a good man. He has a kind heart and is a wonderfully decent guy. Not everything in life will turn out like you want it to. But not all things that seem bad at the moment are bad in the long run. Good can always be found. Especially when your motives are pure. Now, let's walk and get a Coke."

"I really don't feel like that right now."

She got off the bed, and I could see the affection in her eyes. "I'm sorry you're so hurt. It breaks my heart to see you cry."

"But—"

"But nothing. This is the man created for you. It's as clear as the tiara attached to Amber's head. So, I warn you, be careful what you reject while you're seeking perfection." And with that she left me with my self. My perfectly cataclysmic self.

They abandoned me for Nicole Kidman. She was playing in a new movie, and they all decided to go. Mother and Amber both stared at me with suspicion as they left. I stared at Thomas and Paige with suspicion as they left. And Dad just kissed me on the top of the head as he left.

It was all fine for two reasons. First, because it meant I could be alone. Second, because my mother had become addicted to Kernel Season's popcorn shakers. Her favorite: parmesan and garlic. Can I just say once she starts, you don't want the woman anywhere near you. You can smell that stuff three rows down and over. Truth be told, for a woman who doesn't eat anything out of a box, I was surprised she even tried it.

"This is a seasoning, Savannah, not a food product," she claimed.

Whatever a food product is.

As all things Victoria, when she likes it, she likes it big. Or in multiples. Finds a pair of shoes she likes, buys them in every color. Finds a suit that fits perfectly, usually comes home with two. Finds a popcorn shaker that can raise the peach fuzz on a newborn and, well, let's just say the movie theater doesn't run out. Thus, not having to sit beside that putrid smell for two hours was reason enough to be glad.

The Adirondack chair held me perfectly. The book lying across my lap hadn't been opened all afternoon. Who did that surprise? So this was my time. I noticed the young couple across the street but refused to let them distract me. Their parents must have gone to a movie too. They were sitting on the front porch singing to each other. I'd never heard any of the songs before, but that didn't surprise me either. A twenty-four-year-old who loved Barry Manilow and Donny Osmond obviously didn't get out much. Or just didn't get out anymore. They giggled and nuzzled and made me want to throw up. I even threw a couple rocks at them to get them to shut up. They were completely oblivious. And partially hidden by the dark screen of the porch and the sumac planted in their front yard.

I gave a glance up the street, both ways, just to make sure. I even looked back in the house to make sure Maggy was in her kennel, alive. She was, and Duke was at my feet. All was okay. I could now begin. *"Happy families are all alike; every unhappy family is unhappy in its own way."*

I heard the sound of the little voices before I caught a glimpse of the stroller. The pair of little feet dangled and bounced in time with the bumps of the street and were followed by Adam.

I looked at my book and huffed, slamming it shut and darting down the walkway. "Hey, Adam," I chided.

He stopped the stroller by the fence. He never said a word. Just stared at me blankly.

"I talked to Kate." I could see the puffiness in his eyes. I had no sympathy, because I knew they were equally matched by the puffiness of my own, caused by another scoundrel.

"You did?"

"Yeah. And she told me the real reason for your separation."

He stared at me with the most pathetic expression. I almost felt sorry for him for a moment, but my own turmoil refused it. He didn't reply.

"Yeah, she told me all about it, and frankly, she deserves better than that, Adam. I just can't believe you. She is one of the most beautiful and loving women I know."

"Savannah, I really don't want to talk about this today." I

could hear a break in his voice. "It's over anyway. She's served me with divorce papers. Think what you will, but I've done everything I know to do. I've apologized. I've begged. I got rid of that girl immediately. But none of it means anything to Kate. Nothing is enough."

I thought the poor man was going to cry right there. I could feel my tone soften. "There are some hurts too hard to forgive, Adam. Some consequences that leave people unable to deal with the memories."

"Well, you're right. So this is how my life is going to be now, and I have to live it the best I can. But in my heart . . ." He paused, and I saw the deep pain in his eyes that even the tears couldn't hide. "In my heart I just hope that she can forgive me and let me come home and be a husband to her again, and a father to these beautiful boys."

You could hear the kids jabbering, oblivious to the sorrow that surrounded them. "Well, it's just a shame it all turned out this way. Your family was perfect."

"Nothing's perfect," he said. Then he pushed the stroller up the street amid the sounds of little boys being little boys. I'm sure he wished he could have avoided the severity of his growing pains. When would they learn?

CHAPTER THIRTY-THREE

Abigail at Aquarius Spa pummeled my body into submission.

"How firm would you like your massage?" she asked.

"Beat me," I replied.

She laughed. "Hard day?"

"Hard life."

"You're way too young," she said over the recorded sounds of the ocean in the background.

"I know. All the more cruel is the world we dwell in."

And for the next hour there was no more talking. By the time I left, every part of my body was relaxed. Too bad she couldn't massage the furrow from my brow.

The slamming of the car trunk caught my attention. "Savannah!" Lucy hollered with a wave. "You've got to come meet my kids." The one who was lugging the beach chairs from the trunk he had just slammed must have been one of the twins.

Because child number three was the only boy. Or maybe he was the boyfriend of one of the girls.

The last thing in the world I felt like being today was Miss Social. I wasn't Vicky, who could be social regardless of how she felt. Or Amber, who was never upset enough *not* to be social. Even through her tears she was social. But me? Not happy, not social.

"Come on," she crooned. "I've told them all about you."

I made my legs turn in the direction of her house. There was an entire village sitting on the front porch. Three children, one boyfriend, and one girlfriend. Too many names for me to remember. But they were stunning people. The twins with exotic features and captivating dark eyes. But the baby had mousy brown hair and blue eyes and seemed out of place with this lot. Her golden skin tone even more so. But she had her mother's dimpled chin. And her smile. She was evidently theirs with a distant grandmother thrown in.

They kept me for dinner. I resisted. They insisted.

And when the smell of grilled shrimp and sizzling steaks filled the air, I realized I hadn't had a bite to eat all day and was starving. The crew up the street at my house would have wanted details of *my* day. The crew on Natchez Street let me listen to the tales of *their* life. And what an exciting life it was.

There was a concert pianist who was a Harvard graduate, a medical school student, and the baby was the senior class president of her high school. She and I talked campus policy for an hour, and I threw in my own presidential expertise from my senior year of college. She was quick-witted and crazy about her dad. She patted him softly every time she passed him. Teased him throughout the dinner conversation and called him Daddy. And the feeling was mutual. He called her baby and lit up like a runway during a snowstorm every time she called his name. And Lucy watched the whole thing with the admiration of a proud mother.

She hovered over them like a mother hen, and they teased her accent, theirs being virtually nonexistent. They told me stories of how she and Manuel met and how life had treated them kindly. And when the last dish was taken to the kitchen for washing, Lucy and I were the only two left on the front porch.

"Aren't they great?" She smiled as she gazed across the street.

"They're wonderful. And beautiful. But I do believe that baby girl must be the milkman's," I said with a laugh. A strange silence passed between us. I turned to look at Lucy's beautiful face. It had grown solemn and pensive. "I'm sorry, Lucy. I was just joking. I shouldn't have said that. It was very thoughtless of me."

She never turned my way and spoke with no inflection. "Actually, her father was a banker."

I chuckled nervously. "Manuel was never a banker." I nudged her.

She turned and looked at me and smiled softly. "Manuel isn't Alexandra's father. Her father was a banker. A banker who was my boss when I was teller. A six-month affair led to Alexandra."

I heard myself gulp. I was certain she did as well.

She laid her hand across mine on the armrest of my rocker. "The banker had an eye for women and a thousand-dollar-a-day drug habit. And I was lonely and made a terrible mistake that led to one of my greatest treasures. When I found out I was pregnant, I felt surely it was Manuel's until she was born. And then I knew. Manuel knew too."

She turned her gaze back across the street but left her hand atop my own. "I confirmed both of our fears, even though I stopped the affair as soon as I found out I was pregnant. By the time Alexandra was born, her birth father had lost his job at the bank and was serving two years in prison on drug charges. I told him he had a daughter. He told me he didn't care. A year after he was released, he died of an overdose in a crack house on a borrowed sofa."

She stopped, causing me to feel like I needed to say something. But I had absolutely nothing to say.

"When I found out I was pregnant, the news gave new life

to my marriage. It was as if Manuel and I were newlyweds. And when he found out she wasn't his, and the truth of the affair, he was completely devastated. He moved out. I did nothing but ask his forgiveness every day, begging him to come home. And one day, with no phone call and no indication that he would return, he shows up on the doorstep with his bags, and he takes me in his arms and tells me he forgives me. And from that day forward he loved Alexandra as if she were his own. And on the day we found out her father had died, he set into motion the legal efforts to adopt her." She turned to look at me again. "And that is why Alexandra looks like the milkman," she said with a wink.

I sat in silence for what seemed like an entire century. Finally I spoke. "I don't know what to say, Lucy."

"What is there to say, Savannah? I made a tremendously devastating and wrong decision. And somehow grace turned it into one of my life's greatest blessings. All I know is I'm amazingly grateful. Had I been married to any other man, Alexandra and I would have been put out on the street to figure out life for ourselves. But instead, God gave me a man who loved me at my most unlovely moment. And he loved the little girl that came with me."

"How could you do that to Manuel?"

She registered no shock. "Selfishness. Stupidity. All the reasons affairs happen. Because you think someone will love you better, deeper. Then you realize that anything created out of disobedience only leads to disaster. And no matter how fulfilled you may think you'll be, you end up with a thousand other moments that leave you empty and confused and wishing you could turn life back to the place before you were tainted and used."

"But didn't you love Manuel?"

She laughed softly. "I loved him madly. And hated him at the same time. I thought this would make everything better."

"Maybe you shouldn't have married Manuel. Maybe he wasn't the one."

The dimple in her chin deepened as she smiled. "Oh, he was

the one. But even if I thought he wasn't, he became the one the day I married him. That's just how it is. No excuse I wanted to apply to our marriage would have made my decision right. I've heard a thousand excuses out of the mouths of people who have affairs. 'He doesn't treat me the way I should be treated,' they say. None of that matters. I am responsible for every decision I've ever made. And I am responsible for the commitment I made to Manuel the day I promised to love him until death do us part. I broke that promise. It was wrong. And I have paid a heavy price for it."

"But you seem so in love," I asked, bewildered.

"We are in love," she said patting my hand and looking into my eyes. "More in love than we've ever been before. We almost lost everything. And when people almost lose everything, they realize how much there is to lose. And neither of us ever want to know what that feels like again. That man makes me weak. He makes me better. He makes me, well, me."

Footsteps came up behind us, and fair-skinned hands offered us two bowls of home-churned peach ice cream. Alexandra placed them in our laps and then sat on the stairs at our feet. Lucy and I ate in silence while Alexandra jabbered away, and as she talked I thought of Adam, and I saw him differently in that moment. I saw him like Lucy. When I got up to leave, they all waved goodbye from the front porch. And I noticed Alexandra waved just like her father. Her father, Manuel.

I heard music coming from the amphitheater as I headed back toward the house. The sounds came from the play *The Fisherman and His Wife,* presented by the Seaside Repertory Theater. Families were laid out on their Seaside beach blankets from the Seaside store, while some kids rolled down the hill. Others sat in their lawn chairs, which came in all colors and styles. An older couple had chairs that looked like La-Z-Boys, while another couple's chairs could have sung the national anthem. I smelled beer and aloe.

All had come to enjoy the first play of the summer season. And by the looks on the kids' faces, the large marlin on stage and the animated actors and actresses had not disappointed. The lights that lit the stage illuminated most of the faces and spotlighted the American flag that flies atop the post office. The music from Bud & Alley's could be heard in the background as well. But the spring delights fell on tired ears and failed to rally my spirit.

These ears had been through it over the last twenty-four hours. I had heard things I had no desire to hear. And now as I sat down on the grass, weary, I watched as lovers old and young held hands, and children made from bonds of love created their own entertainment. Perusing the crowd, I saw Curly Locks's curls across the lawn. They were still and motionless. And then they got up and walked dejectedly back toward Proteus.

My heart wanted to follow. My self-righteousness held me still.

The yapping was unmistakable. The little mongrel was sporting a Tommy Hilfiger dress, and its backside was sticking out of a pentas plant, where it had apparently gone to explore and gotten hung up.

"I think bridesmaids dresses in pink are the way to go. You know, the blush shade like Julia Roberts's character chose in *Steel Magnolias*." Amber's voice rose over the dusk and the yapping. Even the sound of the swarming locusts, which had eaten up the very threads of my heart, were drowned out by her vibrant vibrato.

"Why did you buy a wedding book?" Paige retorted. "Joshua hasn't even asked you out on a date. You're out of control."

Mother was oblivious to the conversation because she was picking red petals from the pink outfit of her progeny.

"I am going to need this book someday, Paige, with someone. You are the one who thinks I got this because of Joshua. Ooh, Savannah look! Look! I just got this at the bookstore. What do you think? Don't you think every girl should be prepared for the day she gets married?" She waved her new purchase in my face.

Paige jerked her from my line of sight, then jerked the book from her hand. "Because I like you, Amber, I'm going to urge you to sit down and shut that book."

"It's just a book about weddings," Mother finally chimed in as she mounted the stairs, wiping off Magnolia's pink toenails. "Every girl should dream of such, but you better be thinking in the far distant future, Amber." Mother gave her that look.

Maybe my mother wasn't crazy after all.

"And every girl should be saving themselves for their wedding day as well." She eyed me on that one.

Okay, so she was crazy.

I opened the screen door to leave them all to their thoughts of wedded bliss.

"What's wrong with our Savannah?" Amber inquired.

"She's hormonal," Paige responded.

"Ooh, is this the week for that monthly visitor, Mrs. Not So Friendly?"

"Sure. Whatever you say, Amber. Whatever you say."

CHAPTER THIRTY-FOUR

The first promise of morning touched my pillow. The newborn rays of sun caressed my face. I had fallen asleep lying across my bed, fully clothed. I could still hear the chatter from the front porch when I had drifted off into a fitful sleep. This morning, my head felt as if an earthquake had rattled my brain for the duration of the night. I slipped into the shower quietly. Of course, the eruption of Mount Saint Helen wouldn't wake Paige. The smell of a man's cologne could raise her from the dead, but the pitter-patter of my feet wouldn't even roll her over. The water cascading over me reminded me that reality really was as bad as it seemed. But no matter how miserable I felt, I would feel far more miserable if I ever had to endure something like what Manuel had endured in his life. Or what Kate and Adam were experiencing at this very moment. No, reality may feel like the pounding of a hurricane right now, but if I could hold on, I could weather the storm and avoid a worse battering in the future.

My wet ponytail flopped on the back of my neck, causing a portion of my T-shirt to become moist against my skin. Duke must have already been out with Dad, because he never made his way to the door. So I headed straight up Seaside Avenue and toward the Town Center to see if they were in their usual spot. And that was the only reason I went that direction. Just to check on Duke. I'm serious. It was for no other reason at all.

Dad was sipping coffee with Mr. Modica in front of the market. It was the crack of dawn, so I'm sure they were already fully vested in each other's accounts of the previous evening. I almost wondered how these men survived the other fifty-one weeks of the year that they didn't share their coffee together.

"Savannah, you look a little tired this morning," Mr. Modica said, his snow-white beard moving below his small curved lips.

"Why don't you join us, baby girl," Dad said, patting the seat next to him.

"Sit down with your father here," Mr. Modica said, standing up and holding the back of his chair for me.

"I can't risk seeing Joshua," I said, scanning the streets, wondering where his curls might pop up.

"He's come and gone," Dad said, taking a sip of his coffee and reaching over to pat Duke's head.

"Oh really? Already? Well, that's as it should be." I sat down slowly. Mr. Modica pushed my chair under and patted me firmly on both shoulders. "Mr. Modica, may I ask you a question?"

"It's my day off from questions," he said. "But not from statements." So he gave one. Of course. "He's a fine boy, Savannah. Those don't come along often." Then he sighed a heavy sigh. "Well, back to the rest of the world."

Yet none of his world was awake yet. They never were. Just him and Jake and a few other insomniacs who meandered through.

The metal seat beneath me felt cold. Everything had felt cold since I watched Joshua's curls bounce their way right out of my life. Even the Southern humidity felt cold without him.

"How was he?" I asked nonchalantly.

"About as pathetic as you."

"Really? Oh, who cares . . . and I don't want any of your

advice this morning. Just keep that for your little blackboard at your coffee shop."

"I don't have advice for you. But I do have this." He reached into a brown paper bag and pulled out a Coke.

I almost cried. "How did you know I would be here?"

"I didn't. Joshua did. And he bought this and said to give it to you when you got here. He's crazy about you, you know." He rubbed the side of his cup but never took his eyes off of me.

"Well, like I said, it's a beautiful morning, and we don't need to worry ourselves with Joshua. So, how was your movie?" I asked. I took a sip of the Coke and let it burn all the way down. Maybe it would burn out the yuck in the pit of my gut.

"It was good."

"You know, this wasn't how I wanted to spend my vacation."

He chuckled. He knew I was incapable of *not* talking about it. "I'm sure it wasn't."

"I mean, my life was perfectly fine until he showed up and wrecked it."

"You're overreacting, Savannah."

"How do you even know? You don't even know what I'm so angry about."

"Yes, I do actually."

I felt the last swig of Coke shoot up into my nostrils and singe the nose hairs. "You do not!"

He looked at me calmly. "Yes, I do. Joshua told me everything."

"There is no way he told you *everything*."

"He told me that he had been intimately involved with his last girlfriend. The one who is getting married this weekend. The one that you saw him kiss. The one you jumped to conclusions about."

I felt my jaw come unhinged. "He told you all of that?"

"Yes, he told me all of that. And then he asked me to forgive him for hurting you."

"He asked you what?"

"You heard me."

"And what did you say?"

"I told him that if he felt he needed my forgiveness, then he had it."

"Why does everything have to be forgiven?" He took a sip of his coffee. He loved to make me wait, because he knew I'd get impatient and ask another question. "Plus, if you forgive, then you're basically saying it's okay."

"No, I'm not. That's absurd. Forgiveness is releasing. Letting something go. Or letting someone else go from their own mistakes. Just like the city let you go from that first horrible article you wrote. They did that because you asked them to forgive you."

"Well, that could be debated. I still get hostile letters."

"He's a wonderful man, Savannah. A man who loves you, I might add. Though I'm not sure why."

"What did you just say?"

"I said I'm not sure why. You've hidden him all week from your mother and Amber. You're holding something over his head that he dealt with years ago and was forgiven of by a far greater authority than yourself. And now you're worried about *your* precious little vacation being ruined. A vacation, I might add, that is actually mine, that you claimed you were coming on because you needed to work. So, like I said, maybe you don't deserve Joshua."

"I cannot believe I'm hearing this!" I threw my hands up in the air for added measure. "I have waited all my life for the man of my dreams, to give him the gift of myself. And let me add for the record I cannot believe that I am even having this conversation with my father. If I leave this conversation scarred, you will pay the therapy bills. *I* am the one who didn't cave in those moments with Grant, when I could have, I might add, because I am a very desirable woman, and *I'm* the one who doesn't deserve *him*?"

"I believe that is what I said."

"So, you don't think, after the hell of losing Grant, having to move back near my mother, and suffering through her interference in my life, you don't think I have a right to be upset that my vacation has been held hostage by a blubbering beauty queen and a man who can't keep his britches up?"

Dad stood, and I could see the minutest amount of seething in his eyes. I'm not sure I had ever seen that look on his face before. He took Duke by the leash firmly and spoke to him instead of me. "I'm going to give the frightened little girl in front of me a vacation from the back of my hand, only because I know she's scared to death. But she better not talk about my wife that way again. Because she is a mother who loves her daughter very much. And you're just scared, Savannah. You're scared of loving anyone completely. Because the last relationship you gave your heart to didn't work out the way you thought it would. Well, not everyone or everything will, Savannah. Not everything will run according to the Savannah playbook." I felt the hot tears burn their way into my eyes. I blinked hard, refusing to allow another dam to break in the same twenty-four-hour period. "You're even scared that Amber is trying to come in and steal the love your mother and Joshua and I have for you, and for you alone."

I puffed.

"But that can never happen." He started walking off with Duke, then turned around to add one final thought. "And remember this, baby girl, the junk in your life and the junk in Joshua's life aren't really all that different when you compare them to the holiness of the One who forgives them both. They're both just pretty much junk."

He left me there. Staring at his backside. His always right backside. Wishing I could kick it. Or kick myself. I kicked the table instead. "Ow!" I hollered.

Who knew mornings could last so long. I wish Duke would have stayed with me. At least then my angst would have a companion. I rounded the corner of Natchez Street. I saw

Manuel and Alexandra sitting on the front porch and could hear their laughter from the street.

"You won again!" She laughed.

"I can't help it!" He chuckled in response. "You took your hand off. You can't take your hand off."

"Hey, Savannah," Alexandra called out.

Oh, for a less memorable face. "Hey, Alexandra."

"Want to join us? My dad always wins, but you can still play. Maybe together we can take him down."

"I could use some aggression release this morning," I said, joining them on the porch. We played cards for well over an hour, and I listened as they talked and laughed and Manuel gave advice and Alexandra gave way too much information to us both. But it was beautiful and perfect and unbelievable that he could love her so.

She left us for a few moments to talk on her cell phone.

"You look like you've had a bad morning already," Manuel observed as he scooted his chair back and propped his feet up on the table.

"I'm having a bad run of it lately, to be honest." I scooted my chair back as well.

"Lucy told me you and Joshua have had a temporary crisis."

"Temporary?" I coughed. "I'm not sure about that."

He put his hands behind his head. "She also said the two of you had an interesting talk last night."

"Interesting might be an understatement. I mean, you're amazing, Manuel. The way you love Alexandra. The way you act like you're so in love with Lucy."

"It's not an act, Savannah. We're more in love now than we've ever been. Difficult seasons often do that." He removed his hands from behind his head and placed them in his lap.

"But how? How could you love her after all that she did? How could you take her daughter and make her your own?"

"Because there are two options in life, Savannah. You can live with regret and bitterness, or you can forgive. I chose to forgive."

"But how do you forgive, well, all of that?" I said, waving into the wind.

"I didn't have an option." He put his feet down and leaned on the table, letting his deep ebony eyes peer into mine. They looked like Joshua's.

"But you just said you had two options."

He ran his hand through his thick black hair. "I said *there are* two options. I only had one. Forgiveness is the only option for my life. There was no other option for me. I've been forgiven of too much myself, Savannah. And forgiveness is the only way for me to continually be forgiven. If I don't give it, I don't get it. And I make mistakes every day. When I lose my temper—"

I chuckled. "I can't imagine you losing your temper."

"That's because you saved that gate from my wrath that first day we met." He smiled. "And I need forgiveness when I'm impatient, and I need forgiveness when forgiving is the last thing I feel like giving."

"But it's so hard." I leaned my forehead on the table.

I felt his hand rub the top of my head, like my father used to do before he started seething at me. Maybe I'd better refrain from excessive criticism of his wife. "Yeah, it's real hard. And there are times you'd just rather wallow and moan and get angry then forgive. But withholding it only destroys you."

I lifted my head. "But what did you do, I mean, after you found out? You had to have some sort of reaction."

"Oh, I reacted all right." He looked across the street, remembering. "I cried. I screamed. I threw a few dishes. I did all the things men never do, because this is never supposed to happen to a man. Affairs are what men do, not women. And then I looked into the face of the woman that I've loved since I can remember, and when she asked me to forgive her—and I could tell she meant it with everything inside of her—then I went away so I could think about it."

"Ooh, good one." I laughed.

"Well, I had to know that her repentance was genuine and not just desperation."

"How were you sure?"

He leaned into me, and his eyes got big as he whispered, "I was brutal."

I leaned in and whispered back, "What did you do?"

"I made her cut off all ties with the people she'd worked with, leave her job, and commit to weekly meetings with a counselor for the next year."

"She left her job?"

"Desperate places require desperate measures. Plus, how could I expect her to stay in the same place and us get a different result for our life? There was no way. Then I committed to work on the things in me that needed to change. The things that had aided the entire situation in the first place."

"How could you have had anything to do with her choice?" I asked incredulously.

"More than you think. Now, at the end of the day, the choice was hers. And I know that I am not responsible for that. But she had spent years being underappreciated, second to my job, and respected more as a mother than a wife. I had abandoned the fact that she was a woman who needed to feel like a woman. She needed to be romanced and loved and treasured and nurtured. And I had reduced her to housekeeper and financier. So I changed all that. Amazing how almost losing one of life's greatest treasures can cause you to value it in a whole new way."

"But how could you love a child that your wife made with another man?" Even saying it, I couldn't imagine it.

"Because I was able to see Alexandra as a child who was completely innocent of her circumstances. And when her father died, I knew that she needed a daddy. Every day my heart swells with more and more love for her." The tears in his eyes told the truth of his heart.

"I can tell. She's crazy about you. Like she's really your daughter."

"Couldn't feel like it more than if I had given birth to her myself." He chuckled.

"Now, that's a visual." I laughed. "You're amazing, Manuel. Dare I say a saint."

"No, I'm no saint. Sometimes, Savannah, I think that the people who overcome their demons are far more amazing. I never had her temptations to overcome. But every day she fought them, and now she has won. Well, actually we've won. And our Alexandra has won."

"Forgiveness, huh?"

"Haven't found any substitute for it."

"Ever have bad days?"

"Every now and then they'll wash over me like a summer thunderstorm, or sometimes just like a fine mist. I deal with them in whatever form they arrive. And I remind myself that there is nothing in my life that won't turn out for good. Because I have spent my entire life loving God, and I know that there is a purpose for my life, and everything that Lucy and I have traveled. Plus, she's a spicy little chick, you have to agree." He winked.

I winked back. "I'd definitely have to agree with that." I stood up and wrapped my arms around his neck. He held me there. He really was a perfect father.

"We'll see you before you leave, I hope?"

"I'll make sure of it."

From the street I looked back and watched him walk into the house. A man far beyond my ability to comprehend. A hurt I couldn't conceive of. A forgiveness far greater than I was capable of. At least it felt that way today.

CHAPTER THIRTY-FIVE

The sun beat us like we were delinquents.

"I'm sweltering." Paige wiped the beads of perspiration from her top lip.

"You're not near as hot as she is." I motioned to Mother, who was sitting at the base of the East Ruskin Beach Pavilion. She wore a huge hat tied atop her head, and she sat in a fold-up chair, painting the canvas along with six other women and their painting instructor. She was dabbing at her face with a handkerchief, but it was pretty futile, because all of her makeup had slid into one of the creases of her neck. A crease she would assure you did not exist.

"Why is she doing that?" Paige asked.

I pondered the situation myself. "She's into torture for some odd reason."

"You two are going to look fifty by the time you're thirty," Amber surmised from beneath her umbrella, while eating a Milky Way.

"Who cares?" I mumbled. "We'll be living together in a retirement village. The only two we'll have to look at is each other. At least *we'll* think we look good."

"Besides," Paige interjected, "why come to the beach if you're not going to lie in the sun?"

"To see the sights, of course," Amber responded, looking at Mother across the sand and shaking her head. Now, that was a sight if ever we'd seen one.

I was running and it was dinnertime. That only meant one thing: perilous times. The last two days had been too much. The abandonment of every dream I had ever entertained. Every emotion. Every thought. Every buried feeling that had tried to resurrect itself was officially placed right back in its grave. Today, people mocked me instead of mourned me. At least they did in my head. And a very imaginative head it was, I'd come to discover.

On top of that, I had written and submitted my second article. That led to a horrible phone call and a tongue-lashing and a rewrite by 10:00 p.m. or else. It was five o'clock, and I had nothing.

I passed Adam again. How does something so perfect go so wrong? How can you think you have a love so secure and certain only to watch it disappear as suddenly as it arrived. Love is cruel and mean, and who would want it?

I jogged away to the secret place I had discovered on the outskirts of Water Colors yesterday morning with Joshua. I just wanted to be there. Maybe I could understand a little better there. Wynonna sang to me from my iPod. "Heaven Help Me If I Ever Lose Your Love." The words reverberated inside of me. Long gone was Barbra Streisand singing songs from *Yentl*.

As I stood on the edge of the dock and looked out over the glassy water, I watched a turtle's head bob up for a second, only to disappear before I could catch a closer look.

"Well, aren't you Mr. Lucky today. You can just bury yourself."

He didn't respond.

The thoughts, compounded by the music in my head, must have camouflaged the clip-clopping of high heels that sneaked up on me. When the perfectly manicured hand tapped me on the shoulder, I about threw us both over the railing.

"My word, Mother, would you announce yourself first!" I said, pulling the earphones out of my ears.

"If you would actually listen to the sounds around you instead of having your ears crammed full with hullabaloo all the time, you might have heard me. I've called your name the last one hundred feet."

"It's music." I turned back to face the water. "Want to tell me how you found me?"

"Want to tell me what you're doing out here?"

She had followed me. Her question was proof. She had followed people for years. I just never realized until that moment she had perfected the art of spying on *me*. "Thinking."

"Thinking about what?"

"Thinking about how life sucks."

"Savannah Phillips, what did you say?"

"If you would let me finish, I was going to say . . . I was thinking about how life sucks the life right out of you. And your breath smells rank!"

"It's garlic and parmesan."

"No? Really? And you ate it yesterday. What should that tell you about that stuff?"

"You are pitiful."

I didn't offer a different analysis. That one felt accurate.

"How long have you been in love with Joshua?" She used the tone that she always gets when she's about to turn into a friend instead of a mother. It's more sympathetic and not quite as Southern. Imagine that.

I jerked my head around to look into her eyes, which were staring right through me. "I should ask how long you've known."

"Since the other night at dinner."

"There's no way. You all thought he was there to see Amber."

"Give me a break, Savannah. Amber's the only one who didn't realize that Joshua wasn't there to see her."

Mother's discernment continued to amaze. "Now, why would you say that?"

"Well, first, because he never looked at her; second, because he only looked at you; and third, because you chatted like Chatty Cathy, which you always do when you get nervous; and fourth, because you ate a total of two bites of your favorite meal around here. And the last one alone would have been proof enough."

I threw my head down on my arms, which were resting on the railing. "I think I'm completely in love with him. Who knows? Maybe I even liked him the day he almost ran me over and started tormenting me with his quirky smile and his annoying comments. I mean, the day he knelt by my desk and consoled me over my horrible debut story, he was so goofy and charming. And I know you hate him, Mother, but—"

"Savannah, I don't hate Joshua." She said this convincingly enough, causing me to raise my head. "Granted, he needs a few minor lessons in editing his pieces before they go to print"—she caught herself—"but I don't hate him, darling. I don't hate people. I just deal with them. With whatever means are necessary." Not that I knew a single soul who wanted to be on the other end of "whatever means are necessary."

"Well, I hate him!"

"Why do you hate him?" she asked, forcing me to catch a whiff of her parmesan and garlic breath. That stuff was rancid.

"If we are going to talk, you have to promise not to breathe on me." She puffed harder. She could be completely obnoxious. "I hate him because I'm such an idiot," I said, slapping my hands on my forehead. "Just a complete idiot."

"Why do you hate him because *you're* an idiot?"

I raised my eyebrow at her.

"Don't sass me, child."

"Because he's not what I thought. And it's better to find out now than to be like Kate and get married only for him to wake up one day and decide he doesn't want to be married anymore.

Or to be like Manuel and have your spouse get tired of you and have an affair with a . . . with a banker!" I wailed then. Every pent-up emotion rushed to the surface. I lost all control. I had officially become Amber.

"You are not saying Lucy had an affair," Mother asked in horror.

"That's exactly what I'm saying. Now your world's completely wrecked too, isn't it?"

"Darling." She laughed softly. "No one is ever what we think they are. Everyone has issues that you won't know until years down the road. There are things in your father I still uncover every day."

"Please don't tell me what they are. I will be damaged."

"And things don't just happen in marriage, no matter how much someone wants to believe that. There are always little signs. The pulling away. The silent dinners. The unreciprocated touches. But love requires faith."

"I'm plumb out." I sniffled, pulling the sleeve of my T-shirt up to wipe my nose.

"Please don't ever let me have to observe that again," she said with her face contorted. She recovered quickly. "Savannah Phillips, you have more faith than 90 percent of the people I know."

"But not for myself."

"Well, you'll never have love if you don't have faith. And be honest with yourself: you don't hate Joshua. You're madly in love with him."

I sighed heavily. "No, I don't hate him. I just hate the fact that I'm the only one in this entire whacked universe who actually thought she would marry a virgin. Now, if that isn't whacked in and of itself, here I'm talking about him being the kind of man I want to marry when we've had only one unofficial date. And it wasn't for hanky-panky, no matter what you might believe."

"Savannah, don't mock me." She nudged my shoulder playfully. "I know you didn't do such a thing. I could tell by the look of horror on your face when I confronted you. And it's okay, darling, to want things in life. It's okay to want your husband to have never known another woman. And if you feel like that is a criteria of yours, then I will respect that decision as well. But you do need to know that people aren't perfect, and life isn't perfect. Even tans aren't perfect." She eyed me knowingly.

I eyed her back. "This coming from the woman who married perfection and whose life is perfect."

"Your father isn't perfect, despite what you think, Savannah. Now, he's pretty doggone close, I must agree, but the man . . . well he has his own failures."

"I don't want to know them."

"Okay, then I'll tell you yours. Yours are thinking that life won't have them. That marriage is perfect. That you get perfection from imperfect people. No, all you get are imperfect people trying to make things work the best they know. And if Joshua doesn't fail you now, he'll fail you later."

"But what if it's a failure that leads us to divorce?"

"There are no guarantees in this life, Savannah. People will make horrible choices. Some will ignore every tug on their heart and walk away from everything that is right. But all you can do is make it clear that divorce isn't an option for *your* marriage. And don't get married unless you know beyond a shadow of a doubt that he's the man destined for you. That kind of certainty will keep you sane when other things won't."

She wasn't to be stopped. "And you'll fail him. But you don't have to let something that isn't perfect keep you from the perfect thing."

Her words hung in the air like the smell of manure. Hard to handle but full of good stuff for growth.

"What went on between the two of you the other night at dinner, without any words, was exactly what happened with me and your father. I saw a different Savannah."

"How?"

"I saw your vulnerable glances and how you were completely incapable of keeping your eyes off of him."

I raised my eyebrow.

"Well, those are two traits lost on you."

"Wonder how in the world I got so screwed up," I asked the source of my screwed-upness.

"Some children just learn these things." Well, that couldn't be defended. "Joshua loves you, baby girl. I can see it all over his handsome face."

"Well, love isn't always enough, Mother."

"No, the emotion of love isn't, Savannah. But the decision to love always is. And trust me, many years are spent loving because of decision alone." She stared at me revealing her own ability to be completely vulnerable. "Just ask your father."

With those words she revealed that she actually had knowledge of her own imperfections. This changed the playing field.

"But what if I think about it all the time and I can't ever get past it?"

"Savannah, be serious. Now, how many times have I done things that have hurt you or embarrassed you?"

"You're not serious."

"Yes, I'm serious. How many?"

"Numbers don't go that high."

She smacked my hand. "Can you remember all of them?"

"Tons."

"Do you think about them all the time?"

I thought through that one. "Hardly ever."

"See. Hurts never go away, I'll give you that. You still remember. Every now and then something will prick you and cause you to remember. But you don't sit around all day rehashing the hurts of the past. If you do, you have far deeper issues than Joshua and his old girlfriend."

I leaned across the railing. "So let me ask you this."

"What, darling?" she leaned in, a little too close. I held my breath. "Ask me anything."

I knew I could. I knew despite our countless differences that there wasn't a thing in the world I couldn't ask this woman. "What if we got married and he . . . he compared me . . . you know . . . to Celeste. What if I wasn't any good?"

She smiled. Not a Vicky smile. A mother smile. "Darling, if that boy loves you like I think he loves you, he'll have trouble remembering Celeste's name. When something is right, perfectly right, it can never compare to what was wrong."

"You think he'd think I was hot?"

She cackled and threw her head back. Every hair stayed in place. "I think he would think you were totally hot."

"Oh, don't say *totally*."

"Well, what should I say?"

"Say *completely* or something, but not *totally*."

"Okay, completely hot." She patted the top of my hand. The sun sparkled on her massive diamond that could have downed a small aircraft. "Life always has loss, Savannah. But you would miss far more if you let this man go than if you let go of your expectations of him. Because I guarantee you he will not be able to meet them all. But he will tot—completely blow others out of the water. Now, don't think accepting this will change what it is. If you accept Joshua, you have to accept every part of his past as well. His past won't change. But I have a feeling it was the past of that man that changed the man."

I studied her quietly. She let me. Then she kissed me on the top of my head and started back up the long walkway that led out to the street. I turned to watch her go. She could saunter in high heels better than anyone I knew. Until her heel got stuck between two of the wooden slats. She tried daintily to get it undone. Dainty didn't work. She pulled her foot out of it and jerked the entire thing out of the wood slat. She got the shoe all right, but the heel stayed right where it had lodged itself. She left it. Right there, to be contemplated by a thousand spectators for years to come. And away she walked. One heel touching the ground. The other foot walking on tiptoes. Her sauntering never missed a beat. Maybe Amber was her child. Had she ever worked at a bank?

CHAPTER THIRTY-SIX

I ran back onto the streets of Seaside and around Quincy Square until it deposited me in front of Ruskin Place. I walked slowly in front of the stores that were closing up shop. At the second row of townhouses, I worked my way into the center of the Ruskin Place park called Park de Leonardo de Bicci. I made my way along the dirt path that meanders through the covered garden. It's almost as if the trees bent to follow me. When I was finally exposed to a clearing again, directly in front of me stood the Interfaith Seaside Chapel. How poetic to discover at the end of your path the place where you should have begun: the place of faith.

A lone man in a white linen shirt was closing the door behind him. The remnants of white lawn chairs and strewn rose petals were evidence that I had just missed the departure of the latest bride and groom. I stood silently as the young man made his way quietly up the brick street.

The door caught my eye. The rich pecan tones of the wood caused the door to seem small amid the sea of white. The opening looked only large enough for two small people or one rather large one. And seeing it there reminded me of the verse that says, "Small is the gate and narrow the road that leads to life, and only a few find it." I couldn't take my eyes off of that door. It drew me.

The way may be narrow, and only a few may find it, but it wasn't impossible to find. I knew in that moment that my judgmental attitude had prevented me from finding my way. Joshua had been so kind and so loving and so hurt. He needed forgiveness from only One in this life, and yet he asked for mine too, and my father's. And I had been too condescending and selfish to extend it.

My heart ached. I sat down on the concrete wall surrounding Ruskin Place and stared at the church as best I could through the burning tears welling in my eyes. As I looked above the door, I noticed the three stories of paned windows above it. They matched the three stories of windows on the other end of the church, allowing you to see straight through. The One who was worshipped inside that sanctuary could see straight through me as well. And though every part of me wanted to recoil, He wouldn't allow it. He gently prodded the yuck in my life, and by the time He was through, I realized the gate may be narrow but it was open.

I walked quietly to the small door and opened it as if it were the secret passageway at the end of the secret garden. The smell of fresh flowers and extinguished candles lingered in the air. I walked silently up the aisle toward the front of the church. The only two in the place were me and the cockroach that had come in with me. He fortunately went his way and I went mine.

Small baskets of red roses and spring flowers hung from the first three pews. I sat down on the front pew, where mothers sit and cry over daughters and sons they don't want to give away and over sons-in-law and daughters-in-law they don't want to gain.

I stared at the pulpit. I could see so clearly the memories of Sunday morning. The pastor walked to the small raised lectern in his vibrant blue shirt and red tie, the sport coat left at home for a business lunch, not a Sunday service by the sea. He caught my pew's attention immediately. He simply mentioned the name of John Wesley, one of the city of Savannah's most notables, and one of my heroes.

"John Wesley arrived in Georgia to preach the gospel to the ruffians. The ones who had maxed out their credit cards in England." Everyone snickered.

"He fell in love. But his love was not returned." I laughed to myself.

"He got angry."

I could relate to angry.

"He wanted her banned from the church."

How bad an idea could that be?

"But he was the one who was banned."

Okay, not so great.

"And on Wesley's way back home by boat, there was a horrible storm. And the crew was afraid. And Wesley was afraid. But there was a group of Moravians aboard. A strange religious sect of the time that focused on knowing God relationally. Their calm caught Wesley's attention. So, in his priestly getup, he asked their leader why it was that his people weren't afraid. 'Sir, do you know God?' the man asked Wesley. Wesley was angered. He wrote books about the things of God that this man knew nothing about. But Wesley realized afterward that his answer to that man's question was no. And Wesley's honest answer resulted in his genuine conversion. Life's passions are powerful things. But the greatest passion would be knowing God more.

"Not for just a moment. Not until everything works out like you want it to. But every day, seeking to know God more. His heart. His thoughts. His plans. They may not match your own. But the question is, are you willing to let yours match His?" With those words he stepped down.

The memory of my first story crashed into my thoughts. I had hurt a local woman viciously with my first story. She hated me for it. Told me so in no uncertain terms. Knowing she held such animosity toward me ate away at me. I wanted her to forgive me. She hadn't yet, not completely. And then I knew. I knew what it felt like not to be forgiven.

Back to my heart came the words of last Monday morning: be still. I had been anything but still this week. I had been crass; I had been obnoxious; I had been downright ugly, but not still. I turned and knelt by my pew. I asked for the forgiveness I needed. For my arrogance. For my pride. For my self-centered plans. I trusted God could handle my stuff, just like He had handled Joshua's. Just like He had handled Lucy's and Manuel's. Just like He could handle Adam's and Kate's if they would let Him. And just like He had handled millions before us and would handle millions after us.

With the burning tears streaming down my face, I longed for some of that waterproof mascara that was Amber's best friend. And for a long moment, I simply sat still.

The sand-and-seashell cross sitting on the altar table reminded me that forgiveness wasn't a choice, but a way of life. A way of life promised to us by the One who had the most to forgive. As I sat there, I considered what I had once heard, that "one will come to man's Creator by either desperation or revelation." I came by way of one and left by way of the other.

"Ugly before age," I said to the cockroach that waited by the door.

As it swung open, he headed back to his own family, while I headed back to find the man who would, I hoped, one day become a part of mine.

The first pellet of rain hit me as I closed the church door. By the time I jogged my way across Forrest Street Park and through Ruskin Place toward Proteus, well, the rain was beating me mercilessly. I picked up the pace to a brisk run and landed on the front porch of Joshua's beach house with a thud. I knocked twice, hard and loud. Johnny greeted me with his illuminating smile.

"Savannah, my word, woman, what are you doing out in this mess?"

I panted. "I'm looking for Joshua. Is he here?"

"No. He's out in this mess too. Aren't you two a pair." He laughed.

"Do you know where he is exactly?"

"I left him on the beach about an hour ago. He hasn't been much company lately. I have a distinct feeling it has something to do with you."

I didn't have time to confirm or deny his feelings. "If he comes in before I can find him, tell him to stay right here until I get back. Please?" I begged.

"Scout's honor." He crossed his fingers or heart or something like that.

I stood on my tiptoes, but he still had to bend his six-foot-four frame so I could kiss his cheek. "Thank you."

"Make him smile, Savannah."

"I'll do my best."

I ran out through the Savannah Beach Pavilion. How fitting. The rain still mocking me as I scanned the beach. My eyes finally fixed on the dark curls walking slowly up the beach in swim shorts, a sopping beach towel hanging from his left hand, making lines in the sand as he dragged it behind him.

The run down the stairs to the beach seemed to take forever. There must have been hundreds. The thud of my heart echoed on every step. We met at the bottom. He almost walked past me, until I called his name and reached for his arm.

"Please, Joshua! Wait!"

He stepped back down to the soft white sand and looked eye to eye with me as I remained on the bottom step. "Savannah, it's pouring down rain. What in the world are you doing out here?"

"I needed to see you. It's so important."

"What? Has something happened?"

"Yes. To me. Something's happened to me," I said, thankful that the water was running so heavy down my face that he would never be able to tell how many tears were mingled in. "I've been so stupid! I've been so judgmental and condescending and so . . ."

"Arrogant."

"Yes, arrogant!" I blubbered.

He smiled.

"And I'm so sorry. I know the kind of man that you are now. And I know that you didn't even have to tell me; you didn't even owe me an apology."

He stopped me. "No, I do owe you an apology. It wasn't the right decision to make. And I made it. And even though I never dreamed all of those years before that it would ever affect someone else so deeply, the way it hurt you made me realize that all decisions have consequences." He dropped his towel to the sand and placed his hands on my hips. "And I'm so sorry. And I do need you to forgive me. Because what I did has consequences for our future." I could see the puddle of tears that rested on the tip of his long black lashes. At least they might be tears.

"That decision is a part of you. That decision, no matter how wrong it was, is part of what has made you the man that you are. And you are the man who I am completely in love with. And I forgive you! I completely forgive you." I peppered his face with kisses. I wrapped my arms around his neck and then leaned back to stare into those eyes that welcomed me. "But now you have to forgive me. You have to forgive me for my meanness and for not being willing to give you the very thing that I've needed myself more times than I can count. And forgive me for not telling my mother and not telling Amber and not telling the world how much I absolutely love you. And forgive me for continually having to learn lessons over and over. It's like every month something new happens in my life and I go backwards instead of actually growing and changing and maturing and—"

He leaned in closer and wrapped his arms firmly around my waist. "You love me?"

"Yes, I love you! And I won't let my head hit the pillow until everyone who needs to know knows! You hear that, world?" I yelled, throwing my head back to the deluge. "I love—" A raindrop hit the back of my throat and about choked me to death. By the time I got through coughing, my throat was raw. But we laughed. And then I threw my arms around that strong neck, and those strong arms wrapped themselves firmly around me, and the man who I had been waiting for, though I never even realized it, kissed me in a way that let me know he was in love with me too. And by the time we were through, entire books could have been written. They might even have been. We could have written one ourselves. But there would be time for that.

"Let's get out of this mess." He reached down and grabbed his sand-encrusted towel.

We walked slowly up the stairs. There seemed much fewer going up now than there had been coming down. When we reached the Savannah Street Beach Pavilion, I thought that the strong columns gave it almost a rather stately presence. Very much like the man next to me. Clean strong lines. Not a lot of fuss or pretense. But a beautiful statement. He sat down in one of the Adirondack chairs that rested underneath the tin roof, and I sat across his lap and laid my head on his shoulder. The rain fell straight down, so we were covered from any more of its onslaught.

"Oh, excuse me," said a feminine Southern voice as it crested the top of the stairs and shook out its mane of blonde highlights underneath the pavilion. When she threw her head back, we all caught a glimpse of each other. My eyes reached hoot-owl proportions. Hers were even bigger.

"Savannah? Joshua?" Amber screamed. "What are you two . . . oh my . . . oh my . . . you two are . . . are . . ." Her bottom lip began to quiver.

I leaped off of Joshua's lap and ran in her direction. "Amber, you need to let me explain." I reached out to take her arm.

She jerked her arm away. "Explain? How can you explain the fact that you're . . . you're . . . you're . . . a liar?" Her neck jutted out in my direction, causing me to stumble backward.

Joshua stood up and came to help the remotely helpless situation.

"And you!" she said, pointing to him. "Well, you're just nothing but a tease! A tease, I tell ya!" She sounded reminiscent of Carol Burnett when she played Eunice on *Mama's Family*. It was all rather frightening.

"I can't believe this, Savannah. You were my best friend. My sister. The daughter of my mother and father." The child was ill. "And you have turned your back on me in sheer mockery. Well, I disown you!" she screeched. "You are no longer part of our family." She was officially removing me from my own family.

"If you'll just let me explain."

"No. I will hear no more of your Benedict Arnoldness. You and I are through, finito, arreviderci, benediction, amen and amen! And you, mister." She pointed to Joshua. I could see the hurt for her in his eyes. And the entire thing was my fault. "You have just said farewell to—to . . . to, well to me. All for . . . for . . . this . . . this . . ." She waved her fingers at me.

"Careful," I warned.

"For . . . this . . . this heresy!"

"I think she means *heretic*," I said to Joshua.

"Oh."

"What does it matter what I mean! You are what you are! A thief! A liar! A floozy!" Then she sobered up immediately and turned toward me with fire in her eyes. "Is this the man you had the date with the other night?"

I couldn't lie. Well, I could have. Probably should have. But my recent church encounter destroyed that possibility. Plus the fact that she was absolutely right. I had lied to her. Lied to her over and over. Me, the one who demanded honesty, was nothing but a filthy liar. I needed to head back to that church again as soon as she got through with me here. "Yes," I whimpered.

"You mean to tell me, you wore *my* clothes on a date with Joshua?"

"I didn't—"

"I don't want to hear another word from you. But know this, missy, I will never—and I do mean never—not ever, ever, ever, be your friend again." Her tears fell, and her mascara firmly remained. "You either," she said to Joshua as she made a beeline past us. "I hate you! I hate you both!" she screamed as she cried and ran down the footpath to 30-A.

Joshua and I looked at each other and then took off after her. Berserk chasing berserker. What a perfect way to complete a perfectly normal evening.

CHAPTER THIRTY-SEVEN

"How does she run like that in those heels?" Joshua tried to yell over the rain while in a full sprint.

"She can do anything in those heels!" I panted.

We turned down a footpath off Savannah Street, where we had last seen her blur. But once we crossed over to East Ruskin, she was nowhere in sight. We bent double in the middle of the street. "I can't believe this. It's all my fault. If I hadn't been so stupid!"

"Savannah, you can't worry about that now. We just have to find her and make sure she's okay."

I stood up and tried to wipe the rain from my eyes. "Let's go back to the house. Hopefully that's where she is."

"But what about your mother?"

"My mother knows everything."

"Everything?" he said, standing up himself.

"Everything."

"I knew it. I could tell at dinner she knew."

"Yeah, yeah. You know everything. So since you know everything, tell me this is all going to be okay."

He wrapped his arm around me and led me in the direction of home.

That was reassurance enough.

Mom, Dad, and Paige were sitting on the front porch watching the rain fall. Pink Toes cowered on a pink leopard-print pillow not too far from Duke. He had his butt stuck in her face, a posture that meant multiple things, I was certain.

They saw us coming, and Mother jumped to her feet. "Oh, darlings, what are you doing out in this mess? Let me get you some towels."

She returned with two large dry towels by the time we reached the top of the stairs. "Is Amber here?" I asked.

"No, we haven't seen her since she went to take a walk on the beach. I had a feeling she was really going to see if she could run into you, Joshua." Mother gave him the once-over.

I wiped my face with the dry towel and relished the warmth that it brought. "Well, she ran into us all right."

Mother threw her hand to her mouth. "Savannah, what in the world happened!"

"She happened. She happened upon me sitting on Joshua's lap. Called me some rather crude names, I might add."

"Like what?" Paige asked.

"Like not important right now." I glanced at her, allowing my face to make an even clearer statement than my words.

Mother grabbed my arm. "Well, where did she go?"

"We're not sure," Joshua said, wrapping his towel around himself. "We were hoping she came back here."

"We haven't seen her since after dinner," Dad said.

"Well, we've got to find her," I said, laying my towel across the chair and heading back to the steps.

"You're not going back out in that," Joshua said. "I'll find her."

Dad got up from his chair. "I'll go with you."

Joshua turned to my mother. "I know you and I need to talk, Mrs. Phillips."

She smiled at him warmly. "I think you've had to do enough talking lately, Joshua. Don't worry about me right now. You just go try to find Amber."

Dad grabbed a raincoat, his galoshes, a T-shirt and raincoat for Joshua, and a couple umbrellas, and they left in search of Savannah's brightest jewel.

I changed clothes and pulled my hair up in a clip, then returned to the porch. Thomas had arrived while I was inside.

"So tell me what she called you, really," Paige inquired again.

"I think floozy was amongst the carnage."

"Ooh, floozy." Paige snickered.

"She did not call you a floozy," Mother said, shocked.

"Among other things," I confirmed.

"What other things?" Paige leaned in closer.

I sat down in an Adirondack chair next to her. "I will answer no more of your questions."

Thomas entered the conversation. "So, were you getting some smack when she caught you?"

"Thomas Phillips," Mother scolded. "I don't know what smack is, but if I ever hear it come out of your mouth again regarding anyone, but especially Savannah, I will move into your dorm at the Citadel and put some smack on you."

He said not another word the rest of the evening. He knew she absolutely would perform every word she had just spoken.

"I've hurt her so bad."

"She's been out of control," Paige responded.

"She has, darling. She just has never been loved, well, by her own family. And so she has never grasped a clear perspective of what love is or how it works. That's why she lives for pageants. This really has nothing to do with Joshua or you," Mother assured.

"It sure sounded like it did a minute ago."

"She's hurt. That's all. She'll be okay, darling." Mother rested her french manicure across my shoulder. Where was the red? Maybe she was mellowing. "Your father and Joshua will find her, and we'll straighten this whole mess out. It's just been a long week for her."

"It's been a longer one for me." Paige sighed as she leaned back in her chair.

Terror struck me. "My story! Oh my stars! My story!" I ran into the house and up the stairs. The computer sat on the bed. Mr. Hicks wanted a story on storms. I'd give him a story on storms.

For an hour, I wrote about how all the storms of honesty and forgiveness and need had converged on this little part of the panhandle. I hit *send* before I had time to think. He responded an hour later with nothing but a smiley face.

Thomas joined the search party while I was typing furiously. So had Paige. That was rather disturbing in its own right. Mother and I never heard the four of them return. But when morning broke over Seaside, all six of us were sound asleep in our own Adirondacks.

The smell of coffee woke us all up. Dad was sporting five cups of it and a Coke. He had awakened first. Shocker. He passed out the liquid sanity, and we all sat there, peering at the house across the street.

"No sign of Amber at all?" Mother asked as she blew her breath into her hand. I'm not sure what she expected. But the sweet fragrance of roses she would not find. Her own face contorted.

"No, nothing at all. She'll be back. She's just trying to deal with all her emotions, I'm sure," Dad said.

"I need to freshen up." Mother rose slowly from the chair. Her body cracked as she did.

We all turned our attention back to the house across the street. This morning gave all of us a glimpse of the young man's blue-jean-clad behind as it exited the second-story bedroom in these wee hours of the morning. When his eyes caught sight of us, he took off like a firework on the Fourth of July.

"He better hope her daddy doesn't have a gun," Dad said as the steam rose from his cup.

"Savannah used to sneak out her window," Thomas offered.

"Did we ask for your thoughts on sneaking out of windows?" I asked.

"I knew she did," Dad said.

"No, you didn't." I laughed.

"Yes, I did. I knew every time you left and every place you went."

"Really?"

"Really."

I should have known. I caught a whiff of my own breath. "Y'all excuse me. I need to brush my teeth."

Mother was picking up shoes from the family room as I came in. The television had been left on through the night.

"News from the world of the Georgia pageant scene" were the words from the perky morning-news anchor that caught my ear.

"It seems that the reigning Miss Georgia United States of America has been caught in a scandal . . ."

My feet stopped abruptly behind the sofa. "Everyone, you might want to hear this!" I hollered. Feet came scrambling in from every corner.

The anchor continued while a picture of the queen with her sash draped around her filled up the screen. "Sources have confirmed the beauty queen was divorced. A pageant no-no. And because of that undisclosed divorce, she will be forced to surrender her crown."

The coanchor who sat next to her, wearing a pink tie, interjected, "I bet the first runner-up has never been so happy to hear about a divorce in her life."

The thought registered with each one of us in the room. The first runner-up was Amber Topaz Childers herself. She was, finally, the reigning Miss Georgia United States of America.

"She will freak out." Paige always had something profound to say.

"I can't believe this!" Mother said, disgusted. "Someone has defamed the name of our pageant. Will it ever end?" She threw up her hands and marched upstairs.

"Someone's gone through a divorce," I reminded her.

She looked at me for a moment. Then nodded her agreement.

"This means she's won!" Paige screamed. "This means our girl will actually get to live out her dream. And it's only a couple of weeks into her reign. And oh my word, this means she'll get to compete for Miss United States of America. We have got to find her! This is huge! This is so huge!"

"I'm going upstairs to shower," Dad said. "You ladies take the morning shift. And I'll meet you as soon as I get cleaned up."

Joshua turned to me. "I'm going back to the house to do the same. Come by in an hour or so and we'll see what we can find. But if we don't find her this morning, we really need to tell the Seaside security and get some help looking for her."

"I agree," Dad said. "We can't let this go on much longer without getting some help."

"I'm sure she's fine. But I have no idea where she would have spent the night. I'll come find you later," I said, still feeling the need to shake Joshua's hand. Everyone was watching. He saw my face. And rubbed my arm with both acknowledgment and approval. "Come on, Paige," I said grabbing my friend and thanking Joshua with my eyes.

"She'll freak! She will absolutely freak!" Paige could be so articulate.

"Yes, she will. She will freak!"

We searched nooks, crannies, and footpaths. We searched the beach just in case she had actually taken that walk to China via the ocean. We decided to go ahead and head to the Seaside security office, which would open at 7:00 a.m.

We were on our way there when we heard the familiar snore. There she lay, stomach down, on a bench in the screened-in porch in front of the Seaside Sales Center. Her head and left arm were hanging over the side. In her left hand was a cup with a few remnants of overripe fruit inside. Drool was coming from the side of her mouth and had formed a rather nasty ravine on the hardwood planks underneath her.

Her sky-blue halter top and white linen pants looked like they'd been through a cat fight. So did the poor thing's hair. It was not what you'd find beneath a tiara, I assure you. It was more what you'd find underneath a bridge. Actually, on a vagrant underneath a bridge. Not a picture that would fare well in the *Savannah Chronicle*.

"Okay, upsy-daisy," I said, reaching underneath one arm as Paige positioned herself on the other side.

"Please don't ever say that again."

"What?"

"Upsy-whatever. That sounds so your mother."

"Just get an arm and leave me alone," I said, returning to the mission at hand. We tried to hoist her, but she was deadweight. "Let's just sit her up."

Paige pulled from one side, and I pushed from the other, and we just hoped we didn't break an arm in the process. She didn't budge. That left Paige with no more viable options, so she slapped Amber right across the face. That did the trick.

She awoke with a startle. Her glassy eyes passed over us, and she brought the back of her hand to her mouth to wipe away the drool. "I gotsasome good frooth in myyycaup. You wanthsomeofits?" she asked, looking at Paige.

"Are you drunk?" I asked. What a stupid question.

Her eyes registered me and sobriety returned. Well almost. "Whathareyoudoingthhereyoulifflefllussy?"

"I think you mean *floozy*, and I'm here to get your behind out of a major indiscretion," I said, grunting as Paige and I finally got her back to her feet.

She tried to jerk away, but drunks don't jerk. "Ith caf tathe fare of myfelf!"

Paige gave her the once-over. "And we can see that's worked real well for ya."

We dragged all six feet of Amber out the screen door and down the stairs before the morning shift arrived and decided to make Amber the morning news. "You've had us worried sick," I scolded.

"Youmakethmethick!" she spat.

"Well, we can talk about all the things I make you when we get you sober. I can't believe you have been out all night drinking."

"I haventhbinf thrinking. If justh binf eatfing thisth fruiths."

"The liquor's in the fruit," Paige said.

"What?"

"You wouldn't understand," Paige assured.

"But she probably had no idea there was any liquor in it."

"Thats rithe, thisther."

"What did she say?" I asked.

"She said, 'That's right, sister.'"

"Oh. She's gone to calling me *sister* now?" I inquired. Paige shrugged. "Well, call me sister if you want to, but you still have major explaining to do." We made our way up Seaside Avenue.

"Idonthwanththoothalkthooyou."

It was best. And there was no need to tell her anything until she reached the land of sobriety. We would shield her from the inevitable phone calls until it arrived. And then we'd talk. We'd talk long and hard.

We called everyone from our cell phones on the way back to the house. No one was complaining about my phone now. By the time we got there, she was asleep again. Dad and Joshua hauled her upstairs and laid her across the bed. She never even knew where she was.

"Where in the world did you find her?" Mother asked, with her cell-phone earpiece clipped around her ear and Maggy strapped to her chest.

I sat down on the front porch and took a drink of a Coke I had grabbed from the refrigerator. "She was passed out on a bench in front of the Cottage Rental Office."

Mother gasped. "Oh my Lord, have mercy, do you think she's hurt herself?"

"She doesn't look too damaged. But her mascara was rather smudged."

"That's not funny."

Dad sat down next to me. "Did she say what happened?"

I was about to answer when Joshua walked out of the house onto the porch and got my attention. "I think she'll be out for a while," he surmised. "Is she drunk?"

"Wasted," Paige offered with no explanation.

"She got a hold of some happy fruit," I interjected, rolling my eyes at Paige. "Some fruit soaked in liquor. And no, Dad, she's still too mad at me to tell us what happened."

"Hello," Mother said into her chirping earpiece. "Yes, Amber is fine, and she will be back in town on Sunday. She has a few loose ends to tie up here, but I'll have her call you this evening with a statement for the paper. Now, don't bother her anymore. She's on emotional overload right now with all the excitement." Vicky's eyes bugged out in our direction.

"Who's that?" Paige asked.

"Probably the *Chronicle*," Joshua replied. "They've called quite a few times." He leaned against the wood railing on the front porch. He crossed his legs at the ankles and rested each arm on the railing behind him. "You look exhausted," he said to me.

"I am pretty tired."

"I'm starving," Paige said.

"I'll get you kids something to eat," Mother said, prancing herself and Miss Magnolia into the kitchen.

"If there's dog hair in it, I ain't eatin' it!" Paige hollered to Vicky's backside. Maggy barked. "Little rat," Paige mumbled. Duke came and laid his head in her lap. He loved likeminded women.

Mother returned sans doggy pouch but with a feast. She had made eggs, bacon, home fries, sausage gravy, and homemade biscuits. We were licking our elbows, it was so good. An hour later, we all found a sofa or a chair to crash on. Joshua and I shared the sofa, and I nestled my head underneath his arm. I closed my eyes so I wouldn't have to look at Mother's raised eyebrow. But no one moved until well past lunch. Because it was about then the gagging started. And this time it wasn't from the princess with the pink collar.

"I'm dying," Amber said, her face hovering over the toilet seat.

"Well, that's what it smells like," I agreed. "How much of that fruit did you eat?"

"I have no idea. It was just so . . . so . . . so . . . oh, Lord, deliver me . . ." And then she disgorged the rest of it.

I handed her a wet towel to wipe her face, and she leaned back and sat against the wall. Mother and Paige were standing at the door, and Maggy's face was buried in Mother's chest. Here was an animal who would throw up as look at you, yet clearly couldn't handle someone else's pain.

"Why don't you try to get a shower and clean up. We have some things we need to tell you, and I'm sure you won't want to hear them like this," Mother said from the doorway.

I found that a little odd. I thought Amber would want to hear the exciting news no matter what. It might even make her forget she had to throw up. But then I remembered that I always wanted to be dressed up whenever I finally got a marriage proposal. So, then again, I could understand wanting to look half decent when you finally receive some of the most exciting news of your life. Well, exciting news of your life if you're Amber . . . or Victoria.

"I'm not going to be able to do that right now," she wailed, hugging the porcelain god once more. Her news would wait another day. Because sister had apparently eaten fruit with only slightly fewer repercussions than that apple of Eve's.

CHAPTER THIRTY-EIGHT

There are moments in life that cause a dog to snap. I didn't know it was possible, but even good dogs can reach their limits. And apparently Duke's came at about ten that evening. For years, Duke had been relegated to the floor of Mother and Dad's bedroom. He only made it onto the bed when Mother had overnight trips away, and few of those were traveled without Dad, because, well, Dad didn't want his princess traveling alone. So, eventually Duke grew weary of the floor and relegated himself to Thomas's bed.

But around ten on this day, Duke left Thomas's bed and decided to meander his way to Mother and Dad's room. The two, needing a little "peace and quiet," had been watching a rental movie—alone—just to avoid the company of *anyone*. Must not've been that great a flick, because both Vicky and Dad were sacked out when a pint-size *Hack!* sounded from between Mother's feet. And that must have been when Duke saw the little ball of fluff nestled at the foot of *his* bed. Well, to be honest, that might have done me in too. And before anyone could catch their breath, Duke jumped on the bed, clenched the back of that little critter's neck in his teeth, and plopped it on its bum in the middle of the bedroom floor.

Mother screamed, thinking for sure Duke was about to eat her Magnolia alive, but all Duke wanted was the attention he deserved. And when we all arrived in the bedroom because of mother's scream, Duke was lying on top of Mother's chest, with his nose touching hers. All the poor thing wanted was for her to love him. Mother was mumbling. Maggy was whining like a whipped puppy, and Dad rolled over just to see what Duke might do next. Thomas, Paige, and I all stopped dead in our tracks, just to see if Mother might throw him a bone.

She eyed him.

He eyed her.

Maggy whimpered.

Duke turned his head, gave her a hack, then turned back to Mother and smiled. He nuzzled her chin with his nose, and she spat out dog hair. As she rolled him back over toward his true companion and extricated herself from the bed, she had, I do believe, a flash of compassion for the old boy in her eyes. She scooped up her princess, surveyed for broken bones. "My sweet precious baby girl. What has he done to you?"

Mother turned her face back to Duke.

He gave one low whimper, and I wanted to go wrap him in my arms and console him myself. Poor thing had spent all of his years being rejected by this woman, and now she had not just rejected him, but had replaced him. Dad rubbed Duke's head and whispered something in his ear.

Mother turned to all of us standing at the door. "Show's over," she announced. "Now, scoot."

But Maggie started a low, gutteral moan, and Mother decided they both could use a warm glass of milk. That poor dog of hers would need doggy Prozac by the time this trip was over. Mother "shooed" us and headed down the stairs. Duke scooted over and rubbed his head all over her pillow. If she refused to love him, he would leave her with a gift until she did.

Morning had Amber descending the stairs with wet hair and a pink Juicy Couture sweatsuit on. We were all in the kitchen, sitting around the table, still fielding calls from our own paper. Her eyes were bloodshot and puffy. It was the worst I had ever seen her. But she still looked good for a drunk. "Where'd you get the fruit?" my father asked as soon as her feet hit the kitchen floor.

She caught sight of Joshua, and her upper lip began to quiver. "Joshua? What are you doing here?" I suspected she nursed an ounce of hope that he had returned to his senses and was sitting here for her.

"I, um . . ."

Dad cut him off. "Amber, I asked you a question."

His stern tone caught her off guard, and her eyes darted in his direction. Her surprise was momentarily replaced with shame. "I was tired and wet, and there was a whole bunch of people who were out on a porch having a party, I think." She rubbed her head. "And they just thought I was another one of them, and before I knew it they had invited me in, and I realized how starving I was, and the fruit was sooooooooo good. I just had another and another, and by the time all the guests were starting to leave, I figured I should go too, but I was feeling a little woozy and thought I might need to sit down, and that was where the girls found me." She eyed Paige. "And then Paige slapped me."

"You acted very irresponsibly," Dad stated plainly. "We were worried about you and spent the entire night looking for you, and there's no telling what could have happened to you."

Her lips began to quiver. "I . . . I didn't realize . . . I was just so mad." Her eyes landed on me. "Mad at Savannah and mad at Joshua."

"I don't care who you were mad at." Now Dad was making *me* uncomfortable. "We brought you with us, and you shouldn't have put any of us through this. We were about to call the police after you."

She turned her attention back to my father, and then the tears began to flow. "I'm . . . so . . . sorry, Mr. Phillips. No one's ever cared where I've been before." She wailed more. "I could do whatever I wanted or be gone for a month, and my parents wouldn't even care where I was."

He stood up, his face softer now, and walked over to her and placed both of his hands on her shoulders. "Well, we do," he assured her. "We do. So don't ever do that again, okay?"

"I WOOOONNN'T." She threw her arms around his neck, sobbing.

"Now, we'll leave you three to figure out the rest," Dad said when he was finally able to remove her arms from around his neck and helped her sit at the table as he and mother left. But Thomas and Paige just sat at the table as if this were some freak show they were too afraid to miss.

"Get!" I said.

"Well, we had plans anyway, didn't we, Thomas?" Paige said, huffing as she rose.

"Sure, yeah . . . plans." He stood up. I should have been scared.

Joshua laid his hand on my arm. "Amber," his rich voice began. "I don't even really know you. That makes it hard for me to understand how you could be so enamored with me."

"But I know you." She sniffed. "You had me at *hello*."

Paige snorted.

"Get!" I yellspered at the door.

"It's true!" she said, glaring at Paige's invisible carcass outside the door. "I just thought you felt the same way, you know, coming to dinner and all. And there are some great opportunities that come with my committed relationships." I noticed she didn't say marriage. "There is the Mrs. United States of America Pageant."

"Amber, you don't fall in love with someone because you

"Amber, you don't fall in love with someone because you want to get back what you've lost," Joshua replied softly. "You fall in love because you can't stand to spend another day without that someone. Because to wake up again without them being a part of your life is something you can't imagine. You fall in love when every quirk and every defect is okay with you, because these make a person what they are. And you know that time will change you and make each of you what the other needs and longs for." He turned his head to me. "And those are the things I feel every time I look at Savannah. I love Savannah," he said, turning his attention back to Amber. "And I've loved her for a long time. And I'm sorry, but you want love for all the wrong reasons."

I noticed the volcano across the table about to erupt. And as much as I wanted to savor the lavish words Joshua had just spoken—all except the defect part, which we'd have to deal with later—I didn't want any more eruptions. It had been a turbulent enough week as far as I was concerned.

"But you don't have to worry about any of that now!" I interjected. "Because we just found out that the reigning Miss Georgia United States of America was divorced, and she's out and you're in!" I said, standing up and throwing my arms out to hug her as if this were the most jubilant news since Mother found out about waxing.

Amber's eyes glazed over.

"Do you know what this means? This means you are now the reigning Miss Georgia United States of America!" I sure hoped she was getting the picture.

Her hand slowly began to move to her chest. Either she was having a heart attack or getting a clue. "Me? I've actually won?" Her voice registered complete shock.

Mother came running in. She must have been standing by Paige. That's why Maggy's hacking had sounded so close. "This means you finally get to go to Miss United States of America, just like you've always wanted."

"You mean . . . you mean . . . I actually won?" she said, slowly rising from her chair.

"You actually won," I assured her.

The look in her eyes was worth all the pain of the week. Everything she had been hoping for was coming true. Well, almost everything. Joshua was still sitting by me. "I'm the reigning Miss Georgia United States of America?"

"Yes!" Mother said, clapping her hands together. "You won! You won!"

"I'm going to the Miss United States of America pageant?" She was getting it. The girl was getting it.

"Yes, can you believe it?" I asked.

Life flowed back into her face. Her color returned to her cheeks. The dancing in her aqua eyes would take a while to return, because she had forgotten to put her contacts in, so her chestnut eyes were just kind of dancing. "I knew it!" she said, throwing her arms to the sky. Amber was back. "I knew that little miss prissy had something in her closet. I could tell when she wouldn't tell me her daddy's name. So she was divorced, huh? Well, oh, who cares!" She squealed. "Who cares how it happened! It happened! Oh, this is wonderful! It's incredible! It's unbelievable!" She danced around that kitchen with her arms spread-eagle.

None of us could help but smile. She deserved it. Her persistence had paid off, because had she been any other runner-up, she would not now be dancing around our kitchen.

She turned her attention to me and Joshua. "Oh, I'm so happy for you two. You just make the perfect couple! I'll make an appearance at your wedding!"

I coughed. "Uh, we're not at that stage yet," I assured anyone wanting to know.

"Well, I'll be there whenever. And I'll wear my tiara, I promise." I started to protest. "Ah, you don't have to ask me, it will be my pleasure."

"Well, that is very sweet of you," Joshua said casually.

"Oh, my goodness. I'll need to make a statement. I'll need to greet my people! I'll need to get ready for Miss UNITED STATES OF AMERICA!" she screamed. She and Mother jumped up and down in the kitchen. The coffee cups rattled.

Thomas entered the kitchen about the time Amber broke into song. He stood in the doorway for a moment and then turned right back around and headed out the door. We all followed single file. She never knew we were gone. Why should she? Vicky and Maggy were singing with her.

The sun was starting to set, and I could see the brilliant hues of red looking back at me as they reflected off the water. "Is this what life with you is going to be like?" Joshua asked as he took my hand for a walk down the white beach.

The sand felt cool between my toes. A far cry from the heat it had held the day I watched him kiss Celeste. "What? You don't like adventure?"

"Adventure I can handle. But this is certifiable."

"I tried to tell you. I come from crazy people. I mean, have you ever had trouble actually reading more than the first line of a book?"

His head cocked as he looked at me. "Maybe you're right. Y'all might be crazy. But at least your mom likes me."

"You're really concerned about that, aren't you?" I took his hand and laced his fingers between my own.

"It was important to me that both of your parents like me. I thought she might react about like you did when she found out about my . . . indiscretions."

"Actually, you'd be surprised. She was the one who made it clear that I was the one with the issues to deal with, not you."

"Really?" His concern dissipated with my words.

"You gloat."

"No, I . . ."

"Yes, you gloat. It's okay. I love to gloat."

He stopped in the cool sand as the water washed over the edge of his feet. I looked down and watched as they sank deeper into the wet earth with each wave. He turned and looked at me with that look. The one that made everything inside of me liquefy. "I'm really not gloating. I know you've dealt with a million emotions over the last couple of days. You probably wouldn't believe it, but I have too. When I thought I may never see you again, or hold you again or . . . "

"Shush." I placed my finger to his lusciously soft lips. *My, my, this boy is just fine.*

"No, I need to say these things." He wrapped his arms firmly around my waist. "I don't ever want to lose you again. I won't play games with you, and I won't run away. If we have problems, we'll face them. If we have disagreements, we'll deal with them. But we won't run. I'm not a runner. My dad was runner. My mother was an avoider, and I refuse to be either. So promise me, no more running." His eyes swallowed me whole, allowing me to enter the very recesses of his heart. "And I will never again, well, not intentionally at least, do anything to cause you pain."

"Okay, I promise, no running. Not even after lunatics who think they love you."

He leaned in closer, laughing. "She's forgotten my name by now."

"I never will," I assured him. And the passion in his kiss assured me that he would make sure I wouldn't. Shoot, if he kissed me like that much more, I was liable to tattoo his name on my booty.

Nah. Sister don't do pain.

CHAPTER THIRTY-NINE

"Oh, this feels like a dream," I said, crawling into the bed and pulling the covers up around me.

Paige was sitting on her bed, touching up her toenails.

The pitter-patter of paws made their way into our room and came to sit in between our beds.

"What do you want, you little rat?" The white ball of fur whined and scratched its front paws on the edge of my comforter. "Do you think she wants me to pick her up?"

"I have no idea," Paige said, leaning over the edge of the bed.

"What if she bites?"

"Bet you could gag her quicker than she could draw blood."

"You think?"

"Try it and see."

Maggy scratched harder and whined louder. "Okay, but if you bite me or pee on my bed, I'm shipping you to Siberia, where it's cold and animals are mean and eat little things like you for treats." I reached down, and she planted her little soft belly in the palm of my hand. "Paige, look! She's laid herself across my hand."

"Oh my goodness, isn't that the cutest thing?"

I scooped her up and laid her on the bed, and then I leaned back against the headboard to see what she would do. She crawled up on my chest, the nonexistent one, remember, and laid her body across it and started to lick my chin. Her puppy breath was unmistakable. "I love puppy breath," I said, melting quickly.

"Oh, Savannah, she really is a cutie."

I rubbed her back and scooted her down before she could stick her tiny tongue up my nose. "She is cute, isn't she? But don't ever let Mother know we've had her up here. She'll want me to wear her around my chest when she has board meetings."

About that time we heard the thudding of louder paws coming up the stairs. I looked at Paige, and her eyes got huge. "I can't let him see her on my lap," I said, tossing the ball of fur onto Paige's bed.

Duke stuck his head in the door and sniffed. Paige covered Maggy with her pillow. Duke turned around to head to Dad's room and then turned back one more time for one last sniff. By the time he made his way up the hall and Paige removed the pillow from Maggy's head, Maggy had christened Paige's comforter. "You've got to be kidding me!" Paige hollered. That made poor Maggy squat again.

"You're scaring her to death!"

"I don't care," Paige said, jumping out of the bed. "I slept in a wooden chair last night, I got snacked on by mosquitoes, had to take care of a drunk, and now a dog has gone and peed on my bed! Is nothing sacred, I ask you?" She put Maggy on the floor, and the thing scurried out of our room quicker than she had arrived, that's for certain.

She threw her comforter to the floor and walked over to my bed. "Scoot."

"You're not sleeping with me," I announced.

"Scoot."

I scooted.

She propped her toes up on the bed with the dividers still

firmly in place. She wiggled in, and we both lay there, leaning against my pillows. "I'm very proud of you."

"Proud of me why?" I asked.

"Proud of you for forgiving Joshua."

"Oh, that. Well, I guess I realized all the depths love has gone for me, and I had to figure out the depths I was willing to go for love."

"So, if you would forgive him for anything, would you forgive me for anything?"

I looked over at my friend of a lifetime. She turned her blue eyes to face me.

"What have you done?"

"You've got to promise. Before I tell you a thing, you've got to promise you'll forgive me."

"I would forgive you for anything. Okay, now, quit scaring me, what did you do? Have you been dipping in stranger's fruit too?"

She laughed. "No, no fruit here. But there was an incident with Steve Weisler."

"What are you telling me?"

"I'm telling you about those virgin T-shirts you wanted to make for us. Well, I couldn't wear one." My heart dipped. "You promised," she said, her eyes pleading.

I studied my friend. My friend of over thirteen years. I wondered why she had never told me this before now. And then I knew. She knew the reaction she would have gotten two days ago would have been very similar to the one I gave Joshua.

"It was stupid. I was stupid. The whole thing was stupid. I didn't even really like him. We were eighteen. I was completely infatuated, and he drove a BMW. And I was desperate to be loved back."

I turned my body toward her. "Why? Why are you so desperate? I've never understood that about you. You come from normal parents who love you. You're talented. You're exceptionally beautiful, and you will chase anything that says hello. Why?"

"I'm not like you, Savannah. I'm not as confident. I wasn't president of the student body. I was the head of the sorority. I always wanted to be approved." Her voice began to shake. "And when Steve found me attractive, I felt approved. And when I paint, I feel approved. And when I'm the center of someone's attention, I feel approved. And when I thought you wouldn't forgive Joshua, not even with how much you love him, I knew you'd never forgive me."

She had never been more vulnerable.

"Anything else?"

"What do you mean anything else?"

"I mean is there anything else you need to tell me?"

She scrunched her nose. "I don't think so. Should there be?"

"Any more Steves?"

"No, no more Steves. It was horrible."

I leaned back on my bed and put my arm around her. She snuggled up underneath. "Do you know how completely beautiful you are, and talented?"

"I do look pretty good in my new suit."

"You look wonderful in everything. But I'm talking about your heart, Paige. Your sense of life and adventure and passion. Few people have such life. And you didn't get that because you were standing in the full-of-oneself line before you got flung to earth. You are all of those things because God knew He could trust you with them. He knew you would create beautiful artwork and bring happiness into people's lives. But until you learn that for yourself, no man will ever bring those things to you."

"But Joshua brings you those things."

"No, Joshua didn't bring me my passion for life. He just accentuates it. He complements it. That's what the right person does. But they don't create it. Only a Creator can create. You look too hard. You've got to deal with your heart. Because until you can be trusted with your own heart, you can't be trusted with someone else's."

"Trusting always came easier for you. You till, you listen, you trust."

"I screw up. Over and over and over and over. But I keep going back, Paige. I get up each morning and I till again, and I'm forgiven again, and I try again. But deep down inside I know that nothing this side of heaven, not even Joshua, will ever fill what heaven alone can fill."

"How'd you get so smart?"

"Trial and error. Trial by fire. Trial by . . ."

"I get the picture," she said, raising her hand for me to stop. "So, does this mean you forgive me?"

"In the words of our dear tiara-wearing queen, 'You had me at *scoot*.'"

Only crazy people get up at sunrise on vacation. Say hello to crazy. But I love that moment at just around daybreak when all that's heard on the streets of Seaside are the morning melodies of the recently arrived northern deserters, whose wings carry them across the sky with their songs, and the hum of the air conditioners as you pass by each home. Nestled inside are sunburned sleeping beauties and surf-weary young men who gave their souls to the sea the previous day.

In the same moment, heaven breaks open with its treasure trove of talents and just plumb shows off. This morning, the edges of last night's darkness still hung over the far side of the ocean. Yet the morning sun was creating a brilliant display as it pushed the night away. And the ocean does nothing but flutter about underneath it all.

I sat down in the sand with the Tupelo Street Beach Pavilion behind me. Duke was at my heels. It was the perfect way to end the week. The first rays of the sun had warmed my face, and I closed my eyes and let it caress me for a moment. "What do you think about it all?" I asked the golden-haired creature next to me.

He laid his head down across my knees.

I opened my eyes and gently stroked the top of his head. He in return closed his eyes. "I'm in love, old boy. What are we going to do?"

He kept his eyes shut.

"You've got a new housemate."

His ear twitched.

"Amber's the reigning Miss Georgia United States of America."

His breathing deepened.

"And life as we knew it will never again be the same."

He snored.

I looked down on this old friend of mine and smiled. As long as we stuck around to throw the ball, fill up his bowl, cook him steak, scratch his itches, and rub his head, life was all the same to him. I kissed his soft head, and he opened his eyes and looked at me. "Let's go get Curly Locks. We're going to a wedding."

Joshua had asked me to come with him to Mark and Celeste's wedding. I hesitated. He assured me I didn't have to go. Then I said yes. Sometimes the past has to be relegated to its proper place. This was how we would have to begin doing it in our lives.

I watched as Dad, Mr. Modica, and Joshua enjoyed their last vacation coffee. Even Thomas joined them this morning. He must not have found a willing soul to hit golf balls with him at daybreak, and Paige would be asleep until noon. I wouldn't intrude. I had disrupted enough of their vacation. So Duke and I sneaked back and walked around Quincy Circle.

The shutting of the car door caused me to turn my attention toward Kate and Alex's house. Kate had just buckled in the last twin, whose face I could see peering through the window.

"Good morning, Kate," I said, walking over to her car. The look on her face made it clear she really didn't desire adult conversation at this hour of the morning. "Where are you and the boys headed?"

She walked around to the driver's door. "I'm taking them out of town for a couple days. Adam's been coming by every day to see them, and I just need some time away."

"Do you think it's a good idea for them to be away from their dad when everything is already in such an upheaval?"

"Whose side are you on?" she snapped as she placed herself into the driver's seat.

"Doggie! Doggie!" came the shouts from the backseat.

I placed my left hand on the top of the door and let my eyes rest on her. Duke scooted back. "I'm on your side. And Adam's side. And the side of your marriage. And the side of those little boys back there."

"Savannah," she stated, rather resolute and loud. "Are you married? I don't think so. So until you are, you need to stay out of married people's business." She started the car.

"I know I'm not married, Kate—"

"That's right, you're not."

"But this isn't the way this is supposed to be. Adam loves you. He loves this family."

"He destroyed this family."

"What he did was horrible, destructive, and selfish."

She set her hands firmly on the steering wheel, her stare fixed straight ahead. "You're absolutely right, and now those can be his companions."

"I don't get you."

"You don't know me!" she spat. "You come here once a year and bop in and bop out, and now, when my home's fallen apart, you want to save the day."

"I thought I knew you."

"Well, you don't. And you don't know anything about betrayal or how it feels to know your husband has touched another woman and shared things that only you and he should share." The anger in her voice began to give way to sorrow.

Her words made me cringe for a moment. Memories trying

to resurface. I made them leave. Forgiveness had been given. It wouldn't be retracted.

I knelt down by the car door. "You're right. I don't. I've never been married, so there is no way I can understand your pain. But I know someone who does."

She gave me a sarcastic laugh.

"Get out of the car," I said.

"What?"

"Get out of the car, just for a minute. I need you to trust me for just a minute."

She glared at me, frustrated, but slipped out anyway. I grabbed her by the shoulders and turned her body in the direction of Lucy and Manuel's house. "You see that house up there, the blue one with the white trim?"

"I see it, Savannah."

"Well, Lucy and Manuel are living there. And, they know what you feel." I turned her back to face me. "I may pop in only once a year, but you and Adam are part of some of my best memories here. And I don't know what betrayal is like, the kind you've gone through, but I've learned a thing or two recently about forgiveness. And you may think Adam is selfish, but this entire week, all you've talked about is how you've been hurt and you've been betrayed. I've never heard you say a peep about what those two little fellas in that backseat need."

Her body went rigid in my hands. I let her go. She slipped back into the car and buckled her seat belt.

"Please, Kate. I'm begging you. Ask them their story. Tell them yours and see what they can offer you. If you drive out of Seaside without ever doing that one thing, I guarantee you, you will spend years wondering 'what if.' Adam was stupid and selfish and all of those things. But the man I saw the other day was devastated and heartbroken and wants his family back."

She turned and looked me square in the face. "I need to go, Savannah."

"They even have twins too!" I would try anything.

She just stared at me.

"I hope I'll see you again." And with that I closed the door.

As the green Tahoe pulled out into the street and headed to 30-A, she slowed up in front of Lucy and Manuel's. I turned around to head home. This would be her decision. To go or to stop. To forgive or let bitterness eat away all the beauty in her.

I tilled a little longer. I tilled for Kate and Adam. Duke never complained.

I sneaked into Sundog Books one last time. Duke was more than willing to take a breather on the steps. I had a gift I wanted to buy. If I couldn't get a good book in this week, maybe someone else could. I found it tucked away in the far corner of the back wall. I picked up a bookmark and paid the cute store manager with the dark brown ponytail, then started back up the street. As I walked past Lucy and Manuel's, I saw a green Tahoe parked by their white fence. The two car seats were empty. I walked quietly up the steps and laid the first Chronicles of Narnia book on the seat of Lucy's favorite chair. Inside I had scrawled, *To my friends, Lucy and Manuel, and the bag of groceries that caused our paths to cross. Thank you for sharing yourselves. Whenever you read this, remember me. Your friend, Savannah.*

I patted the green Tahoe as Duke and I headed back up the street.

CHAPTER FORTY

Vicky was sitting on the front porch, painting Maggy's toenails a color in the loud orange family. She and Maggy were wearing matching Hawaiian-print numbers. Life deteriorated so quickly. Duke and I sneaked around the back. He grabbed water; I grabbed a Coke and my book. I had a few hours to kill before the wedding and a book that I really did want to read.

"Happy families are all alike; every unhappy family is unhappy in its own way."

"Insufferable!" Paige hollered in my ear. "Insufferable, I tell ya."

I looked at the book. Laughed to myself and closed it quietly, laying it on the table beside me. Books could be read anytime.

"Having trouble with your new queen?"

"She's made me watch her try on ten different outfits. I've had to listen to her sing. Watched her dance and helped her adjust her bra straps. I'm never coming on vacation with you again. I need a vacation from my vacation." She dropped into the chair beside me.

I laughed. Duke came from his water bowl and shook his

head right between us. Water flew in our faces. "This is when you must admit he really is a dog," I said, wiping the water from my face. "So what's on your agenda today?"

"Peace and quiet."

"How's that?"

"Well, your dad paid me twenty bucks to get lost for the afternoon."

I stuck my fingers in my ears. "La, la, la . . ."

"I know. It's disgusting. So Thomas and I are going to the movies while you and Amber go to the wedding."

My eyes furrowed. "What do you mean while me and Amber go to the wedding?"

"I don't know. You'll have to ask her. But she says she's going to that same wedding you're going to this afternoon."

I leaned back in the rocking chair. "She makes me crazy."

"No, you were already crazy."

"Okay, crazier."

"That'll do."

She got up to leave. "And why are you and Thomas going out together again anyway?!" I hollered. She never turned around. Well, she couldn't get far.

"Somebody get the door!" I hollered. No one answered. I tottered down the stairs in two-inch heels, trying to put on my earrings, catch my breath, and not break my neck all at the same time. When I opened the door, Johnny Deal, Joshua's college friend, was standing at the door in a seersucker suit, crisp white shirt, and navy blue bow tie with pink stripes. He held a bouquet of white daisies tied together with raffia.

"I'm here for the reigning Miss Georgia United States of America."

I stared at him, befuddled. "You're what?"

"Are you going to invite me in?" he asked.

"Sure, sure . . ." I said, stepping aside and motioning him in. "I'm sorry. But how in the world did you meet Amber?"

"We met yesterday at Dawson's Yogurt. She was getting a lemonade. I was getting a yogurt, and I fell in love with her pink lipstick." He winked.

"You're a mess."

"I know. Ooh, how beautiful," he said as his attention turned toward the staircase. Beautiful was an understatement. Amber glowed like I had never seen. She descended like royalty. Well, technically she was a queen. Her flowing silk scarf dress encased her in rich blue tones and made her eyes sparkle exceptionally.

"Amber, you do look beautiful," I said as she reached the bottom of the staircase.

"Did you meet Johnny?" she asked, not even looking at me. She actually had to peer up into a man's eyes. Her tall frame matched his nicely.

"I did."

"These are for you," he said, extending his bouquet.

"They're beautiful. For me?" Her hand went to her chest.

No, for me.

"Yes, they're for you."

"Savannah, would you put these in water?" she said, passing them into my chest, still not looking at me. She took his arm and he opened the screen door to the front porch, and they descended the stairs.

I headed back to the kitchen to put the princess's flowers in a vase. I laughed to myself as I watched the water fill up the vase. "Psst. Hey, Savannah," came the noise behind me.

I turned around to see Amber in the doorway.

"I told Johnny I needed just one minute. I tried to find you this morning."

"Find me for what?" I asked, still holding her flowers.

"To apologize. I've been brutal. I've been selfish and stupid and have acted totally inappropriately." Her face registered complete sincerity.

"I owe you just as much an apology, for not being honest with you and telling you what was going on with me and Joshua. You deserved to know. I just honestly . . ." I laughed at the idiocy of the statement. "I just didn't want you to hurt anymore."

She walked over to me. I was glad I was wearing heels. "I know you were trying to protect me. You let me invade your vacation. You've let your mother fall in love with me. And your dad." She huffed. "Oh my goodness, you would think I came from that man's loins."

I raised my hand. "I get the picture, really."

"It's just I've never had people care for me like this. Honestly, never."

Something different about her caught my eye. "You look different."

"What do you mean? I don't look nice today?" She examined her dress.

"No, you look breathtaking, but something's different . . . Oh my stars, you're not wearing your contacts."

She smiled sheepishly. "I know. I wouldn't have believed it myself if I hadn't seen it. 'Johnny likes my real color.'"

"I like your real color too."

"Honest?"

"Completely honest."

"So you forgive me?"

"If you forgive me."

"Awwww." She shuffled over in her heels with her arms extended like a wind-up doll. "Come here, you." She pulled me into a bear hug. I hoped my hair survived. I finally extricated myself. "You and Paige are my best friends in the whole world."

"Well, as your friends, no more eating happy fruit."

She laughed. "I promise. But it was doggone good."

She turned to go; then she paused. "And Savannah, I really do hate that a divorce is what got me here."

She really could amaze me. I smiled in agreement. Then I walked her back to the door, and felt almost like a proud mother watching her daughter go to the prom as I watched her leave.

Joshua rounded the corner, eyeing the departure himself. "Johnny's been beside himself," he said as he reached the screen door.

I stared at him through the mesh. The tan linen suit and crisp white shirt made the sun that had saturated him this past week radiate. His pale blue tie was the perfect complement.

"You look wonderful," I said, too transfixed to open the door.

"May I come in?" He chuckled.

"Oh, yes," I said, opening the door. "I'm sorry, I've had trouble with that today."

"Where'd you get the flowers?"

I forgot I had been given flower duty. "Oh." I laughed and walked back to the kitchen. "Johnny brought these for Amber. I do think they're a perfect twosome."

I set the flowers down on the kitchen counter and felt Joshua's warm breath come up behind me. His arms encircled my waist. His lips brushed my ear, and every hair on my legs grew an inch. "We are the perfect twosome," he said, kissing me on the cheek. "Now let me go introduce you to the world as the woman I love."

I turned to look at that face. That beautiful face. The lone curl loose over his left eye. "I'd love that. And then can I tell them how I feel about you."

We headed to the front porch. "You look beautiful, Miss Phillips. Brown suits you," he said.

The knit V-neck halter felt soft against my sunburned skin. Amber assured me the V-neck would give the illusion of breasts. I looked down to check. It was an illusion all right. The teal and brown floral silk skirt swished against my legs as we walked up the brick street, hand in hand.

"Do you think I should go change? Maybe put on my khaki sundress? We'd match, you know. Just in case people wondered if we were really together. It really would only take me a minute." I started to turn around to head back into the house.

"I think they'll know we're together," he said, pulling me back around.

"You think? Because you know, since we're an item and all, we really need to let people know. And coordinating outfits really have a way of doing that. You know, Donny and Marie."

"They were brother and sister."

"Oh, yeah, okay. Bad example." I chewed my lower lip. "Sonny and Cher."

"They divorced."

"The Captain and Tennille. I know they're still together. They were just on *Fox and Friends* the other morning."

"Who?"

"Okay, so maybe brown is good on me." I ran my hands down my sweater for good measure.

"Brown is fine. Perfectly fine."

My feet began forward motion again. We were going to a wedding. Me and my man. I liked weddings. Come to think of it, I liked the color white too. Come to think of it, I looked fabulous in white. The love bugs flitted past us, and in the distance I heard the church bell ring. Come to think of it, love bugs weren't so bad after all. And I've always liked the sound of bells. Yeah, there is definitely something about the sound of bells.

ACKNOWLEDGMENTS

As with all books, they come about by far more people than just us rather lone individuals who sit behind a computer screen and type away for endless hours. Okay, maybe only two hours a day, but there are times it feels like an eternity.

But I couldn't do this without the ceaseless and immense talents of:

Ami McConnell: who continues to challenge me to go places I don't even want to go, yet when I get there, I realize it really is actually better than where I was. And who refuses to allow me my "implausible" moments.

To Erin Healy: once again your talents took Savannah to new and better places, and me too, even if I bucked a time or two!

To Allen Arnold: thank you for creating an enviornment where we can truly explore those facets of life that no one would believe unless we called them "fiction." You allow our imaginations to explode.

And to the entire Thomas Nelson team: Caroline, Jennifer, Lisa, Natalie, Mark, Elizabeth, and Heather, thank you for helping what I do actually make it onto the shelves and into the hands of the readers.

To my faithful friends: who hear me rant, who listen to me send up urgent prayer requests, and then so graciously pray me through my crisis moments: Deneen, Beth, Lawana, Paige, April, Joan, Theresa, Jackie, and Janey. I wouldn't make it through if I didn't have you there to watch my back.

To my precious family: I count it a privilege to tell your stories and change your names and spend the rest of the time listening as people ask, "Is Victoria really like your mama?!"

To my beautiful and endlessly giving husband: In a year with more twists and turns, your faithfulness to allow me the time to do what I've been called to do still humbles and touches the deepest places in me. And even though you let me read to you over and over again, you still smile, even though you've heard it a thousand times. So, on the days when you wonder if I notice how hard you work and how tirelessly you give, let the record show that I do, and that I am ever so grateful. Thank you for warming my feet and letting me eat Parmesan and garlic seasoned popcorn at the movies even though I stink for two days. What more could a woman ask for in the man that she loves?

And to the Creator of my life: once again, I'm an inadequate vessel. I get weary and sometimes irritable. I get scared and often remind you of how I can't come up with another story to save my life. And yet everyday you meet me so graciously, giving and giving and giving again. The words on this page aren't because I'm a writer. No, they rest on these pages because you are so kind to give such wonderful dreams. Thank you for giving me a dream. And thank you even more for showing up in my life each day to make sure it actually comes to pass. You give good gifts. And thank you for your best gift. The one that changed my life: Jesus Christ.

And to those of you who will pick up this book. I thank you once again for giving me your most gracious treasure, that of your time. (You thought I was going to say your money didn't you?!)

Truth be told, I am continually amazed that people actually buy what I write. So, to each of you I say a special thank you. And even if you pick up these pages and don't agree with all that I say, please know the heart with which it all comes from is, at the end of the day, a heart that desires to share the things life has taught me. We all travel different roads. And these are the lessons I've learned on my journey. May your journey teach you many valuable lessons as well. And may we all be changed for what we've learned.

Blessings,
Denise

Reading Group Guide for
Savannah by the Sea available at
www.thomasnelson.com/readingguides
